To Track a Killer,
You Had To Think Like a Killer.

Live like one. Act like one. And if necessary, even kill like one.

That was the challenge facing Gail Walton—and nothing in her quiet, contented life as a suburban housewife had prepared her to hunt down a human savage.

But that was what she was doing, using herself as bait in every seedy rooming house and every haunt of twisted pleasure—until she could flush him out of the sordid hell he inhabited.

There was no law she wouldn't break to find him, no danger she wouldn't risk. Because Gail was going to bring her daughter's killer to justice . . . even if she had to administer it herself. . . .

Life Penalty

Great Reading from SIGNET

LIFE PENALTY

Joy Fielding

Ⓢ
A SIGNET BOOK

NEW AMERICAN LIBRARY

PUBLISHED BY
THE NEW AMERICAN LIBRARY
OF CANADA LIMITED

First Signet Printing, October, 1985

2   3   4   5   6   7   8   9

Ⓢ SIGNET TRADEMARK REG. U.S. PAT. OFF. AND FOREIGN COUNTRIES
   REGISTERED TRADEMARK—MARCA REGISTRADA
   HECHO EN WINNIPEG, CANADA

SIGNET, SIGNET CLASSIC, MENTOR, PLUME, MERIDIAN
AND NAL BOOKS are published in Canada by The New American
Library of Canada, Limited, 81 Mack Avenue, Scarborough,
Ontario, Canada M1L 1M8

PRINTED IN CANADA
COVER PRINTED IN U.S.A.

In memory of my wonderful father,

LEO TEPPERMAN

Chapter 1

The nightmare began at exactly seventeen minutes after four on the last afternoon of an especially warm sunny day in April. Up until that moment Gail Walton had considered herself a lucky woman, and if one of the reporters who later thronged to her house at 1042 Tarlton Drive had asked her to name her reasons for so considering herself, she would have been able to do so easily.

Holding up the hands she would later use to shield her face from their cameras and the relentless, blinding flashes of lights, she would proudly enumerate the reasons for her good fortune with her long, elegant fingers. The first reason had to be Jack, a man as straightforward as his name, nothing fancy about him and perhaps a little rough around the edges, but a giving and honest man to whom she had been married the last eight years. The next two fingers would mark off each of her daughters, Jennifer and Cindy, two very different children by two very different men, which would bring down the fourth finger, the fourth reason Gail Walton considered herself a lucky woman, her ex-husband Mark Gallagher. Not all women enjoyed the easy, relaxed relationship Gail could claim with her ex-husband, and though it hadn't always been such, the last few years had brought each of them to the pleasant realization that perhaps their five years together had not been so misspent after all.

She was approaching forty with the energy and appearance of a woman at least a decade younger, and her health had always been good. She lived in a nice house in a nice city, and if Livingston, New Jersey, didn't exactly spell the excitement and romance of New York, it was still a safer and calmer place in which to live and raise a family. Besides, New York was less than an hour's drive away, even in the worst of traffic, and thanks to Jack's very substantial income—he was a veterinarian—they were able to make the trip into the city as often as they liked. Jack's income also afforded her the luxury of not having to work at a full-time job herself. She'd had enough of that in the years following her separation and divorce from Mark, when she'd been forced through necessity to leave her small daughter with her mother while she worked as a bank teller to support them. Now she was able to relish long lunches with her friends who, more often than not, had to dash off to return to their jobs, leaving her to linger over her coffee and to contemplate their parting looks, filled with an equal mixture of envy and confusion. Envy because she didn't have to rush to a job she found less than satisfying, and confusion because didn't she know that working outside the home, having a career, was essential to a woman's satisfaction? What was she doing spending all her time at home looking after a six-year-old?

She'd given up trying to explain her motivations to her working friends. The fact was that she simply *enjoyed* being a stay-at-home mother, being there for her daughters when they returned home from school, and it was her deep conviction that her sixteen-year-old needed her there every bit as much as her six-year-old. She remembered how much she'd liked having her own mother at home in the years when she was growing up. Besides, she was not entirely without outside ambitions. A gifted piano player all her life, she had recently taken to giving piano lessons to a number of children in the area, and her pupils now numbered five, one for every day of the school week. Ranging in age from eight to twelve, they came to her house at four o'clock every afternoon for half an hour. Jennifer was busy with her homework at that time; Cindy was addicted to "Sesame Street."

Another reason to be considered lucky, she would have told anyone who asked, was her parents. Both were alive and well and retired to Florida where they lived in a bright and spacious condominium right by the ocean. In the four years since they had moved to Palm Beach, Gail and Jack had visited them at least once a year, always with the girls, and once a year her parents journeyed back to Livingston to look after the children while Gail and Jack took some much needed time to themselves. Their close friends, Laura and Mike, both professionals, he a lawyer, she a social worker, childless by choice, were always chiding them over their seeming rut. Florida with the kids in the winter, Cape Cod by themselves in the summer. Laura and Mike were always disappearing into the more exotic locales on this earth—India last year, China the year before that. Gail had no deep desire to see India or China. They seemed so far away from everything that made her feel safe—her home, her family, the city she grew up in.

Maybe she *was* in a rut, Gail would have had to confess, but it was one of her own choosing. She had never felt comfortable with too much excitement. It was one of the reasons her first marriage had ended and her second was so successful. Mark had been unpredictable; Jack plotted out every move. Mark would get into his car—always a foreign sports car, sleek and metallic and bright—and just drive. He never knew where he was headed; he never consulted a map. If he got lost— and he was always getting lost—he would drive for hours rather than stop to ask for directions. He didn't seem to care if he ever got where he was supposed to be going. Jack Walton, on the other hand, was a man of lists. His time was highly organized and each minute was accounted for. As each item on his list was accomplished, it would be crossed out with a neat black line. If Jack was going anywhere, to another city or just another part of town, he would get out the map the night before and plan his route. He drove a new car every two years, always American, always white, and he was never late. Mark had made Gail very nervous; Jack made her feel secure.

More than anything else about her life, Gail liked this feeling of security. Her sister Carol was entirely different, more like Mark, and Gail had often thought her first husband would have been much happier with her younger sister. But Carol, who had obviously adored him, was too restless to wait out the five years it took for Gail's marriage to fall apart and had moved to New York, where she had taken up residence with first one painter and then another before moving on to dancers and then, probably for the sheer perversity of it, a stockbroker with whom she had been living for the last two years. Mark himself had gotten married again three years ago to a wonderful woman named Julie who seemed devoted to him and who treated Gail's daughter Jennifer as lovingly as if she'd been her own. It was something else that Gail felt thankful for.

Life, she would have told the newspapers that later clamored for her statements when she was too weak and sick to answer them, was exactly as she would have wished.

She rarely varied her routine. Her alarm went off at precisely seven-fifteen on school days and she never had any trouble getting out of bed. Always an early riser, mornings were her favorite time. She would shower quickly and dress and then go downstairs to get breakfast ready, giving everyone else in the house the extra time to sleep. She liked this time to herself, her hands busy setting the table and making the coffee, her mind free to wander without having to think about anything in particular. It relaxed her for the next hour when she was rushing around frantically trying to get everyone ready and out of the house in time for school and the office.

Jennifer was the worst. A typical teenager, she stayed up too late at night and had trouble waking up in the morning, no matter how long Gail tried to let her sleep. In the end, after gentle shakings and soft words had inevitably failed to reach her subconscious, Gail was forced to physically drag her older daughter out of bed, and only then, when she was sprawled across the floor like a rag doll, would Jennifer's eyes begin gradually to open.

Cindy was much easier, as she had been in every respect since she was a baby. It took only a soft stroke of Gail's hand across the child's forehead to get her to open her big blue eyes. Immediately, Cindy's arms would reach up and pull her mother to her, locking her in a warm, loving embrace. Gail would then go through the motions of trying to select something for her daughter to wear. Whatever she picked was invariably wrong, for Cindy, a child who was remarkably easygoing about every other aspect of her life, was unaccountably stubborn about what she wore. Many a day Gail would silently pray that Cindy's teacher realized that the child dressed herself and that her mother was neither color-blind nor a hopeless eccentric. Today, despite the heat, Cindy had insisted on wearing a purple velvet dress which had been a gift from her grandparents and which was at least one size too small for her, because it was her favorite dress and she hadn't worn it in a long time. When Gail pointed out that the reason she hadn't worn it in so long was precisely because it was too small, Cindy merely fixed her mother with an icy stare and protruding lower lip, and waited for Gail's inevitable capitulation.

By this time, Jack would be in the shower and the coffee would be ready. Breakfast was always noisy and rushed, and by the time everyone left the house at eight-thirty, Gail was ready for another cup of coffee and some time to relax and read the paper before straightening up the kitchen and then heading back upstairs to make the beds. Jack drove the kids to school on his way to work. Since both schools were in the neighborhood, both children walked home, Cindy always in the company of one of her classmates and the child's nanny. Gail was always at home waiting for their return at approximately three-thirty. She then had almost half an hour to go over the events of their day with them before her student arrived for her lesson.

The hours while her daughters were away at school were spent the way most middle-class housewives spent them: running small errands, making phone calls, grocery shopping, the occasional appointment at the hairdresser's, lunch with a friend, more errands, preparing dinner, waiting for her family to come home. If anyone had asked her to describe her life up until the moment she had turned the corner onto Tarlton Drive at exactly seventeen minutes past the hour of four on that sunny April afternoon, Gail Walton would have said that she was the face of average America, middle-aged, middle-class and middle-of-the-road. While she recognized that it was a description virtually all her friends would shun, it summed up everything Gail felt comfortable being.

She had no desire to stay young forever. Her own youth had been something less than spectacular. Shy and flat-chested, she had been largely spurned by the more popular cliques in high school, virtually ignored by the boys she admired. Only in her thirties had Gail begun to feel truly at home in her own skin. She was probably the only person she knew who actually looked forward to turning forty. So far, anyway, she had managed to avoid the mid-life crises her neighbors all seemed to be suffering through. She was neither frustrated by her lot nor bored with her lack of ambition. She was well read, kept abreast of current affairs, and was increasingly confident of her ability to hold up her end of any conversation. She belonged to no political party, and had somehow managed to avoid being radicalized by the sixties and the war in Vietnam, possibly because of her natural shyness and an innate tendency to avoid any kind of overt confrontation. The only vaguely radical thing she had ever done was to leave college before her last year was completed to marry Mark Gallagher. She often regretted her lack of a university degree, but never enough to go back to school to get it. She belonged to no groups. She respected everyone's right to be whatever he or she wished to be, and expected the same consideration from others. Her friends admired her inner peace, her seeming serenity. They sought out in her all that was normal. They asked for her advice; they relied on her common sense; they looked to her for the reassurance that all could be right with the world, and that if you were basically an honest individual, you would be justly rewarded. If asked to sum herself up on one word, Gail Walton would have chosen "content." She was everything she had ever wanted to be.

And then it was seventeen minutes after the hour of four on an especially warm, sunny April day, and everything changed.

Chapter 2

She saw the police cars as soon as she turned the corner, and knew immediately, instinctively, that they were parked in front of her house. Her first reaction was panic. She dropped the few parcels she was carrying and stood, unable to move, staring straight ahead, her breath holding her stomach in tightly, pressing into her back. In the next instant she was running toward her house, unmindful of the bags she had dropped, seeing only the police cars, knowing as she glanced down at her watch and saw that it was seventeen minutes after four, that for her time had stopped.

Later, much later, when the sedative they would give her was starting to take effect and her mind was hovering in the mid-ground between dreams and reality, her thoughts would keep returning to how her day had been spent, how things might have been different. That somehow it was her fault. She had changed the routine.

Lesley Jennings' mother had called first thing in the morning, just after Jack and the girls had left, to tell her that Lesley had spent the better part of the night throwing up and must have picked up some flu bug at school and therefore would not be able to have her regular Friday afternoon piano lesson. Gail had commiserated with the young mother, remembering how upset she used to get whenever Jennifer came down with anything, realizing how calm she was with Cindy, and telling the young woman what she was sure her doctor had already told her, to keep the child quiet and in bed, no solid foods and lots of liquids. Mrs. Jennings seemed grateful for the advice, confiding with obvious guilt that she was desperately trying to locate someone to come and stay with Lesley while she ran off to work. Gail told her about the daughter of a friend who had recently dropped out of school and might be interested in picking up a few extra dollars by baby-sitting, and again Mrs. Jennings was grateful, adding that she hoped Gail's children would be spared the flu bug which seemed to be sweeping the Livingston school system, probably because of all the rain they'd been having lately and wasn't it just typical that the child would get sick when it finally looked as if the weather was starting to break. Children were just little incubators for germs, Gail remembered thinking as she hung up the phone.

On impulse, and because it was such a surprisingly nice day, too nice to spend indoors, she had picked up the phone again and called her friend Nancy, the most frivolous of all her friends, frivolous because Gail doubted that a serious thought had ever passed through the woman's head. She was forty-two years old; her husband had left her five years earlier for a younger woman, and now Nancy Carter divided her time between visits to her masseuse and tennis lessons at her club. She was an avid, no, a *fervent* consumer, and she was never happier than when spending money, specifically her ex-husband's money. She was a follower of astrology, the occult and ESP. She believed that she could tell the future, although when her husband had announced his intention to leave her for the woman who regularly manicured his nails, she had been the only one in their immediate circle who was surprised. She never read past the entertainment section of the newspaper, and would have been hard-pressed to name either of her state's senators, although she knew all about Dustin Hoffman's private life and Joan Collins' rather more public affairs. Despite what her other close friend, Laura, referred to as Nancy's lamentable lack of depth, Gail had always found her shallowness and utter self-absorption entertaining, and today a little light gossip and some heavy-duty shopping seemed just what the sunshine ordered. The girls needed some new spring clothes, and for that matter, so did she. Gail had reached Nancy just as she was about to leave the house for a reading with her psychic and they arranged to meet for lunch at Nero's.

Lunch had been entertaining and fun. Gail didn't have to contribute much. She just had to sit there and smile as Nancy did the talking. Nothing was required of her except to listen and look attentive. If Nancy said something about which she disagreed, she kept this to herself. Nancy was not interested in her opinions; she was interested only in her own. Gail thought as she listened to Nancy talk about her visit to the psychic that Nancy Carter was probably the most self-centered woman she had ever met. No matter what anyone said, no matter what was happening in the world, she would find some way to relate it to herself. If the talk turned to Margaret Thatcher and the volatile political position she found herself in, Nancy Carter would say, "Oh, I know just how she feels. The same thing happened to me when I was running for president of my club." It was her greatest failing as a human being and her greatest charm. Gail's friend Laura professed shock at this attitude, rolling her eyes skyward at the slightest provocation whenever the three women were together, but Gail had long ago learned to accept the fact that if you wanted to talk to Nancy Carter, you talked *about* Nancy Carter.

Gail listened as Nancy explained that her psychic had told her she was suffering from lower back pain (not bothering to interrupt to tell her that most people over the age of forty suffered from some sort of lower back pain), knowing that for all the faults she could find to list about her friends, they could undoubtedly list an equal number where she was concerned. In the end, as with a marriage, a successful friendship depended upon accepting people for what they were. The only alternative was learning to live alone. Gail had never liked living alone. She liked having friends. She liked being part of a family.

Nancy had dragged her to shop at the Short Hills Mall. They went from store to store, ostensibly looking at clothes for Gail's daughters, but Gail quickly noted that Nancy grew restless after only minutes in the girls' or teen departments, and relaxed only when she found something that she herself could try on. The afternoon had proceeded at a faster pace than Gail had been prepared for, and when she looked down at her watch and saw that it was after three and that she could never be home in time for her daughters' return, she had called the school and left a message for Jennifer to be sure to go right home so that someone would be there for Cindy. It was only after Nancy had rushed off to make a three-thirty hair appointment that Gail was able to accomplish any real shopping for herself and her children. Since Gail had not taken her car, and since the day was such a lovely one, she found herself walking a good part of the way home, turning the corner onto her street at just after four-fifteen. Normally, she would have been home by three-thirty. Normally, she would have been there for her children when they came home from school. Normally, by this hour, she would be halfway through her piano lesson, and thinking ahead to what the family would be doing over the weekend. But she had changed her routine.

"What's going on here?" she cried, pushing against the cordon of police officers who blocked her front door.

"I'm sorry, ma'am, but you can't go in there," one officer said.

"This is my house," she shouted. "I live here."

"Mom!" she heard Jennifer yelling from inside.

The front door flew open and Jennifer threw herself into her mother's arms, sobbing hysterically.

Gail felt her entire body go ice-cold, then numb. Where was Cindy?

"Where's Cindy?" she asked in a voice she didn't recognize.

"Mrs. Walton," a voice said from somewhere beside her, "I think we better go inside." She felt an arm around her shoulder, felt herself being drawn across the threshold of her front door.

"Where's Cindy?" she said again, slightly louder.

The hands led her into the living room and sat her down on the peach and green print sofa. "We've called your husband. He's on his way."

"Where's Cindy?" Gail screamed. Her eyes sought out those of her older daughter. "Where is she?"

"She didn't come home," Jennifer was crying. "I got home from school right away like you asked me to, and I waited but she didn't come back. So I called Mrs. Hewitt's to see if Linda was home yet, and her nanny said that Linda had gotten sick at school and she'd had to go pick her up early. She said she called to tell you but no one was home."

"She must have gotten lost," Gail said quickly, blocking out the knowledge that her house would not be filled with policemen had her younger child simply gotten lost on her way home from school. "She's never gone home by herself before. I would never allow it."

"Mrs. Walton," the policeman beside her said gently, "can you tell us what your daughter had on when she left for school this morning?"

Gail frantically looked around the room trying to picture what Cindy had been wearing, able only to see the child's dark blond hair falling over her forehead and into her eyes, remembering that she had thought about clipping the bangs before they got so long that Cindy wouldn't be able to see. She saw the laughing blue eyes, the once fat cheeks now slim and finely structured, the small, full mouth with its missing two bottom front teeth. And the purple velvet dress at least one size too small. "She was wearing a purple velvet dress with smocking across the front, and a little white lace collar," Gail told them as quickly as she remembered. "I told her that it was too small and that it was too hot to wear velvet, but once she makes up her mind, there's no talking to her, and so I just gave in and let her wear it." She paused. Why had she told them that? She could see by their expressions that they had no interest in the suitability of the dress to the weather. "She was wearing white socks and red shoes," Gail continued. "Party shoes. She didn't like running shoes or shoes with laces. She only liked shoes with buckles. And dresses. She would never wear trousers. She was a very feminine little girl." Gail's hand flew to her mouth with the shock of what she had just said. She only *liked* shoes with buckles. She *was* a very feminine little girl. She had been talking about her daughter in the past tense. "Oh my God," she moaned, falling back against the pillows, wanting to pass out, trying to will her body into oblivion. "Where's my little girl?" she asked in a voice so low and distant it was barely audible.

The front door opened and suddenly Jack was beside her, his arms around her, his lips brushing against her cheek. "Do they know yet?" he asked.

"Know what?" Gail demanded.

The policeman who had brought her into the room now sat down across from her on a chair. Gail found her eyes being drawn to his face, surprised to find that it was quite a young face. "A child's body was discovered about half an hour ago in the bushes by the small park just down from Riker Hill Elementary School," he said evenly, careful to keep his voice nondescript. "It was found by some boys on their way home from school. Apparently, they cut through the park every afternoon. They heard some sounds coming from the bushes. They saw something running off. When they went to see, they found the girl's body." He stopped as if waiting for Gail to interrupt, but she said nothing, kept staring at the light beige broadloom at her feet, waiting for him to continue. "At about the same time that we got there, your daughter came running up the street looking for her sister. We brought her back here and called your husband. We didn't know where to get in touch with you." He stopped again. "We're not sure it *is* your daughter, Mrs. Walton. We didn't want to ask Jennifer to try to identify the body . . ."

Gail was suddenly aware that Jennifer was sobbing uncontrollably from somewhere in front of her, and she reached up and grabbed the trembling girl to her, rocking her back and forth on her lap as if she were a baby.

"Where is the child . . . the body?" Jack corrected. Gail was aware of a strain in his voice, knew he was trying to hide his own fears from her and her daughter.

"Down at the station," the policeman said. "We'd like you to come down and make an identification if you can."

Gail stared at him, thinking how odd it was that policemen really did say things like "down at the station."

"But you're not sure it's Cindy?" Jack stated more than asked.

Gail was quick to agree. "Just because she's missing, because she got lost coming home, that doesn't mean that the body you found—" She broke off, falling back into her silence. It hurt too much when she tried to speak, as if someone were plunging a knife into her chest.

"How was the little girl killed?" Jack was asking. Gail tried not to listen to the answer but was unsuccessful.

"It looks like she was strangled," the policeman answered. "And it looks as if she might have been sexually assaulted." He lowered his voice, as if aware that he was beginning to sound too clinical. "We won't know, of course, until all the reports come in."

Gail shook her head. "Those poor parents," she began, feeling the tears stinging her eyes and running down her cheeks. "Those poor people when they find out about their daughter. Such an awful thing to have happen."

"Mrs. Walton," she heard someone say from what seemed a great distance. "Mrs. Walton." The voice continued to retreat each time it called her name until it sounded as if it weren't coming from the same room at all. Even the hand touching her arm felt as if it were touching someone else. "Mrs. Walton," the voice said again, but she could hardly hear it with all the other noise that had suddenly seized control of her brain. "Do you recognize this?" the voice was asking. "Mrs. Walton, do you recognize this?" The hand was forcing her face to look at something she did not want to see, something her eye had caught a fleeting glimpse of moments before when her husband had entered the room, but something that her mind had refused to allow her to accept.

"Oh my God," Jack whispered, his head falling into his hands, his shoulders starting to shake with a grief he no longer tried to hide.

Gail felt Jennifer's head bury deep into her chest, felt her own head being pulled as if by a magnet toward the policeman's outstretched hand, saw in that hand the purple velvet dress stained by the mud of the recent rains. She tried to speak, but when she did, she again felt the pain shooting through her body, felt the force of the invisible knife as it was thrust deeper into her chest. She looked down and saw the knife slicing down the center of her stomach like a zipper opening a jacket, watched as her insides tumbled out, and waited eagerly for her own life to be over. Instead, she only fainted, and when she was revived, she stayed conscious only long enough for the doctor to give her a sedative.

Chapter 3

Gail watched as the next few days passed through her drug-filled mind like scenes from a play— early dress rehearsals where the blocking wasn't quite right and the actors had trouble remembering their lines.

The setting was a small private room in St. Barnabas Hospital. Decorative prints hung at suitably spaced intervals along pleasantly off-white walls. A large arrangement of flowers occupied much of the window-sill. At center stage sat a modern hospital bed, its crisply white sheets and neatly stacked pillows attractively appropriate, if a touch severe. Various people, dressed as doctors and nurses, alternately fussed over her, wiping her forehead, taking her temperature, administering needles and drugs, tripping over their lines of condolence or comfort, occasionally unable to hold back their tears, forced to retreat temporarily and then run through the scene again.

She was the center of all their attentions, the understudy pushed reluctantly into the lead role, totally unprepared, terrified of her new status, speechless despite the fact that all the best lines were supposedly hers, that they were all waiting for her to speak.

"What are these?" she managed, looking into an out-stretched palm that had suddenly appeared.

"Valium. Take them. They'll relax you."

Gail took them. The actress in the white uniform withdrew her hand, seemingly satisfied, and exited stage left. She collided with a distinguished-looking actor wearing a white coat who was coming over to take Gail's pulse.

Gail closed her eyes, and when she opened them, Jack was sitting beside her, his hand stretched through the bars at the side of the bed, encircling her fingers with his own. She could feel him struggling to keep his emotions in check, but the strain showed in his face, swollen with the bloated cheeks and vacant eyes of a drowned man, his skin pale and even pasty, touched by splotches of red, like misplaced rouge. In the almost overbearing stillness, she could hear his breathing coming in irregular spurts, nothing for many long seconds, and then a number of short, quick breaths following in rapid succession, as if he had to remind himself to breathe. He cleared his throat often and mechanically, and when Gail's eyes finally managed to travel the distance to his without closing, she found him staring straight ahead at something only he could see, and she turned her head away, back against the pillows, afraid that she might stumble across his vision and have to share it.

"Jennifer . . . ?" she groped.

"She's okay. She's staying with her father and Julie."

"Have you spoken to her?"

"Last night. And again this morning. She's better this morning. She said Julie slept in the same bed with her."

"That was nice," Gail said, hearing her words slur together. "Julie's a nice woman." Jack nodded. "How about you?"

"I took one of those pills the doctor gave me. Didn't help much. I was up most of the night. I kept hearing Cindy calling me."

"Oh, Jack . . ."

"Once I guess I must have dozed off for a few minutes, I could have sworn I heard her asking for a drink of water, you know how she always does, and I got up and went into the bathroom and started pouring it for her, and then I realized . . .''

"I should have been there for you," Gail said. "I have no business being in the hospital. You need me. Jennifer needs me. I have to get out of here." Gail struggled to sit up. Immediately, she felt Jack's strong hands at her shoulders, laying her back against her pillows.

"You'll be home soon enough. Give it another day. Get your strength back."

"My strength," Gail repeated, trying to assign meaning to the word. "Every time I feel my head starting to clear, someone's here to give me another shot or another pill. They keep telling me it's going to relax me, make me feel better. But it doesn't. The drugs don't change anything. They just delay it. They don't make *me* feel better; they make the *doctors and the nurses* feel better. I guess they think they're helping." She paused briefly. When she spoke again, her voice was very low. "Do you know what I keep wishing?"

"What?"

"Every time a doctor comes over with a fresh syringe, I hope that there's been a confusion at the lab, a mistake in the drugs, a wrong dosage on the chart. It happens you know, they make mistakes . . . and I keep hoping that this shot will be the last shot—"

"Gail . . ."

"I'm sorry," Gail apologized quickly, seeing the fright that flashed across Jack's eyes. "I shouldn't have told you that. It wasn't fair."

"I love you, Gail."

"Do you know what Cindy asked me?" Gail said, suddenly switching gears. "Maybe a month ago. She said, 'Mommy, when we die, can we die together?' Out of the blue. Just like that. 'Mommy, when we die, can we die together?' What could I say? I said yes. And then she asked, 'Can we die holding hands?' And I said yes. And she said, 'Do you promise?' " Gail was silent for several seconds. "And I promised. Oh God, Jack!" Her body began an unconscious sway.

She heard the sirens wail in the distance, felt her body rocking with increasing violence to the sound, saw Jack take a step back, to be replaced by a blur of white uniforms against her bed, and realized that the sirens were coming from inside her and that soon another needle would emerge to rescue them all from that awful cry, to make all those who didn't actually have to suffer feel temporarily soothed.

"Did someone call my parents?" Gail asked Jack sometime later. She wasn't sure if it was another day or the same one.

"I did," he answered. "They're flying in this afternoon. Carol's already at the house. The doctors thought it was best for you not to have too many visitors at the hospital."

"She's my sister."

"If you want, I'll bring her over later," he offered.

"Who sent the flowers?" Gail asked, having trouble focusing her thoughts.

"Nancy."

"That was nice."

"Everyone's been calling, asking what they can do. Laura's been terrific. She's organizing everything, making sure there's food . . ."

"What about your mother?"

"I haven't been able to reach her. She's on a boat somewhere in the Caribbean. Laura's trying to track her down."

"I should get home," Gail repeated numbly. How many times had she said that lately? How long had she been here? "Were there reporters?" she asked, recalling a barrage of notepads and eager faces.

"Outside the house when we were taking you to the hospital," Jack told her. "They're still there, a couple of them."

"What do they want?"

"Answers. Like the rest of us."

Gail closed her eyes.

"The police are outside," Jack said, and Gail wondered if she had fallen asleep in the space between his words. "They want to talk to us. Are you up to it?"

"Yes," Gail told him, raising her body up against the pillows and watching as an attractive, young-looking man with light brown hair and a sad smile approached her bed.

"I'm Lieutenant Cole," he told her, pulling up a chair. "I was at your house yesterday."

Was it only yesterday? Gail wondered. So many dreams in so short a time. "Have you found the man?" Gail asked, her voice barely audible.

"No," the lieutenant replied. "But we have a description from the boys who discovered Cindy's body." He said the last few words as gently as possible. "It's not much, I'm afraid. We even had a doctor hypnotize the boys, but all they could agree on was that the man had dirty-blond hair, was slim, of average height, and appeared youthful."

"That's all?" Jack asked.

"They only saw his back. He was wearing blue jeans and a yellow windbreaker. It's a pretty vague description. It could fit any one of a thousand guys, myself included." He paused, collecting his breath. "Your ex-husband, Mark Gallagher, for another."

"Mark?" Gail was incredulous.

"Can I ask you some questions about your ex-husband, Mrs. Walton?"

"You can," Gail said clearly, shocked out of her drug-induced lethargy, "but you're wasting your time. Mark would never have hurt my little girl."

"How long have you and Mr. Gallagher been divorced?"

Gail had to think for several seconds, her mind running back through the years. "Uh, almost thirteen years."

"Do you mind my asking *why* you were divorced?"

"There were a lot of reasons, I guess. We were very young, very different. Mark wasn't really ready to settle down. He had . . . he had other women." Lieutenant Cole looked up from his notepad. "Women," Gail repeated. "Not children. Believe me, his taste in women is anything but puerile."

"What was his attitude when you remarried?"

Gail shrugged. "He wished me well. I'm not sure what you want me to say." Jack's hand gripped hers tightly.

"How about his relationship with his daughter?"

"He loves Jennifer. He's a wonderful father to her."

"How did he feel about Jack replacing him?"

Gail stared into her husband's eyes. "I think he might have been a little uneasy initially," she began, "but after he saw that Jack had no intention of trying to replace him, as you say, he relaxed. Jack and Jennifer get along beautifully. She loves him and he loves her, but Mark is her father, and she knows that."

"How did Mark feel when you had a child with another man?"

Gail tried to recall Mark's reaction. "I don't remember," she said at last. "I don't think he felt too much about it one way or the other."

"He wasn't jealous?"

"Not that I know of. Why would he be jealous?"

"You don't think that he harbored any feelings of revenge?"

"Revenge? For what? I don't understand what you're getting at."

"Take it easy, Gail," Jack cautioned.

"What's he trying to say?" Gail asked her husband as if the police lieutenant were no longer present.

"Your ex-husband has no verifiable alibi for the

time your daughter died," Lieutenant Cole said simply.

"He doesn't need an alibi," Gail protested weakly, trying to come to grips with this new information.

Lieutenant Cole checked his notes. "He says he was photographing a woman in West Orange from two to three o'clock. His next appointment was at four, twin boys not too far from where you live." He paused to let these facts sink in. "It doesn't take an hour to get from West Orange to Livingston."

"You're wasting your time, Lieutenant," Gail told him, feeling her eyelids growing heavy.

"What about Jennifer's boyfriend?"

"Eddie?" Gail asked, her amazement jolting her awake again.

"Eddie Fraser," Lieutenant Cole pronounced, reading from his notes. "Age sixteen, eleventh-grade student, straight A average."

"Eddie and Jennifer are in the same class," Jack embellished. "They've been going steady for almost a year."

"Eddie didn't do it, for God's sake," Gail whined, panic mounting in her chest. "You're wasting valuable time. Eddie is a nice boy. He's a serious student. He wants to be a doctor or a lawyer. He's crazy about Jennifer. He's crazy about Cindy." She stopped abruptly.

"Did you ever notice anything untoward in his behavior with Cindy?"

"Untoward? What do you mean?"

"Did you ever see him staring at her in a way that made you uneasy? If they played together or roughhoused around a bit, did you ever notice his hands brushing up against her legs? Maybe a pat on the posterior that lasted a touch too long . . ."

"Stop it!" Gail cried. "This is crazy. Eddie didn't hurt Cindy! He's a kind, gentle boy, always polite, always helpful and sweet." Gail looked to Jack for confirmation. "Isn't he?" Jack nodded silently. "We like Eddie. He likes us. I mean, initially, we weren't thrilled about the steady arrangement. We thought that Jennifer was too young to get involved with one boy, but he was so nice that we decided she could do a lot worse, and probably would in years to come, because after all, they are only sixteen. We didn't want to encourage their . . . passion," she stumbled, "by trying to deny it. We made certain conditions. No middle-of-the-week dating, home by one o'clock on Friday and Saturday nights. Eddie was very agreeable. We've never had any trouble with him. Don't you see?" she asked, looking back at the young lieutenant. "It can't be Eddie. He loved Cindy like she was his own little sister. I know that's how he thought of her."

"He has no alibi for the time period involved," Lieutenant Cole said, as he had said earlier in the conversation about Mark Gallagher. "He claims to have gone right home after school to study for a test."

"If that's what he says," Gail protested, "that's what he did."

"Unfortunately, there was no one else at home at the time to back him up."

"This is ridiculous," Gail said, firmly closing her eyes. She would not listen to any more of his questions if he wasn't going to listen to her answers. Eddie was not a child molester. He certainly wasn't a killer. Neither was Mark Gallagher. The police were wasting their time when they could be out trying to find the man responsible.

"What are you doing to find the killer?" she asked, and knew immediately it was the next morning, though no one seemed to have moved. The sun was hitting the floral arrangement in the windowsill at a wider angle; the nurses looked crisper, more efficient, their actions more defined. They traveled from point A to point B as if there were really a reason for doing so. Nobody had thought to tell them that there were no reasons.

Gail had spent most of the night in the park, confronting the faceless killer of her young child, wanting to kill him but unable to do so, missing the opportunity to avenge her child's death, to alleviate some of her guilt. She knew it was the next morning because, if it were possible, she felt even more tired than she had the night before.

"What are you doing to find the killer?" she repeated, not sure whether the lieutenant had heard her the first time, whether she had, in fact, asked the question aloud.

Lieutenant Cole's assurances were quick and automatic. "We're doing everything we can," he stated, almost by rote. "We have all our available men working on the case; we've rounded up all known sex offenders in the area. Your husband's already gone through our file of photographs to see if anyone looks familiar. We'd like you to do the same when you're feeling a little stronger."

"I'll look now," she told him, and he immediately produced several sheets of photographs. Gail slowly perused each face, some young, some not so young, some distinctly unpleasant in appearance, others quite good-looking. No one was familiar. She handed the photographs back to Lieutenant Cole. "They're all so . . . ordinary," she said at length, surprised by the word. She had expected evil to be more striking in appearance.

"We're conducting numerous tests," Lieutenant Cole continued.

" 'Tests'? What kind of tests?"

"The killer left a pretty clear footprint in the mud, which we're making a cast of. Then there are saliva tests, blood tests, semen tests."

The full impact of these words hit her square in the stomach like a fighter's fist. She felt the bile that lay lodged in her throat beginning to move up to her mouth, and in the next instant she was retching violently into the bedpan. Within seconds a nurse was beside her, holding her head, and the lieutenant was gone.

Sometime later, her head back against the pillows, Jack's hand still in hers, the room quiet except for the sound of their dull breathing, she wondered how she could still be alive when she felt so altogether dead inside.

The reporters were waiting for her when she left the hospital, hurling their questions against her like hard, fast pebbles, surrounding her with their bodies and their cameras.

"Do you have any idea who might be responsible?"

"Have the police given you any indication in which direction they're heading?"

"Are there any leads?"

Just like on television, she thought, without answering them.

"How do you feel about the death penalty?"

Someone had answered, and she was surprised to see in later newscasts that it had been she who had answered, that she was not out for blood or vengeance, that she wanted only for the killer to be caught, and that she was confident he would be. Where had she found the strength to say that?

Jack fixed his eyes on the road, his hands covering hers, as they sat in the rear of the police car on the drive back to their home. Lieutenant Cole sat in the front seat beside the driver. There might be more reporters waiting at the house, he warned them. Gail nodded but said nothing, her mind on the results of the autopsy.

The police had informed her, as she had struggled with the image of her beautiful child being cut open in the name of acquiring evidence, that Cindy Walton had been sexually assaulted and then manually strangled by an unknown assailant on April 30 at approximately three-thirty in the afternoon, essentially the same information they had given her before they thought they knew anything at all. In two days, despite constant assurances to the contrary, they were no further ahead, no closer to catching the man responsible. They had only confirmed what they had known all along. But her small daughter's body had undergone the further indignity of the coroner's knives, the trail her killer had left was two days older, and despite her statements to the reporters that the police were sure to catch the man responsible, Gail wasn't sure at all. The fact that their two prime suspects were men she knew to be absolutely incapable of such an act did nothing to increase her confidence. The police would never find the killer, she acknowledged silently, staring at Lieutenant Cole's straight shoulders.

He was a nice enough man; he meant well; he obviously wanted to help. But Cindy was just a case to him, as she was to all the others, a sad, even tragic occurrence, but not an uncommon one in today's world. Her death had touched their lives, perhaps, but it hadn't changed them. The police would do all they could, but in the end, what could they do? She'd read enough to know that after a few days, a killer's trail grows increasingly cold. There was very good reason to believe that if the police hadn't found the murderer by now, they never would.

The thought of her daughter's killer evading capture, of his walking freely through the city streets, disrupted the buzz of her most recent sedative. The final obscenity, she thought, her mind curling itself around the corners of a plan, something she could never permit. If the police could not find her daughter's killer, she would have to find him herself.

This realization surprised her only slightly, as if her unconscious mind had been aware of it all along. It was simple really. She would avenge her daughter's death by bringing to justice the man who'd killed her. She would not remain the helpless figure of her dreams.

But first she would give the police a chance, she decided, leaning against Jack, and at the same time give her body a chance to renew its strength. She looked out the side window.

She would give them sixty days.

Chapter 4

They were waiting for her when she walked through the front door, their faces like the tortured wood etchings of Edvard Munch, drained of the colors of life, frozen in grief and bewilderment.

"Mom," Gail whispered, unable to say more as her mother's arms surrounded her and their bodies trembled one against the other.

"My darling," she heard her mother cry before she felt her body being pulled away by stronger arms.

"Daddy," she sighed, feeling the word rush from her mouth. Her father, a big man with a deep tan, held her tightly against his chest, his head buried against her shoulder. He said nothing, and she recognized, as the weight of his body pressed against hers, that she was supporting him as much as he was supporting her.

"Such a terrible thing," he muttered. "Our beautiful little Cindy."

Gail tried to move her head but couldn't. Her father held her in too tight a grip. She felt suddenly straitjacketed, her arms pinned to her sides, unable to turn her head in either direction. Her father's arms seemed to tighten their hold when she tried to move, and she felt like a small animal being slowly asphyxiated by a python, the snake's coils tightening with each of its victim's last desperate breaths. She couldn't find any air.

He was smothering her, squeezing the life right out of her. My God, Cindy, she screamed silently, is this how it felt? She pulled herself violently out of her father's puzzled arms.

"They'll find that son of a bitch," her father said forcefully, "and if we're lucky, somebody will shoot the bastard."

"Dave," her mother cautioned.

"They'll find him," her father continued, ignoring his wife's admonition, "and then someone should kill the animal slowly. Shooting's too good for the man. So's gas, and the chair. They should cut off his balls and pull the rest of him apart with their bare hands. I could do it. I know I could do it."

He sat down in a crumpled heap, his energy spent, his voice gone.

"Doing those things isn't going to bring our Cindy back," Gail's mother said quietly, returning to her daughter and drawing Gail back into her arms.

"At least the animal wouldn't be able to do this to anyone else," her father said angrily. "At least they'd wipe his smile off the face of this earth."

"I'm with you, Pop," a voice said from a corner of the room. Gail looked past her mother's shoulders at her younger sister Carol, who stood slim and pale. Gail felt herself drawn toward the young woman, and seconds later the two sisters were in each other's arms. "Oh God, Gail, it's so awful," Carol cried softly.

"I know," Gail gasped, feeling increasingly numb, the numbness spreading to her legs. "I need to sit down." Her knees suddenly buckled.

Immediately, she was led toward the sofa, where many arms arranged pillows and leaned her against them. Her sister sat to one side of her, her mother to the other. Her father sat on the wing chair across from the sofa, his head in his hands. Jack remained standing, unable to move. He had no one to surround him, Gail realized. His father was dead; his mother, with whom

Gail had a cordial, if distant, relationship, had yet to be located. Jack had been an only child, so there was no one else for him now. No one except herself, Gail realized, moving over to include him in their tight circle of grief. He walked quickly to sit down between her and her sister, but when he did, it was *his* arms that did the comforting. It was so like Jack, Gail thought, leaning her head against his broad chest.

They sat frozen for what felt like a very long time. Nobody spoke. In fact, there was nothing to say. The stranger in the bushes had said it all.

The knock on the door was quiet and tentative. Lieutenant Cole, whom Gail had not realized until now was present, went to answer it. Gail watched as her daughter Jennifer came running inside, and she stood up just in time to catch the teenager as she collapsed into her arms. Gail quickly covered her daughter's wet cheeks with kisses, noticing out of the corner of her eye that Jennifer was not alone. Mark and Julie, Gail's ex-husband and his wife, were with her. So was Jennifer's boyfriend Eddie. Mark and Eddie, Gail thought, glancing at the lieutenant, his two prime suspects.

Mark and Julie were instantly at her side, Mark's arms moving easily around her. He was taller than Jack; she had forgotten how much taller. But after only seconds pressing her head against his chest, she felt the same shortness of breath she had experienced when her father had held her, and she pulled away. She felt easier with Julie's embrace.

"If there's anything we can do," Julie was saying, "anything at all, please don't hesitate to ask. If you want Jennifer to stay with us . . ."

"Thank you," Gail said sincerely, "I think she probably needs to be here right now, but I appreciate everything . . ."

"Do the police have any idea . . . ?" Julie began, looking helplessly around her toward the lieutenant.

"They think Mark did it," Gail laughed, her laugh startling everyone in the room. Had it really been as loud as it sounded?

Gail looked toward Jennifer's boyfriend. "And if it wasn't Mark," she said, hearing her voice echo loudly against her ears, "then it was you, Duane." Why was everyone looking at her in so strange a manner? "Eddie," she corrected herself, then began laughing at her mistake, thinking how the subconscious associations of the mind could be so interesting, so unexpectedly funny. She wondered if Lieutenant Cole, who was looking fairly uncomfortable at this moment, could see the humor of her mistake. Or was he too young to remember the early days of rock and roll?

Someone, she wasn't sure who, led her back to the sofa and sat her down, lifting her legs up and propping a pillow behind her head. Someone else covered her with a blanket. Yet someone else gave her a drink of water. She heard the front door open and close and knew that some of the people in the room had left, but her eyes were shutting and it took too great an effort to open them to see who had gone. As she closed her eyes and allowed the monster fatigue that had been hanging onto her muscles for the last several days to envelop her, swallowing her whole, the last image she had was of her father, his tanned and lean body doubled over against itself, at least a decade older than when she had seen him the year before.

She opened her eyes to the sound of new voices.

"Hi," her friend Laura said gently, trying to smile. "How are you feeling?"

Gail swung her feet off the couch and pushed the blanket away from her. "What time is it?" she asked, looking around, aware that it was dark outside and that her parents, sister and daughter were no longer in the room. Neither was the police lieutenant. Had they been there at all or had she dreamt them?

"It's eight o'clock," Jack told her, coming to her side. "Lieutenant Cole left some time ago. I sent everyone else out for dinner."

"The flowers are from Nancy?" Gail asked, seeing the enormous arrangement of roses and carnations which sat on the glass coffee table. Jack nodded.

"Are you all right?" Laura asked.

Gail let out a long, deep breath. "I don't know how I am. I feel so numb. I guess it's all the drugs they've been giving me."

"And the shock," Laura added.

Gail nodded silently, her eyes drifting in a desultory fashion around the room, coming to a stop at the red and pink flowers. "Pink was Cindy's favorite color."

Laura lowered her head to the floor. "It used to be my favorite color too when I was a little girl."

"Really? Mine too," Gail confided, a small smile reaching the corners of her mouth. "I guess it's every little girl's favorite color."

The conversation stalled: the small smile disappeared.

"Has Nancy been here?" Gail asked, her mind back on the flowers.

Jack shook his head.

"Don't expect too much from Nancy," Laura advised gently.

Gail almost laughed. "I never have," she said. "Nancy is Nancy. We all have our own way of handling grief."

Laura's face turned serious. "How are you handling it?"

"I don't know." Gail shook her head from side to side, first slowly and then with increasing speed. Suddenly, she felt Laura's arms around her, her hand at the base of her neck, gently stopping the movement, bringing her forehead down against the soft cotton of Laura's blouse.

"Let it out," Laura whispered. "Don't keep it bottled up inside."

"I can't," Gail said, panic creeping into her voice. "I don't know what I'm feeling. I'm feeling so many things."

"What are they?"

Gail's eyes searched the room as if looking for suitable adjectives. "I don't know," she repeated helplessly. "Anger, I guess."

"Good," Laura told her. "You should feel anger. You have every right to feel anger. That's healthy. Feel as angry as you damn well please."

"And I'm angry at myself—"

Laura cut her off abruptly. "No," she said forcefully. "That's not anger. That's guilt. Don't you dare feel guilty. Do you hear me? You have absolutely nothing to feel guilty about. Look at me," she commanded gently, and Gail found her eyes being drawn directly to Laura's. "Guilt is a totally useless emotion. It accomplishes nothing. And you have nothing to feel guilty about."

"You don't understand," Gail stammered. "You see, it was partly my fault."

"It was no way your fault."

"Listen to me," Gail pleaded, and Laura was silent. "I went out. With Nancy. I wasn't home and I should have been."

"Gail, for God's sake, even mothers are allowed out of the house on occasion. It wouldn't have made any difference if you'd been home."

"Yes, it would have," Gail answered, vigorously nodding. "You see, if I hadn't gone out, I would have been home when Mrs. Hewitt's nanny called to say she'd brought Linda home from school early. I would have been there to pick Cindy up from school. We would have walked home together. She'd be safe. She'd be alive if only I had stayed at home. But I didn't. Oh God, it's all my fault."

Laura's voice was suddenly strong and hard. Her hands around Gail's arms were no longer comforting but demanding, her fingers pressing into Gail's flesh. "Now you listen to me," she said, "and you listen good, because I want you to remember every word I'm going to say and play each one back whenever you start having thoughts like those. What happened was not your fault. There was absolutely nothing you could have done. If, if, if, if. There isn't a worse word in the English language. If only I hadn't done this, if only I *had* done that. Well, you didn't. And there isn't a damn thing you can do about it now except make yourself crazy. Do you understand?"

Gail's hand reached out and stroked her friend's soft blond hair. "Yes," she said, trying to reassure her. "Thank you. For everything."

Laura's husband, Mike, was suddenly at his wife's side. Gail was startled. She hadn't been aware he was present. "I think we should go now," he said gently. "Let Gail get some rest."

"I've been doing nothing but for the last few days," Gail reminded him.

"Do you want us to stay?" Laura asked.

Gail shook her head. "No, you go. Mike's right. I'm tired despite all the rest."

Laura leaned over and kissed Gail, then she backed away as her husband approached Gail for the first time. Gail felt the warmness of his breath as it brushed against the side of her face, his lips grazing her hair. She caught a fleeting glimpse of a man behind a clump of bushes, his obscene mouth rubbing against her small daughter's cheek, and she pulled back sharply, an involuntary shudder traveling the length of her body. Mike ran a gentle hand across her cheek in a gesture that Gail knew was meant to comfort, but his fingers suddenly felt like razors against her skin, and when he withdrew his hand, she felt mauled and exposed. "Take care," he said, then shook his head. "I just realized what an empty expression that is."

The phone rang just as Jack was closing the front door behind them. Gail made a slight effort to raise herself up, but Jack was quicker, sprinting back into the room and picking the phone up on the fourth ring.

"It's Nancy," he said, his hand over the mouthpiece. "Are you up to talking to her?"

Gail nodded, pushing herself off the sofa and taking the receiver from Jack's hand, suddenly looking forward to the sound of Nancy's voice.

"How *are* you?" Nancy gushed. "Oh God, I couldn't believe it when I heard the news. I felt so awful. Are you all right? You must be a mess, you poor thing. To think that we were out shopping when it happened. I feel so . . . responsible somehow, like it's my fault . . ." she drifted off.

"Don't be silly, Nancy," Gail said gently, trying to comfort her friend in much the same way Laura had done for her just minutes before, "how could what happened possibly be your fault?"

"Well, I know it isn't really," Nancy concurred, and Gail marveled at how subtly Nancy had been able to shift the focus of the conversation to herself. There was no way that Nancy could relate to what she was going through, Gail realized. Nancy's two children only rarely had anything to do with their mother. She had largely ignored them during their so-called formative years, only to dismiss them as ungrateful when they chose to live with their father after the divorce. Whenever Gail made the mistake of glowing over her own offspring, Nancy's mouth would curl into a knowing smile and she would say, "Just wait till they get a little older and they start dumping all over you. You'll see." How could Nancy possibly understand what Gail was going through? For that matter, how could anyone?

"Thank you for the flowers," Gail said sincerely. "It was very thoughtful of you to send such beautiful arrangements."

"Are they all right?" Nancy asked, suddenly unsure. "I didn't know what to do, whether you'd consider flowers appropriate . . ."

"Pink was Cindy's favorite color." Gail repeated her earlier statement, wanting to share something of her child with her friend.

There was an uncomfortable silence. "I better go and let you get some rest," Nancy said finally. "I'll call you tomorrow. Or listen, maybe *you* should phone *me*. I don't want to disturb you or interrupt anything, so why don't you phone me. Will you do that? Gail?"

"What?"

"Will you phone me tomorrow when you get the chance?"

"Oh sure," Gail agreed flatly.

"Do you promise?"

Mommy, when we die, can we die together? Can we die holding hands? Do you promise?

"I promise," Gail said, and hung up the receiver.

That night in bed, Gail dreamt that she and Cindy were boarding a crowded bus, which seemed to get more crowded as they pushed their way into the middle of it. There were no seats and she and Cindy were forced to stand, their bodies pressed tightly against those around them. After a few minutes, the air seemed to grow thinner and one man collapsed next to her, but because of the number of others squeezed like sardines together, he remained standing. There was nowhere for him to fall, and Gail was forced to bear his weight, his chin pressed against the back of her neck. She could tell by the man's absence of breath that he was dead. Suddenly, the doors sprang open and the crowd surged outside, tearing Cindy from her mother, propelling her out onto the street. Gail's hands flailed vainly about, searching for her child, but she caught only air, abruptly finding herself at the entrance to Memorial Park, stunned in the realization that she was utterly alone. She began racing frantically through the park, seeing nothing, finding no one.

She turned a corner and suddenly she was in the Short Hills Mall, in Bloomingdale's. The crowd from the bus had reappeared and was frantically buying up everything in sight.

Gail looked beyond the crowd and saw a small clump of bushes and the receding figure of a young man. He was carrying a plastic bag from Bloomingdale's. The bag seemed to be moving. Gail gasped with the realization that Cindy was inside the bag. She started pushing her way through the crowd.

"Can I help you?" a saleslady asked, approaching and taking hold of Gail's arm.

Gail pushed the woman aside, hearing her voice pledging assistance, as Gail shoved her way past one person and then another.

The young man disappeared behind the clump of bushes just as Gail extricated herself from the mob. She raced toward the bushes, but there was no one there. She spun around. The crowd had disappeared. She was, once again, alone.

She heard a sound and threw her body in its direction. But there was nothing there. And then she saw it lying on the ground, half buried by the mud. She lunged to pick it up—the bag from Bloomingdale's. She tore it open, hearing strange, masculine laughter emerging from the bushes which were now closing in around her. Frantically, her hands pulled at the contents of the package. She tossed the bag aside and stood staring at what she had found.

A child's purple velvet dress.

She woke up screaming.

"It's all right," she heard Jack telling her parents at

the door of their bedroom. "She had a bad dream. She's all right now."

When Jack got back into bed beside her, he moved his body close against hers. "*Are* you all right?" he asked quietly.

Gail nodded without speaking, pulling Jack close to her, opening her eyes wide, as if her eyelids could force back the images of her nightmare and keep them from reappearing.

"Do you want a sleeping pill?" he asked.

"No," she whispered, forcing out the words. "No more pills." She felt the warmth of his body easing the shivers in her own. "Did I wake you?"

"No," he said. "I wasn't asleep."

"Maybe *you* should take a pill," she suggested gently. "What time is it?"

Jack stretched his body to see the clock. "Three-thirty," he said.

"Three-thirty," Gail repeated, both silently acknowledging the significance of the hour. Cindy had died at approximately three-thirty.

Jack closed his eyes and Gail studied his thick lashes, thinking of the horror those eyes had been forced to endure when he'd had to identify their child's lifeless body.

How did our baby look? Gail wanted to ask but didn't because she couldn't bear to hear the answer.

She burrowed her body in tighter against her husband's as if to compensate for the newly imposed distance between them. They were essentially alone in this, she realized, despite all their years of closeness. Death demanded solitude.

From the spare bedroom she could hear her parents talking quietly, the worry in their voices audible even through the walls. She remembered, when she was young, lying in her bed listening to their soft chatter, trying to make out their words, understand the reasons for the laughter she heard sneaking out from underneath their closed door. There was no laughter now.

Still, she found the simple sound of their presence comforting. Taking her back as it did to her childhood, it made her feel secure.

Chapter 5

She had grown up in a house full of music. Her father was always singing, and all Gail's earliest and strongest memories were built around her father's vibrant baritone raised in song. Opera had been Dave Harrington's particular favorite. His record collection was the envy of all who knew him, consisting as it did of at least three different versions of all the great classics. While most other small children were busy singing about Mary and her little lamb, Gail and Carol were stumbling their way through the complicated arias of *Aïda* and *La Bohème*. While other children were weaned on the bedtime stories of the Brothers Grimm, the small sisters went to bed with *The Tales of Hoffmann* and *La Traviata*.

The Harrington household staged minioperas of its own, Gail's father always assuming the lead role of the dashing suitor, with Carol as his tragic lover. Lila Harrington, who fancied herself something of a dancer, played a multitude of parts, most of them involving long, flowing chiffon scarves, of which she never seemed to run out. Gail provided the musical accompaniment on the piano.

Gail never told anyone at school about these home productions, embarrassed the way children often are by what they consider their parents' peculiarities. She wanted only to be regarded as normal by the other kids, whose parents never answered questions about homework by bursting into song. Carol, on the other hand, reveled in the family theatrics, won the lead roles in all the school musicals, and went on to become a professional actress, struggling for the past decade to make a name for herself on Broadway.

It wasn't until Gail was almost out of grade school that she realized her father was not the opera singer she had always assumed he was (and had listed as such on all school forms under father's occupation) but was, in fact, a wholesale furrier. This news came as something of a shock to her, and for a while caused her to think twice before answering any questions at all, even on subjects of which she was very sure. A naturally intense, somewhat anxious child, Gail became increasingly shy as she grew older, possibly a reaction to all the extroverts at home, but more likely because it was simply in her nature to be quiet.

Carol was her opposite. Outgoing where Gail was introspective, mischievous where Gail was cautious, argumentative where Gail was diffident, Carol was like a little tank that rolled over anything and anybody who stood in her path. She did it in the sweetest of ways, however, and nobody seemed to mind, especially Gail, who admired and adored her younger sister. The admiration was mutual, and despite the fact that Carol was almost four years younger, it was Carol who was protective of Gail, and not the other way around. Carol watched out for her and made sure that Gail was not lost amid all the hoopla and noise generated by the rest of the family.

Aside from singing, Dave Harrington was a prolific painter and part-time mad inventor. The recreation room of their home was covered with his exotic, expressionistic works of art. Gail was too embarrassed to bring any of her friends down to this room lest they be frightened away by the barrage of green and purple faces that would greet them. On one occasion, when

Gail had been asked to take the furnace man downstairs to check the oil, he had stumbled across a large bright pink and orange painting of a nude woman, standing with her back to the viewer, her ample buttocks overhanging a large bucket of water in which rested her right foot. The furnace man had looked from the bright pink body of the nude woman to the brighter pink face of the teenager beside him, and asked with a leer, "Is that you?" Later, Gail's mother confessed that she had posed for the painting. She had also posed, she confided, for another nude which depicted a red-haired woman (Gail's mother was a strawberry blonde), her pendulous bosom fully exposed, reclining against a bright green background, a small purple dog positioned discreetly in the area of her hips, one of its large floppy ears pointing toward the sky.

The paintings, however, paled in comparison to Dave Harrington's inventions. Among his many ideas were a chastity belt for dogs, umbrellas that could somehow attach themselves to hats, leaving one's hands free for parcels, and sunglasses with built-in eyelashes. He swore everyone in the house to secrecy with regard to his inventions, but Gail would have rather died than divulge any of these secrets to her friends, who all seemed to have perfectly normal fathers.

It wasn't until Gail was divorced from Mark Gallagher and forced to leave her own small daughter, Jennifer, with her parents to go off to work as a teller in a nearby bank, that she realized how truly special her mother and father were. By that time, of course, that phase of her life was over. It had begun with a simple introduction.

"I'm Mark Gallagher," he had announced confidently, a man who obviously knew who he was, and Gail had looked up from the book she had been studying to see the handsome, if somewhat morose-looking student of art at Boston University, studying her just as intently.

"I know," she said shyly, her instincts telling her to get up and run, her curiosity dictating that she stay.

"You know?" He sat down on the bench beside her. It was a beautiful October day, the trees surrounding them with brilliant shades of red and orange. "Just what do you know?" She said nothing. "How old are you?" he asked. "You can't be very old."

"I'm nineteen," she replied, somewhat defensively.

"What's your name?"

"Gail. Gail Harrington." She struggled with herself to look directly into his eyes, lost, and focused her gaze on her lap instead.

"What are you so afraid of, Gail?" he asked, his eyes mocking her. "You're not afraid of me, are you?"

"No," Gail answered, terrified.

"Do you want to come up and see my etchings?" he asked, and promptly burst out laughing.

"I see enough etchings at home, thank you," she replied, resolutely serious.

"Oh?"

"My father's a painter," she said, and then looked back at her lap, wondering why she had told him that. She had never told anyone that before.

"Has he ever painted you?" Gail shook her head. "I'd like to paint you."

"Why?"

"Because you have a very attractive quality about you, a stillness you surround yourself with that I'd like to try to capture on canvas."

"I don't think so."

"Why not?"

"Because . . ."

"Because what?"

"Why do you want to paint *me*?"

"I already told you. A more interesting question is why you don't want to let me?"

"I don't know you."

"And you don't like what you don't know?"

"I just don't think I'm your type, that's all."

"Who said anything about type? I don't want to make love to you. I just want to paint you." He paused to let this last line take effect. "For such a shy kid, you're pretty conceited."

Gail shook her head, embarrassed now more than ever, wishing he would go away, terrified he might. "All right," she said finally, when it became obvious that he would say no more. "All right," she repeated, nodding her head up and down. "All right."

Mark Gallagher had overwhelmed and frightened Gail. She felt the danger of the man even as she walked along the street beside him. He radiated a certain static that manifested itself most clearly in his paintings, wild moving swirls of violent color. Unlike her father's art, which was primitive, almost childlike, but innately well balanced, there was no discipline to Mark's work, no structure, no limits. One color ran into another. The combination of hues was no less disturbing, even alarming, setting one color into conflict with its nearest neighbor, almost deliberately undermining what with a little more thought could have been a much more satisfying painting. But Mark Gallagher was not a man given to a great deal of thought, and he was interested in satisfying only himself. His portrait of Gail was strange and otherworldly, frightening in its lack of definite boundaries, her skin spilling out into the background of the wall behind her.

When Mark was called up before the draft board— and he threatened vociferously to flee to Canada if he were drafted—he was turned down on the grounds that he was hopelessly, *dangerously* color-blind. For Mark the knowledge that he was not producing for others the vision his mind was creating, and that his erratic genius was the result of a physical handicap and not a product of any wayward artistic spirit, caused him to abandon painting. He turned instead to photography. Portraits and landscapes. Black and white only.

Very early in the marriage Mark took to spending more time than he should with several of his subjects, and after half a decade of grand gestures and casual infidelities (he bought her a baby grand piano with the money he had made from a number of the subjects with whom he was carrying on affairs), Gail called it quits. She had never confronted him with any of his indiscretions; it would have been too painful. Instead, she busied herself with taking care of Jennifer and with her piano playing. When she moved out, she took only those two things, and for a long while, her life was shared only by her baby and her baby grand.

Mark supported his daughter whenever he could, but his earning power had always been erratic at best, and he tended to spend money as soon as he got it, if not before. Gail's feeling when she abandoned the marriage was one of relief, not regret. And while the first few years following their divorce had been fraught with the customary tension common to former spouses, the years soon brought a certain calm and mutual affection. By the time Gail married Jack Walton, she and Mark could legitimately refer to each other as friends.

Her first encounter with Jack had been completely different.

"There's a man here with a problem."

Gail had looked up from her desk at the nervous teller who stood before her. "What is it?"

"We bounced one of his checks for insufficient funds and he claims he had more than enough money in his account to cover it."

Gail, who had recently been promoted to the role of supervisor, took the passbook from the teller's hand and studied it. "He seems to be right," she said, glancing at the somewhat gruff-looking man waiting patiently on the other side of the counter. "I'll talk to him," she said, approaching him with a smile, unaccountably nervous, liking him even before they were introduced, though she was unable to pinpoint why.

Jack Walton was shorter and stockier than Mark had been, but bigger somehow, occupying more space. He reminded her of a Viking, she thought, despite the fact that his hair was brown as opposed to blond, and he had no beard. He just looked . . . capable, she decided, as if there was nothing he couldn't handle.

"What kind of medicine do you practice, Dr. Walton?" she asked him after the error had been straightened out.

"I'm a veterinarian," he smiled. "Do you have any sick cats that need taking care of?"

It was Gail's turn to smile. "I'll get one," she said. A year and a half later they were married, and Gail had never, for an instant, regretted her decision. Just as she had known from the first minute she laid eyes on Mark Gallagher that he was wrong for her, she knew Jack Walton was right. Despite the roughness of his features, the surprise with which they seemed to come together on his face, he had gentle blue eyes and a smile that sent creases to his forehead.

Gail startled all her friends by immediately abandoning her job and staying at home to be a full-time mother to Jennifer, who, like herself, had always been a nervous, intense little girl. She seemed to blossom under Gail's patient, quiet supervision, and, as with her second marriage, Gail had never for a moment doubted that her decision to stay at home was the right one. Jack made every effort to befriend the initially recalcitrant girl, and eventually his persistence paid off. They became the best of friends, a factor which helped when, a little more than a year later, Gail found herself pregnant with Cindy.

Everything about Cindy, from the moment of her birth, was different than it had been with Jennifer, in much the same way that Gail had been different from her own sister. While Jennifer's birth had come after twenty-eight hours of painful labor, with Mark out somewhere getting drunk in a nearby bar, Cindy's delivery, assisted by Jack, had been relatively easy, and the infant proved to be one of those babies who did everything right at just the right time, making things that much easier for Gail and that much more difficult for Jennifer, who took an instant dislike to the new arrival. Still, with almost ten years separating the two girls, the problems were not what they could have been, and Gail had always been grateful. Every year became easier, passing more quickly than the last, it seemed, as times changed and people moved on to other places and other lives.

Her parents eventually gave up on the cold New Jersey winters and, aided by her father's retirement, moved down south, where they had occupied the same Palm Beach condominium for the last four years. Her mother constantly rearranged the furniture (Gail was never sure where anything was liable to be from one visit to the next) and contented herself with long walks on the beach. Her father, who still liked to sing and paint—although he had grown disillusioned with the world of inventions—was considered something of an eccentric by the other more conservative residents in the building. He had discovered the bliss of the Sony Walkman and now tuned most of them out with one switch of a button, wearing his radio like a hearing aid whenever he decided to lie out by the pool. At first, his loud singing along with the music disturbed some of the other sun worshipers, but those who didn't enjoy Dave Harrington's impromptu concerts soon learned to sit at the other end of the pool; those who did, and their numbers increased over the years, formed their own little coterie around his chair. His groupies, Lila Harrington would laugh, referring to the mostly wealthy widows who were her husband's most adoring fans.

Carol had settled in New York after obtaining a degree in theater arts at Columbia, and had achieved a modicum of success in the theatrical worlds on and off Broadway. Her name often appeared on the backs of original cast albums if rarely out front on the theater marquee. She had never married, moving from one man to another at fairly regular two-year intervals.

Even Mark Gallagher had developed into a different

man in the years since his marriage to Julie—steady, successful, monogamous. Or so Gail had thought until Lieutenant Cole had called to tell her that her ex-husband had been eliminated as a suspect, that he had furnished the police with the name and address of a woman with whom he claimed to have spent the better part of the missing hour between his two appointments, and that this woman had verified his alibi. Gail wondered if Julie knew about the woman, and felt a keen sense of disappointment as she remembered the old hurts from her previous marriage.

Gail had watched the passage of time and the changes the years had brought with a calm, even detached amusement. She had seen friends switch partners and ideals, exchange one cause for another, and complain bitterly about children who were exact duplicates of themselves.

Somehow, despite the daily atrocities she read about in the newspapers, she had grown up with the idea that people living in the free world got as good as they gave, that ultimately one ended up with exactly what one deserved.

In the days immediately following Cindy's death, it was the first of her illusions to vanish.

Chapter 6

"We'd like you to keep an eye out for any unfamiliar faces at the church, even at the cemetery," Lieutenant Cole was saying.

"What? What are you talking about?" Gail's voice was unsteady, her fingers ice-cold as she twisted her hands one inside the other.

The lieutenant reached over and took Gail's hands in his, a gesture she was sure was nowhere in the police instruction manual, an instinctive act of compassion. The move was typical of Lieutenant Richard Cole, a man Gail had come to regard in the last seven days as more than just an investigating officer and something of a friend. He was in contact with Gail and her family every day, keeping them apprised of what the police were doing, of any leads they were following, of the crank confessions they had received and discarded, the standard debris of any murder investigation. On more than one occasion, he had dropped over on his way home from work just to talk. He had even sat with Gail and Jack as they pored over old photo albums, filled to overflowing with pictures of their dead child. He had listened to their memories, and even if Gail had recognized in the back of her mind that he was hoping to hear something that might provide him with much-needed clues to the killer's identity, she was grateful nonetheless for his attention, for his willingness to listen. So many of her friends, those who called to voice their concern or who dropped over to the house, grew quickly uncomfortable as soon as Gail tried to talk about Cindy. They kept telling her it was better for her not to think about such things, and so Gail had stopped talking about Cindy, for their sakes, not for hers.

"It's not uncommon for murderers to show up at a victim's funeral," Lieutenant Cole was explaining. "It gives their sick minds a sense of power, I guess, kind of like the author of a play sticking around to catch the audience's reaction after the last act. Part of him is daring everyone to catch him; the other part is relishing in the misery he's caused. When has he been that powerful before?"

Gail felt sick to her stomach. "You think he'll be there?"

"It's just a possibility. We'll have men all over, of course. If you spot anyone you don't recognize, or think you see someone that looks uncomfortable, a little off in some vague way, someone who smiles maybe or who does something equally out of place, point him out as soon as you can. I'll be right at your elbow."

Gail nodded, forcing herself to concentrate on what the lieutenant was saying. The man who murdered her little girl might also come to her funeral! The thought was too grotesque, too appalling. Her mind quickly sifted through the many crank phone calls she had received this past week: the angry voices which condemned her as a parent, the religious quacks who told her it was God's punishment for her sins, the simply vicious who taunted her in little girl voices with cries of "Mommy!"

A week ago she would not have thought such monsters existed, that people could be so willfully cruel to another human being already suffering so much pain. And yet the week had shown her that there was nothing human beings were incapable of doing, no level to which they could not descend. How had she failed to live in this world for almost forty years and not realize this before?

Exactly seven days had passed since the thirtieth of April.

Gail looked toward the coffee table in the living room. The morning paper lay stretched open across it. "The paper said there might be some connection between what happened to Cindy and that little girl who was killed a year ago . . ."

"There's no connection," Lieutenant Cole stated immediately. "I don't know where these reporters get their information sometimes. Karen Freed was run over by a hit-and-run driver. There was no sexual assault, nothing at all to connect the two cases." Gail winced to hear her daughter referred to as a case, and looked back toward the newspaper.

All the papers were making a great theatrical show of anger, screaming at the police in large black headlines to find the child killer before he struck again. But the effect of all that anger was only an increase in sales for the people who put out the papers. Perhaps the killer had purchased a copy.

Perhaps the killer would be at the funeral.

The television cameras followed them from the car to the church and later to the cemetery. Gail watched them with the detached curiosity of a spectator, which, she realized, in the last week, was the way in which she had come to view her life. Only when her thoughts turned to finding the man responsible for her daughter's death did she feel any stirrings of life within her. Outwardly, she was there for those who needed her, to put her arms around Jennifer, her hand into Jack's, her cheek against her mother's. Inwardly, she watched her every move as if she were watching someone else, observing herself as if she were the central figure in a foreign film with subtitles she was unable to follow or to understand. She moved from room to room on cue, ate when she was directed to do so, even managed a smile when supplied with the proper motivation; but inside, she felt nothing.

She listened to the words of the minister with seeming concentration, and if pressed, could probably have repeated his sermon word for word, and yet she had no comprehension of anything he had said, just as the minister, for all his kind words, had no idea of anything she was feeling. How could he? she asked herself. She was feeling nothing.

The church was filled with flowers. Gail spotted the arrangement from Nancy immediately. It was the biggest. Nancy had dropped by the house several days before to explain that she wouldn't be able to attend the funeral because it would just be too painful for her, and she hoped, she *prayed*, that Gail would understand. Gail had tried to talk about Cindy, but Nancy had promptly burst into tears and begged Gail to talk about something else. Gail had grown silent and let Nancy do the talking.

And now the minister was speaking about her child in the safe way one can talk about someone one never really knew, and Gail was unable to listen. *We'd like you to keep an eye out for any unfamiliar faces at the church . . . it's not uncommon for a murderer to show up at his victim's funeral.* Gail twisted her head around. Was he here?

Gail's eyes drifted purposefully over the rows of people, the degree of whose grief seemed to magnify the closer they got to the front. The church was crowded, and Gail was initially astonished to find that there were many faces she didn't recognize at all. She spotted Cindy's teacher, the young woman's face a tear-streaked wall of pain, and Gail quickly turned away, feeling the sharp stab of the invisible knife at her chest. Gail also saw, even nodded at, several of her neighbors. When she caught sight of the slightest quiver of a lip or the first swallow at a throat, she turned immediately in another direction.

She felt safer with the members of her family. The

last week had numbed all of them somewhat. Waiting for the police to release the body for burial had been strain enough on everyone, and today, Gail recognized, was thought to be some sort of conclusion, as though the act of putting Cindy's body in the ground was a signal for the rest of them to start picking up the threads of their own lives and begin carrying on again. In the next little while, she knew, probably in the next few days, Jack would be returning to work, Jennifer would be going back to school, her parents would be disappearing to Florida, and her sister would head back to New York. Routines would be reestablished. The public's outrage would continue only until fresh headlines appeared. She would move from the status of human being to that of a statistic.

Gail looked toward the end of the row at her father, his skin dark and leathery, his hair thinning and gray, his blue eyes, in the past rarely without a twinkle, now pale and watery. Her glance back-tracked to her mother, her face drawn and pale despite its tan, her short strawberry-blond hair hidden beneath one of her many chiffon scarves, her fingers intertwined and trembling. She saw Carol, sitting to her mother's right, reach over and cover her hands with her own. Carol's hand was steadier, calmer, though her face was no less distraught. Always thin and fragile-looking despite her toughness, she appeared to have lost weight during the last week, and had resumed her two-packs-of-cigarettes-a-day habit, a habit she had supposedly kicked the year before. Carol hadn't known Cindy that well. She was glamorous Aunt Carol from New York who visited several times a year with presents and a nice smile, and whom Cindy had seen last year in the chorus of *Joseph and the Amazing Technicolor Dreamcoat;* but for the most part, niece and aunt had remained attractive mysteries to one another. Still, her eyes were puffy and her face drawn. Her other hand held tightly onto Jack's. He stared straight ahead, as Gail had caught him doing often in the past week. He looked the same as he always did, and yet he looked completely different. Something had been stolen from him, she realized, knowing in that instant that the same thing had been taken from her. When she looked at Jack, it was like looking in the mirror. Did he feel as dead inside as she did?

Jack's other hand moved restlessly from his knee to Gail's lap. Occasionally, they had clasped hands tightly. Now both her arms were around Jennifer, who sat staring at the floor, her white skirt dotted with the tears that kept falling into her lap. Her shoulder-length straight brown hair fell against her cheeks, virtually blocking out her face. Her hands twisted in her lap, tearing at a tissue and banging at her legs. To Jennifer's right sat Sheila Walton, Jack's mother, who had only just flown in the night before from wherever it was that Jack had been able to reach her in the Caribbean. She had that otherworldly look of a person suffering from jet lag, Gail thought, then decided that the look was one they all shared.

Behind her sat Mark and Julie, Laura and Mike, and several other of their friends. Gail looked around for Lieutenant Cole but couldn't find him.

Beyond the first few rows, the faces grew indistinct, and though Gail tried to find a face that didn't belong, it was impossible. They all belonged. None of them belonged.

"That man over there," she said to Lieutenant Cole as he appeared out of nowhere to take her arm and escort her up the aisle when the service was completed. Gail indicated a dark-haired man with a forward thrust of her chin. Lieutenant Cole whispered something to the man beside him. "And I don't recognize that man in the blue and white suit." Gail watched the fair-haired young man with slightly slumped shoulders disappear through the church doors. She remembered that the suspect had been described as having dirty blond hair. "And that man," she said, pointing quickly with her hand before realizing what she was doing and dropping it to her side.

Lieutenant Cole's lips creased into a narrow smile. "That's one of our men," he told her.

Gail's face registered surprise. "He's a policeman?"

"Undercover."

Undercover. Gail repeated the word silently as they continued their walk to the front of the church.

As they filed out the door, Gail noticed Eddie Fraser flanked by his parents. Gail tried to smile in his direction but her lips only twitched grotesquely and she abandoned the attempt. Jack walked with his arms tightly around Jennifer. In the past week Jack and Jennifer had pulled closer together than ever, while Gail had felt herself pulling farther away. Had anybody noticed?

Gail watched the burial service, the small coffin being lowered into the ground, hearing the sobs of those around her, without any movement of her own. Her eyes were dry; her body was still. To a casual observer, to the man behind the camera and to those who would watch the events later on television, she appeared, as one newscaster would comment, a pillar of strength, a remarkably controlled woman. One commentator went so far as to wonder publicly what she had been thinking, and would have been undoubtedly disappointed to learn that she was thinking nothing at all. Her mind was a complete blank. A stranger lurking in the bushes had wiped it clean.

They knew as soon as they pulled the car into the driveway that something was wrong, that the house was not the way they had left it. They saw glass strewn across the front entrance as they approached.

"My God," Gail whispered.

"What's happened?" Jennifer cried.

"Call the police," Jack said, his voice calm.

The police were right behind them, and within minutes had surrounded the house and searched inside it, thoroughly dusting the house for fingerprints.

"I doubt we'll find anything," Lieutenant Cole told them later as the extended family sat in stunned silence in the middle of their ransacked living room. The stereo was missing, and the color TV, as well as any money that had been left lying around, and some jewelry. "Whoever did this probably knew from all the publicity that no one would be home because of the funeral and selected his time accordingly. Break-in artists are no respecters of grief."

"Do you think whoever killed Cindy might have . . ." Gail began.

"Unlikely," Lieutenant Cole answered, cutting her off gently. "Very unlikely."

"But not impossible," Gail stated.

"No," he agreed. "Not impossible."

"Animals," Dave Harrington kept repeating to whoever was nearby. Gail stared blankly at her father and felt nothing. This further indignity was too far removed to touch her.

After the police had left, and Jack was driving Jennifer over to Mark and Julie's where it had been decided she would spend the night, Gail set about picking up the objects that had been carelessly thrown around the house. Drawers had been emptied onto the floor, coffee tables had been overturned, several little knickknacks lay broken or crushed into the carpet. The cutlery had been emptied onto the dining-room floor and discarded, silver plate not being a good enough substitute for the real thing. Gail leaned over and picked up one of the long knives, running it along the side of her finger, and was surprised a second later to see a small river of blood.

"Gail, my God, what did you do?" Carol said urgently from somewhere beside her.

Gail stared at her blankly, not sure how to respond. Ultimately, she said nothing, letting her sister and her mother lead her into the kitchen, where they washed her finger and wrapped it in a tissue.

"I'll put away the cutlery," Carol said, abruptly stopping. Gail suddenly realized that the radio was missing. "Daddy's right," Carol continued, "people who do things like this are no better than animals. They don't deserve to live. Somebody ought to round them up and shoot them."

"Carol, please," her mother said quietly, "it doesn't help to talk like that."

"It helps me," Carol retorted sharply. "What's the matter with some people? Don't they have any feelings at all?"

"Apparently not," Gail answered in a voice so calm it surprised even her.

"Are you all right?" Carol asked, moving very close to her. "You don't look well. You look kind of funny. Gail, can you hear me?"

Gail saw her sister's lips moving and recognized the panic in her eyes, but the force of her sister's breath against her face blocked out the words. Gail tried to get away from her sister's concern, the touch of her hand, the feel of her eyes. Carol was taking away her air; she was giving her no room to breathe.

Gail tried to speak, to tell Carol to please move over and give her some room, that there was nothing wrong that a little distance wouldn't cure, but when she opened her mouth, the same twitching that had overtaken her in the church resumed and her lips were unable to form any words. Before she fainted, she remembered noticing that aside from the radio, the thieves had also stolen the kitchen clock right off the wall.

"Are you okay?" her mother was asking her, sitting beside her on the bed and holding her the way she had when Gail was a little girl. Gail nodded speechlessly. "No," her mother said, "that's not good enough. This is your mother. Tell me what you're feeling."

"I wish I could," Gail told her honestly. "It's like I've

been run over by a big truck and every time I think I can stand up, it comes back and mows me down again. I feel numb from the top of my head to the bottoms of my feet, but not quite numb enough. I wish I was dead," she said simply, even objectively.

Her mother nodded and said nothing for several minutes. "We have to go on," she said finally. "That's all we can do. There are other people who need you, are counting on you. Your husband. Your daughter."

"Jack's a grown man," Gail said analytically, "and Jennifer is almost a woman. They'd manage without me."

For the first time, Lila Harrington's eyes grew frightened, betrayed alarm. "What are you talking about?" Her voice was filled with a quiet intensity Gail had never heard in it before.

"Nothing," Gail said, shaking her head.

"Don't shake me away," her mother demanded. "Don't do anything stupid, Gail," she cried. "This family has had enough tragedy. Don't give us any more." Her shoulders started to shake and then heave, and soon it was Gail who sat with her arms around her mother.

"I won't do anything foolish, Mom, I promise you I won't. I'm sorry. I don't know what I'm saying half the time."

"You were talking like you were going to kill yourself," her mother sobbed.

"Just talk," Gail told her, "crazy talk. I don't have the guts to do something like that." She laughed, knowing she shouldn't have. "I don't have the gun," she said. "Sorry, I'm talking crazy again."

Her mother pulled away from Gail's arms. "Gail, maybe you should see a doctor. Laura called before, she gave me the name of a man she says—"

"A psychiatrist?"

"Yes. She thought it might do you and Jack good to get some professional help."

"He'll tell me I had a mixed-up childhood and a

crazy mother," Gail said gently. "I already know that."
Her mother's face remained unmoved. "Mom, I don't
need a psychiatrist. I know what's the matter with me,
and I know that I have to deal with it in my own way.
It's just going to take time."

"He could help you deal with it. Laura also gave me
the name of a group she says it might be wise for you to
contact . . ."

Gail smiled. "Laura's a good friend. She wants so
badly to help."

"Then let her. Please, Gail, let her. Call these people."

"Who are they?" Gail asked.

"I wrote the name down on a piece of paper. It's in
the kitchen. Something like Families of Victims of Violent Crimes, some organization where the families get
together and try to help each other."

"I've never been one for groups, Mom," Gail said,
wishing now that she had been. "I don't see how they
could help."

"Could it hurt?"

Gail shook her head. "I don't know. I guess not."

"I'm afraid for you," her mother cried, putting her
hand to her lips.

"Don't be afraid," Gail sighed. "I'll be all right. I just
need some time."

"Will you give yourself that time?"

The phone rang, and the question hung suspended in
the air between them as Gail reached over automatically to pick it up. "Hello?"

"Gail," Lieutenant Cole's voice was soft, reassuring.
"How are you?"

"Fine," Gail replied automatically. "It's Lieutenant
Cole," she whispered to her mother, who leaned forward anxiously. "Everything's more or less back in its
proper place," she said. Except my life, she thought.

"About those two men you pointed out at the
church . . ."

"Yes?"

"The dark-haired man is Joel Kramer. His daughter Sally is apparently one of your piano students." Gail nodded into the phone without speaking. "He came out of respect. His alibi is airtight."

"And the other man?"

"Christopher Layton, a fifth-grade teacher at Cindy's school. We've checked him too. He's okay."

"So, there's nothing," Gail said.

"Nothing *yet*," the lieutenant emphasized. "But it's still early and we're not giving up."

"You'll keep me posted?" It was half question, half statement.

"I'll call you tomorrow."

Gail replaced the receiver and looked at her mother. "He'll call me tomorrow," she said.

Chapter 7

"Time to wake up, sweetie," Gail said gently.

Jennifer twisted around in her bed and stared up at her mother. "I'm not asleep," she told her.

"Neither am I," Carol said from the daybed at the other side of the room, "so you don't have to whisper."

Gail walked to the rose-colored curtains and pulled them open, letting the bright, summery day inside. "Are you nervous?" she asked, looking back at her daughter whose eyes betrayed her almost total lack of rest.

Jennifer shook her head. "Not really. It's just English. I've read all the books. I always do all right in English."

"I remember how upset I used to get over final exams," Gail told her.

"You were a real pain," Carol laughed. "We couldn't even talk on the phone when she was studying," she embellished for Jennifer. "The world had to come to a complete halt until her exams were over. I remember Mom actually taking the phone into the closet once so she wouldn't disturb her."

"No," Gail protested. "I don't remember that."

"It's true. You were a real tyrant."

"The only exam I'm really concerned about is math,"

Jennifer interrupted, "and Eddie's going to help me with that."

Gail tried to smile, but the sound of Eddie's name was like a finger poking sharply into her ribs. He had been unable to provide the police with an alibi; he was still their prime suspect.

It was June 1. Thirty days had passed since Cindy's murder.

"Well, you just get this set of exams out of the way, and then you can start work for your father in a few weeks."

"I can hardly wait," Jennifer said, though her voice lacked the enthusiasm it had once held when she spoke of the opportunity to work as Mark Gallagher's photography assistant over the summer holidays.

"I'll go get breakfast ready," Gail said, heading for the door.

"I'm not very hungry," Jennifer called after her.

"Just coffee for me," Carol concurred.

"You'll eat," Gail told them, and went downstairs.

Jack had already left for work, called in early with an emergency. Gail set about making a fresh pot of coffee, dropped an egg into some boiling water, and cut a grapefruit into appropriate wedges, laying everything out on the table and waiting until she heard footsteps on the stairs before lowering the bread into the toaster.

"This is too much," Jennifer protested. "I can't eat all this."

"Eat as much as you can," her mother told her.

"Just coffee for me," Carol said again.

In the end, coffee was all anyone could manage, and Jennifer kissed her mother and aunt goodbye and ran out the front door.

"Good luck," Gail called down the street after her.

When she got back to the kitchen, Carol was already clearing the table. "What should I do with the egg?"

"Put it in the fridge," Gail shrugged. "Maybe somebody will eat it for lunch."

"We're getting quite a collection of five-minute eggs

in here," Carol laughed, putting the egg alongside the others that had been cooked and abandoned over the last week.

At exactly eight-thirty the phone rang.

"Who's going to answer it this time?" Carol asked.

"I'd better," Gail said, moving to the phone. "It's me they want to check on." She put the phone to her ear. "Hi, Mom," she said, without waiting to hear who it was.

"How are you, darling?" Lila Harrington asked.

"The same as yesterday," Gail told her, trying to smile through the telephone wires. "You really don't have to call every night *and* every morning."

"Yes, I do. I'm not convinced we did the right thing coming back to Florida as soon as we did."

"Of course you did," Gail assured her. "Mom, you and Dad can't keep me company forever. You have your own lives. You were here almost a month."

"It wouldn't have hurt to stay one more."

"I'm all right, Mom, really I am."

"Have you cried?" her mother asked, as she had been asking for the last three days.

Gail toyed with the idea of lying, but she'd always been a notoriously poor liar. "No," she answered truthfully.

There was a pause. "Anything new with the police?"

"Not since I spoke to you last night."

"I'll speak to Carol for a few minutes."

Gail handed the phone to her sister and tried not to listen to Carol's end of the conversation. Her parents had reluctantly returned to Palm Beach three days before, after Gail had convinced them it would be better for everyone to return to at least a semblance of normal life. They had to get on with their own lives, she heard herself telling them. They had agreed only after Carol had promised to stay around for a few more weeks. And they called twice a day to check on Gail's behavior.

For some reason they felt that Gail wouldn't be

really on the road to recovery until she had broken down and cried, something that she hadn't been able to do since the tragedy. Gail would have liked to accommodate them, but her eyes remained persistently, even stubbornly, dry.

Gail studied her younger sister as she talked on the telephone. People said they looked alike, both tall, slender and pale, with a kind of careless grace about them. Carol lit a cigarette while continuing to talk, drawing the smoke into her hollow cheeks. She was at least ten pounds lighter than herself, Gail calculated, her eyes dropping down Carol's body. Her stomach was still the flat midriff of a woman who had never carried babies inside her. Gail inadvertently stroked her own stomach as Carol laughed at something her mother had said. It was a pleasant, subtle laugh, one that warmed the air without overpowering it, inviting the listener to join in without insisting. It was nice having Carol stay with her, she thought.

"Does Jennifer ever say anything about Cindy?" Gail asked when Carol got off the phone.

Carol shook her head. "No. She's not sleeping very well either. I hear her tossing and turning all night. She's usually up around six. Sometimes I open my eyes and I see her sitting on the side of her bed just staring off into space. I asked her once if she felt like talking about what happened but she said no, so I didn't push it."

"I hope she'll do all right on her exams," Gail said, changing the subject.

"She will. Don't worry." Carol put her arms around her older sister. "Would you mind if I went back up to bed? I didn't get much sleep myself last night."

"Of course not. Go ahead."

Gail was alone in the kitchen when the police phoned half an hour later.

"We're checking on a lead we have in East Orange," Lieutenant Cole told her. "A report came in last night about some guy who's been acting a little peculiar lately."

"What do you mean, 'a report came in'?" Gail asked, needing to understand exactly the way things worked. "What do you mean, 'peculiar'?"

"It's probably nothing," the lieutenant cautioned. "But one of our informants says there's some young guy, a drifter, who's been talking a lot lately about the murder, nothing specific, just a lot of nervous talk, so we're sending somebody in to check things out."

"What do you mean, 'sending somebody in'? Are you going to get a warrant? Search his room?"

"We need a little more than what we've got before we can go searching his room. Just because some guy shows interest in a recent murder doesn't mean we can just—"

"So what exactly are you going to do?"

"We'll send someone in undercover."

"What do you mean, 'undercover'?" Gail interrupted, recalling the word from the funeral. "You mean like on television?"

Lieutenant Cole laughed. "Sort of. Undercover work isn't quite as exciting in real life, I'm afraid. It works a lot slower than what you see on TV."

"What exactly will this man do, this undercover man?"

"He'll move into the same rooming house as this fellow, follow him around, try to make friends with him, gain his confidence, that sort of thing. If we think there's anything, we'll go in, make an arrest if we can. But don't count on it, Gail. We follow through on tips like this one every day. Usually nothing comes of them."

"I understand. I appreciate your keeping me involved."

"I know you do. And one of these days, hopefully soon, something will pan out. I promise."

Jack phoned just after Gail sat down to her second cup of coffee. The little mutt he had rushed in to save that morning had died. Gail tried to comfort him, knew how depressed he always felt when he lost an animal, especially one that had been run over by a car as this one had because its owners thought it cruel to keep him on a leash. "I'll try to be home early," he told her.

Gail informed him of her conversation with the police, and he told her the same thing Lieutenant Cole had, not to get her hopes up. She didn't try to explain that her hopes for finding Cindy's killer were all that were keeping her going, that while the rest of them had returned to the semblance of normal life she had advised, for her normal life had largely consisted of taking care of a six-year-old child, and now both that child and that normal life were gone.

Mommy, when we die, can we die together? Can we die holding hands? Do you promise?

Oh, Cindy, my sweet angel, Gail cried silently, the image of her beautiful daughter before her still-dry eyes, don't you see I did keep my promise? When that monster killed you, he killed me too. When he took your life, he took what was left of mine. We did die together, baby. Just like I promised.

Gail let these thoughts sink in, realizing she had been denied the right to hold her daughter's hand. The killer had denied her that right along with everything else he had summarily taken from her.

Gail let her eyes drift toward the kitchen window. She pictured the killer walking freely past her house, a lazy grin across his face.

She stood up abruptly, her hand knocking over her coffee cup, its dark contents spilling across the white of the table and dripping, like blood, to the floor. Gail made no move to wipe it up, her mind still focused on her daughter's killer. She would find him and bring him to justice, she told herself with fresh resolve. It was all he had left her. She glanced at the calendar hanging on the wall beside the telephone.

Thirty days had passed since Cindy's death. Thirty days remained in her deadline.

Chapter 8

Gail pulled the morning edition of the Newark *Star-Ledger* across the kitchen table toward her. What was she going to do? She had no plan. She knew nothing of the criminal mentality or the minds of madmen. Where would she start? The police followed "leads." She had none, she realized, her eyes falling across the front page of the paper and quickly focusing on a story of an assault on Raymond Boulevard.

An eighty-year-old woman was in critical condition in the hospital after an attempted purse-snatching. Her youthful assailant, described by onlookers as tall and fair-haired, had fled without the woman's purse—which had contained three dollars—after repeatedly kicking the woman in the head and ribs. It was doubtful the victim would survive.

Without stopping to consider why, Gail jumped up and ran into the small den off the living room, searching through the built-in bookshelves which lined the wall opposite the television for the place where Jack stored his maps, locating them and rifling through them until she found an assortment of New Jersey street maps. She promptly returned with them to the kitchen. Quickly, she unfolded the map of Newark, and several seconds later, she had located Raymond Boulevard.

Somewhere on that street, a young, fair-haired boy had left an old woman to die.

She turned the page. A robbery on Broad Street had left two men wounded. Gail immediately located Broad Street on the map. James Rutherford, age nineteen, of no fixed address, had been charged with the crimes and later released on bail.

Gail read the paper from cover to cover, from the initial black headlines to the final advertisements, poring over each crime story as if she were a detective, marking on her maps the spots where an attack had taken place, carefully reading to secure a description of the assailant.

There had been no further attacks on children in the last month; articles on what had happened to Cindy had virtually disappeared. As far as the public was concerned, a little girl named Cindy Walton had existed only as long as she was newsworthy, and then only in small black letters and a few smiling photographs. It was sad, tragic even, they would have conceded, but then it was also old news.

It became a daily routine.

As soon as she was alone in the morning, Gail would get out her maps and go through the morning paper. Even after only a few days, a pattern was beginning to emerge: certain areas of her maps were more marked up than others; definite concentrations of high crime activity could be found.

"What are you doing?" Carol asked her, catching her off guard one morning.

Gail hurriedly folded up her maps and pushed aside the paper. "There's a new condominium complex going up in Newark," she lied, keeping her face turned away from her sister, feeling the lie blush red against her cheeks. "I wanted to locate exactly where it was."

"Any more coffee?" Carol asked, accepting the untruth easily.

Gail poured her a cup.

"Mom call?" Carol asked.

"Mom called," Gail answered. "And Jack. That little poodle he was so worried about pulled through okay, but a relatively healthy Dalmatian, which was just in for a routine clean-out or whatever, died under the anesthetic."

"Was Jack upset?"

"He didn't sound too bad," Gail realized out loud. "I guess the poodle made him feel better." She paused. "The police phoned."

"And?"

"That lead they were following—the drifter in East Orange—didn't pan out. Turned out the guy was in jail the day Cindy was murdered." Gail let out a deep sigh.

"Do you remember that I have to go into New York this afternoon?" Carol asked after a lengthy pause. "I have that audition I told you about, for Michael Bennett's new musical. Do you want to come with me?" Gail shook her head. "I don't like to leave you alone."

"I won't be alone. Jennifer will be home studying."

"I won't be late."

"Don't worry."

"I'll be home in time for supper."

"I'll have it waiting on the table," Gail smiled.

"You sure you don't want to come with me?" Carol asked again as she was getting ready to leave the house.

"I'm fine," Gail told her, settling herself down in the den to watch the new television that had replaced the one the thieves had stolen.

Gail flipped on the remote-control unit, hearing the front door close, carelessly changing the channels with a repeated flick of her finger. She tried to concentrate on what she was watching, but the problems of the soap operas bored her, and the hysteria of the game shows alarmed her. She continued to change the channels, suddenly hearing the familiar music and gasping audibly at the sight of Ernie and Bert cavorting on "Sesame Street."

Gail sat transfixed for the better part of an hour, lost in the show Cindy had so loved, her arm around her daughter's imaginary shoulder, laughing where she knew Cindy would have laughed.

"What are you doing, Mom?" a worried voice asked from the doorway.

Gail turned to face Jennifer. She said nothing. She didn't know what she was doing, so how could she answer. Gail watched as Jennifer walked into the room and took the remote-control unit out of her hand, pressing the television off. For several seconds, no one spoke.

"Are you finished studying?" Gail asked as soon as she could find her voice.

"I thought I'd go over to Eddie's for some help. This math is a real bitch."

"They always save the best for last," Gail smiled.

"I'll be glad when this week's over." Jennifer put the remote-control unit down on the coffee table. "Maybe I shouldn't go out."

"Don't be silly. You need help in math. I'll be fine. In fact, I was thinking of going out for a walk myself."

"That's a good idea," Jennifer said rather too loudly, noticeably relieved. "You can walk me over to Eddie's."

They walked side by side, not speaking, lost in the warm summer breezes, totally absorbed in the movement of their feet.

"Here it is," Jennifer said suddenly, and Gail found herself staring at the red brick house, startled to realize how close to them Eddie Fraser lived.

"Study hard," Gail called after her as Jennifer ran up the front steps.

Jennifer waved and disappeared inside the front door. Gail caught a fleeting glimpse of Eddie before the door closed. His hair was brown, she thought, wondering if anyone would ever describe it as dirty blond. Perhaps if the sun were to catch it in a certain light, she decided, striding with seeming purpose down the street.

A few minutes later she passed Riker Hill Elementary School, where Cindy had been a first-grade student. A minute or two after that she found herself in the small park where Cindy's body had been found on that April afternoon.

The sun was shining brilliantly and the soil was dry and firm. Gail took a deep intake of breath, feeling like a trespasser on hallowed ground. It wasn't much of a park, she thought, more like a parkette, if such a term existed. Just a clump of bushes and a freshly painted bench, its dark green surface glistening in the sunlight.

Gail approached the bench gingerly, as if it were still wet. She lowered herself slowly onto it, feeling her breath released in equally measured exhalations. She sat there for the better part of the afternoon, not moving, not aware of any movement around her. And then suddenly the park was full of children returning home from afternoon classes, of boys running boisterously past her, of curious eyes upon her. She got up quickly and returned home, rushing to make sure she had supper ready for everyone's arrival.

Carol came back with the dispiriting news that her audition had not gone well, that she had forgotten the lyrics to a song she could sing in her sleep, for God's sake, and that the rest of the audition had proceeded downhill after that. Jack was still brooding about the Dalmatian that had died that morning, and Jennifer was nervously fretting about her math exam. As a result, no one was very hungry, and the dinner that Gail had prepared sat largely untouched.

On the afternoon of Jennifer's last exam, Gail sat nervously waiting for her to return.

"She's late," Gail told Carol, reluctantly acknowledging the new clock on the wall.

"She's probably discussing the exam with her friends," Carol said casually.

"She was never this late after her other exams."

Carol shrugged. "It's her *last* exam today. Maybe some of the kids went out celebrating."

"Did she say that's what she was going to do?"

"No," Carol smiled. "But you know teenagers. They probably decided to go somewhere on the spur of the moment."

"That's not like Jennifer," Gail said, panic edging into her voice. "She'd call if she was going somewhere. Oh God, Carol, do you think something could have happened to her?" Gail's face went from its natural pallor to stark white in the space of a second.

"Gail," Carol began slowly, moving toward her, "come on, calm down. Jennifer is perfectly fine. She's just a little late coming home from school, that's all. Now sit down and I'll get you some lemonade."

"You know there are a lot of crazy people out there," Gail said, as if she hadn't heard her sister's words. "Some lunatic who decides he's already killed one sister, so he might as well finish off the other one—"

"Gail . . ."

"Or some monster who's read about Cindy, and decides it would be fun to go after her big sister . . ." She walked quickly toward the front door.

"Gail, for God's sake, where are you going?" Gail opened the door and stepped outside. "Come on back in the house. I promise you that Jennifer is all right."

"I'm going to find her."

"What? Where are you going to look?"

It was too late. Gail was already halfway down the street. She heard a door close and a second later she felt Carol right behind her.

"Oh God, oh God," Gail was muttering over and over.

"Gail, please, calm down. You can't do this to yourself every time Jennifer is a little late. Do you know where you're going?"

Gail said nothing, turning the corner onto McClellan Avenue. Carol had to walk quickly to keep up, abandoning her attempts at conversation. Though Gail said nothing, she felt grateful for her sister's presence. She turned another corner, then another, walking briskly up the front stairs of the neatly structured red brick house and banging on the door.

"Where are we?" Carol asked.

"Maybe she's with Eddie," Gail said by way of a reply. She knocked loudly, frantically, on the front door, but it soon became obvious that there was no one there. Even so, Gail continued to knock.

"There's no one there," Carol said finally. "Gail," she repeated, touching her sister's arm, "nobody's home."

Gail said nothing. She looked around helplessly for several seconds and then hurried back down the front steps. "Where are we going now?" Carol asked, following close behind, running to keep up.

They passed a small shop called Anything Goes that had recently gone into receivership. Everything Went, Gail thought through her panic, and quickened her stride. They were soon standing in front of Jennifer's school, but even as Gail ran up the front steps, she knew the doors would be locked. The grounds were deserted. Gail raced from the yard, seeing a small gathering of teenagers smoking by the side of the road.

"Have any of you seen Jennifer Walton?" she asked desperately.

The two girls and the boy regarded Gail anxiously, frightened by the tone of her voice. They shook their heads in unison.

"You're sure?" Gail persisted.

"I don't even know who she is," the boy said, and Gail noted that he was slim and his hair a light brown that might qualify as dirty blond.

"Gail," her sister beckoned. "Come on. They don't know her."

Gail turned on her heel and fled down the street, disappearing around first one corner, then another in rapid succession until even she was confused. And suddenly, there it was, the small park, the clump of bushes, the newly painted bright green bench.

"Is this where—?" Carol began and quickly broke off.

Gail said nothing, her eyes locked on the ground behind the bench.

"Let's go home," Carol said.

"There's nothing to be afraid of," Gail told her, her voice suddenly, eerily calm.

"I'm not afraid," Carol said. "I just don't think that it's a good idea for us to stay here."

"It's quiet here." Gail sat down on the bench, not seeming to hear the noise of a nearby group of boys who were tossing a ball back and forth. "I came here a few days ago, when you were in New York. I sat here all afternoon." She could see the startled expression on Carol's face.

"For God's sake, why?"

"There weren't any kids playing here then," Gail said, ignoring Carol's question. "I guess their mothers have told them to stay away from here. So only a few brave kids cut through. But now it's more crowded again. Soon even the dirty old men in raincoats will begin coming back. I'll have to start keeping track of who comes and goes."

"Shouldn't you leave that to the police?"

"How many policemen do you see?" Gail asked.

"I don't think that you should come here anymore," Carol told her, sounding more like the older sibling than the younger.

"What's wrong with here?" Gail asked.

"What's right with it?" Carol demanded in return. "Why torture yourself? Why go looking for trouble?"

"I'm not looking for trouble."

"If the rock hits the pitcher or the pitcher hits the rock," Carol said, "it's not so good for the pitcher."

Gail stared at her sister for several seconds and then burst out laughing. "Where did you hear that one?"

"Mom used to say that all the time."

"Really? I never heard her."

"Maybe she only said it to me," Carol said, reluctantly sitting down beside her sister. "I was the one who was always getting into trouble, remember? Couldn't keep my big mouth shut. 'Don't go looking for trouble,' she used to tell me, and I'd say that I never went looking for trouble, it always came looking for me. And then she'd say, 'if the rock hits the pitcher or the pitcher hits the rock . . .' And now here I am, carrying on the proud family tradition."

Gail smiled and put her head against her sister's shoulder. She allowed Carol to put her arm around her and slowly pull her up beside her. They walked side by side out onto the street.

"What's happening with you and Frank?" Gail asked, suddenly aware that Carol had said nothing about the man she lived with since her return from New York.

"We called it quits," Carol said matter-of-factly. Gail looked surprised. "We took an hour when I was back in the city, and settled everything."

"Oh no! Oh, Carol, it's all my fault. If you hadn't been with me—"

"If I hadn't been with you, it would have happened that much sooner. Frank and I, or more specifically, Frank and his *children* and I, haven't been getting along well for quite some time now. I wish I could say that we had this big dramatic falling out or that he caught me in another man's arms, but the truth is that after slightly more than two years together, we discovered it wasn't worth all the arguments. So we decided to split everything down the center—he got the stereo, I got the records; I kept the apartment, he got most of the furniture. He retained his children, I retained my sanity. We all live happily ever after." She shrugged. "Anyway, it was time to move on."

Time to move on, Gail repeated silently as the two woman found themselves back on Tarlton Drive.

"How much do you want to bet that Jennifer's inside

now and wondering what the hell happened to her mother and her wayward aunt?" Carol asked, hugging Gail to her. But when they walked inside the house, there was no one home and Gail's panic returned. "She'll be back soon," Carol said quickly. "Don't worry, please. I know she'll be home anytime now."

Jennifer finally walked through the front door at ten minutes to five.

"Where have you been?" Gail demanded, suddenly bursting into tears for the first time since Cindy's death.

"A bunch of us went over to Don's Restaurant for a hamburger to celebrate after the exam," Jennifer explained with growing alarm. "What's the matter? Did something happen?"

"Your mother was very worried," Carol explained, her eyes riveted on Gail. "You should have called to tell her you'd be late."

"I did. A few minutes after we got there, I called, but no one was home. What's the matter? I didn't think anybody would mind if I went out with the kids. I've done it before . . ."

"This isn't exactly like before," Carol reminded her, watching as Gail sank sobbing into one of the kitchen chairs. "Your mother was afraid that something might have happened to you. She was very worried."

Jennifer approached her mother. "But I *did* phone. Oh, Mom," she said, kneeling down beside her, "please, I'm so sorry. Don't be frightened. Nothing happened to me. Nothing's *going* to happen to me. I'm a big girl and I know how to take care of myself. You shouldn't have worried." Gail continued to cry, unable now to stop. "Oh, Mom, I'm so sorry. Please, Mom, talk to me."

"I love you," Gail stammered. "I couldn't bear it if anything happened to you."

"I love you too," Jennifer told her, the words barely escaping her throat before she too started to cry. "I'd give anything to make things better for you. Oh God, I wish it had been me who died and not Cindy!"

Gail's fingers shot to her daughter's mouth. "No, no, darling, don't ever say things like that! Don't even think them!"

"I saw your face that afternoon when you came home and saw that I was there and Cindy wasn't. I know that you wished it was me who was dead . . . I even understand . . . She was your baby . . ."

"Oh my God," Gail cried, "is that what you've been living with all these weeks? It's not true. I swear to you. It's not true. I love you. I love you more than anything in the world."

She threw her arms around her sobbing youngster, Jennifer's arms immediately wrapping themselves around her mother.

"Oh, I love you so much, my beautiful girl. I do. I'm so sorry. I didn't realize what you've been going through. I thought you just didn't want to talk about your sister, that it made you uncomfortable."

"I was mean to her, Mom," Jennifer cried.

"What are you talking about?" Gail asked, her tears now falling in a steady rhythm, making no move to wipe them away.

"She was pestering me when I was trying to study and I told her to get out of my room." Jennifer's whole body was trembling. "And once she came in and was trying on all my shoes, and I yelled at her to stop and told her that she'd made a mess and that she'd have to clean it all up, and I yelled at her until she cried. And another time I found her in my purse and she'd put on my lipstick and she had it all over her face, and I told her that she looked stupid and that she was ugly. Oh God, Mom, why was I so mean?"

Gail's hands ran frantically through her daughter's hair, smoothing down the sides. "You weren't mean to her. You were the best big sister any little girl could have asked for. Do you hear me?" Jennifer nodded. "And just because you yelled at her a few times when she did something wrong or because she just plain got on your nerves, don't you blame yourself for that. It's natural. We all do things like that. What's important is how you really felt about her."

"I really loved her," Jennifer whimpered.

"I know you did," Gail cried. "And what's more important, Cindy knew you did. And she loved you. Very, very much."

Gail buried her head in her daughter's hair and continued to cry. When Jack walked through the door a half hour later, she was still crying, and both he and Carol looked noticeably relieved, as she was sure her parents looked when her sister phoned them later that evening. Gail was going to be all right, she heard Carol telling them. She had cried. And then she started crying every day, and everyone began worrying again.

Chapter 9

"People keep expecting you to get over it," the woman was saying softly. "They keep expecting you to come around eventually, to become your old self again. They don't understand when you tell them your old self is dead. They think you're wallowing in self-pity; they think you'll get over it in time. Then time passes, a lot of time, maybe years, and they begin to get impatient. They start to think you've gone a little crazy. It's one thing to grieve, they tell you, as if they could possibly understand, but it's not normal to let it consume you. You try to explain that what happened to you *isn't* normal, and they tell you that life goes on. And you nod and agree. What else can you do? If there's one thing you've learned, it's that life goes on." She laughed in sharp, bitter acknowledgment of the fact.

The woman was barely five feet tall and couldn't have weighed more than ninety pounds. Her hair was several shades of blond; her mascara was smeared and running in a watery black line down the length of her cheek as she spoke. Her voice came in whispered waves. Though she spoke to everyone in the room, it was clear she spoke to no one but herself. Though there were ten other people around her, she was unmistakably alone. They all were.

"She'd gone out to study with a friend," the voice quivered, "the same way she always did. I used to ask her all the time—to bug her, she used to say—if it was such a good idea to study with a friend. I mean, how much work did they really get done? But she'd insist that she got a lot out of it, that Peggy, that was the girl she studied with, was so much smarter than she was, and that she learned a lot this way. So, how can you argue? I mean, I'm only the mother, right?" The woman swallowed and lowered her head, wiping at her eyes. "What do I know?" She raised her eyes to Gail, who sat staring at her from across the room, unable to move, barely able to breathe. "So, she went out as usual. It was a Tuesday night, about seven-thirty. She said she'd be home by ten o'clock.

"Well, I'm watching some movie-of-the-week on TV. My son, Danny, is already in bed asleep; my husband and I are divorced. So, I'm not too aware of the time at first, but then I look over at the clock during a commercial, and I see that it's a quarter to eleven. Well, that's not like Charlotte. She always comes home when she says she will. She was a good girl. Well, at first I thought, maybe it's taking them longer to do the work than they thought; give them a chance to finish up. Or maybe she had to wait a long time for a bus coming home. Peggy didn't live that far way, but I didn't like for Charlotte to walk home alone at night, and the bus stop was right out in front of Peggy's house. Well, I waited, and pretty soon it was eleven o'clock and the movie was finished, and I started to get a little angry. I didn't know whether to call Peggy's house or not. You know how embarrassed they get when they think you're checking up on them. But I thought, damn it, if she's embarrassed, then let her get home on time the next time out, and I picked up the phone and I called. Peggy's mom told me that Charlotte had left over an hour ago. Well, it only takes a few minutes by bus, so I started to get worried. By midnight I was quite hysterical wondering what had happened to her. I called all her other friends, woke everybody up. No one had seen her. Then I called the police. That was a real waste of time. Charlotte was probably with a boyfriend, they said. I told them she didn't have a boyfriend, that she was a very shy girl, and they laughed and said that all seventeen-year-old girls had boyfriends, and that only their mothers thought they were shy. They asked if we'd had a fight about something or if there was any reason for her to run away from home. I told them no. They asked where my ex-husband was. I said I had no idea; I hadn't seen him since the divorce. They said that Charlotte was probably with him. I said how could that be when she didn't have any more idea where he was than I did? They said that teenagers knew all kinds of things their mothers didn't, and that I should just relax and wait until the morning, because she'd probably call, and that there was nothing they could do until she'd been missing for twenty-four hours anyway. They told me to try and get some sleep; they'd send someone around the next afternoon if she hadn't come home already.

"Well, I knew she wasn't with any boyfriend or a father she hadn't seen in eight years, and I knew that something had happened to her or she would have at least called, but the police insisted on treating it like just another runaway, even after they'd talked to all her friends and her teachers and everybody said the same thing, that Charlotte wouldn't run away, that she never even talked about wanting to see her father.

"Then one afternoon, six days after she'd disappeared, I was lying down in my den trying to sleep—I hadn't slept since she'd been gone—when I saw this police car pull up outside, and I jumped up happily, because my first thought was that they had found her and that they were bringing her home, but then I saw that they were alone, and that they were walking very slowly, like they didn't really want to come to the house at all, and suddenly I felt sick to my stomach. Charlotte and me, we'd always been real close, especially since her father had left.

"Well, then the rest gets kind of blurry. I blocked out as much as I could. They said they'd found a body and they thought it might be Charlotte but that they'd have to get hold of her dental charts. The body had been found out in some field and was pretty badly decomposed and the animals had gotten to it. It was another day before we knew for sure that it was Charlotte. They said that she'd been raped and beaten to death, probably with a blunt object. It didn't take much. She wasn't any bigger than I am.

"I didn't go out of the house for almost a year. Danny moved in with my brother. I didn't hear from Charlotte's father till about a month after she died, and when he did call, he blamed me. I didn't try to argue with him. I thought he was probably right. I blamed myself too." She stopped talking and for several moments no one made a sound. Then she resumed speaking.

"Like I said, I didn't go out of the house for almost a year. I lost close to forty pounds. A neighbor finally forced me to see a doctor and he put me into the hospital for about a month.

"When I got out, I tried to kill myself. The first time, my neighbor found me and got me to the hospital in time. The second time, Danny came home—he'd run away from my brother's—and he found me, and that was when I knew I couldn't do anything like that again. And I haven't. Even if I've never stopped wanting to.

"That was four years ago. Danny's failed twice in school since then and he still has nightmares almost every night. His teachers have warned me he's going to fail again this year the way things are going. I can't hold a job. Oh God, it just gets worse and worse. What am I telling you for? You all know. You're the only ones who *do* know."

Her eyes searched those of the others, who blinked

back tears in silent understanding. Gail held her breath, afraid to release it. Why was she here? Why had Jack been so insistent that they come? She wanted to leave. She had to get out of this room, away from these people.

"About a week after they found Charlotte's body," the woman continued, "the police arrested two boys. Juveniles. Both under eighteen. They confessed. There was no particular reason for what they did, they told the police. They just wanted to see what it would feel like to watch somebody die. They picked Charlotte. They saw her standing at the bus stop, and they shoved her into this car they'd stolen earlier and drove off with her to that field." The woman looked helplessly around the room. "They were juveniles, you understand, so they don't actually go to jail. They go to a reformatory for a little while. One boy's out already. The other one still has another few months left on his sentence. But I'm sure he'll be out in time for summer camp, and of course, being a juvenile, his record will be wiped clean." She looked at the floor. "I don't know what I expected. I guess I still had some sort of faith in the justice system. The fact that my daughter's killers were caught at all gave me reason to believe that justice might somehow be served. Now, of course, I know better. I know there is no such thing as justice, that the right of my daughter to a long and happy life pales in comparison to the rights of her killers, that a good lawyer can make mincemeat out of already weak laws, all in the name of justice. Can somebody please tell me one thing?" the woman asked, her eyes moving from face to face, although it was clear her question was purely rhetorical. "Can somebody please tell me why there seem to be so many brilliant defense lawyers and so few competent prosecuting attorneys?" She swallowed audibly. "How long," she continued, and this time her voice begged for answers, "before I can vomit up this bile of hate that's slowly choking me to death?"

Gail felt the final question aimed directly at her. She

turned to Jack. She wanted to leave. Why had he brought her here? Couldn't he see how desperately she wanted to get out?

"Jack," Gail whispered, but Jack was lost in thoughts of his own. Gail touched his arm, trying to indicate her desire to leave without disturbing the rest of the group, ten other people whose lives had all been touched, been irreparably shattered by random acts of violence over which they had no control. How many other meetings like this one were taking place around the country? How many other lives had been altered in similarly gruesome circumstances?

"I brought some pictures of Charlotte," the woman continued, reaching into her purse and pulling out several photographs, passing them around. "The first one is Charlotte when she was a baby. I don't know why I brought that one," she giggled self-consciously, "except to show you what a pretty baby she was. The other two are Charlotte when she was fifteen, that last one taken just three weeks before she died. She had such pretty long blond hair. She loved long hair. Couldn't even get her to trim it half an inch." She paused, watching as the photographs were passed from hand to hand, her eyes stopping directly on Gail's at the same moment that the pictures reached her. Gail glanced down at the photographs of the chubby and proud infant, of the smiling, fair-haired girl that was no longer. She quickly passed the photos over to Jack, trying to grab his attention as she did so, to tell him that she had to get out, that she couldn't stand to be here any longer.

How could he sit here? How could any of them sit here? she wondered, looking at the ten other people who huddled together in the tight circle of grief.

The meeting was being held in the pleasant West Orange home of Lloyd and Sandra Michener. They had organized the group three years previously, six months after their own daughter had been stabbed to death on her way home from a movie. Despite Laura's information about what went on at these get-togethers—they were run along the same lines as Alcoholics Anonymous, she had told Gail—Gail had nonetheless been taken aback by the degree of honesty that she encountered.

"This is Gail and Jack Walton," Lloyd Michener had said, introducing them to the others. "Their six-year-old daughter, Cindy, was murdered seven weeks ago." No gentle euphemisms, no attempt to hide or soften the facts. The people in this room were clearly past gentle euphemisms.

There were Sam and Terri Ellis whose teenage son had been shot and killed during a holdup at their neighborhood 7-Eleven; Leon and Barbara Cooney whose twelve-year-old boy had been stabbed to death by an older boy in a fight during school recess over lunch money; Helen and Steve Gould whose infant daughter had been strangled by a spaced-out baby-sitter; and Joanne Richmond, whose seventeen-year-old daughter, Charlotte, had been raped and beaten to death in a field four years before.

Gail had silently acknowledged each one, the nervousness in the pit of her stomach building into nausea and then to panic. She had been fighting the urge to turn around and run from the moment she had stepped through the front door.

"We understand what you're feeling right now," Lloyd Michener had said, reading her thoughts. "Believe me, we've all felt exactly the same way." He took her hands. "We want you to feel free to say anything at all to us. Our motto is 'Judge not lest you be judged.' There's nothing you can say that can shock us, nothing so disgusting that we haven't all felt it ourselves. Let us help you, Gail," he had said, sensing, *no, feeling,* her reluctance.

He had let go of her hands and turned to Joanne Richmond. "Joanne has offered to tell her story tonight. You don't have to say anything," he said, turning back to Gail. "New members don't usually contribute anything the first two or three times. But, of course, that's completely up to you."

Gail had remained silent throughout his speech, and she remained silent now that Joanne Richmond had finished her story and retrieved her photographs.

"Why don't we take a break for a few minutes and have some coffee?" Sandra Michener suggested pleasantly.

"I want to go," Gail told Jack.

"Gail . . ."

"I mean it, Jack. I have to get out of here, and I'm going to go with you or without you."

The look in her face told Jack that she would permit no argument. "I'll go with you," he said reluctantly.

Gail immediately headed for the hall, and stood waiting by the front door for Jack to join her. She heard him talking to Lloyd Michener, who, once again, seemed to know what was on their minds before they did.

"This isn't uncommon," she overheard him telling her husband. "Often, new couples leave before a meeting's half over. It's very difficult to sit and listen to all the pain, especially when it strikes so close to home. Try to persuade Gail to come to our next meeting. If she won't, then I'd strongly advise that you come without her. People are under the mistaken impression that tragedies like this bring people closer together when, in fact, the opposite is true. There's simply too much guilt for couples to handle by themselves. We're finding that in marriages where husbands and wives don't get help, seventy percent end in divorce. Please try to come back. It's important."

If Jack answered, it was with a nod only. A few minutes later, he and Gail were in their car heading silently for home.

Chapter 10

On the last morning of her self-imposed sixty-day deadline period, Gail checked in with the police.

"It's me," she said almost guiltily when Lieutenant Cole answered the phone.

He recognized her voice immediately. "You can always call me, Gail, you know that. How did the meeting go?"

"Fine," she answered abruptly, not wishing to talk about it. She had already been through similar discussions with Jack, Carol and Laura, all of whom were urging her to attend the next meeting. Gail was adamant that she would not.

"I understand groups like the Micheners' are a big help to a lot of people," Richard Cole continued.

"I'm sure they are. Tell me," she said, cutting him off, "is there anything new today?"

"We've come up with a psychological profile of the killer," he answered.

"What do you mean, 'a psychological profile'?"

"We've formed a mental picture of this man based on the opinions of a number of psychiatrists. Give me a minute, let me find it for you." Gail heard the rustling of papers. "Here it is." He paused dramatically. "The general consensus is that the killer is a loner with a possible history of arrests for minor crimes. He's most likely the product of a broken home, although who isn't these days? His mother was either too domineering or too weak."

Either way, Gail noted to herself, it was the mother's fault.

"He has few, if any, close attachments," Lieutenant Cole went on, "was a poor student, and has a possible history of cruelty to animals. His father was most likely either abusive or nonexistent."

"Basically, what you're telling me is that the killer could be anyone," Gail said, digesting the information.

"I think we've narrowed it down a bit more than that."

"Tell me."

"Well, even given all the either-ors, we're looking for a young man who doesn't relate well to other people, who's quiet, a loner, the product of a broken home. My own theory is that he's a drifter, lives in a rooming house somewhere in the New Jersey area, and sooner or later he's going to say or do something to trip himself up."

"What if he's not in the New Jersey area anymore?"

Lieutenant Cole took several seconds before responding to Gail's question. When he did, it was with a question of his own. "Do you play bridge?" he asked.

"Bridge? No."

"My wife and I play once a week. Talk about cutthroats. Well, bridge is a game of strategy as well as luck. And when you're playing a hand in bridge, and the only way to win that hand is if one particular player has one particular card, then you have to assume when you make your move, that that card is where you want it to be. It's the same with finding a killer. If we assume that he's moved to another state, we might as well give up now. Our only hope to catch this man is if he's still in New Jersey, so we have to play the hand as if that's where he is. Do you understand?"

"So what exactly are you doing?" Gail asked, choosing to ignore his metaphor, asking the question she had asked at least a hundred times over the last two months.

"We're keeping our eyes and ears open. We have men in various rooming houses throughout Essex County. We're keeping tabs on possible suspects. We're thinking of posting a cash reward for information that would lead to the killer's capture."

"Is there anything I can do?" Gail asked.

"You can get lots of rest," the lieutenant answered with obvious concern. "Get your strength back. Keep going to the meetings and try to put your life back together."

"I know all that." Gail tried not to sound as impatient as she felt. She knew he was only trying to help. "I meant, is there anything I can *do?*"

"I know what you meant. But there's nothing."

"I feel so helpless."

"I know you do."

"You *don't* know!"

There was a worried pause. "Try to be patient, Gail. We're doing all we can." Gail nodded without speaking. "I'll call you soon."

Gail hung up the phone and walked into the den where the photo albums she had been looking through the night before were lying, still opened, on the dark green leather sofa. She sat down and lifted them into her lap, opening one up, momentarily startled, as she always was, when first confronted with the smiling reminders of her once-happy family. There were pictures of the jolly little group at Halloween, on birthdays, in Florida: Cindy, age two, sitting precariously on a large rock in the ocean during low tide, her nervous mother just out of the camera's range; Cindy lounging on a chair beside her proud grandfather; Cindy swimming with water wings at the age of three in an otherwise empty pool, swimming unaided a year later, diving from the diving board at the age of five.

Yet for every happy time, Gail could recall a time in which she had spoken too harshly, reacted too quickly.

Pictures of Cindy at the piano were particularly difficult for Gail to look at.

Despite her patience in most areas and despite her patience with her other pupils, Gail found that she turned into a virtual tyrant behind the keyboard where her youngest daughter was concerned. When Cindy balked at practicing or spent too much time in front of the piano scratching and fidgeting, Gail's voice would grow heavy with sarcasm and shrill with annoyance until by the end of the practice period, Gail couldn't bear the sound of her own voice for another minute and Cindy had been reduced to tears.

Now whenever Gail looked at the piano, she saw Cindy's bright eyes filled with tears, and so she had stopped looking at the piano. She had informed the parents of her pupils that lessons were temporarily suspended. They had seemed more relieved than disappointed.

"Gail," a voice said softly from the doorway, "don't you think it's time to put the albums away?"

Gail looked up to see her sister, still in her nightgown, walking into the room to sit down beside her. "I yelled at her," Gail whimpered. "There was no need." She shook her head in disgust.

"So you yelled at her a couple of times," Carol said with genuine astonishment. "So you weren't always the perfect mother. Who is? You're a human being. You're going to make mistakes. There are times when you're going to yell when you shouldn't. We're all guilty of that." Carol paused, looking around her helplessly. "I know I'm going to sound like our mother again, but here goes." She forced Gail to look at her. "The important thing is that you did the best that you could, that you were the best mother you knew how to be. Christ, I sound like *you!* Can't you remember what you said to Jennifer? That the important thing was that she loved Cindy and that Cindy knew it? That she was the best big sister anybody could want? Why can't you say the same thing to yourself? Why can't you realize that you were the best mother any little girl could have? Gail, for God's sake, how many children have the luxury these days of having their mothers at home all day? Cindy was such a lucky, *lucky*, little girl." She broke off when she saw the look in Gail's eyes. "All right, don't hang me because of semantics. You know what I meant."

Gail sat on the sofa, the books of photographs still in her lap, open to the last page. She stared at the delicate face of her younger sister, her eyes puffy with lack of sleep. Slowly, with deliberate care, she closed the albums and put both down on the leather cushion beside her. "What am I supposed to do? Am I supposed to forget about her? To put away the albums and all my memories and just pretend that she never existed?"

Carol was shaking her head. "No, Gail, no," she whispered. "Nobody is asking you to forget about Cindy. Just don't forget about yourself. You have to go on living. You have a family that loves you, a wonderful husband who loves you. We all have to carry on somehow . . ."

Gail laughed sadly. "You *do* sound like Mother," she said softly.

"I knew it," Carol said, laughing and crying at the same time. "I knew it was going to happen."

"That's all right," Gail cried. "She's not such a bad person to sound like." She hugged her sister, then reached over and picked up the leather-bound book of photographs. "You're right," she said, crossing to the other side of the room and stacking the photo albums at the far end of the bookshelves before returning to her sister as if possessed of a new strength and purpose. "I'm very lucky to have you," she said. "But I think it's time you took your own advice and got on with your life. You've put things on hold for long enough because of me."

Carol nodded. "I have to admit that I've been thinking the same thing these last few days." She looked toward the albums on the bookshelves. "You seem much stronger now. You have Jack and Jennifer. I know you're going to be all right." She broke off. "Besides, I'm only a phone call away. If you need me . . ."

"I'll call, don't worry. When do you think you'll leave?"

"How about just after the July 4 weekend?"

Gail nodded her approval. "I think I'll go out for a walk," she said.

"Want me to come with you? It'll only take me a few minutes to change."

"No," Gail told her. "I won't be long."

Gail was secretly pleased that Carol felt it was time to return to New York. Not that Gail was tired of her company, far from it. Just that some things were better accomplished alone.

Gail looked around at the small clump of bushes, the well-trodden grass around the dark green bench, and knew that Carol was right. It was time to get on with the present, time to start getting things done. It was time, as Lieutenant Cole had told her earlier, to start putting her life back together.

There was only one way she could do that and that was by finding the man who had torn it apart.

A drifter, the lieutenant had postulated. Gail thought the term a good one to describe herself as well. It contained just the right touch of irony, she decided, as she walked behind the bench and into the trees, no longer a grieving mother searching for memories, but a detective, as it were, ferreting out clues. She knelt on the ground and ran her hand along the soft earth, feeling for the spot where her daughter had fallen, feeling for the weight of the stranger as he fell on top of her. Gail looked toward the bushes, letting her fingers bounce haphazardly along their branches. She wasn't sure what exactly she was looking for, but she was determined to keep looking until she found it.

Her eyes traveled back and forth between the bushes and the ground. The police, despite their valiant efforts, had found nothing. All their tips, all their "hot leads," had led exactly nowhere. She had given them all this time and they hadn't been able to do anything with it but apologize and advise patience. They would never find the man responsible. She would have to do that herself as she had known all along she would.

It was the end of June. The murder had occurred on April 30. In a few days it would be the Fourth of July. She stood up and took a final look around the small park. Enough time had been wasted.

The sixty days were up.

Chapter 11

Gail spent the better part of the holiday weekend reading every article she could get her hands on concerning deviant sexual behavior. She learned that the world was full of people who like their sex in groups, in graveyards or on church pews; that others preferred members of their own sex, members of the animal kingdom or members of the dear departed. There were those who were into bondage and those who were into buggery, those who liked to exhibit and those who chose to watch. Some liked to beat; others preferred being beaten.

She learned all the terms. There were the standards with which she was already familiar such as homosexuality, lesbianism and sodomy. There was the masochist, the sadist and the rapist. There were also words like necrophilia, coprophilia and pedophilia.

Pedophilia—sex with children.

The articles confirmed much of what Lieutenant Cole had already told her, that sex offenders were almost exclusively male and usually young, that they hated women or feared them, that they hated themselves and feared their desires. They had often been abused or neglected as children, born to monsters, and so destined to become ones themselves. Small cruelties grew larger with the passage of time. There was little that could be done to help these people, even less to protect others from them.

Men who preyed on little girls were characteristically quiet and cowardly. They killed more from fear of discovery than from desire to inflict further pain, although there were those demented minds who regarded the kill itself as the ultimate in thrills.

Society's attitudes toward the more sexually adventuresome had changed through the years, moving from one of strict condemnation to a more casual acceptance. It was now generally assumed that consenting adults could do whatever they wished in the privacy of their own homes. There were private clubs and even public bathhouses to accommodate what was becoming increasingly acceptable social behavior.

Even the hard-core deviant, the sexual psychotic, who didn't ask but took, who violated and destroyed regardless of age and beyond all reason, was being viewed in a more sympathetic light, no longer held responsible for his actions.

The papers and weekly newsmagazines were full of stories of the gross indecencies of so-called justice. Gail sat on the wing chair in her living room, a newspaper on her lap, a cup of coffee and a stack of magazines at her feet, and mentally reviewed what she had read in the latest editions of *Time* and *Newsweek*.

There was the story of a twelve-year-old girl in Canada whose grandfather had been accused of molesting her. The judge had dismissed the case after extensive questioning of the girl revealed that she couldn't remember the last time she had been to church. The judge reasoned that with no religious upbringing she couldn't properly understand the seriousness of the oath she would be asked to take, and since she was the prosecutor's only witness, the case against the accused was dismissed.

Gail had read this item three times through to make sure that she understood it, that she hadn't left anything out. When she was satisfied that she had indeed read it correctly, she lowered the magazine to her lap and let her eyes drift to where Jack sat reading a spy novel on the sofa. The message of the article was fairly clear, she decided. Children were somehow less than people; the deviant would be set free.

Another story concerned a woman, two of whose children had died previously under highly suspicious circumstances—one had drowned in the bathtub at the age of seven months, and the other had apparently swallowed some sort of poison—who was now accused of causing the death of her three-month-old daughter by willful neglect. She had been found guilty and was sentenced to a grand total of two years less a day in prison. She vowed that once she got out, she intended to have many more children, that no one could stop her from having as many children as God intended.

Again Gail had lowered the magazine to her lap, pondering the meaning of what she had read. It was all right to kill a child, she reasoned, especially if it was your own child. Again children were considered less than people. The murderer of probably three defenseless children had been sentenced to only two years in jail.

There were similar stories in the Sunday New York Times: a man who had shot and killed his wife had been given the same sentence as that of the woman who had killed her babies, because he had shown genuine remorse and was unlikely to commit such an act again; two men were freed after a judge ruled that the woman they had raped and sodomized had consented to the acts. He cited the photographs one of the men had taken which showed the victim smiling through her tears while she was being buggered as sufficient evidence to dismiss the charges, despite the victim's testimony that the men had threatened to kill her if she did not smile for the camera. The judge had ruled that the woman was obviously enjoying herself. He dismissed evidence of her two subsequent suicide attempts and lingering depression. It was obvious, he had ruled, that she had been remorseful only after the fact.

Toward the back of one of the newspapers were two more stories of a slightly different nature. A man in Florida had shot and killed two young men who had attempted to rob his store. Apparently, he had actually killed one as the youth was ordering him at gunpoint to open the cash register, and then he had calmly walked over to the by now cowering second young man and fired a bullet into his brain. The shop owner was now considered something of a local hero and was happily giving interviews on the right of the American people to protect their property.

In another incident, a group of irate New Yorkers, who upon seeing an old and well-liked shopkeeper shot dead by a robber, had, rather than calling the police, taken off after the killer themselves. They caught up with him and fell on him, tearing out his eyes in furious revenge.

Gail read both these last stories again with a mixture of revulsion and curious satisfaction.

"Are you all right?" Jack asked suddenly. Gail looked up to find him staring at her, his book in his lap.

"Yes," she answered. "Why?"

"You were shaking."

"Was I?" Gail asked in surprise. She shrugged and folded up the paper.

Jack looked at his watch. "It's almost midnight," he said. "I think I'll call it a night. You coming?"

"I thought I'd wait up for Jennifer."

"What for? She's with Eddie, isn't she?"

"Just thought I'd wait up in case she felt like talking. You know that I never really fall asleep until I hear her come in anyway."

"Maybe *you're* the one who feels like talking," Jack pressed gently. "Upset because Carol leaves tomorrow?"

Gail shook her head. "No. It's time."

"It's time for a lot of things," Jack said softly, walking over to her chair and taking her hand in his. "Time we started seeing some of our friends again . . ."

"I know."

"Laura and Mike invited us for dinner again next week . . ."

"I'm sorry about this weekend. I just didn't feel up to celebrating."

"I understand, and so do they. I didn't feel much like celebrating either. But a quiet dinner with friends might be something to look forward to."

"Maybe."

Jack knelt down beside her. "I love you," he said.

"I love you too."

"How are you? How are you *really?*" he probed. "Look at me when you answer. Don't try to hide anything from me."

"I could never hide anything from you," she said, pushing the newspaper deeper into her lap. "How am I? What can I say? I'm lonely," she said after a long pause. "More than anything else, I guess I'm lonely. I miss her so much."

She saw Jack's eyes instantly well with tears and he turned his head to face the wall. "Look at me," she told him softly, repeating his words. "Don't try to hide anything from me."

"I miss her too," he said, his voice husky and strained.

"You have your work, at least that's something. It keeps your mind occupied, keeps you busy."

"Yes," he agreed, "and it's been a lifesaver in many respects. But there are days when some guy will come in with his little girl and they'll both be crying over some runover cat, and I can hardly see the cat for the little girl, and I wish I'd had more time with my own little girl. You were so lucky, you know, lucky because of all the time you got to spend with her, although I guess that's one of the things that makes it so hard for you now." He shook his head. "It's affected my work," he said after a pause.

"What do you mean?"

"I guess it's a question of caring. I don't care as much anymore."

"But Jack, you've always loved what you do."

"I know. But after something like this happens, it's hard to get too worked up over whether a cat lives or dies. They're just animals, for God's sake." He paused, shaking his head. "Although I must admit I had the cutest little dog in the other day. I've been as busy as hell, you know; you'd think I was the only veterinarian in Essex County, probably because of all the publicity. Whatever the reason, I've never seen so many sick animals."

"Tell me about the little dog," Gail said.

"It was a mixed breed, part poodle, part Pekingese, which sounds like a terrible combination, but it wasn't at all. It was a beautiful little thing, apricot in color. Smart as a whip. Mixed breeds usually are. Much smarter than thoroughbreds. This was a female. She was in because her back legs were bothering her. You see that a lot with poodles. It's very interesting," he continued, lost in his own recollections, "because she really doesn't look like either a poodle or a Peke. She looks more like a cocker spaniel. I don't know where that comes from." He stopped, smiling at Gail sadly. "It looks like *I'm* the one who felt like talking."

"That's all right. I feel like listening."

"They're thinking of breeding her," Jack continued. "They've offered me the pick of the litter."

"You want a dog?" Gail asked in surprise. "You always said you saw enough animals at work."

"This one sort of got to me. I don't know. Something to think about."

"A puppy," Gail said, turning the thought over in her mind. "They're more work than having a baby."

"We could do that too."

Neither said anything for several long seconds.

"You can't replace one child with another," Gail said carefully.

"I know that."

"I don't think I'm ready to talk about this yet," Gail whispered.

Jack patted her shoulder. "I'm going up to bed." He stood up and held out his hand. "Come with me." There was a question in his voice.

Gail looked into his eyes. "I'm not ready for that yet either," she said quietly. "Please don't be angry."

"Why would I be angry? I'm a very patient man."

"I love you," Gail told him, thinking he deserved better.

"I know you do. Don't stay up too late."

Gail watched him leave the room, wondering how her ex-husband, Mark, would have handled such a tragedy. Most likely, he would have suffered through a month full of stiff drinks and then disappeared. Their marriage never would have survived the strain. He would have hopped into his metallic sports car and driven off into the sunset, buried himself and his memories in liquor and women. Certainly, he would never have displayed the compassion and understanding that Jack Walton just had.

She pictured Jack up in the bedroom, taking off his clothes, his strong body exposed and strangely vulnerable. They hadn't made love since the tragedy.

Sex had been one of the wonderful surprises about Jack. While sex with Mark had been probably the best thing about him, Mark looked as though that was the way things were supposed to be. He carried his sex appeal like a portfolio, and anything less than a superb performance in bed would have been a profound disappointment, a form of false advertising. Gail was aware that many good-looking men were less than sensational in bed, too preoccupied with their own bodies to give much attention to their partners, but Mark had not been like that. He really appreciated a woman's body. Unfortunately, Gail came to realize, he appreciated *any* woman's body, and after a while this came to alter her perception of their lovemaking. With Jack, Gail had expected a competent lover. She assumed he would be as workmanlike as his appearance, forceful yet caring, but not terribly original or demanding. She was only partly right. As a lover, Jack Walton was a constant well of surprises. He was indeed forceful and caring. He was also, as befitted the occasion, passive and shy, aggressive and abandoned, playful and gentle. After almost nine years of marriage, they had still made love often and eagerly.

But that was before the afternoon of April 30. Before some stranger lurking behind a clump of bushes had, with his own perverse desires, robbed her of any desires of her own.

Gail waited until she heard Eddie's car pull up outside and knew Jennifer was home safe before she folded up her papers and went upstairs to bed.

Jack was already asleep when Gail crawled in beside him. She stared through the darkness at his face until she was able to make out his features clearly, her eyes focusing on the soft curves of his barely parted lips.

He was so strong, she thought. So caring. He was trying so hard. She knew that despite his assurances to the contrary, she was disappointing him, letting him down.

Gail lay her head on the pillow next to his, staring up at the ceiling, thinking that her husband would be better off without her.

Chapter 12

She was asleep when she heard the noise.

There was someone at the front door. But the bell had not rung; she knew that no one had knocked. It was a different sound, and it took her a few minutes to realize that it was the sound of glass breaking. She sat up in bed and realized immediately that Jack was not beside her, that it was morning and that she seemed to be the only one in the house. She glanced quickly at the clock by the side of the bed. It was ten o'clock.

Her mind raced through the subsequent ramifications. Carol's bus had been scheduled to leave for New York at eight forty-five. Jack was going to drive her to the bus stop. Jennifer was starting to work for her dad at nine o'clock sharp. That meant she had missed them all.

Had she really slept so soundly?

Had they tried to rouse her and failed? She'd been very tired, it was true, her mind weighted down with the information of her recent research, and Jennifer hadn't arrived home until almost 2 A.M. She'd have to speak to Jennifer about that. Two o'clock was too late to be coming home even during summer holidays.

Gail got out of bed and walked to the window, pulling back the blue curtain and looking into the backyard. Her senses felt dulled. She seemed to walk as if in slow motion, every action exaggerated and heavy. Her sister had left without saying goodbye, she puzzled, hearing the sound of more glass breaking.

She froze. Someone was trying to break in.

She stood absolutely still for several long seconds, not sure what she should do. Whoever it was obviously thought that no one was home. What would they do if they found her here? In an article she'd read recently, an old woman had been killed when she had surprised a robber in her home. The killer-thief had received a sentence of five years in prison.

Gail looked toward the phone and wondered if she had time to call the police. Then her eyes shot to the silver button on the wall above the phone, the "panic button" which rang directly into the police station when pressed, signifying an emergency. She had protested when Jack had insisted on installing it along with the burglar alarm system he'd had put in just after the robbery. "They won't come back," she had argued. But they obviously had.

She heard someone forcing the lock on the inside of the door and knew that whoever it was was only moments away from getting inside, that in several seconds his feet would be on the stairs. She had time to get to the button, she realized, and the sound of it would undoubtedly frighten the burglar away. She made a move toward the button and then stopped, holding her breath with the sudden realization that she didn't want to frighten the man away. Maybe it was the same man who'd murdered Cindy.

Lieutenant Cole could have been wrong when he'd said it was unlikely that Cindy's killer had also been the man who robbed their house. The police profile postulated that the killer had a past record of arrests for petty crimes. It was possible, she thought, catching her breath. God, anything was possible. At any rate, she was going to stand right where she was and wait for him. She was not going to move.

Suddenly, she heard a voice coming from the hall-way.

"Mom," Jennifer was asking, "what's that noise?"

Gail stared at her daughter who stood staring back at her from the doorway. "What are you doing home?" she asked.

"I slept in. I was out kind of late," she admitted sheepishly. "I called Dad. He said it was okay to start this afternoon instead." A look of fear crept over her face. "What's that noise, Mom?"

So, she was not alone in the house. Jennifer was there. She couldn't stand there and wait for the man at the door. She had to protect her child.

An instant later, she heard the front door as it gave way. "Oh my God," she muttered, grabbing Jennifer's hand, aware now that footsteps were circling the inner hallway and moving into the downstairs rooms. "Quick," she shouted at Jennifer, pulling her hand and running with her to the hall, not sure in which direction to turn. She started to her left, then quickly back-tracked to her right, Jennifer's feet tripping over themselves in the confusion, her hand slipping out of her mother's, her body careening toward the floor, a loud gasp escaping her mouth.

Gail raced back and grabbed her hand, pulling Jennifer to her feet and dragging her along the hallway. Jennifer cried out in dismay. "Be quiet," her mother admonished with growing panic as the men—there were two of them, she noted quickly, one young with light brown hair—reached the top of the stairs. Gail pushed her daughter back into her bedroom and they slammed the door behind them. "Help me," she yelled to Jennifer, and the two women pulled first a chair, then a small table toward the door. "Press the panic button," Gail commanded, and Jennifer rushed in its direction as Gail dragged the heavy dresser which sat across from her bed to further block the entrance to the bedroom. Jennifer pressed the button in the same second that the men began pounding against the newly erected barricades. It sounded immediately, but the noise from the alarm did nothing to deter them. Gail grabbed Jennifer, hugging her close, then ran with her into the adjoining bathroom. Frantically, with Jennifer now starting to weep, Gail pulled the contents of one of the cupboards under the sink out onto the floor. "Get in there," she commanded, surprised at how easily her daughter was able to fit inside. "Don't move or make a sound." Someone would come to help them soon, she tried to reassure her, and it was imperative that Jennifer not let anyone know where she was until she knew she was safe. Then Gail quickly piled the contents of that drawer into another before racing back into her room, to the intercom on the bedroom wall. Flipping the button which connected to the front door, she began screaming for help. Surely people would hear her screams as they walked past the house and someone would rush in to save them. She stared at the panic button—where were the police? Gail saw that the furniture was beginning to give way in front of the bedroom door, and knew that she had only a few minutes before the men on the other side would succeed in breaking through. She resumed her screams into the intercom, finally abandoning the attempt when she saw the bedroom door beginning to open.

She ran quickly, her heart thumping wildly, into the bathroom and locked the door. The lock could be easily picked with a bobby pin and wouldn't hold for long, she knew. One good slam would send it flying open. She looked to the bathroom window and toyed with the idea of jumping out. Even though they were on the second floor and the fall to the ground would probably injure them severely, she decided it would be better than risking certain death at the hands of the lunatics who had now succeeded in breaking into her bedroom. She looked around for something to hurl through the window, to shatter the glass. There was nothing. The men were at the bathroom door. They were laughing, arguing loudly and playfully with one another over who should have the honor of busting it, which woman they would have first. Gail hurried to the medicine cabinet and pulled out Jack's straight razor, lunging back behind the door just as it burst open.

"Come out, come out, wherever you are," one of the men sang in a gross parody of the children's song. While his companion began tearing apart the bedroom, the first man—the young one with the light brown hair—strode purposefully toward the cupboard under the sink as if directed by magic. As he lowered his hand to pull open the small door, Gail lunged in his direction, her arms grabbing his head and pulling it sharply back, the straight razor slicing across his throat like a line of red ink. He fell back gurgling, his eyes filled more with surprise than pain, as the second man—and now Gail noticed that he too was young, with the same color hair as the first—came rushing to his aid.

Gail felt strong arms around her waist, lifting her into the air. Flailing about wildly, she brought one foot up, then kicked it furiously back, catching her assailant square between his legs. He bellowed sharply with the sudden, intense pain, releasing his grip on Gail's body as she spun about and caught him with her razor as he was about to fall. The blood flew from his throat and splattered against the walls, his jugular vein severed. Gail walked between the man's legs and kicked him there again. Then she picked up the gun that had fallen to the floor in the scuffle, and of which she had only now become aware, and held it to the man's head. She pulled the trigger three times in rapid succession. When there was nothing left of his face, and his light brown hair was soaked in red, she walked calmly over to the second man and shot him too. Then she dropped the gun to the floor and sank down beside it.

"Mommy," she heard the small voice cry from underneath the sink, and she ran toward it, opening the door and preparing to pull her daughter out. Arms reached up and surrounded her neck as Gail closed her eyes in relief, cradling the small body in her lap and against her bloody nightgown. The two of them rocked gently back and forth together.

"I saved you," Gail repeated over and over to the rhythm, looking down to see Cindy, not Jennifer, in her arms. She crushed Cindy tightly to her breast. "I saved my beautiful baby."

Gail sat up abruptly in bed and looked toward the clock. It was a few minutes before seven. Jack lay asleep beside her. She reached over gingerly and turned off the alarm so that it wouldn't ring.

It had all been a dream.

But a dream of a different sort, she recognized immediately. Up until now, her dreams had been inconclusive, fraught with frustration. What made them nightmares had been her inability to act. Night after night, she had confronted her daughter's murderer and each time she had been unable to move, unable to take even the smallest of steps toward avenging her daughter's death. She had awakened from those dreams screaming, her body bathed in a cold sweat, her head and heart racing.

Now she felt only a curious calm and the same sort of strange satisfaction she had experienced the night before when reading about the shop owner in Florida who had gunned down his two would-be robbers and the irate New Yorkers who had taken the justice system into their own hands.

Jack stirred beside her. Gail watched him balancing on the border between sleep and consciousness. Did he have such dreams? she wondered.

She looked down at the front of her nightgown. The pale pink bodice was untouched by the rude red stains of her imagination. Her hands were clean and dry.

Soon she was standing inside the bathroom, beside the tub, looking at the gaily papered walls, feeling the hard, cool tile under her toes.

Normally, she would have taken a shower. But this

morning, a shower seemed too abrupt. She needed a slower, gentler awakening.

She reached over and began running the tub. A few minutes later she was soaking peacefully inside it, seeing the blood splattered artfully across the walls and lost in the dream that she had saved her little girl.

Chapter 13

Over the next few weeks the routine in the Waltons' household subtly shifted. Gail was still rising early, before everyone else. She still prepared breakfast for her husband and daughter, cleaned up when they were through and watched them leave in the morning, Jack for his office, Jennifer for her new job assisting her father. Gail would clear the table as always, go upstairs and make the beds, and take meat out of the freezer for the evening meal. She would then go over the morning paper, her maps of New Jersey spread out in front of her.

She remembered Lieutenant Cole's advice: for the purposes of her investigation, she had to assume that Cindy's killer had stayed in the state. She had no hope of finding him if he had moved elsewhere. Gail made up her mind that the young man with the dirty blond hair who had raped and murdered her six-year-old child was still somewhere within easy grasp. He was quietly living in New Jersey, perhaps still in the Livingston area. It was only a question of ferreting him out.

She decided to concentrate on the same areas as the police—East Orange, Orange, possibly Newark, districts where transients drifted in and out in comfortable anonymity, streets where the words "of no fixed address" were more than just a convenient expression for the newspapers. But unlike the police, she would not be defeated.

Despite her resolve, she was nervous. She was an amateur, after all. The police were professionals and they had gotten nowhere. Still, she had spent the better part of the past two weeks preparing. There was little else her maps could tell her, only so much more she could learn from books and magazines. Lieutenant Cole had nothing new to report. She had delayed long enough.

On the morning of July 18, Gail knew that it was time to put the maps away and get out into the streets. Hadn't Sharon Tate's father grown a beard and donned hippie garb, living with the undesirables on the Sunset Strip when he was trying to find his daughter's brutal killers? Gail would have to do the same.

Jack had seemed unusually talkative at breakfast, perhaps sensing her preoccupation. "I had a German shepherd in the office yesterday," he began. "Funniest damn thing. The dog's been trained as a watchdog supposedly, but it's one of the gentlest dogs I've ever seen. I can't imagine it hurting anyone."

"So, what was funny?" Jennifer asked, already smiling, eager to laugh.

Gail looked across the table at her husband, trying to appear interested, her mind already behind the wheel of her car.

"Well, apparently, their house was robbed. Everybody was asleep. The dog was downstairs in the front hallway where it always sleeps. Everything was quiet. The next morning Mr. and Mrs. Simpson came downstairs, and half the house was missing. And this damn dog is sitting there wagging its tail. Didn't make a sound all night. Not a bark out of him. Meanwhile, they've been cleaned out. They called the police, who came right over, and wouldn't you know it? The dog bit the policeman."

Jennifer shrieked with delight.

Gail continued to stare at Jack pleasantly but otherwise failed to react.

"Mom?" Jennifer asked, "didn't you think that was funny?"

"What?" Gail said, startled back to reality. "I'm sorry, my mind must have wandered. I didn't hear the punch line."

Jack shook his head. "It wasn't important."

"Your mind's been wandering a lot lately," Jennifer pouted.

"I'm sorry," Gail said genuinely. "I thought I was paying attention. Tell the story again, Jack. I'd really like to hear it."

Jack dutifully repeated the slender tale and Gail concentrated hard on listening, but the spontaneity was missing and when it was over, nobody laughed. "I guess you had to be there," Jack concluded, obvious disappointment in his voice.

"No," Gail objected weakly, "that was a very cute story. The dog bit the policeman. That's funny."

"I have to go," Jennifer announced with some agitation. She stood up and leaned over to kiss her mother's forehead. "See you later."

"Goodbye, baby," Gail said. "Be careful."

Jennifer stopped halfway to the kitchen door. "I'm not a baby, Mom," she said with slow deliberation.

"No, of course you're not," Gail agreed. "What was all that about?" she asked Jack after they heard the front door close.

"Jennifer claims you've been treating her like a little kid lately."

"Like a little kid? Why? Just because I call her 'baby'? It's a term of affection, that's all. You know that. *She* knows that. I've always called her 'baby' and 'doll' and . . ."

"That was before. She didn't mind being called

'baby' as long as she felt she was being treated like an adult."

"She's not an adult. She's sixteen."

Jack shrugged. "I don't want to argue with you. You asked me what was going on with Jennifer."

"What else? She's obviously talked to you about this at some length."

"That's all."

"Jack . . ."

"She's a bit hurt that you haven't shown more interest in the work she's doing with her father. She says she's tried to talk to you a number of times about her job with Mark, but that you just kind of drift off when she's in the middle of telling you something. She's afraid you might be angry with her."

"Why would I be angry with her?"

"She thought maybe you didn't like the idea of her working with Mark."

"That's silly. She knows I have no problems with that."

"She's afraid you're angry with her because of what she told you about Cindy, that she'd been mean to her . . ."

Gail was growing rapidly impatient with the conversation. "That's ridiculous. She knows how I feel. We've discussed it. I told her—"

"Tell her again. She needs to talk to you, Gail. She needs your love and approval."

"She *has* my love and approval!"

"She needs your attention." He smiled sheepishly at her. "*I* need your attention."

Gail lowered her head. "I'm sorry. I've been preoccupied lately, I know. And moody. I'll try to watch it."

"Jennifer's really very excited about her work with Mark," Jack laughed. "You should hear her talk about tripods and camera angles, and it's pretty fascinating stuff actually. Gail . . ."

"What?"

"What did I just say?"

Gail saw the look of irritation that passed through Jack's eyes. "I'm sorry, I didn't realize you'd said anything . . ."

Jack stood up. "I better go." He leaned down to kiss her forehead as Jennifer had done moments before. "I'll call you later."

"I might be out," she said quickly.

"Oh? Where are you going?"

"I thought I'd go for a drive."

"It probably wouldn't be a bad idea to take the car in for a tune-up," Jack said on his way out. "We missed the last one."

Gail poured herself a second cup of coffee after he had left the house, feeling edgy and uncomfortable. She hadn't realized she'd been so distracted lately, that Jennifer had sensed it and been hurt. Jack too. She put her coffee cup down. She would have to make a special point of showing appropriate interest in all of their recent activities. It was important, she told herself, reaching for the morning paper.

There was an interesting story on page 2. A young man of eighteen, while stoned on a variety of drugs, had brutally bludgeoned to death with a hammer the mother of his best friend. A sympathetic judge, citing the boy's already pronounced suicidal tendencies, had sentenced the boy to a three-year suspended sentence. "Suspended," Gail repeated aloud. Though she had heard that word a thousand times in the past, it was only lately that the full impact of its meaning was becoming clear. A woman was dead; her killer was out on the streets. Suspended. Society would be serving his sentence.

A small story on page 5 captured her attention. She read it quickly and then got up off her chair and hunted by the phone for a red pen. She found one and brought it back to the table, reading through the article again and underlining the appropriate information. There had been three robberies on one street in Newark over the weekend. She underlined the street—Washington Street. A pawnshop, a men's clothing store and a savings and loan had all been held up by a lone gunman. The man, who had shot and injured one customer when he tried to block his escape, was described as Caucasian, around twenty-five years of age, with dirty blond hair. He stood about five feet nine inches tall and had a slim build. He fit the description of the man the boys had seen running from the park after Cindy had been killed. Gail lowered the paper to the table. The description could fit any of a hundred young men in the Livingston area alone.

The phone rang.

"I don't care what you say," Laura began cheerfully as soon as Gail said hello, "but I'm taking you to lunch today. Name a spot."

Gail tried to protest. "Laura, I can't . . ."

"If you have a meeting with the dentist, cancel it. If you have an appointment with your gynecologist, forget it. If you already have a lunch date, then break it. I am taking you to lunch and I won't take no for an answer. Now, where would you like to eat?"

Gail nervously fidgeted with her newspaper. "I'm not very hungry for lunch these days—" She broke off suddenly when she saw the ad. "Maestro's," it proclaimed gaily. "The very best in Italian cooking." It was located on Washington Street.

"Gail, haven't you been eating?" she heard Laura asking.

"Maestro's," Gail told her.

"What?"

"You told me to name a place. I'd like to go to Maestro's."

"I've never heard of it."

"It's supposed to have the very best in Italian cooking."

"Well, I love Italian food. Where is this place? Is it new?"

"It's on Washington Street."

There was a second's silence. "Washington Street? You mean Washington Street in Newark?"

"Yes," Gail said firmly. "I've heard it's wonderful."

"Christ, Gail, isn't there somewhere a little closer to home? A little nicer? I was thinking more of Mayfair Farms."

"Maestro's," Gail repeated firmly.

"Maestro's it is," Laura agreed after a pause.

"I'll pick you up at noon," Gail told her.

Before Laura had a chance to ask any more questions, Gail had said goodbye and hung up the phone.

"Gail, what are we doing here?" Laura asked, speaking in a low voice and bending conspiratorially across the table.

"We're having lunch," Gail said, smiling.

"Maybe you're having lunch. I'm too nervous to eat."

"Salad's delicious," Gail laughed.

"Gail, have you looked around you? This is a mob hangout, for God's sake."

"Laura, you're being a little dramatic . . ."

"No, I'm not. Take a good look around. Go on. Just don't be too obvious about it."

Gail put down her salad fork, and slowly let her eyes circle the large, dimly lit room, though there was really no need. She had absorbed everything about the place from the minute she had stepped inside, just as she had taken in every shabby detail of Washington Street, every crack in each window they passed, absorbing the shuffling footsteps of a nearby wino, the cackling laugh of an elderly bag lady as she sifted through a corner garbage bin. Inside the restaurant, Gail's eyes had needed only a few seconds to adjust to the shift in light, to determine that the clientele was mostly well dressed and business-oriented. Instantly, she understood that Cindy's killer would not be here, but at least she had made a beginning.

The two women ordered salad and pasta, and Gail had found herself surprisingly hungry, digging into her salad while Laura nervously picked at hers.

"Relax, Laura," Gail told her, her eyes returning to her friend across the table. "Nobody's going to come in and gun us down."

"Yeah? You remember that restaurant in New York where those four guys were having a drink at the bar and somebody opened up with a machine gun? And it turned out that he shot the wrong four guys."

"Innocent people die every day," Gail said matter-of-factly, watching as Laura stopped cold in the middle of a halfhearted stab at a piece of lettuce. "Sorry, I didn't mean for it to come out that way."

"What are we doing here, Gail?" Laura asked again slowly.

"We're having lunch," Gail repeated as before. "Tell me, have you seen Nancy lately?"

"She managed to fit me into her busy schedule for one lunch last week. But it wasn't easy. Between getting her hair done, having her back rubbed and planning for the next fashion show, it's all she can do to find time to have her nails done, let alone have lunch."

"I think she was very hurt when Larry left her," Gail mused, almost to herself. "The rest of us weren't as understanding as we could have been."

"Maybe," Laura said. "But she lost me when she got so vindictive, taking Larry to the cleaners the way she did."

"Larry could afford to go to the cleaners. Who's to say who was right?" Gail thought back to the evening in Lloyd Michener's living room. " 'Judge not lest you be judged,' " she said aloud, recalling the group's motto.

"I guess you're right," Laura agreed quietly. "Anyway, you can expect your invitation in the mail sometime in September."

"Invitation?"

"For the fashion show. Nancy's organizing it this year. October 15, I think she said."

"I think I'll pass."

"You'll do no such thing. Come on, a couple of hours in the middle of a cold afternoon with a bunch of silly, shallow women is just what you need. I always wondered how such vacuous minds could make so much noise."

"Laura . . ."

"Yes, I know, I'm being judgmental again, but that's the whole point of clubs like Nancy's. They're there to give the rest of us something to be nasty about. I wouldn't miss this fashion show for the world. And neither will you. Come on, do me a favor and come with me. I won't enjoy myself if I don't have anybody there I can bitch to. Please. For me?"

Gail nodded agreement. October 15 seemed very far away.

Laura speared a large cherry tomato and raised it to her mouth. "Have you thought about getting a job?" she asked, catching Gail by surprise.

"A job? What kind of job could I get?"

Laura shrugged and swallowed the tomato. "Maybe you could go back to school. Work on finishing your degree."

"That's a possibility."

"In the meantime, what about your piano lessons? Have you given any thought to starting them up again?"

"I can't," Gail answered quickly as the waiter approached and cleared away the salad bowls, reappearing a minute later with the pasta of the day. "I've tried to sit down and play a few times and I can't even do that. My hands start to shake. I see Cindy—"

"It's probably just as well," Laura said, cutting her off gently. "I think you need something that gets you out of the house."

"I was thinking the same thing," Gail told her, digging into her pasta, knowing they were not thinking the same thing at all.

Chapter 14

For the rest of the summer Gail divided her time between her home in Livingston and her excursions into Newark and East Orange.

Her days were spent traveling in her car from one run-down street to the next, casing the stores that had been recently robbed in much the same way she envisioned the perpetrator of the crime had done, watching those who went in and out, those who loitered nearby, her eyes watchful for anyone who might fit the vague description of her child's killer. In the beginning, she rarely got out of her car.

She was always home by four o'clock, in time to get supper ready for Jack and Jennifer. When her husband and daughter walked through the front door at the end of the day, they invariably found Gail in the kitchen putting the finishing touches on dinner. They had no idea how she spent her days.

"Oh wow, I'm tired," Jennifer exclaimed one evening, falling into her seat at the kitchen table.

"Tough day?" Gail asked, putting the roast on the table for dinner. "Careful, it's hot."

"Looks good," Jack said, starting to help himself.

"I hope so," Gail worried. The traffic out of East Orange had been bad, and she'd been late getting home. She wasn't sure the meat had had enough time to cook.

"I don't know how Dad does it every day," Jennifer continued. "Some of these people . . . they can't sit still for two seconds, or it's like pulling teeth to get them to smile. They're so stiff, and some of them think they're God's gift to the camera. You should see the poses! But Dad's terrific. He's so patient with everyone. He listens to them telling him which is their best side or what kind of mood they want to capture, and he agrees, and then he just goes ahead and takes his pictures the way he intended to all along."

Gail smiled. It sounded like Mark.

"Sometimes I think a picture is going to be beautiful, because the woman he's photographing is beautiful, but Dad will tell me to wait and see, and sure enough the woman doesn't photograph well at all. And other people who aren't all that good-looking, their pictures turn out gorgeous. Dad says that some people are naturally more photogenic than others."

Gail sat down and put a small amount of food on her plate. "So, you're having a good time, are you?" she asked, very proud of her daughter and pleased that she was enjoying herself as much as she obviously was.

"I can't believe the summer's half over," Jennifer sighed.

"It is?" Gail was genuinely astonished.

"It's August 1 tomorrow."

"August 1," Gail repeated numbly. Time was passing so quickly, passing her by. She'd accomplished nothing.

"Gail . . ." Jack's voice was puzzled. "Are you all right?"

"Oh sure," Gail said, quickly jumping back into the conversation. "Is the meat too rare?"

"Just right," Jack told her. "Does anybody feel like a movie tonight?"

"Sounds great," Jennifer said immediately.

"I don't think so," Gail said at the same time. "You and Jack go," she added.

"Come on, Gail. It'll be good for all of us to get out together."

"We're going out together on Friday," she reminded them. Carol had called over the weekend with the announcement that she had managed to get tickets for the latest Broadway smash and that they were all to be her guests, no arguments permitted.

"That's Friday," Jennifer protested. "This is Tuesday."

"That's enough excitement for one week," Gail said, the tone in her voice indicating that as far as she was concerned the discussion was over. "Eat your dinner," she told her daughter.

Jennifer stared across the table at Jack.

"We'll go," he said to her. "If your mother changes her mind between now and the time we leave, she can always come with us."

Gail smiled, but she knew, and they knew, that her mind was made up.

On her excursion into East Orange the following afternoon, Gail decided it was time to get out of her car.

She began this new phase of her plan by opening an account at a branch of a savings and loan that had suffered a spate of recent robberies. While she waited in the long line in front of the teller's window, she perused the other customers, an almost even mixture of middle-aged whites and blacks, the women marginally outnumbering the men. The place itself was typically nondescript.

Gail wondered what she was doing here, turning toward the main entrance just as the door opened and a young man with a slim build and dirty blond hair came inside. He stood for a few minutes in the lobby and looked around, balancing on one foot and then the other, his head turning restlessly from side to side. Gail watched him, transfixed. He moved back and forth, his hands now going to the insides of his pockets. His eyes quickly passed over the other customers in the bank, stopping momentarily on Gail, looking her up and down before turning away again. Had he been measuring her for a bullet? Gail wondered, trying to will his eyes back to hers. But the youth had discarded her for a young girl in a pair of tight red elastic pants. Gail watched as he sauntered over to one of the counters containing the withdrawal and deposit slips, his eyes never leaving the pants of the teenage girl.

Gail moved forward in the line, felt someone come up behind her and half turned to catch the side of the youth's face. She was about to speak when she felt the stab of something sharp against her ribs. She lifted her elbow and saw the black tip of the gun. She waited breathlessly for his next move. But nothing happened and when she looked again, it wasn't the youth at all, just a man with a briefcase nudging her to move ahead. It was her turn with the teller.

She opened a small account with ten dollars. The teller made no comment, and the entire transaction was accomplished in a quarter of the time Gail had spent waiting. She hung around for a few minutes afterward, pretending to fumble in her purse by the door, waiting to see what the youth would do, keeping track of who went in and out, realizing again how many young men could be described as slim and fair-haired. She could not allow herself to get discouraged, she decided, as the young man, having connected with the girl in the red elastic pants, pushed past her at the door as if she weren't there.

In the next two days Gail opened similar accounts in a variety of banks and savings institutions throughout the shadier sections of Essex County, spending hours in her car, still more hours on her feet, patrolling the streets, all the while watching and waiting.

She began frequenting the numerous pawnshops in Newark and East Orange, startled at first by the amount of merchandise she found there. The first day, she took no part in the transactions, shaking her head and muttering a feeble "just looking" whenever someone asked if there was anything specific she was after. The next day Gail took in several items (an old brooch, some trinkets that had been lying around the house for years) and pawned them. She received eighteen dollars in total and deposited the money in one of her new accounts.

On Wednesday afternoon Gail ate lunch in a local greasy spoon, carefully photographing with her mind the noontime customers. On Thursday she brought her own lunch in a paper bag and ate in a nearby park with the men whose own paper bags concealed only bottles of cheap wine. She received many strange looks and realized it was the way she was dressed. She looked simply too well-off to be a frequenter of parks and greasy spoons. She'd have to do something about that, she decided, mentally reviewing her wardrobe for potentially suitable items.

On Friday she drove reluctantly into Manhattan to meet her sister for lunch. Carol had insisted, and Jack had agreed, that she drive in early so that the two sisters could have some time alone together. Jack and Jennifer would get a lift into town later with his receptionist.

Gail had gone along with the plan, afraid to make waves, to do or say anything that might be misconstrued. She felt it was important that everyone feel she was looking forward to this outing as much as they were, even though inside she felt nothing at all.

Jack had his work; Jennifer had her summer job, and her father as well as her stepfather. They both seemed able to function quite well without her. Gail simply wasn't needed anymore, despite what everyone kept telling her. Except for brief lapses, Gail's family and friends accepted her outer persona as genuine, and she was increasingly careful not to let her real feelings surface.

What were her real feelings? she wondered on the drive into Manhattan. She had none. She was dead inside. A Broadway show would hardly be enough to bring her back to life, although she would laugh and clap and pretend to enjoy it as much as everyone else.

The truth was that the only time she felt alive was when she was searching for death. But it would be pointless to try to tell anyone that. They would suggest anxiously that she seek professional help. They wouldn't understand. Did she?

Carol had made reservations for lunch at the Russian Tea Room. "I know it's touristy and kind of hokey, but what the hell?" she laughed, and Gail laughed with her. "You look good. A little thin."

The two sisters walked along Broadway toward Fifty-seventh Street, Gail taking careful note of the hawkers and seedy shops that lined the streets.

"I'd forgotten how filthy it is," Gail remarked, sidestepping a pool of fresh vomit that lay in the center of the street.

"This is clean," Carol said with sincerity. "A few years ago it was worse than this."

Gail looked in the windows of all the stereo stores, but they seemed filled more with pornographic video tapes than with traditional stereo equipment. As they approached the corner, Gail saw a small crowd surrounding a lone man whose hand was waving something in the air, his voice raised and strong.

"Let's cross the street," Carol advised.

"What's he saying?" Gail asked, ignoring her sister and drawing closer to the crowd.

The something in the man's hand turned out to be a petition advocating stiffer penalties for violent crimes. Gail listened enthralled as the man told of his son-in-law having been knifed to death in an attempted robbery ten months before. The man collecting the signatures went on to say that the youth responsible had been found soon after the incident and brought to trial. After many delays the case was finally heard and the guilty party sentenced to twenty-one months in jail for manslaughter. The shock of this light sentence was further aggravated when the man was informed by the police that the killer would probably be out on the streets in seven months.

"Let's go," Carol whispered uneasily, tugging on Gail's arm.

Gail extricated her elbow gently from her sister's grasp, watching the faces of the people in the crowd as the man spoke, studying their reactions. The growing crowd listened attentively, almost respectfully, their faces reflecting concern, even fear, and perhaps admiration, as the man went on to explain that he had subsequently quit his job and begun traveling across the country, launching a national petition campaign calling for stiffer penalties for violent crimes. So far, he boasted, he had almost one million signatures. Gail quickly added her own to the list, and Carol did likewise, as the woman beside them exclaimed that it probably wouldn't do much good, that politicians were notoriously deaf unless an election was around the corner. The woman had signed anyway.

"I've signed every petition that's ever been drawn up," she told them. "I've campaigned till I'm blue in the face for the return of the death penalty . . ."

"What good does the death penalty do?" another woman interjected. "It's never deterred anyone. We've got to learn to rid our minds and bodies of all this hate or we'll never live in peace. We have to find God and accept that His way is the only way . . ."

"I can't believe that God wants innocent people to die and their killers to go free."

"Spare us these high-school diatribes on the existence of God," a plump man stated vehemently. "If there is a God, then He has absolutely no bearing on my life." The woman who had mentioned God now silently crossed herself and whispered a prayer in the crowd's behalf. "The point is that it doesn't matter what you sign or even whom you elect in New York. We have a governor who's promised to veto any capital-punishment statute that the legislature passes, just like his predecessor did. Just getting capital punishment back on the books doesn't mean it's going to get anything accomplished."

"It's a start," someone said.

"I'm not in favor of capital punishment," a man said loudly from behind Gail. "It doesn't solve anything."

"I'm with you," a woman who had not spoken before agreed. "It only makes us as barbaric as the killers."

"Baloney," the plump man shouted.

Carol was once again tugging on Gail's arm. "Gail, let's go."

"If we could only be sure that the courts would lock these people away forever . . ."

"Never happen."

"They're out on the street before you are," the man with the petition exclaimed bitterly. "Everyone feels so sorry for them. They're misunderstood. They had miserable childhoods. Well, that's too bad. I, for one, say that we should stop worrying so damn much about the criminals and start paying some attention to the victims and their families. We're the ones who have to live the rest of our lives with what these murderers have done."

"That's a tired old argument."

"There's nothing tired about it."

The voices began coming very fast, falling one on top of the other like a stack of dominoes. Gail could no longer keep track of who was speaking. She closed her eyes and listened to the sound their confused and angry voices made. Their faces were unimportant. She didn't have to see them to know them. She saw them every day in her own reflection.

"Gail, I've had enough. Let's go to lunch."

"I want to hear this."

"I don't," Carol said forcefully, starting to move away. "Look, we've signed the petition. There's nothing else we can accomplish here. Let's go." Gail didn't budge. "Gail, I'm going. Half the people signing this stupid thing are pickpockets and muggers. I'm getting out of here."

"I'll meet you at the restaurant," Gail told her.

"Gail!"

Gail turned her attention back to the crowd, peripherally aware that Carol had vacated the space beside her and someone else had replaced her.

"Capital punishment tries to vindicate one murder by committing another. How can you say that's right?"

"Society has a right to take force against injustice."

"No one has the right to take a life."

"Nothing will bring our murdered children back to us."

"That's not the point . . ."

"The point being?"

"The point being," Gail heard someone saying as she pictured her daughter's body discarded in the dirt, "that some people just don't deserve to live."

"Exactly," nodded the man beside her.

After that, the gathering seemed to run out of steam and the people began to disperse.

Gail looked around the corner for Carol but she was gone. She'd have to find her and apologize. Gail turned in the direction of the Russian Tea Room, catching sight of a fair-haired youth who was studying her from a distance of several feet.

When her eyes caught his, the youth turned his head quickly and moved away, more than a touch self-consciously, looking back at her over his shoulder several times. Gail kept careful track of his movements, only to lose him in a fresh onslaught of pedestrians.

She peered with great concentration through the people, but the youth had virtually disappeared. Gail proceeded carefully, looking into each store window, wondering what there was about the boy that was pulling her forward.

He had been watching her. Had he recognized her from her photographs in the newspapers? Had he known who she was? Was it possible that Cindy's killer had fled to New York, seeking to lose himself among the other illegals and undesirables? Could she possibly have stumbled across him in so miraculous a fashion?

No, this was crazy, she thought, remembering her sister, about to turn back toward Fifty-seventh Street.

And then she saw him across the street, going into what was euphemistically referred to as an adult bookstore. Gail took a deep breath and crossed the street, reaching the bookstore and pushing open its door, feeling several pairs of eyes turn in her direction as she walked inside and down the first aisle after the boy.

Whatever she had been expecting, whatever her mind had prepared her for, she was still sickened and surprised by what she saw. *Twenty New Cunts*, one magazine proclaimed simply, its pages filled with appropriate close-ups. Gail riffled quickly through several of the least offensive magazines she could find, all the while edging her way to the rear of the store.

The next aisle dealt mostly in bondage and discipline. There were photographs of women being whipped, women being chained, women being tortured with branding irons. *How to Rape a Virgin*, one article advised. In one memorable photograph, a woman was being stuffed into a meat grinder.

Gail closed her eyes and tried to will the rising flood of nausea back into her stomach. Her hands shaking, she returned the magazine to its appropriate slot. She thought of Jennifer, studying the art of photography with her father. What of the people who took *these* pictures? she wondered. What of the men and mostly women who posed?

She reached the last aisle. More of the same, only worse. *Men Loving Boys*, she read, picking up the magazine and studying a picture of a perhaps thirty-year-old man with a boy no more than fourteen. *Little Girl Lost*, another title announced, the accompanying photographs depicting a young girl made up to look much younger. Her long hair was braided with ribbons, her boyish body was clad in a short, open pinafore; she wore little-girl socks and shoes. And no underpants, revealing a shaved pubic area. She was being ogled and fondled by several middle-aged men.

What was she doing in here? Gail wondered, suddenly panicking, bolting for the front of the store, desperate for some fresh air. An outstretched arm appeared out of nowhere and blocked her way.

Gail looked up to see the young man whom she had been following. He was taller than she had been prepared for, possibly over six feet, and very muscular despite being slim.

"Looking for me?" he asked with a taunting grin.

Gail gasped with surprise, focusing her attention on the sign behind him which directed patrons to the back room to see the impressive display of films.

"Can I take you to the movies?" he sneered.

Gail forced herself to look at him. His eyes were small and piercing, his skin bad, his nose and mouth thin, his hair uneven and uncombed, neither blond nor brown. He was possibly twenty years old, she estimated.

He moved closer to her. "Why are you following me?" he asked, his lips moving closer to her face. "Think I can do something for you? Want me to do it for you right behind one of those curtains back there? You name it, lady, I'll do it."

Gail struggled to find her voice, but no words came. He pushed his face closer to her, his hand reaching for her and catching the back of her hair.

"Nice hair," he said, moving still closer.

"Please . . ." she said softly.

"Please? Oh yeah, please. I like my women nice and polite."

Gail's hands shot wildly into the air, catching both herself and the boy by surprise. He dropped his arm and stepped back, not sure what had happened. In the several seconds it took him to reassess the situation, Gail raced past him, knocking over a row of magazines and watching in horror as pages of bound and gagged women fell lifeless before her eyes. In another instant she was out on the street, straining to catch her breath and praying that the youth would not follow her.

What could she possibly have been thinking about when she'd followed him inside? Even discarding the odds on finding the killer here, this boy couldn't be the one she was looking for. He was too tall, too bold, too forward. And he obviously had no trouble dealing with older women. He was not the sort to attack a child, she decided, unless the child was old enough to give him a good fight back. His interests would run to bigger prey. Gail slowly straightened her shoulders and headed shakily toward the Russian Tea Room.

Carol was on her second glass of wine when she arrived. "Sorry I left you like that," she apologized before Gail had a chance to speak.

"I'm sorry too," Gail said sincerely.

"Enough said," Carol decreed, signaling for the waiter. "I'm starving."

Carol was as good as her word, saying nothing about the incident to either Jack or Jennifer when they met later at the theater.

It was a pleasant evening, and everyone agreed when the day was over that they would have to do it again soon.

Chapter 15

After a particularly vicious series of late-night murders along Highway 280 into the New Jersey Turnpike, Gail began to drive there daily. At first, she was curious to pinpoint the exact location of the killings. However, even after her initial foray told her that there would be nothing to mark the spot, no police blockade of the area, no blood left splattered along the roadway to interrupt the tedium of the drive, she continued to cruise there every day.

The newspapers were frustratingly vague. Highway 280, they reported, west of the New Jersey Turnpike. About the details of the crimes themselves, they had been appallingly explicit.

The first of the four killings had occurred sometime after midnight on the sixteenth day of September. A young woman, age thirty-two, had been returning from an evening spent visiting friends who lived in New York. She was alone in her car when she was waylaid and forced off the road by another car, which police surmised from the tire tracks found near the scene, had been waiting for just such an opportunity. The woman had been led into the grass at the side of the highway, stripped of her clothing, sexually attacked with a sawed-off shotgun and then murdered.

Two nights later another car was forced off the road

in a similar fashion at just past ten. According to a near-hysterical motorist who was driving by but didn't come forward until several days later, the middle-aged couple inside were forced out of their car at gunpoint and led into the tall grass by the side of the road. No one but the killer was around to appreciate the depth of their fear, the degree of their horror. The police could comment only on the savagery of their wounds. Both had been sodomized and shot repeatedly; both had been mutilated after death and left by the side of the road for early morning motorists to discover on their way to work. The driver who had witnessed the couple being led to their doom claimed he saw only one gunman, that the man was white and appeared to be young and blond, but it was dark and he had been terrified and couldn't be sure.

Police insisted that they were keeping a sharp eye on that stretch of highway, but the following week, there was yet another killing: a young man returning from a late date had been edged off the road and slaughtered in the identical manner of his predecessors. The police, though they voiced strong doubts in print that the killer was likely to strike again in the same spot, were nonetheless advising motorists who had to travel between the two states at night to take 24 or a suitable alternative. The traffic between New Jersey and New York after dark along Highway 280 came to a virtual stop.

During the day it was as busy as ever. No one thought that the killer, or killers, would strike before dark. Gail was usually on the highway before twelve noon and home by four, giving her enough time to travel back and forth between the two states twice. Occasionally, she pulled over to the side of the road and stopped for several minutes, trying to internalize the terror of being pulled from her car and being forced to walk into the high grass at gunpoint. A walk toward death.

After a few days she began leaving the car, walking along the side of the busy highway. Passing motorists regarded her strangely, then averted their eyes, not stopping to ask if she might need help. She began concentrating her attention on the tall grass, kicking at it with her feet and wondering if there were snakes.

She imagined being led into the thick of it, being told to remove her clothes and lie down, disappearing into it as if into an open grave. She felt the coldness of a gun's metal as it inched up her thigh and forced its way rudely inside her. She heard the squeeze of the trigger, saw her body exploding around her, felt . . . nothing.

"Hey, what the hell are you doing out here?"

Gail turned around sharply at the sound of the man's voice and saw a late-model silver car with its driver, a balding, middle-aged man, leaning out of the window on the passenger side. "What's the matter with you?" he continued angrily. "Are you crazy? Don't you know what happened on this road? It's goddamn dangerous to leave your car! You gotta take a leak?! Wait till you hit a service station!"

Gail thanked the man for his concern and retreated timidly to her car. He waited until she was safely inside before resuming his own journey, shaking his head in dismay as he passed her.

She was getting nowhere, she thought restlessly, her mind not on the traffic at all. Her excursions into Newark and East Orange were proving fruitless. Everyone was guilty, she decided cynically. There were no innocents left.

She'd certainly never find anybody driving along the highway in the middle of the afternoon. It was an exercise in futility.

A few days later Gail ceased driving along Highway 280 in the afternoons, and went there at night.

She waited until the evening that Jack was scheduled to attend one of Lloyd Michener's group meetings, declining once again to accompany him. Soon after he was gone, she informed Jennifer that she was restless and felt like going to a movie. When Jennifer offered to go with her, Gail reminded her she had homework, and left the house before Jennifer could protest further.

The highway at night was a different world. The darkness took away its cloak of civility, making the serpentlike twists and turns a tangible menace. Even before the murders she had felt this, driving home with Jack and Jennifer after their recent foray in New York. Gail had never been a creature of the night. As a child, she had slept with the bathroom door wide open, its light spilling over into her room. With the daylight, she felt in the middle of things, included, protected, secure. But with the darkness came the isolation. She felt like an observer on an alien planet, and the feeling had always frightened her. Now, along this dark stretch of highway, aware that hers was the only car in sight, that feeling of isolation intensified and overwhelmed her. She fought the urge to turn back, to return to the safety of her well-lit kitchen and wait until morning. And then she remembered (as if she had ever for a moment forgotten) that Cindy had been killed in the bright, friendly light of day, that monsters did not always require the glow from the moon to guide them. Her eyes searched out the darkness at the side of the highway. ("Are there such things as monsters, Mommy?" "Of course not, sweetie.") She tightened her grip on the wheel and continued full speed ahead.

And then she saw the other car.

She was almost at the New York border when she saw it hidden behind some trees and camouflaged by its own dark color. Within seconds it was behind her, edging closer and closer to her rear fender. Gail stepped on the accelerator. The other car stayed right behind. Gail checked her rearview mirror but the darkness and the glare from the other car's headlights made it impossible for her to get a good look at the men inside. All she could make out was that there were two of them. She saw the other car veer suddenly to the left, out of her sight line. In another instant it pulled up beside her, trying to force her off the road. Gail pressed the gas pedal to the floor but the other car matched her speed, the man in the passenger side waving her frantically over. Then she heard the siren and looked toward the other car with measurable relief. But the man on the passenger side was flashing something in her direction, something that looked like a badge, and she realized that he was responsible for the siren, though the car was unmarked. She took her foot off the gas pedal and slowly reduced her speed, gradually pulling over to the side of the road. The car was right behind her. She heard the sound of car doors slamming and saw two men racing in her direction, guns drawn. It suddenly occurred to her that no one knew precisely how the other victims had been waylaid. What better way, she thought, as the men approached her door, their guns clearly visible, than to pretend to be the police. Everyone stops for a cop. No one questions the authority of a uniform and a badge.

She felt the gun at her head and stepped wordlessly from the car. No one spoke as the men led her away from the automobile, into the high grass. No other cars drove by to witness her forced striptease, to see her laid bare against the cold earth, one gun at her temple, the other snaking its way up her leg. Perhaps they would just shoot her and spare her the pain of their tortures. She'd been tortured enough, she thought, looking past her window into the worried—even frightened—eyes of the young man at her car door. She pressed the button which automatically lowered her window.

"Police, ma'am," he announced, pushing forward his badge. Gail gave it only a cursory glance. There was no way she could differentiate between the real thing and a fake. "Would you mind getting out of the car, ma'am." It was a command, not a question.

Gail took a deep breath and released it slowly. Her knees were shaking as her feet touched the ground outside. The grass licked at her ankles. The air was cool, much colder than when she had begun her drive. Fall had definitely settled in, she realized, wondering how it had escaped her notice, amazed by the inexorable progression of time.

The second man went around to the passenger side of her car, peering into the back seat with a flashlight. "We'd like to take a look inside," the first man said. Gail nodded. Was this part of the game? Get the victim to relax, make her feel secure before leading her to the slaughter? "Can I see your driver's license, ma'am?" the officer—she decided to think of them as such for the time being—asked politely, if warily. He watched closely as she opened her handbag and took out her wallet, handing it over to him. He declined, pulling his body noticeably back. "Take it out of the wallet," he told her. Gail smiled. It had been a test. She knew that policemen were required to ask you to remove your license from your wallet before handing it over. If this man had done otherwise, she would have known he was not who he claimed to be. But he obviously knew his part well. She watched him as he studied her license.

"Everything's fine in here," the other officer said. "Would you mind opening your trunk, please?" he asked, and Gail reached inside the car and pulled the keys out of the ignition, then handed them to the young man beside her. He, in turn, threw them over the hood of the car to the other policeman, who walked to the trunk and opened it up. It was empty except for the spare tire.

The first man now returned to his own car and phoned in her driver's license number for verification. He came back a few minutes later, seemingly satisfied, his gun now safely in its holster. "Mind telling us just what the hell you're doing out on this highway alone at this hour?" he demanded with an equal mixture of curiosity and anger.

"I had a fight with my husband," Gail lied, saying the first thing that came into her mind. She was still not sure these men were who they claimed to be. She pictured Jack's face, wondered if he was home yet from the meeting. Would they call him? Tell him where she'd been? "I needed to get out for a while and calm down."

"On this highway?" the second man demanded incredulously. She saw that he was the older of the two and swarthy where the younger man was fair.

"It seemed as good as any," Gail said, not sure what else she should say.

"Don't you read the papers?" the younger officer asked. "Don't you know what's been happening along this highway?"

"We've been away," Gail said. "Florida. We just got back."

"You don't have much of a tan," the second policeman observed, shining the flashlight in her face.

"I don't like to sit out in the sun," she told him. "It's not good for you."

"Neither is driving alone this late at night down a highway where four people have been murdered in the last two weeks."

"I didn't know," Gail stammered. "We've been away."

"Yeah, well, make sure that you don't do anything stupid like this again," the older man said. "If you want to cool off, drive around the block, not out on the highway. Better still, don't fight with your husband. Poor guy's probably got enough on his mind."

Gail thought that was probably true. "Do you have any idea who's been doing the killing?" she asked.

"We're working on it," came the standard response.

Gail nodded, feigning assurance. "Can I go now?" she asked timidly. She wondered if Lieutenant Cole would ever find out about tonight, what he would say to her if he did.

The younger officer handed her back her driver's license after first rechecking her name. "Look, Mrs. Walton," he said softly, and for a minute Gail thought he might have recognized her, "we didn't mean to scare you, but this isn't a television program where the good guys show up just in time to save the damsel in distress. People are getting killed out here. Innocent people are being butchered. It's not kiddies' day at the exhibition. You're damn lucky it was us and not some lunatic who stopped you." Gail nodded contritely. "We'll follow you back till you get off the highway," he said.

"You don't have to do that," Gail protested.

"Oh yes we do," she was told.

"Thank you," Gail acknowledged.

"After you," the policeman said, and Gail climbed back into her car and started the engine. The police car stayed behind her until she was safely off the highway. She honked her horn in appreciation, which was acknowledged with a wave of a hand.

Jack was in the living room waiting for her when she walked in the front door.

"How was the movie?" he asked, his voice flat.

"Not very good," she told him, avoiding his eyes, heading directly for the stairs.

"What did you see?"

Gail stopped on the second step, her mind a blank. "I can't remember the title," she said. "One of those dumb car chase films, you know the type. Cars racing down the highway. Cops and robbers." She stopped. "How was the meeting?" She asked the question to avoid more questions from Jack.

"Good," he answered slowly. "I'd like to talk to you about it."

"Could it wait till morning?" she asked quickly. "It's just that I'm so tired now . . ."

"Sure," Jack said immediately, not trying to hide his disappointment.

"I'm really so exhausted," she continued, realizing it was true.

"Good night, Gail," he said softly.

Gail managed a weak smile. "Good night," she told him, and went upstairs to bed.

Chapter 16

On October 1, the body of a twenty-nine-year-old mother of three was discovered buried in a shallow grave just past the outskirts of Livingston. She had been raped, and shot twice through the heart. The woman was the wife of a local real estate tycoon. The newspapers were suddenly filled with photographs of the attractive young woman and her now grieving family.

"Do you think there's any connection?" Gail asked Lieutenant Cole when she was finally able to reach him two days later.

"No," he said firmly.

"Why not?" Gail's voice was terse, anxious.

"Too many differences," Lieutenant Cole explained, enumerating the details of this latest murder. "Veronica MacInnes was a grown woman; she was shot, not strangled . . ."

"She was raped . . ."

"Men who rape children rarely rape women old enough to have them."

"But it could be . . ."

"Gail," Richard Cole said steadily, "it isn't."

Gail lowered the phone to her chest and looked toward her kitchen door. "What happens now?" she asked, suddenly bringing the phone back to her mouth.

There was a pause. "I'm not sure I understand the question."

"Do you know who killed this woman?"

"Not yet. We have—"

"I know, you have several leads."

"Gail . . ."

"What happens to Cindy's case now?"

"We're still working on your daughter's case."

"Veronica MacInnes was the wife of a prominent man, a very rich man. Are you trying to tell me that you haven't got all your men out searching for her killer?"

"That doesn't mean we aren't still searching for the man who murdered your daughter."

"Doesn't it?"

"No."

Gail was about to argue, thought better of it and said nothing. There was no point in further discussion. She understood the facts even if Lieutenant Cole was unable to admit them, and the sad fact was that her daughter was old news. The police would concentrate their attention on a case they still had a chance to solve. The hunt for Cindy's killer would be abandoned. Whatever undercover men were still wandering the streets of New Jersey would undoubtedly be sent elsewhere, where their time could be spent more productively.

She was about to hang up the phone when Lieutenant Cole's voice caught her off guard. "What did you say?" she asked quickly.

"I asked you where you've been the past month," he repeated.

"What do you mean?"

"I mean that I've called many times and you're never home. I just wondered what you've been doing with yourself."

Gail tried to clear her throat and wound up coughing into the receiver. "I've been in and out," she finally sputtered nervously. "Nowhere in particular."

"Feeling all right?"

"Fine," Gail answered, anxious now to get off the phone.

As she replaced the receiver, she knew she had reached yet another plateau. It was time to press forward, to act on the next phase of her plan.

She had been watching a number of rooming houses for the past several weeks, making mental notes of the various inhabitants, keeping a careful check on who went in and out.

It was time now for her to move inside, to join them. She had been delaying such an action, hoping the police would discover something.

They had, Gail laughed with bitter irony as she got behind the wheel of her car and pulled out of her driveway.

Another body.

Johnson Avenue was a narrow, uninteresting street that ran perpendicular to Broad Street. It was lined on either side by run-down brick houses, their wood trim in need of paint, their front steps cracked and uneven, covered with the leaves of autumn, which no one had bothered to rake up.

Gail chose this street over several of the others because it seemed the most nondescript. It wasn't the best such street, nor was it the worst. She had followed several young men here, always trailing half a block behind, her face concealed inside the upturned collar of her fall coat.

Once she had caught a fleeting glimpse of herself in a store window as she turned the corner, collar up, head down, shoulders slumped, feet shuffling forward, and she had almost laughed out loud. After that she had toned down the stereotype somewhat, careful not to let herself drift into caricature, making herself as real and therefore as invisible as the others who wandered these streets. It wasn't difficult. In many ways she felt she was truly one of them—alone, angry, desperate. There were days she felt more at home on these avenues than on the streets around Tarlton Drive. At least here she knew the dangers. Back in Livingston, in the comfortable upper-middle-class section called Cherry Hill where she lived, there weren't supposed to be any dangers.

The killer was somewhere in these streets, she felt sure, in one of these old, worn-out houses, hiding himself from the world. But not from her. And not for much longer.

She chose No. 17 because it appealed to her in some strange way. Looking past its chipped paint and collapsing eaves trough, Gail could almost imagine what it had looked like a long time ago—straight, sturdy and even warm. She had watched at least one slender, fair-haired youth pass through its front door, and several others whose vital statistics could be stretched to accommodate the description of the man she was seeking. Hair could be dyed, after all. Beards and mustaches could be grown. Pounds could be added. Heads could be shaved.

The sign in the front window proclaimed a vacancy. Rooms could be rented by the day, week or month.

"I'd like a room," Gail told the woman peeking out from behind the first door downstairs.

"For how long?" the woman asked, keeping a growling Doberman at bay with her slippered foot.

"I'm not sure," Gail answered, thinking that she would probably move on to another house in a week's time if she should find nothing here.

"Pay by the night then. Cash in advance," the woman told her, and Gail saw a cigarette dangling from the woman's fingers. "Get in there, Rebecca," she snarled at the dog, who instantly backed off. Gail thought the name Rebecca an odd one for a Doberman.

"How much?" Gail asked, wondering if the woman had chosen the dog's name for its irony. This was certainly no Sunnybrook Farm.

"Fifteen dollars a night," the woman said.

"Fifteen dollars a night?" Gail repeated, searching through her coat pocket for fifteen dollars. "That's a lot."

"You might find cheaper down the road," the woman told her, "but it won't be as nice. Fifteen dollars a night. Take it or leave it. I haven't got all day to waste talking. My soaps are on."

Gail wondered what soaps the woman watched but didn't ask. "That's fine," Gail said, handing the lady the fifteen dollars, which she promptly counted.

"I'll get the keys," the woman said.

As the landlady led her up the stairs, Gail noticed stains along the otherwise blank wall that appeared to be blood. "What are these stains?" she asked.

The woman's eyes followed Gail's fingers to the ugly faded maroon streaks. "I have no idea," she said, as if she could barely be bothered answering the question.

"It looks like blood."

The woman smiled for the first time since Gail had knocked at her door. "Yeah, it could very well be."

Gail preferred not to think how blood might have gotten there, and gave her attention to the woman's legs as she preceded Gail up the second full flight of stairs. The woman was more than just thin; she was anorexic, her thighs the size of wrists underneath her dirty slacks. Oddly enough, her hair was immaculately coiffed, cleaned and curled, and her nails were carefully and expertly manicured and polished a bright, vibrant red.

"Are all the rooms filled now?" Gail asked when they came to a stop outside a locked door, the landlady jiggling the key in the keyhole.

"Got one more," the woman said, pushing the door open, and handing Gail the key. "There it is. Well?"

"Well?" Gail asked, not sure what the question meant.

"Are you going in or what?"

"I'm going in," Gail told her. "It's very nice."

"You can get cheaper down the road," the woman

told her again, "but it wouldn't be as nice. I try to keep the place as neat as I can. I only ask a few things from you—no loud noise after midnight, no smoking in bed, don't want to burn the place down, and no drugs or drinking in the halls. I don't care what you do in the privacy of your room except that this ain't no brothel. That's the word, isn't it? You know, whorehouse. You can have guys and all that. Just don't make it too obvious."

"There won't be any guys."

The woman regarded her strangely. "No? Well, that's your business. I just don't want any hassles from the police, you know what I mean."

"Well, I don't drink, and I don't smoke, and I don't take drugs," Gail started, but the woman was already halfway down the first flight of steps. "Don't you want to know my name?" Gail called after her.

"What for?" the woman asked without looking back. Gail noticed a trail of ashes along the floor from the woman's cigarette. She stood for a few seconds in the empty hallway and then went inside her room.

The room was no better than she had expected. The walls were several shades of green or possibly yellow, and the floor was bare wood. At least it was clean, Gail thought with a sense of relief. There was only the most minimal furniture: a double bed in the middle of the room, covered with a cheap, blue-flowered bedspread; a multicolored overstuffed chair whose stuffing had long since vanished; a cheap lamp on a cheaper plastic table; a chest of drawers.

Gail sat down on the middle of the bed and felt with surprise that it was firm. Not that it mattered; she wouldn't be sleeping on it. She felt a sudden stab of panic, the room closing in around her, and she hurried to the window behind the chair. It was a small window, covered with the flimsiest of blue curtains, and it looked onto a dreary back alley. Gail felt cut off, isolated from the street, from her routine. How could she hope to find anyone behind these unfriendly doors?

She felt queasy and almost fell against the small table trying to find the bathroom. She needed a toilet. Where was the bathroom?

"Where's the bathroom?" she asked the landlady after she had gone downstairs again.

The landlady peered out from behind her door.

"Oh, didn't I show you? It's down at the end of your hall. There's one on each floor."

"You mean there isn't one in the room?"

"Did you see one?"

"I just assumed . . ."

"You know how much it would cost me to put a toilet in every room? Are you kidding? And the upkeep? Having to worry about someone stuffing something they shouldn't down the plumbing, which, by the way, you better not do. I don't get a lot of women to my place, so I forget to mention that sometimes."

"Who do you get here?" Gail asked.

"What kind of question is that?" The woman tightened her hold on her door, closing it further, so that Gail could see only a quarter of her face. "Are you a cop or something?"

"A cop!" Gail's laugh was genuine. "No, I'm just . . . lonely," she confided, surprised to hear the words come out of her mouth.

The woman behind the door relaxed her shoulders and pushed open the door with her foot. "You want a drink?" she asked.

"I'd love a cup of tea," Gail told her before she realized how it would sound.

"Tea's not exactly what I had in mind," the woman said, "but I guess I have an old teapot around here someplace. Come on in."

The room was approximately twice the size of Gail's, with a small adjoining bedroom. Gail noted that it also sported its own galley kitchen and separate bathroom. The walls were the same yellow-green as the rest of the house, and the furniture strictly Salvation Army. The woman was searching through her cupboards for the teapot.

"There it is," she said triumphantly. "I knew I had one somewhere. I think I remember how to boil water. Sit down, make yourself comfortable."

"I'm Gail," Gail told her, deciding at the last minute not to lie.

"I'm Roseanne," the woman replied, filling the pot with water from the sink and putting it on the stove. "Go on, sit down. Don't be afraid of the dog. She won't hurt you unless I tell her to. Rebecca, get down from the couch."

The dog obeyed instantly, jumping down from its comfortable spot on the faded burgundy velvet sofa and settling on the floor in front of the television. Gail sat down uneasily, her eyes traveling between the small black and white television and the large black and brown dog.

"How did you decide on the name Rebecca?" Gail asked, forcing her lips into a smile in the dog's direction.

"It was my mother-in-law's name," Roseanne told her, coming back into the room and gluing her eyes to the TV. "Rebecca here looks just like her. Gotta have a dog, you know, a woman alone. Especially around here. Men come, they think they can take advantage 'cause you're a woman living alone. They think again when they see Rebecca."

"You live alone?" Gail questioned, trying to determine the woman's age.

"Have for sixteen years," Roseanne said. "It's better that way. Husband went out one night for a quart of milk . . ." She left the sentence linger while she listened for several seconds to what was happening on the television. The program broke for a commercial. "At least he brought back the milk before he split," she finished, returning to the kitchen to take the teapot off the stove. "Now, let's see if I have some tea bags." Gail watched as she hunted through several drawers. "Thought so. They're a little old. Tea doesn't go stale, does it?"

"No," Gail smiled.

"Haven't had tea in so long," the woman continued, dropping a tea bag into a mug and filling it with water. "Don't have any milk or sugar, so you'll have to drink it plain."

"That's fine. What about you?"

"I never eat between meals," Roseanne said, holding out the mug for Gail to take. "Do you watch this one?" she asked, indicating the television. Gail shook her head. "It's my favorite. All sorts of things go on you wouldn't believe. Adultery, murder, Russian spies. Everything, all in the same family! This here's Lola. She's the troublemaker. I like her the best, of course. Every time she comes along, you can expect trouble."

Gail watched the beautiful woman with the long, dark hair wrap her arms around a handsome, middle-aged man wearing a doctor's uniform and a worried expression.

"That's Will Tyrell she's got her arms around. He's married to Anne Cotton, a lady doctor and a real goody-goody since they got married. She never used to be that way. Will's her fourth husband in five years. She had a nervous breakdown and murdered the last one, and they gave her all these drugs and she became a drug addict and then she went through a bout of hysterical blindness before she met and married Will and got so boring. I have a feeling they'll be bumping her off pretty soon." Gail was about to laugh when she realized that Roseanne took her soaps very seriously. "But this Lola here, she's a real character. Nobody knows where she came from and she keeps pretty much to herself. You never see where she lives or anything, but she's always beautifully dressed, and she does things like wear full-length mink coats with nothing underneath, and she's always after somebody's husband. The last husband she stole, the poor girl committed suicide.

I wonder if that's how they're planning to bump off poor Anne Cotton."

"I tried to watch a few of these shows for a while , . . uh, 'The Guiding Light,' I think it was called, and 'A Brighter Tomorrow.' "

"Oh, yeah, I used to watch that one. Is Erica still cheating on her husband, Richard?"

Gail had to think for a minute. "I think her husband's name was Lance."

"Lance?! She married Lance? That no-good crook?! Oh, now she's in for it, throwing away a nice guy like Richard. I mean, playing around on him is one thing, but dumping him to marry Lance, well she deserves whatever she gets."

Gail looked restlessly around the room, feeling the walls beginning to close in on her as they had before. "I should be getting home," she said before she realized what she was saying, and turned anxiously in Rose-anne's direction.

But Roseanne was lost in the problems of Will Tyrell and Anne Cotton and Lola-whoever-she-was, and hadn't heard Gail's mistake. Gail wiped the sudden sweat off her upper lip. She'd have to be more careful. A silly slip of the tongue like that one could cost her all her careful planning. She stood up abruptly and the dog jumped to its feet, teeth bared, ready to leap at her throat.

"Down, Rebecca," Roseanne warned softly, and the dog slowly lowered its narrow body back to the floor.

"I'm feeling a little dizzy. I think I'll go out for a walk," Gail volunteered.

"Don't have to explain anything to me. I'm not your mother."

"Thanks for the tea."

Roseanne waved acknowledgment without taking her eyes from the TV. Gail took a last look around the room before stepping out into the hallway and closing the door behind her. She looked at her watch. It was almost three o'clock and she had better be on her way.

She met with resistance at the front door, realized that someone was pushing in as she was pushing out, and backed away. The young man who stepped inside was barely out of his teens and wore his hair in an unfashionable crew cut. It was so short, it was hard to determine its color. He kept his eyes on his feet as he strode with seeming purpose past Gail and up the stairs. If he had seen her at all, he didn't acknowledge it in any way. Gail listened to the sound of his boots as he took the first flight of stairs two at a time, and felt the weight of his footsteps as they passed over her head. She pulled the front door open and hurried into the outside air, colder and damper than earlier in the day. She looked back at the house. The boy lived in one of the front rooms, she had quickly determined from his footsteps. Gail glanced up toward the second floor.

He was staring down at her from the window, and as soon as he saw her look up in his direction, he disappeared behind the curtain. Gail stood for a moment on the front walk before deciding to return to her car. As she ambled down the sidewalk, she felt the boy's eyes following her down the street.

Chapter 17

It was four days before she saw the young man again.

She had taken to leaving her door open when she was at the rooming house, so she could listen for noises from the other rooms and hear the front door open and close. Usually, the house was eerily quiet. Except for footsteps and doors banging, there were almost no sounds at all. Conversation was virtually nonexistent. Occasionally, there was a sudden burst of verbal abuse from the hallway, an angry torrent of words from the stairwell, but mostly, there was nothing. The sounds of silence, Gail hummed in her mind. In the four days she had been coming here, climbing the stairs to her room at approximately ten o'clock each morning and then alternating between the bed and the chair until it was time to go out for lunch, returning a half hour later to fill in the hours until three o'clock, she hadn't uttered more than a few sentences to anyone.

She kept track of who the residents were, if not by name, by what room they occupied. There were five rooms on each of the second and third floors. The first floor, where Roseanne's apartment took up more than the usual amount of space, had only two. Not counting Roseanne, that made for a total of twelve rooms.

Two aging drunks lived in the two rooms on the

ground floor. They wore their unwashed hair long, their beards untrimmed and their scowls fixed. Gail always found them sitting together on the front steps in the morning when she arrived. Surprisingly, each would greet her with a gallant old-world tip of the hat, but when she had tried to speak to them on the third morning, to ask how long they had been living in this place and what they thought of the other residents, they had regarded her as if she were speaking a foreign language and continued in their own erratic attempts at conversation as if she were no longer there.

Most of the five rooms on the second floor had already changed occupants several times since Gail's arrival, inhabited by a succession of aimless, young-to-middle-aged men and, since yesterday, a strange-looking, mismatched couple of indeterminate age. The young man Gail had seen on her first day still occupied the front room on the second floor. She had seen him on two occasions since, staring down at her from his window when she went out for lunch.

The third floor boasted a redheaded woman of approximately Gail's age and height, a sinister-looking man a few years older and several inches shorter, a swarthy male, and a still-empty room. The woman was the only one on their floor who had been living here before Gail arrived. Gail had been waiting for an opportunity to talk to her, but each time she had seen her, the woman had been in the company of a different man, and so Gail had said nothing.

On the afternoon of the fourth day, Gail heard the woman's footsteps in the hallway and jumped off her bed and into the hall.

"Something I can do for you?" the woman asked, startled by Gail's sudden appearance, but unafraid.

Gail hesitated. "I thought maybe we could talk . . ." she ventured, trying to sound casual, aware she was failing miserably.

"What about?" the woman asked skeptically from the door to her room.

"About anything. Just get acquainted, you know."

"I don't do women."

"I beg your pardon?"

"I'm not into women. Sorry, honey, I may be a hooker, but I'm straight as an arrow." She turned the key in her lock.

"I just want to talk," Gail said quickly as the woman disappeared inside. "That's all. Really."

The woman's head reappeared. "What for?"

Gail shrugged. She had no reply.

"You want to talk? Okay, you can come in and talk while I pack."

"Pack?" Gail asked, following the woman inside. Their rooms were identical in fact if not in feeling. While the bed in Gail's room had never been slept in, its covers never turned down, Gail doubted that this bed had ever been made. The chair in the corner was covered with discarded clothing and unruly wigs, and someone had knocked the table lamp carelessly against the wall and not bothered to right them. Bottles of makeup all but hid the top of the dresser.

"Pardon the mess," the woman said with a touch of sarcasm. "I wasn't expecting company."

"You're moving?" Gail asked.

"Got my walking papers," the woman said, pulling an old cardboard suitcase from under the bed and tossing it in the middle of the rumpled sheets. Gail smelled the familiar odor of recent sex and felt her body grow numb, a tingling sensation spreading through her limbs.

"Can we leave the door open?" Gail asked as the woman was about to draw it closed. "It's just that my purse is lying on my bed and I left my door wide open. Anyone could walk in . . . Besides," she continued, desperately needing the extra air, "I have a thing about closed doors."

The woman shrugged and returned to her packing. "Yeah, I noticed that your door is always open. Myself,

I like privacy. It's better for business, if you know what I mean."

"Have you been a prostitute for long?" Gail tried not to sound too naïve.

"Just since I failed my medical exams," the woman sneered, beginning to clear the items from the top of the dresser and throw them into the suitcase. "What's your name? You look like a Carol."

"That's my sister's name," Gail smiled. "My name's Gail."

"I'm Brenda, and I don't make enough money to be called a prostitute. What do you do?"

Gail found herself startled by the question. "I don't do anything right now," she stammered. "I'm trying to find a job, but there doesn't seem to be a whole lot available at the moment."

"You sound like you got an education."

"No," Gail said quickly. "No college degree or anything like that."

"You finish high school?"

"Yes," Gail nodded.

"I took a secretarial course once. Never could type more than thirty words a minute, and half of those were mistakes."

"I can't type at all."

"If you can't type, you can't get a job," Brenda told her matter-of-factly. "Forget the high school diploma. You got any money?"

"A little. Enough to last a few weeks."

"You ever thought of hooking?" Gail's eyes grew wide. "Not that you'd make a whole lot. I mean, let's face it, we're both a little past it, if you know what I mean, but you're pretty enough, you might be able to make a few dollars. I could help you. Introduce you to a few people . . ."

"I don't think so," Gail said quickly.

Brenda shrugged and continued packing.

"Roseanne kicked you out?" Gail asked.

"First thing this morning. Told me I was getting too

obvious, whatever the hell that means. It's not like she didn't know what I was doing right from the beginning. She's probably mad 'cause she's not getting any share of the proceeds. Or maybe she's mad 'cause she's not getting any, period." Brenda laughed. "If you ask me, she's a dyke anyway. Either that or she's got something weird going with that dog."

Gail shuddered as she unwillingly recalled the vile magazines in the "adult" bookstore. "How long have you been living here?" she asked, changing the subject.

"Couple of months." Brenda put the last of her belongings into the bag and snapped it shut. "Time to move on anyway, I guess. Doesn't really matter. One room's the same as the next."

"Do you ever make friends?"

"Are you kidding? You're the best friend I got." She laughed.

"Have you ever talked to anyone in the house?"

"Just the ones who pay me."

"The people here move around so much."

"Yeah? I never noticed."

"Except for that boy in the front room on the second floor. Do you know the one I'm talking about?"

Brenda tossed the question aside. "No."

"He's young, maybe nineteen or twenty. Real short crew cut, kind of sullen-looking . . ."

"Oh yeah, I know who you mean. He's real creepy, isn't he? Yeah, I know who you mean. I sidled up to him once and asked him if he felt like having a good time, and he pulled away from me like I had leprosy. What can you do? Can't be everybody's type."

"Do you know how long he's been here?"

"What?" Brenda asked, distracted, her eyes searching the closet for anything she might have forgotten.

"I asked if you knew how long he's been here."

"How would I know? He was here when I arrived. Keeps to himself all the time, that's all I know about him. Why?" she asked, suddenly suspicious.

Gail laughed. "He looks like an old boyfriend I used

to have," she lied, hoping Brenda would accept the lie at face value.

"Yeah? Well, it ain't him, and you had lousy taste," she joked. "Wait, did you hear something?"

Gail sucked in her breath, her adrenaline beginning to pump. She cocked her head to one side, listening for whatever Brenda thought she might have heard.

"Stay here for a minute," Brenda told her cautiously. "I'll check it out."

Gail sank down on the now empty chair. What was she so afraid of? That the young man had been listening to them from outside the door? Her hands were shaking, she discovered, burying them between her knees.

"Nothing," Brenda said, returning a minute later. "Must be hearing things in my old age." She picked up her suitcase. "Well, I'm on my way." Gail stood up. "Nice talking to you, Gail. Maybe we'll run into each other again some time."

"Good luck," Gail called after her, wondering who the next tenant would be to sleep in this bed.

She heard the downstairs door open and close, and returned to her own room.

Her purse was lying opened, its contents emptied onto the bed. Gail took a minute to assess what had happened, her mind racing as her fingers fumbled through her wallet. Her social security card was there, as were her credit cards and driver's license. Only her cash was missing.

Brenda! she realized. There hadn't been any noise in the hallway. Brenda hadn't heard anything at all. It had been a clever ruse to get into Gail's room and at her money. Gail had told her that the door was open, that her purse was unprotected. Good God, she had even told her that she had enough money to get by for several weeks!

Some detective she was turning out to be, Gail thought as she raced down the steps trying to catch up to Brenda. She was the one who was supposedly doing the pumping for information and yet it had been

Brenda who had gleaned all the pertinent facts, and made off with over a hundred dollars in cash.

Gail found herself staring down a deserted street. The sky was threatening rain. The weathermen were already predicting an unusually cold winter. Gail felt the chill through her thin blouse and returned inside.

He was watching her from the top of the stairs. At first, too lost in her own thoughts, she didn't see him. She'd have to be more careful next time, she scolded herself, leave everything but what she absolutely needed at home, leave her driver's license in the pocket of her slacks. It wasn't until she started up the steps that she saw him on the landing.

"Oh!" she cried, trying to laugh, feeling awkward and afraid, "you scared me. I didn't see you."

He said nothing.

"It's cold out there," she continued, rubbing her arms. "They're calling for rain."

Still he said nothing, just kept staring at her face, and Gail wondered if he recognized her from her photographs in the newspapers, if he was the one who had murdered her little girl. She looked directly into his eyes. Tell me, she commanded silently. You can't lie to *me*.

He stared back at her blankly, telling her nothing. An instant later, he was descending the steps at a fast pace, pushing past her without saying a word. Gail heard the door open behind her, felt the cold wind against her back until the door slammed shut again and she was alone. She took a few seconds to catch her breath, hearing the drone of the afternoon soaps emanating from Roseanne's room, and began a slow climb up the stairs.

Things could be worse, she told herself, trying to banish from her mind the sinister image of the boy. Brenda could have cleaned her out before lunch, or the man at the parking lot could have collected at the end of the day instead of at the beginning. Then, where would she be? Hungry and walking home to Livingston, she answered, trying to make herself smile.

At the first flight landing, she stopped and looked down the hall. The door to the boy's room beckoned her like a door in a nightmare, surreal and terrifying, floating several inches off the floor, attached to nothing. Gail took a first tentative step toward it.

It was unlikely that this boy was Cindy's killer, she told herself with each succeeding step. Despite his strange behavior, despite the knowing look in his eyes, it felt wrong that she should stumble across him so quickly in the first house in which she had taken up residence. Yet, she had begun her search in July. It was now October. She had selected the house carefully. It could be him, she repeated to herself as her hand touched his door knob. He could be the one.

Of course, the door was locked, she realized with a mixture of relief and dismay. Not everyone was as stupid as she was to leave a door open in invitation for anyone to enter.

"Oh my God," she said aloud, realizing that she had done exactly that again, left her door wide open, the contents of her purse spread invitingly across the dismal blue-flowered bedspread. She ran up the second flight of stairs to her room.

The room was as she had left it, everything tossed unceremoniously across the bed. Nothing had been touched, Gail realized with relief as she checked through each charge card and piece of identification. She clasped the white straw bag tightly between her fingers and began tossing each item back inside—her lipstick, brush, a tampon holder, her car keys, her wallet with her driver's license and assorted charge cards.

Gail looked back at the open door. Even locked, it didn't afford much protection. It was an exceedingly flimsy lock. Probably a large bobby pin was all that was necessary to open it. She felt the weight of the wallet in her hand. Or a credit card.

She froze, her head turning toward the hallway,

afraid that somehow someone had overheard her thoughts. Don't do it, she heard a small inner voice cry out, don't go in there. He's waiting for you.

But her feet were already on the steps and then edging across the second floor hallway to the room at the front of the house. What if he came back? What if he returned suddenly to find her searching through his things? She stopped, motionless, outside his door.

She pulled out her American Express card—Don't leave home without it, a little voice whispered giddily—and thrust it forward. She would be able to see him from the window, she told herself; she would be able to hear the front door open and slam shut. She would have lots of time to get back up to her room before he could find her.

She pushed the card in the narrow crack between the door and the wall, rotating it haphazardly around the lock as she had seen in countless television shows. There was nothing to worry about, she assured herself, and then realized with a combination of disappointment and relief that the reason there was nothing to worry about was that she was never going to get inside that room. It might look easy on television, but reality was something else again, and the lock was proving more formidable than she had been prepared for.

And then it opened.

Slowly, almost reluctantly, the door fell back against the inside wall, daring the intruder to enter, to find its hidden secret.

Gail took a deep breath, felt her knees weaken and stepped across the threshold.

She ran to the window and looked down at the street, careful not to let herself be seen. There was no one. Still, she had better move quickly. He could come back at any minute. She couldn't afford to be long. She had to be exact, make sure that everything was returned to its proper spot. He couldn't know that anything had been disturbed.

She backed away from the window and did a quick

appraisal of the room. The first thing she noticed was that it was spotless, *excessively* clean, the bed made with perfect hospital corners, the cheap formica table polished until it actually shone, not a speck of dust clinging to the lampshade, not a stray sock anywhere. And that smell, she thought, recognizing it as disinfectant, so strong, so overpowering. How had she failed to notice it immediately? How could he sleep with that sharp odor covering him like an extra blanket?

The small dresser was shined as brilliantly as the little table. There was nothing on top of it, no pictures, no bottles, no brushes or combs. Nothing but a well-rubbed surface in which she could almost make out her own reflection.

Gail heard a noise and raced to the window, knocking the lamp from the table and watching helplessly as it crashed against the wall. "Oh God," Gail uttered as she looked outside to see the two drunks from downstairs arguing over which one of them was going to get the first sip of a newfound bottle. Gail quickly righted the lamp, hearing her breath escape in short, frantic ripples of fear.

She had made a slight dent in the lampshade. A normal person might not notice it, but there was no question that she was not dealing with a normal person, and that the boy would quickly discover the dent and figure out that someone had been in his room snooping around. Her fingers worked furiously, trying to straighten out the indentation. She told herself to be calm, that even if he did suspect someone of snooping, he was far more likely to assume it had been the landlady.

Gail wasted several more seconds trying to fix the shade, improved it somewhat—not enough, she knew —and then returned it to the table, turning it so that the dent faced the wall. Perhaps this way there was a slight chance it would escape his notice.

She opened the boy's closet. Two pairs of neatly pressed trousers hung side by side. Old, shabby, but hung as proudly and as carefully as if they were expensive imports. On the floor, unobtrusively off to one side, was a large bottle of Lysol and another, smaller spray can of Pledge.

There was no question that this boy had problems, Gail told herself, returning to the chest of drawers, but was he sick enough to have raped and killed a six-year-old child?

She pulled open the first drawer. It was filled with pair after pair of heavy black socks. Gail rifled through the piles. There must have been fifty pairs, all identical, all neatly folded one inside the other, all smelling of fabric softener.

The second drawer contained his underwear. Each pair of jockey shorts was folded carefully in the same manner, sorted into neat little stacks of five. There were six such stacks.

The third drawer was reserved for undershirts. Once again, they were neatly arranged in groups of five, all white, all V-necked. Three stacks.

The last drawer contained two shirts, one black, one blue and gray checked. They sat beside each other, collars pressed, pockets empty, sleeves tucked under.

Gail was careful to return everything to its exact position before moving on. She closed the bottom drawer at the same moment she heard the footsteps on the stairs.

She had been so absorbed in the contents of the dresser that she hadn't heard any sounds at all. Now whoever was on the stairs was headed in this direction, and it was too late for her to escape. She was trapped.

The steps stopped somewhere outside the door. He was waiting for her to try to leave. Gail stood paralyzed in the center of the room. Then she heard the sound of a key clicking into a lock and recognized that it was coming from down the hall. She waited until she heard a door close before allowing herself the luxury of crying.

Stop it, stop it, she admonished herself, wiping away

the tears and taking a last look around. What was it she had been looking for? What exactly had she been hoping to find? Some sort of physical evidence linking this man to her daughter? Some shred of evidence that would reveal him for the man she suspected him to be?

All his room told her was that he had a fetish for cleanliness, and as far as fetishes went, this one was certainly preferable to some of the others she had read about. I wonder if he does windows, she thought, heading for the door. Get out now, her inner voice commanded, her eyes returning to the bed in the middle of the room. She hadn't looked under the bed.

Get out of here, the little voice pleaded.

Gail marched with determination to the bed and knelt beside it, thrusting her arm underneath. She felt something hard hit her hand. Another stack—this time of magazines—she realized before she saw them, and didn't have to look to know what sort. They were the same type as the ones she had seen in that awful store. In rapid succession, photographs of tortured and mutilated women appeared before her eyes. "Oh my God," she wailed, stuffing the magazines back under the bed, becoming aware of some sort of commotion outside.

He was back! She knew it before she reached the window. He was arguing with the drunks, trying to push past them into the house, and, for some reason, they were being difficult and blocking his way. The boy looked up in exasperation and Gail pushed her body back against the wall. Had he seen her? Had she moved fast enough?

There was no more time to wait and wonder. Gail tore out of the room, pulling the door shut behind her at the same moment she heard the front door closing downstairs. They would pass in the hallway, she realized, not sure in which direction to run. She decided she would only trap herself if she ran upstairs; if she went down, at least she had a chance.

She reached the landing at the same time he did, but as he had done on their first encounter four days before, he virtually ignored her. If he had seen her, he gave no clues. His head lowered, his shoulders slumped, his eyes firmly on his shiny brown leather boots, he walked past her as if she didn't exist. Gail clasped the banister for support. She heard the door to his room slam shut.

Chapter 18

When she returned to the rooming house the next day, the boy had gone.

"What do you mean, 'he's gone'?" Gail asked Roseanne, as the landlady was busy laying fresh sheets across the boy's bed.

"Took off this morning bright and early."

"Did he say where he was going?"

Roseanne fixed Gail with the most world-weary of stares and said nothing. Gail looked morosely around the boy's now empty room, its closet open and bare, the drawers cleared of their neat little stacks. She watched as Roseanne lazily tucked in the sheets, tossed the pillow across the top of the bed and perfunctorily covered her poor effort with the tatty blue-flowered bedspread. "I'll say this for him, he was a neat one, all right. Kept everything smelling so clean. Kind of hate to lose ones like that, the ones that are quiet and keep to themselves."

Gail felt a sickening sensation in the pit of her stomach. He was gone. She had lost him. "Did he say why he was leaving?"

The landlady shrugged, not about to waste her time on an answer.

"What was his name? Did you know his name?"

Roseanne stared at the ceiling as if studying a crack.

"Don't think he ever told me, and I probably never asked. Doesn't matter anyway. They never tell you their real names."

"Did you ever talk to him?"

Roseanne returned her eyes to Gail's. "What for?" It was Gail's turn to shrug. "Why are you interested in this guy?"

"I'm just interested in people, I guess," Gail answered lamely. "I like to try and figure out what makes them tick, why they do certain things. The quiet ones are sometimes the most interesting because they're the most surprising. You can never figure out what they're thinking."

"I never *cared* what they were thinking."

"I just find it interesting," Gail continued, trying not to ramble. "You know how you're always reading in the newspapers about some crazy killer, and the police interview all his friends and neighbors and they say that he was real quiet and kept to himself all the time, that they never knew what was going on in his head. They're always so surprised when it turns out that he was busy killing people in his spare time." Roseanne regarded her strangely. "You have to watch the quiet ones," Gail laughed uneasily.

"Guess we don't have to worry too much about you," Roseanne said on her way to the door. "You want the room?"

"What?"

"The room. It's a little nicer than yours 'cause it's got the window onto the street instead of the back alley. Course, it also means you get more noise . . ."

"I don't want the room," Gail said quickly. "Actually, I'll be leaving myself some time today."

Roseanne pushed past her into the hall. "Suit yourself. I don't give refunds."

"You have absolutely no idea where he went?" Gail asked again.

Roseanne stopped. "He did say something about having to dispose of a bunch of bodies," she chuckled, her laugh trailing her down the stairs to her apartment. "I think you've been watching too much television," she called back just before Gail heard the door to her room close.

Gail was out on the street a few minutes later. Where could he have gone? What street would he have picked? He had obviously discovered that someone had been snooping through his things. What secrets had he been hiding? Where had he gone? Gail paced up and down the shabby neighborhood as if she were a cop patrolling her beat. Which house was he staring down at her from now?

The day had not started well. She had slept fitfully and awakened tired. Jennifer had been moody and disagreeable, dawdling over her breakfast, only to tear out of the house when she realized she'd been late for school. Jack had been visibly upset, even annoyed, when she'd refused to consider the possibility of accompanying him to the next meeting of the Families of Victims of Violent Crimes. He changed the subject abruptly, saying something about his mother having returned from her most recent trip to the Orient, and when Gail mentioned that she hadn't realized his mother had been away, Jack only shrugged, not bothering to repeat what he had voiced so often lately, that Gail seemed to be off in her own little world, that they were drifting further and further apart.

She had wanted to tell Jack about what she was doing, the suspect she had found, but she was afraid that he would tell her this was too dangerous and that she would have to stop. Leave it to the police, he would surely say, and so she had said nothing. On his way out the door, he had reminded her again to take her car in for a tune-up before the weather got too cold.

It was almost as if the car had ears, Gail thought approximately an hour later when it refused to start. She had turned the key in the ignition and listened to it sputter and wheeze, trying to connect, yet missing by the tiniest of spasms. "Turn over," she had commanded angrily, pressing her foot to the floor and then having to wait ten minutes because in addition to whatever else was wrong, she had flooded the engine. Why hadn't she listened to Jack? she castigated herself. He'd been telling her for months to take her car in. She was about to call for help when the engine finally caught hold and started. "Thank God," she muttered, determining to take the car to the garage over the weekend.

She had raced into Newark, worked herself into a frenzy of anticipation, only to discover that the boy had vanished. Packed his bags and disappeared. His bags, she thought, capturing in her mind the image of his belongings. She hadn't seen a bag. Yet he had obviously had one. What else had she missed?

Gail spent the rest of the day hunting for another room, and finally settled for one on Howard Street, a block and a half down from the first. It was smaller than her other room, and a dollar cheaper, though as Roseanne had warned her, not as clean. She paid for three nights in advance. The landlord, a sturdy-looking middle-aged man with a pronounced stutter, cautioned her against noisy parties but said little else. She spent the early part of the afternoon on her new bed listening to the couple in the next room argue through paper-thin walls. Was he here? she wondered. When she had asked that question of the various landlords up and down the streets, each had professed ignorance. Could be, they told her. He would have arrived just this morning, she had pressed. Surely they could remember: slim, young, with a very short crew cut. Could be, they repeated, shaking their heads, unable, or more possibly, unwilling, to jog their memories.

At three o'clock, Gail returned to her car, disappointment clinging to her like a second shadow. The car wouldn't start. "Great," she said, smiling to hold back the tears, "just great." She pressed gently on the gas pedal three times, careful this time not to flood it. Then she turned the key in the ignition and waited for the familiar rumble. Nothing happened. The engine was cold and dead.

"My car won't start," she told the short, balding man in the booth of the parking lot. "What should I do?"

"Call Triple A," he advised.

"I can't wait for Triple A. I have to get home."

The man raised his palms skyward. What had she expected? It wasn't his car. It wasn't his problem.

"Can I leave it here overnight?"

"Five dollars," he told her.

"I'll call Triple A in the morning," she assured him, but it was obvious that he didn't care what she did. In the meantime, she'd have to figure out a way to get home. She gave the man his money and walked out into the street, the cold wind biting at her cheeks. "Don't you cry," she said aloud as she searched in vain for a taxi. "Don't you dare cry. Damn car."

She began walking up the street. She couldn't very well walk back to Livingston. Perhaps there was a bus . . .

She didn't see them until they were almost on top of her and by that time it was too late to prevent a collision.

"Jesus Christ, lady, watch where you're going," the first boy snapped angrily. "You don't own the sidewalks."

"Sorry," Gail whispered to the two young men, one dark, the other—the one she had stumbled into—fair. Fair and slender, she noted. There were so many of them, she cried softly, letting the frustrations of the day finally escape.

"Hey, lady, it's okay," the dark-haired youth said quickly. "He didn't mean anything by it. It's just his way, you know what I mean?"

Gail continued to cry, knowing both boys were watching her, unable to stop.

"Weird," the first boy muttered as they moved away.

"You shouldn't have talked to her like that," the other scolded.

When Gail was finally able to wipe her eyes and look around, she found that she was standing alone outside a video-game store. It was filled, she noted, as she peered through the outside window, with youngsters who should have been in school. A second later she was standing inside the doorway, the door held open by the wedge of her back. She stared at the young men wrestling wildly with the various games—there were no girls, which she found mildly interesting—saw their looks of intense concentration and wondered if any of them ever concentrated this hard on their schoolwork. They laughed; they swore in frustration; they continued to pour the required money into the slots. Gradually, they began to feel the cold draft from the open doorway, became aware they were being watched. The noise and activity stopped.

"Hey, you comin' in or going out?" someone called.

"Yeah, it's gettin' cold in here," several voices echoed, their courage growing as peer support increased.

"Can I help you with something?" a man asked from behind the counter.

Gail backed out of the store, taking the sound of laughter with her.

"Guess her kid's over with the competition," she heard someone say as the door closed in front of her.

The boy from the rooming house had not been inside. She had known that he wouldn't be.

Gail approached the corner and stopped. Two girls, no more than Jennifer's age, stood on the curb, their arms outstretched, their thumbs in the air. Gail watched them anxiously. Didn't they know how dangerous it was to hitchhike? Oh well, she sighed, at least there were two of them. A minute later a car containing three teenage boys pulled up and the girls climbed inside.

So much for safety in numbers, Gail scoffed, her feet propelling her to the corner. In the next instant she was standing where the two girls had stood, her right arm outstretched, her thumb wavering in the cold air. Why not? she reasoned. You never know who you might meet.

Six cars passed without stopping.

"You want a lift somewhere?" a voice asked from behind her.

She turned quickly, recognizing one of the boys from the video-game shop. He was about seventeen or eighteen, with dark hair, and jeans that looked as if they had been painted onto his skinny frame. He was staring at her as if he knew who she was. Gail shivered, but not from the cold.

He didn't fit the description of Cindy's killer, Gail reminded herself, but then appearances could be altered.

"These buses take forever," she said, walking beside him toward his car.

"Helps if you stand by a bus stop," he told her matter-of-factly. "Where you headed?"

"Livingston," she said, searching his face for a sign of recognition.

"Livingston? That's kind of far. I'm not going that far."

"Wherever you're going will be fine," she told him quickly.

They reached his car, which was parked around the corner under a No Parking sign. The youth was a fast walker and the cold propelled him more quickly still. Gail had to run to keep up. The car was two-toned, red and gray, at least five years old and impeccably maintained. The interior was plush burgundy velour. There were no errant tissues on the floor or old gum wrappers such as Gail was always leaving lying around the inside of her car. Gail slid into the front seat. A boy and his car, she thought, as he put the key in the ignition and started the engine. It started with no trouble at all.

"Sounds good," the boy said proudly.

Gail silently cursed her own car stuck in the lot. "You obviously spend a lot of time on it," she said.

"Yeah," he agreed. "This here's my baby."

"You're lucky you didn't get a ticket," she told him as he pulled away from the curb. What the hell was she doing?

"They never give tickets," he said confidently. "I park there all the time."

"You come here a lot?" He nodded. "Don't you go to school?" she asked. Where was he taking her?

"Sometimes," he smiled. "You from the truant office?"

"No," Gail said. "Is that what you guys thought?"

"Crossed our minds. Somebody's mother?" he asked.

"Is that why you offered me a lift? To find out what I was doing?"

"Naw, I don't care what you were doing," he said honestly. "I just didn't want you to freeze your ass off with the cold."

"You were worried about me?" Gail laughed, wondering where they were going.

"Well, you're not the usual run-of-the-mill hitchhiker, you gotta realize. I mean, well, you know what I mean."

"I'm old?" Gail asked, surprised to find herself enjoying the conversation.

"Well, not old exactly. Older. You look like somebody's mother," he qualified.

"I am," Gail said quietly. "But I have girls." She didn't bother correcting herself.

"Oh yeah," he said, as if he knew, "girls are a lot easier. My mother's always telling me that."

"She wouldn't be too happy to find out you're not in school this afternoon."

"Probably not," he agreed, and continued driving, turning the corner. Gail wondered again where they were going. She had lost track of the streets and could be anywhere. But the thought frightened her only momentarily. "How come you were hitchhiking?" he asked.

"My car wouldn't start."

"I didn't think you were a regular. You looked kind of

stiff," he said, his voice assuming a curiously paternal tone. "You gotta be pretty careful. There's a lot of crazy people out driving the streets. You never know who's liable to pick you up. A friend of mine was hitchhiking once and this guy stops the car and she's about to get in, you know, when the guy driving motions her over to his side of the car and tells her she'll have to get in from his side because the door on the other side isn't working. Well, man, she backs off right away 'cause of course what's happened is that this guy has rigged the car so that the door on the passenger side doesn't open and once she gets in that car, she's trapped." He let out a deep breath. "Now, this girl hitchhikes all the time, so she knows the ropes. She knows what to avoid, and she's street-smart." He looked Gail up and down. "You don't look very street-smart," he told her.

They drove the rest of the way in silence.

"Thanks for the ride," she told him when he stopped to let her out.

"Don't hitchhike anymore," he told her.

"Go to school," she replied.

She stood on the corner and watched him disappear down the street. Where was she? And what was she going to do now? She checked her watch. It was getting late. Jennifer would be home from school. How was she going to explain where she'd been and how she was dressed? She looked down at her baggy pants and old worn-out shirt, only partially covered by the buttonless, thin gray coat she had recently purchased from the Salvation Army. It would hardly escape Jennifer's notice.

Oh well, she thought, she'd have until she found a ride home to think up a suitable excuse.

She waited until the youth's car was out of sight before she brought one foot down off the curb and thrust her right hand out in the air, hesitantly raising her thumb. It was almost ten minutes later when another car pulled up, and the driver, a well-dressed businessman in his mid-forties, bent over and opened the door on the passenger side.

"Where are you going?" he asked with a smile. Gail relaxed immediately. She was too cold and exhausted to deal with another slim, fair-haired youth.

"Livingston," she told him eagerly.

He looked doubtful but then agreed. She climbed in beside him and he pulled back into traffic.

"Cold enough for you?" he asked after several minutes.

"Freezing," she answered.

"Feel like a cup of coffee?" he smiled after a few minutes more. "Or a drink? A drink would warm you up nicely."

"No, thank you," Gail said. "I've got to get home."

"Husband?" he asked.

"He likes his dinner on the table when he walks in the door," Gail embellished, beginning to feel vaguely uncomfortable.

"What does he think of his wife hitchhiking?"

"I'm sure he wouldn't like it." Gail noticed that the man's eyes kept glancing at her body.

"What else do you do that your husband doesn't like?" he leered. She pulled the thin coat tight across her chest.

Gail ignored the suggestion implicit in his question and looked out her side window. The man made no further attempts at conversation, and gradually Gail began to recognize the familiar Livingston streets. "This is fine," she said, feeling tremendously relieved. "Right here."

He stopped the car. Gail was about to reach for the door handle when his hand on her knee stopped her. "Say, pretty lady," he said casually, an afterthought almost, "I just drove you a hell of a distance out of my way. I think I deserve a little something for my time and trouble."

"Please get your hand off me," Gail said steadily.

"Come on, darling," he continued. "Just French me a little."

" 'French'?" Gail asked, removing his hand and sneaking her other hand toward the door, her eyes holding onto his with an unspoken promise.

"Yeah," he answered, his hands moving to the zipper of his pants. "You know, darling, with your mouth."

He lifted his hand to bring her head down. Suddenly, Gail pushed her door open and jumped out, his hand slapping against the side of her hair as she made her escape.

"Bitch!" he yelled as Gail ran from the car. She heard the screech of his tires as he threw the car into full speed. He obviously didn't want to stick around any longer than she did. Gail stopped running, tears stinging her cheeks. She found an empty garbage can by the side of the road and threw up inside it.

Gail was still feeling shaky when she got home. Jennifer was in the living room playing the piano. She jumped up as soon as she saw her mother.

"Hi. You look frozen. Where have you been? My God, where did you get that coat?"

Gail discarded it quickly in the rear of the closet. "I've had it for years."

"Where's your nice red one?"

"At the cleaners," Gail lied.

"What are you wearing?" Jennifer gasped. "Where on earth did you find those clothes?"

"I was helping Laura move some furniture around at her office," Gail told her, surprised how easily the lie came. "I didn't want to ruin anything nice."

"Laura?" The question was more of an exclamation. "Something wrong?"

"No . . . Just that Laura called before, wondering where you've been. She said she's been trying to reach you for days . . ."

"Did I say 'Laura'? I'm sorry—I meant Nancy."

"Since when does Nancy have an office?"

"Since she decided to get one," Gail said impatiently,

walking past her daughter into the kitchen and opening the refrigerator door. She took out the leftovers from the night before and laid them on the counter. Jennifer was at her elbow.

"Where's the car?" Jennifer asked, catching Gail by surprise.

"I had to take it in," Gail lied again.

"How'd you get home?"

"I walked."

"You walked all the way from Harold's garage?" Jennifer's face registered appropriate shock.

"It's not that far."

"It isn't?"

"Jennifer, have you done your homework?"

"Yes."

"All of it?"

"Yes." Jennifer grabbed a carrot from one of the plates and sat down with it at the kitchen table.

"Don't do that," Gail said.

"Don't do what? Sit down?"

"Grab food off the plates. You know what I'm talking about."

"Sorry. Didn't think you'd mind one carrot."

"Well, there's not a whole lot of food for supper," Gail admonished, surveying the meager fare, then swinging around abruptly. "Jennifer, do you ever hitchhike? I want an honest answer."

"Sometimes," Jennifer answered reluctantly, sensing trouble.

"Jesus Christ," Gail muttered, slamming her fist down onto the counter.

"I don't anymore," Jennifer told her quickly. "I haven't since . . ." She broke off.

"If I ever hear of you hitchhiking again," Gail began slowly building, "for whatever reason, you're grounded for six months. Do you understand me?"

Jennifer regarded her mother with growing concern. "Yes." She lowered her eyes.

"Jesus Christ," Gail cried again. "How stupid can you be?"

"What brought this on?" Jennifer demanded. "Did someone get hurt or something? Has something happened to somebody we know?"

"Does somebody have to get hurt for you to use your head?"

"Why are you yelling at me?"

"I don't want you ever to hitchhike again. Do I make myself clear?"

"Yes," Jennifer cried. "I'm not arguing with you."

There was silence. Gail turned back toward the sink.

"And something else I've been meaning to talk to you about," she said slowly, carefully.

"What's that?" Jennifer asked warily.

"Eddie."

Jennifer's eyes widened in surprise. "What about Eddie? I thought you liked him."

"I do," Gail agreed quickly. "But you've been dating each other exclusively for almost two years now, and I think it might be a good idea if you were to start dating other people."

"Nineteen months," Jennifer corrected. "And I don't want to go out with anybody else. I love Eddie."

"How do you know you love him if you have nothing to compare him with?"

"I don't need to compare him with anybody!"

"Sweetie," Gail pressed gently, "I'm not suggesting that you stop seeing him, just that you see other boys too."

"I don't want to see other boys! Where is all this coming from?"

"Okay, okay," Gail said, backing off. "I just thought I'd mention it. Will you do me a favor and think it over at least?"

"No."

Gail and her daughter exchanged stubborn glances.

"Julie called before and asked me to have dinner over there tonight. I said I didn't think so, but if it's all right with you, I think I've changed my mind. You're only serving leftovers anyway, and this way there'll be plenty for you and Jack. Is it okay if I go?"

"Only if your father picks you up and brings you home."

"He will," Jennifer told her, getting up and reaching for the phone. Gail pretended to be busy as Jennifer talked easily with her ex-husband's wife. "He'll pick me up in half an hour."

Gail nodded but said nothing as her daughter left the room.

Chapter 19

       Friday morning Jack insisted that he and Gail get away by themselves for the weekend. They needed some time together *alone*, he stressed; they needed a couple of days to get away from everything and everybody.

He chose Cape Cod.

The first time that Gail and Jack had been to Cape Cod had been on their honeymoon almost nine years before. Then it had seemed, as everything had seemed to her in those early days, a magic place. Now, though even the most jaded could hardly dismiss its charm, it seemed much more commonplace. While the magic wand had been waved lavishly across certain sections, giving added vibrancy to the paint of the old wooden cottages that lined the streets and conjuring up the word "quaint" from the old Patti Page song, in other areas the magic had been applied in too desultory a fashion. Quaint had given way to tacky. Even in October, tourists seemed to outnumber the natives. The sand dunes seemed smaller, the salty air less pleasing. For eight years Gail had thought Cape Cod to be paradise on earth. Now she knew there was no such place. One town was the same as another. While before, Gail felt only peace and serenity when she and Jack walked these streets, arms intertwined, now she was aware of every automobile horn and faulty muffler. The formerly romantic breezes were harsh against her cheeks. She longed to escape them but was afraid to suggest to Jack that they go inside.

Once she had resigned herself to the trip, Gail had found the drive up from Livingston to be a pleasant one. It was sunny; the weatherman was promising a relatively mild few days. Even the traffic had moved along at a decent clip. There were only two accidents along the way and neither seemed from her vantage point to be particularly serious. She had wondered briefly as they passed one car that had been rear-ended by another what it would be like to be rammed sharply from behind, to collide with another car at a high speed. How would it feel, she wondered, to witness the sudden explosion of her flesh as another automobile plowed right through her body? Would she feel anything at all?

Jack regularly consulted his new map ("What happened to all my maps?" he had asked before they left the house, and had been forced to purchase a new one at the gas station) even though he knew the way, and could probably find Cape Cod blindfolded.

Gail wondered how Jennifer was doing with Mark and his wife. Would Julie be there when Jennifer returned from school today? Would she remember to get Jennifer up in plenty of time on Monday morning or would she be too busy rushing to her own job? Julie worked as a secretary for an accountant. Would she have enough time and energy left at the end of the day to be bothered with a moody teenage girl? Though Jennifer adored her father, would he be strict enough with her about her homework and her bedtime? Would he make sure that she and Eddie stuck to their curfew?

Several times during the lengthy drive, Gail had been tempted to ask Jack to turn the car around and go home, but then she had reminded herself that they would be back on Monday evening and that Jennifer would undoubtedly manage fine without her for a cou-

ple of days. Probably better, she thought, recalling
their frequent bickering of late.

Gail also realized how important these next few days
were for her and Jack. He was right—they did need
some time together alone. They were drawing further
apart from each other with each new day, retreating
rather than risking open argument, burying their anger
and their guilt rather than confronting it, or each
other.

It wasn't Jack's fault, Gail recognized. He had made
repeated attempts to draw her out. At first, she had
also tried, but as much as she admired and relied on his
strength, she also found herself resenting it. Though she
had been the one to press for a speedy return to their
normal lives, she begrudged him his ability to adapt so
readily, to simply pick himself up and carry on.

Stop it, she told herself, knowing she was being un-
fair. There was no reason for her to be angry at Jack (or
at Jennifer, for that matter) because he had somehow
been able to adjust to the tragedy. If anyone had reason
to be angry, if anyone had a right to assign blame, it
was Jack, not herself. How could he *not* blame her? she
wondered.

He *had* to blame her, he *had* to be thinking each time
he looked at her that if only she'd been at home on that
last April afternoon, Cindy would still be alive. Every
time his eyes confronted hers, she felt his unfocused dis-
taste, just as each time she tried to reach out to him, she
resented . . . what?

Gail glanced at her husband as he walked along beside her, his hand in hers, his attention seemingly devoted to the local scenery. Was his mind really on these
old clapboard houses? Or was he seeing, as she was,
Cindy's face behind each curtain, Cindy's smile in each
window? Could he hear their daughter's careless giggle
in each lingering laugh of a passerby?

"They painted that house," he said suddenly.

"What?"

"That house over there. Second one from the corner. They painted it white. Remember? It used to be blue."

"That's too bad. I liked it blue."

"So did I."

"I guess they felt it was time for a change."

"And those people cut down some trees," Jack added, pointing across the road.

"It looks nicer this way," she said, not remembering how it had looked before.

"Really?" He seemed surprised. "I liked it with the trees."

"Gives them more sun like this."

"I suppose," he shrugged, taking a deep breath. "I love the smell of this town."

Gail took a deep breath the way Jack had done, but with the intake came a sharp stabbing sensation in her chest.

"You okay?" he asked quickly. "Want to quit? Go inside somewhere for a cup of coffee?"

"No, I'm enjoying the walk," she told him, trying to sound convincing, knowing he was no longer so easily fooled.

"Do you want to walk along the beach?" he suggested.

"Sure," she agreed.

"It might be too cold," he cautioned.

"We can always turn back," she said, taking comfort in the small choices that were left them, as she had earlier sought refuge in their small talk.

He was right—the waterfront was cold, even unpleasant, though each pretended for a time that it wasn't. Jack had such a kind face, Gail thought, studying him, his nose strong and prominent in profile, his cheeks red with the wind.

Another couple passed them, nodding a chilled hello as they burrowed their faces against the collars of their jackets.

"Crazy tourists," Jack laughed. "You don't see any of the natives out walking the beach in this cold."

Gail's eyes followed the other couple as they hurried along the sand, imagining herself in the other woman's place, wondering what thoughts were filtering through her mind as she strolled with her arm through her husband's, in much the same way Gail walked beside Jack. Just another ordinary American couple, probably entertaining similar thoughts about herself and Jack, Gail surmised, trying to guess what secrets were hiding behind the woman's rosy cheeks and smiling eyes, knowing there were always secrets. And scars. Gail knew that things were rarely the way they seemed, that happiness was only a momentary illusion. Walk a mile in my shoes, Gail thought and then, judge not lest you be judged.

She shook away the unwelcome thought with a prolonged shrug of her shoulders. Jack immediately let go of her hand and put his arm around her, pulling her close against him, trying to make her warm.

"Let's go back," he said. "I've had enough." Gail nodded silently. "Not quite the same when it's cold, is it?"

Gail said nothing. They both knew that the weather had nothing to do with things not being the same.

They returned to the tourist home and spent half an hour talking with Mrs. Mayhew. She had wondered about them, she told them, when they failed to make their usual summer arrangements. The summer season had been slightly slower than usual. Local residents were blaming it on the economy, she embellished. Things were slower all over the country. What could you do?

She asked about Jack's business—had the economy affected it as well? Jack told her there seemed to be no shortage of sick animals, although people were cutting down on certain luxury expenses, such as pet grooming. Mrs. Mayhew then inquired after their family. Jack explained softly that there'd been a tragedy, that their child had died. He didn't say how; Mrs. Mayhew didn't ask. The conversation drifted to an uneasy stop and Jack led Gail upstairs to their room.

How different this rooming house was from the ones she was more recently used to frequenting, Gail thought as they walked down the warm, softly papered hallway. An expensive narrow rug ran the length of the dark hardwood floor; a small antique table with a suitably decorative lamp sat in the corner, its frosted bulb casting a welcome and unobtrusive light.

Their room was equally pleasant, done in well-modulated shades of peach and brown. The bed was queen-size and felt as comfortable as it looked. Folk art from the Canadian Maritime Provinces hung on the walls. Gail took an appreciative glance around. She had always loved this room.

"Remember that little dog I was telling you about?" Jack asked, as he removed his jacket. Gail said that she did. "They finally got around to mating her. It'll be a couple of months, of course, until she has her litter, and then six weeks after that before they're ready to give any of them away. Have you given it any thought?"

"Not really," Gail said, feeling guilty. "But I will."

Jack walked over and stood very close to her. "I don't want to push you," he said, his hands reaching around her, and Gail knew that he wasn't just talking about the dog.

"You're not," she told him, knowing that this moment could be put off no longer, that the time had come for them to make love. She lifted her eyes to his and watched as he lowered his mouth onto hers, her arms stretching under his and around his back.

The kiss was gentle, their lips barely parted. She heard him moan, felt his hands as they stroked her back, careful not to squeeze her too hard. He kissed the side of her face, her eyes, her neck, slowly circling back to her lips, this time his touch a little stronger, his mouth now open, his tongue gently searching for her own.

His hands traveled down across her jeans, cupping

her buttocks, then running across her stomach up to her breasts. A few seconds later, she felt his fingers at the buttons of her blouse, stumbling over them as if he were a teenager, shyly tugging the garment off her shoulders and letting it drop to the floor. He fumbled with the hook on her bra, and for a brief instant, they giggled with the absurdity of what they were doing, until Gail reached behind her and undid the clasp herself.

Jack fell to his knees, his hands lifting up to her breasts, burying his head between them, Gail's hands clutching at his hair. She felt the snap on her jeans come open, heard the sound of her zipper as it separated, felt the tug on her legs as Jack pulled off the heavy denim.

She couldn't remember when he had removed his own clothes, had no recollection of how they had gotten over to the bed, and was not able to pinpoint the precise moment that her stomach began to churn inside her. She had not consciously thrust Cindy's face before her tightly closed eyes; she had tried hard to push away the memory of last April, to not compare what was happening to her now to what had happened to her child six months ago.

And yet it was the same, she realized, opening her eyes wide and looking up at Jack, understanding now the resentment that up until this moment she had been unable to consciously define. It was his very maleness that she resented. This so-called act of love was the same act that had been forced on their daughter just prior to her death.

And suddenly, all she felt was pain, her own pain and that of her daughter, and she cried out in anguish.

"What's wrong?" Jack asked, alarmed. "Did I hurt you?" He pulled out of her when he realized she was crying. "What is it, Gail? Please tell me what it is."

"I can't," she cried. "I just can't do this." She lowered her face to her knees and sobbed. "I tried, Jack. I wanted to. Please believe me. I really wanted to. I love you. I wanted to be able to make love to you, to have you make love to me, but I just can't."

"I pushed," Jack said, instantly berating himself. "I shouldn't have tried to force things . . ."

"You didn't force anything. It's me, Jack. Not you. You've been everything you could possibly be. You've been patient and loving and good . . . and it's not you. There's nothing you could have done any differently."

"I could have waited."

"No," Gail said, shaking her head sadly. "It wouldn't make any difference. That's what I'm trying to tell you. A year from now I will still feel the same way." He tried to protest, but her words stopped him. "I can't make love to you now . . . I won't be able to make love to you later, no matter how patient you are, no matter how long you wait . . . because all I can think of when you touch me is that this is what that monster did to our beautiful little girl. All I can see are that animal's hands all over her. I can feel his weight on top of her tiny body, and I can feel him pushing his way inside her, and my God, I'd give anything not to feel this way, but I can't help it. The sight of your naked body . . ." She began crying uncontrollably now. "I tried. I thought I could do it. For a few minutes, I was able to forget, but then it all started coming back—the loathing, the disgust, the shame. And I know that I will never be able to make love again because the image of that man with our child will never leave me, and no matter how well I am able to suppress it during the day or when I'm alone, being with you this way brings it all back to me. Oh God, leave me, Jack," she cried, seeing that he was crying now as well. "Find someone else and start a new life. Find someone who can love you the way you need to be loved, the way you deserve to be loved, you dear, sweet man." Jack started to speak, but her fingertips against his lips stopped him again. "Please, listen to me, Jack. It's not fair to you. I know that you love me, and it wouldn't be fair of me to go on letting you think that there's a chance I might ever feel differently . . ."

"You might—"

"No . . . I won't. Leave me, Jack. Find somebody else. I'm not the same person I was before. I can never be that person again. Find someone else. I'll understand."

"You will?" he asked, twisting around and pulling a sheet over his torso, "then understand this, lady. Understand that I love you and that nothing that you say or do, or don't do, for that matter, is going to make me leave you. You're stuck with me whether you want me or not, because I love you and I need you, and not only that, damn it, I really *like* you. And even if that maniac has robbed me of my daughter and maybe even my wife, he is not going to take away the best friend that I have in this world, because I'm not going to let him. He's taken enough from us, Gail. Please don't let him take any more."

Gail reached over and cradled Jack's head in her lap. They sat that way until it got dark and then they crawled underneath the covers. By the time Gail closed her eyes to sleep, she was more convinced than ever that Jack deserved more, that he would be better off without her.

Chapter 20

The phone rang as Gail was putting on her coat to leave the house.

"Hello," she said, hurrying her voice, hoping that whoever was on the other end would instinctively grasp that she had no time to talk. She was anxious to get into Newark, to reestablish her routine.

"Well, hallelujah!" Laura's voice responded immediately. "I don't believe I finally reached you. Where have you been?"

"Jack and I drove up to the Cape for a few days. We just got back last night."

"That's great. How was it?"

"Cold," Gail replied, ignoring the more obvious implications of the question.

"Where else have you been?" Laura asked.

"What do you mean?"

"I mean that I've been calling every day for weeks. You're never home."

"I've been looking for a job," Gail said, more comfortable now with lies than with the truth. "No luck yet, but . . ."

"Well, I think that's wonderful. Where have you been looking?"

"Everywhere," Gail laughed. "But don't say anything to anyone yet, Jack or anybody. He doesn't know. I wanted to surprise him."

"I won't say a word. Can I help you in any way? You need a character reference?"

"I'll let you know," Gail told her, eager to get off the phone. "Actually, I was just on my way out the door."

"Okay, I won't keep you. I just wanted to make sure you haven't forgotten about our lunch today."

"Lunch?"

"At Nancy's club. You remember . . . you don't remember. We decided months ago. October 15. The fashion show at Nancy's club. You promised you'd go with me."

"I forgot," Gail said honestly. "It totally slipped my mind."

"No kidding. Well, it doesn't matter. I'm just glad I caught you before you went out. I'll pick you up about twelve-thirty."

"Laura, I can't go."

"Of course you're going. You promised."

"I have an appointment."

"I've reserved two seats. *And* paid for them. You have to go. Make the appointment for another time."

"I have nothing to wear. You know how all those women will be dressed."

"I'll pick you up at twelve-thirty. Come as you are."

The phone clicked in Gail's ear. She looked down at her oldest sloppiest pair of slacks and her ragged black turtleneck sweater. Sure, she thought, replacing the receiver and wishing she hadn't stopped to answer the phone, come as you are.

Gail was struggling with the zipper of a red linen dress when she heard the doorbell. She looked at her watch. It was only twelve and it was unlike Laura, who was usually late, to be this early. "Laura?" she asked into the intercom.

"Sheila," the voice informed her coolly.

Sheila? Her mother-in-law? What was she doing here?

"I'll be right down," Gail said quickly. "Just a minute."

She gave her zipper a final tug and then ran down the stairs. What did her mother-in-law want? She opened the door. "Hi," she greeted her pleasantly.

Sheila Walton stepped inside. She wore a dark brown mink coat and a sour expression. "You're a difficult girl to get ahold of these days. I've called many times . . ."

"Jack and I were away for the weekend," Gail explained, hoping that would satisfy the other woman. When she recognized it hadn't, she continued. "And I've been busy; I've had to go out a lot."

"So I gathered." Sheila Walton glanced at the old coat slumped over the hall chair. "Going out again?"

Gail retrieved the worn gray cloth coat and returned it to its place at the rear of the closet. "Well, not in that coat," she said, trying to smile, feeling increasingly defensive.

"But you are going out." It was a statement, not a question.

"In half an hour."

"I'll try not to keep you."

"Please come in." Gail motioned toward the living room. "Can I get you a cup of coffee or something?"

"No, thank you." Sheila Walton sat down on the sofa. "I don't want to hold you back, keep you from whatever it is you have to do."

Gail braced herself for the neglected–mother-in-law routine, aware that Sheila Walton had at least some justification. "I'm sorry I haven't called you," she began. "I've meant to. How have you been?" Gail had never felt too comfortable with Jack's mother, who was a cold woman at the best of times, and who since the death of her only grandchild, had become even more withdrawn. This aloof quality had never bothered Gail before. She knew it was, as Jack had explained, the way she was with everyone. Since her husband had passed away—she was one of those people who always said "passed away" and never "died"—she had traveled extensively, going on two around-the-world cruises and flying off to Europe or the Orient whenever things got too routine at home.

"I've been fine," the woman answered. "And you?"

"All right. How was your trip?"

"Japan is always nice. I've been back for several weeks now. I called, spoke to Jack. You were obviously too busy to return my call . . ."

"I'm sorry," Gail apologized. "There's no excuse, I know. Just that I've been very preoccupied lately."

"Where are you off to today?" The question was more of an accusation.

"A friend called and invited me out to lunch. Laura. You've met her, I think."

"Yes, the blonde. She's very attractive. I hadn't realized that you had such an active social life," Sheila Walton continued. "I always had this image of you as the little housewife, singing in the kitchen, waiting for her children to come home. You know, the perfect mother . . ."

"I never claimed to be perfect," Gail said defensively, growing uncomfortable, wondering where this conversation was headed.

"But you go out to lunch," Mrs. Walton went on, ignoring the interruption. "You're too busy to call and say hello, to ask how I'm doing, find out about my trip. You have friends to see, places to go." She stopped abruptly. "You were out shopping that afternoon, weren't you?"

"What afternoon?" Gail asked, already knowing the answer.

"The afternoon that Cindy passed away," Sheila Walton said, and Gail knew that she had been waiting a long time to voice these words.

"What are you trying to say?" Gail demanded, feeling her knees starting to shake, her hands to tremble.

"That I'm responsible? That what happened was my fault?"

"Of course not," Sheila Walton demurred realizing that perhaps she had gone too far. "I'm just saying that you're a busier person than I envisioned, and that it's a shame that you had to be out having lunch with a friend, shopping for clothes, on that particular afternoon." She swallowed hard and looked toward the door. "I'm sure I'm not saying anything to you that you haven't said to yourself at least a hundred times."

Gail looked around the room helplessly. "Why are you doing this?" she asked. A hundred times? The number was more like a hundred thousand.

"My only grandchild is dead," the woman said simply.

"A child you saw two or three times a year," Gail reminded her pointedly, seeking to wound, pleased when she saw that she had.

"That's as much as your parents saw her," Sheila Walton countered, as if that made everything right.

"My parents live in Florida. You live around the corner!"

"Don't you dare try to tell me I didn't love my granddaughter!"

"I never said you didn't love her."

"I loved her very much."

"I'm sure you did."

"I wouldn't have let her walk home alone from school, you could bet on that. I never let my son take risks like that. I made sure that I was always home for him, just as I would have made sure that somebody was there for Cindy. I wouldn't have been out gallivanting around . . ."

"Why are you saying these things?" Gail pleaded, unable to listen to more.

"How dare you," Sheila Walton glared across the room at her daughter-in-law, "how dare you suggest that I didn't love my grandchild."

"I never suggested any such thing," Gail cried.

"How dare you," Sheila Walton muttered.

"Please . . . just get out of here before we say anything else," whispered Gail.

"Oh yes, I almost forgot about your lunch."

Gail suddenly threw herself at the seated woman and pulled her to her feet. "Get out of here," she shouted, unable to control herself any longer. "Get out of here before I kill you. Do you hear me? Get out!" She half pushed, half carried the frightened woman to the front door.

"I'll never forgive you," Jack's mother's voice trembled as Gail forced her outside.

"I'll never forgive *you*," Gail answered, collapsing on the other side of the door.

Fifteen minutes later a smiling Laura Cranston arrived to take Gail to lunch.

Chapter 21

Gail was still shaking when Laura's car pulled up in front of The Manor. The valet, a slim young man in his early twenties with neatly trimmed brown hair, ran to open Gail's door. Gail pressed the automatic door lock.

"What are you doing?" Laura asked, startled to find herself locked in.

"I can't do it," Gail whispered. "Please, Laura. I don't think I'm ready for this."

Laura twisted her body around to face her friend. "Of course you are. Come on. It'll take your mind off what happened."

"She said such awful things, Laura. She practically accused me of engineering my daughter's death."

"She was just feeling neglected, and angry because you're going out. She probably has her own demons that she hasn't come to terms with. She wasn't exactly the old-fashioned granny with milk and cookies, was she? She has a lot of her own guilt to deal with."

"I shouldn't have said the things I did to her."

"So, you'll call her later and apologize. It's never too late to apologize. Besides, you expect too much of yourself. You always have." Laura reached over and took Gail's hands in her own. The valet stood beside the locked door and watched the scene with growing interest. "Listen to me," Laura continued, ignoring his prying eyes. "You've handled this awful thing that's happened to you remarkably. Maybe even too remarkably. Outwardly, you're the proverbial pillar of strength. What's happening inside you, Gail? You've been bottling everything up. There has to be a whole lot of rage, and it's going to come out in one way or another. It has to. That little scene you played with your mother-in-law was bound to happen sooner or later. It'll probably happen again with someone else."

"God, I hope not."

"People who love you will understand." Laura looked toward the impatient young man waiting by the car door. "You ready?" Gail nodded, and Laura pressed the appropriate button to release the lock.

The valet promptly held open Gail's door, staring at the two women uneasily.

"You gettin' out?" he asked almost timidly.

Gail studied his face, the small brown eyes and long, even nose. His skin was fair, almost baby smooth, and he had large, straight teeth. She studied his hands on the car door. They were big hands with short, fat fingers and nails chewed down to the skin. She pictured those hands around her neck. "Gail," Laura called, coming around to her side watching as Gail stepped onto the sidewalk. "Nancy's going to love those shoes," she said, trying to smile.

They had to wait in line, and when they were finally led to their table, they found themselves seated with ten other women, none of whom Gail recognized. She felt grateful.

Gail looked around the room as discreetly as she could, keeping her eyes down, willing herself into invisibility. There were approximately two hundred women present, each one extravagantly turned out and glowing with anticipation.

Gail searched the room for Nancy but couldn't find her.

"Have some wine," Laura advised softly. "It's nice and dry."

"Where's Nancy?" Gail asked.

Laura looked around. "Probably backstage organizing things. You know Nancy. She likes to be in total control."

"Total control," Gail repeated, taking a sip of her wine, thinking how meaningless those words really were.

"Your husband's a lawyer, isn't he?" one of the women asked Laura from across the table. Laura nodded, a crooked smile crossing her face. She had never liked to be known for her husband's occupation. "I've been called for jury duty . . ." the woman continued.

"She's been called for jury duty," another woman at the table repeated loudly for the benefit of the others who might not have heard.

"Hang him," someone said immediately.

"I don't want anything to do with him," the first woman whined. "I want to know how I can get out of it."

"You can't," Laura told her with casual authority, "unless you can prove that it would cause great hardship to your family or to your health. It's your patriotic duty."

"Damn," muttered the woman. "Have you ever served on a jury?"

"Can't," Laura reminded her. "Like you said, I'm a lawyer's wife."

"That disqualifies you?" Gail asked, suddenly interested. She realized she knew little about how the legal system actually operated.

"Apparently, the logic is that I know too much. A little knowledge is a dangerous thing, that line of thinking. Also, the fear is that with a husband who is a lawyer, one might be unduly influenced by his opinion."

"I thought you weren't supposed to talk about what went on," someone said.

"You're not supposed to do a lot of things," Laura told her, and, as if on cue, each woman turned away from the table to pick up the trail she left behind before the sudden burst of conversation.

Gail looked down the long, rectangular table. They were seated six women to a side. She noted a total of twenty such tables on either side of a newly erected runway that ran down the middle of the large, ornately decorated room. In the middle of each table sat a centerpiece of fresh flowers. The dishes were of delicate Lalique china. A small champagne glass of fresh fruit sat on each plate, but no one made a move to begin. Gail wondered if they were waiting for someone to say grace.

"So tell me all about your appointments," Laura said suddenly, turning back in Gail's direction, catching her by surprise.

"Oh, they weren't very exciting. Just job interviews. Nothing special."

Her response had been too weak and Laura was too smart and too persistent to let it go at that.

"What kind of jobs? Who have you seen? Where are they? Come on, details, details."

Gail forced a smile. "I've seen so many people about so many different types of jobs . . ."

"Such as?"

"Secretary, receptionist . . ."

"I didn't know you could type or take shorthand."

"I can't," Gail laughed. "Maybe that's why I'm not having any luck."

"Tell me about your weekend."

Gail caught a momentary glimpse of Jack, his nude body covered with the crumpled bed sheet, his shoulders slumped, his posture defeated. "It was fine," she said. "Cold. Very cold."

"Whatever happened to Indian summer?" Laura wondered aloud.

"There's Nancy," Gail said abruptly, pointing

through the crowd toward the head table where Nancy Carter was stepping up to the microphone.

There were a few more minutes of frenzied conversation before everyone quieted down and allowed Nancy to speak. Nancy was resplendent in a bright red taffeta blouse and black skirt. Understatedly overpriced, Gail thought. When Nancy began to speak, her voice was steady and strong.

"She missed her calling," Laura muttered as Nancy finished her welcoming speech and admonished them all to begin lunch and enjoy the show. "She should have been Queen."

"She looks great," Gail said.

"That awful black dye," Laura winced. "She must have had a fresh onslaught of gray." Laura began digging into her fresh fruit salad, and the rest of the women at their table did likewise.

The fruit cocktail was followed by a delicate salmon mousse, framed by asparagus and small white potatoes. Judging from the minuscule portions, the chef evidently assumed all women who came to fashion shows were on a diet.

The waitress cleared away the plates and there followed a bright pink sherbet which one of the women explained loudly was actually a sorbet. Gail thought they looked exactly the same and tasted the same. She took one spoonful and then put the spoon down. She noticed that after several mouthfuls Laura did likewise.

Suddenly, the lights dimmed and the by now familiar rock music that accompanied most fashion shows began blasting from the speakers. A spotlight appeared boldly, then another and another, and at once there were three gorgeous women parading down the runway in next spring's fashions.

The models pranced, hips first, shoulders swaggering, back and forth before their rapt audience. Gail watched their smiles flash on and off, listened to the blare of the music and grew increasingly depressed.

How could they be modeling next spring's fashions already?

As suddenly as the show had begun, it ended. Not that the finale was anything less than spectacular, consisting as it did of two live cheetahs being led growling down the runway by a stunning dark-haired model whose dress was of a similarly bold pattern. Gail wondered if the animals might not suspect some sort of double-dealing and rebel, leaping off the platform and helping themselves to an impromptu lunch of their own, but, despite their growls, they were disappointingly calm.

"Last year's Oscar De La Renta," one woman scoffed, and another agreed as the lights came on again.

"I saw the same thing *two* years ago at Valentino's," the woman who had to serve on jury duty announced. "And that model with the cats—she looked like something the cats dragged *in*." She laughed at her feeble joke.

"What can you expect from a designer from Hackensack?"

"Hackensack? You're kidding!"

"Apparently, he runs a very successful store there."

"Well, you won't find me in it," another woman said, and the others agreed.

Nancy Carter approached the table, glowing with expectancy. "Well, what did you think?"

"Great," said the Oscar De La Renta fan.

"Beautiful clothes," the refugee from Valentino's announced to a general hum of agreement.

"What did you think of the last model?" Nancy asked her. "The one with the cats."

"Gorgeous," she answered without so much as a pause.

"My daughter," Nancy laughed, her voice an interesting mix of pride and envy. "My daughter, the model."

"I had no idea Sloane was so grown up," Gail said out loud.

Nancy turned in her direction, aware for the first time that Gail was there. The color all but drained from her face. "My God, Gail, I didn't know you were coming." She looked accusingly at Laura. "Laura, you never told me you were bringing Gail."

"I wanted to surprise you."

"How *are* you, dear?" Nancy asked, her eyes begging for a simple "fine."

"All right," Gail told her.

"You look wonderful," Nancy said, an obvious lie. "I'm so glad that you could make it. Why haven't you called me? I've been so worried about you!"

Gail shrugged. What could she say?

"How's Jack?" Nancy asked, smiling at a woman at the next table.

"Okay," Gail answered. "Jennifer too."

"Good," Nancy said, starting to inch away. "That's good. I think you're amazing, all of you. I really do." She took a deep breath, as if the effort of what she had just said had been too much.

"You're full of shit," Laura told her as sweetly as if she'd just said how nice she looked.

Gail watched Nancy's face in surprise. It registered nothing. She hadn't heard. She hadn't heard because she didn't listen. "I've got to run," Nancy apologized happily. "You know what it's like being hostess. I have to make sure that everyone's happy." She turned back to Gail, allowing their eyes to connect for only several seconds before looking away. "Listen, you be sure to call me if you need me, do you hear? If there's anything I can do, anything that you need . . ." She moved on to the next table without completing the sentence.

How could I ever have believed that woman was my friend? Gail wondered sadly.

"You used to find her amusing," Laura said, reading her mind. "Come on, we'd better go." Laura pushed her chair away from the table. "I have to get back to work."

"Are you very busy?" Gail asked as Laura was driving her home.

"The usual. Alcoholics, wife beaters, incest. A social worker's life is not a happy one."

"Incest?"

"Yes, right here in River City," Laura chuckled. "You look genuinely shocked. Didn't you think we did that sort of thing in New Jersey?"

"I can't imagine doing it anywhere," Gail said honestly.

"Then you're very much behind the times, my dear. Conservative statistics estimate one in ten boys and one in four girls will be molested before they reach maturity. It's an epidemic."

Gail was beginning to feel sick to her stomach. "But how can a grown man be sexually interested in a child?" she asked weakly. If Laura realized that Gail was no longer referring to the files of nameless statistics that crossed her desk every week, she made no show of it, her concentration on the traffic, her mind slowly being taken over by her professional persona.

"You'd be surprised how sexy some of these five- and six-year-old girls can be," Laura told her matter-of-factly.

"Laura!" Gail gasped.

Laura suddenly realized all the implications of her remark and pulled her car over to the side of the road. "Hey now, wait a minute. What are we talking about here?" she demanded, turning in her seat to face Gail head-on. "I was not talking about Cindy—"

Gail didn't let her finish. "It doesn't matter who you were talking about," she exclaimed. "Did you hear what you said? You said that five- and six-year-old girls are sexy!"

"Some of them are," Laura defended herself shakily. "Look, Gail, you don't know. You don't see what I do.

In my office every day, families come in, all torn apart. I see this little prune of a wife who puts out for her husband maybe twice a year when she has to, and I see a little girl openly flirting with her father. A lot of men aren't strong enough to resist—"

"They damn well better resist," Gail shot back, tears springing to her eyes. "They damn well better stop using their wives as an excuse, and start assuming their responsibility as adults! If they need other women, let them find them! Women! There are plenty of available, willing ones around. A man doesn't have to turn to a defenseless child who doesn't have any choice in the matter!" Gail found herself twisting her body wildly from side to side. "Listen to you," she cried. "You've bought the whole phony bill of goods. If there's a problem with society, don't look to the perpetrator, look at the victim! Don't put the blame where it belongs; put it where it's easiest to disregard. Blame it on the women! If a man rapes his five-year-old daughter, blame his frigid wife. Blame his 'sexy' child. God forbid we place the blame on the man responsible!"

"Gail, calm down. I didn't mean to imply—"

"I am appalled," Gail continued, unable to stop herself, "that you, an intelligent woman, would believe that a five-year-old girl has any overt knowledge of her sexuality, that she would be seeking anything but affection from a man, especially if that man is her father. I am sickened by how easily you allow that man to relinquish his responsibility to his child. To all children. A child cannot make the same kind of rational decisions that an adult can. A child looks to a grown-up for guidance. A child trusts the adult to provide it. We allow that adult to subvert and destroy that trust and then we blame the child? What is going on in this world? What are we doing to our children?"

Gail lowered her head to her lap and wept. After several minutes she became aware of a hand stroking her back.

"I'm sorry," Laura said softly. "I wasn't thinking."

Gail kept her eyes closed. She sensed Laura wasn't finished, that a "but" hung in the air between them. "But," Laura continued, her voice unsteady and unsure, "you have to learn to put things in perspective. You can't keep relating everything that happens to what happened to Cindy."

"I read the papers every day, Laura," Gail whispered. "I see case after case where the victim ends up shouldering the blame. I listen to people talk, people like you who are well-meaning, good people, and I hear what you say, and you say the same thing—that the victim is somehow responsible for the crime. And the guilty parties walk away with suspended sentences or a slap on the wrist, and I am terrified, *terrified*, that the police will one day catch that monster who killed my baby and they will bring him to trial and he will get up there on the stand and say that my little girl, my baby, enticed him into those bushes, that it was all her fault she died, and they'll let him go."

"They won't let him go," Laura said with a certitude that Gail envied. "He's obviously a very sick man. They'll put him away somewhere. They won't let him go."

Put him away somewhere, Gail repeated to herself. Put him away. He's obviously a very sick man.

"In the meantime," Laura continued, "you're the one we have to worry about." She paused. "I want to be very careful how I phrase this. Please don't misunderstand . . . There's a tendency at times like this to glorify the deceased, to turn the person who died into a saint, to change him or her into something that . . ."

Gail looked up from her lap in slow horror. "The deceased," she spat contemptuously, "was my six-year-old daughter, not some anonymous him or her, and, if I want to remember that while she was alive she was a constant joy to be with—"

"Gail, slow down. That's exactly what I mean. 'A constant joy to be with,' you just said. Gail, I can remember days when you were at your wit's end with that child, when I'd call you and you'd be begging for five minutes of free time—"

"Shut up!" Gail shrieked, her frustrations pouring out and frightening Laura into silence. "Is this the kind of counseling you give to people? Is it? Reminding a woman whose child has been raped and strangled that she occasionally wished for five minutes of time to herself? That she was as human as her child? That because the child wasn't always perfect and sometimes got on her mother's nerves, that the mother, that *I*, should think any the less of her? Are you really so insensitive, Laura? Are you really so goddamned stupid?"

The two women sat beside each other as if they were strangers. For a long while neither said a word.

Then Laura spoke, her voice and hands trembling. "I don't understand what's happened here, how we got to this point. I didn't mean to imply those things. I just wanted you to—"

"See things the way you think I should?"

"No, not that at all. I know how upset you are, and I recognize that you're probably still reeling from that scene with your mother-in-law. But this is *me*, Gail. I'm your friend and I love you. Don't you understand?"

"Don't *you* understand," Gail retorted angrily, "that I would trade any of my so-called friends, including you, *especially* you," she emphasized, "a thousand times over for just five minutes with the daughter I lost?"

Both women let their eyes drop and turned slowly to face the windshield. They said nothing, each lost in the realization that there was nothing left to say.

Chapter 22

       Gail sat on the old, lumpy mattress of the single bed in her room at 26 Barton and thought about the events of the last few days.

Everything was falling apart. The facade she had worked so hard to erect was starting to crumble around her. She was fighting with everyone, first her mother-in-law, then Laura. This morning there had been yet another squabble with Jennifer that had led to yet another confrontation with Jack. Over what this time? she asked herself, trying to remember the order of things.

"Laura called again last night," Jennifer had said, and then continued when Gail said nothing. "Why won't you speak to her, Mom?"

Gail continued to sip at her coffee, saying nothing. She noticed Jack look up from behind the morning paper.

"Why won't you speak to her?" Jennifer had asked again.

"Laura and I had a slight disagreement."

"What about?"

"Nothing important."

"Then why haven't you spoken to her all week? Why won't you take any of her phone calls?"

"What's this about Laura?" Jack asked.

"It's nothing," Gail repeated.

"Sounds pretty serious if you're not talking."

"What happened, Mom?"

"Really, Jennifer," Gail said loudly, "it's none of your business. If I wanted to tell you, I would. Now drop it. Please," she said, lowering her voice.

"I'm late for school." Jennifer let her fork fall noisily to her plate of unfinished scrambled eggs and jumped to her feet.

"Jennifer," Jack began, "you have plenty of time. Sit down. I'll drive you—"

"No thanks," Jennifer told him, and hurried out of the room. Seconds later, they heard the front door slam shut.

"You don't think you came down on her just a little hard?"

Gail ran her hands through her hair, feeling it in need of a good wash. "I'm sorry. I didn't mean to. I'll talk to her later."

"What happened between you and Laura?"

"Nothing."

"The same nothing that happened between you and my mother?"

"When were you speaking to your mother?"

"She's very upset," he told her, not answering her question.

Gail took a deep breath, recalling the older woman's startled expression as Gail had hustled her angrily to the front door. "I'll have to apologize," Gail said almost under her breath.

"What happened, Gail? What's *happening*? Can't you talk to me about it?"

I wish I could, Gail thought. "There's nothing to say," she said aloud. "It'll work itself out."

"I'm not so sure."

Gail shrugged, not wanting to argue.

"And this thing with Laura? Will it straighten itself out too?"

She hadn't answered, and eventually Jack had tired of waiting and left the table.

What about Laura? Gail now wondered. A friendship of such long standing shattered in so few minutes. How could Laura have said those things to her? How could she have said those things to Laura? Laura, who had always been there when she needed her, who had cried with her, laughed with her, tried so hard to help her. A real friend, she thought, simultaneously thinking of Nancy, not a friend at all. Interesting the insights that tragedy could provide, she mused.

Now they were both gone, Gail realized. The true friend and the false one. In the end, what difference did it make? Her other friends had stopped calling, stopped asking her and Jack over. They'd been refused too often. People get impatient, she heard the woman from the group meeting repeat silently.

It didn't matter, she thought, remembering how she had always valued these relationships. She could do without friends. If she had to learn to live without her child, she could certainly learn to live without her friends.

Gail looked around the stark, white room. Of all the rooms she had inhabited, and in the last few days she had moved three times, this one was the most prisonlike. It was tiny, the size of a large walk-in closet. Its cracked walls were dull white; the narrow bed was covered with only a thin, faded blanket of indeterminable color. There was no chair, and only a bare overhead light. The dresser consisted of three beat-up shelves. The landlord, a squat middle-aged man with a noticeable paunch, had given her no instructions nor issued any restrictions on her behavior. As far as he was concerned, she could smoke in bed, drink in the halls or shoot up on the stairs. The rent was twelve dollars a night.

The boarders in this establishment were not much different from the roomers in any of the other houses she had stayed in. She had not been in this place long enough to meet anyone, had not even seen anyone except for an obviously deranged young man who lived on the main floor and apparently never left the house. He had the slightly unnerving habit of yelling "Into the trenches!" whenever anyone walked through the front door.

As with all the other rooms she had occupied, she kept her door open, listening for footsteps in the hall, straining to catch bits of conversation. While what little she heard was often angry and contentious, she had yet to hear anything that might link any of these lives to the death of her daughter. She refused to allow for the possibility that she never would.

Gail heard the front door downstairs open and close.

"Into the trenches!" came the immediate cry.

Gail found herself laughing despite herself. Then she heard footsteps on the stairs, and she slid off her bed toward the door.

"The rent's twelve dollars a night," she heard the landlord explaining as she reached the doorway.

"Fine," the man beside him said, fishing inside the pockets of his worn jeans for a handful of crumpled bills. He handed them over just after the landlord pushed open the door to the room and gave the man his key. Gail waited for further pleasantries but they never came. No "Have a good day." No "Enjoy your stay with us." Not even a simple "Thank you." The landlord simply pocketed the money and turned toward the stairs. He stopped momentarily when he saw Gail, but whatever thoughts he had he kept to himself. His raised eyebrow was the only acknowledgment that Gail was to receive.

"Something I can do for you?" the other man asked from across the hall, his voice somewhere between curiosity and contempt.

Gail shook her head and retreated slowly back into her room, feeling her body trembling. There was something familiar about this man, with his bulky frame, his squat neck and barrage of dark, unwashed curls.

She had seen him somewhere before. On more than one occasion.

Gail heard the door to the man's room close shut as she felt the back of her knees knock against her bed. She sank down onto the worn mattress. Where had she seen this man before?

Her mind raced back through her time in Newark during the past few days. There had been nothing particularly memorable. She had talked to no one, had her lunches alone . . .

Lunch. Harry's Diner. Yesterday. She had been seated at a table near the back, facing the door so that she could keep track of who came in and out. The restaurant had been half-filled. Two black men had sat arguing at the front corner table. Another man, white and balding, had sat at the table directly in front of hers, muttering angrily to himself. He had been joined by a slightly drunk, hugely overweight woman just as he was finishing up his meal. An elderly couple stared wordlessly into their coffee cups at the last table in the rear. There were three people sitting at the counter—a woman well into her sixties who sat flirting with Harry as if she were a silly teenager, a black man wearing a green beret and another man, white, maybe thirty years old, who sat hunched over the counter nursing a single cup of coffee, a man with a bulky frame, a squat neck and a barrage of dark, unwashed curls.

Gail leaned slowly back against the wall behind her bed, watching a memory of herself as she finished her lunch, paid her bill and left the restaurant. Out of the corner of her eye she had seen the dark, curly-haired man gulp down what was left in his cup and stand up. She had not paid him any further notice.

And yet she had seen him again less than an hour later, she realized, her body vaulting suddenly forward on her bed, her fingers twitching nervously. She had gone into the National State Bank to make a small withdrawal, and he had been there when she stepped outside again. She had barely noticed him at the time, but now she could see him quite clearly. He had been leaning against a bus stop sign, ostensibly trying to light a cigarette. His head was down, his body hunched forward, his hand in front of his face, seemingly intent on keeping the wind from extinguishing his match. But it was unmistakably the same man she had seen in Harry's Diner. The same man she had just seen renting the room directly across the hall from her own.

Was he following her?

"Excuse me," Gail asked the landlord several minutes later, standing outside his door at the bottom of the stairs. "I was wondering if you could tell me who that man is, the one who moved in across the hall from me." She looked warily up the stairs.

"Why don't you ask him?" the landlord asked, already bored with the conversation.

"I'd rather not," Gail tried to explain. "I was hoping you could tell me."

"Don't run no dating service," the man said. "You want to know who he is, you ask him yourself."

Gail understood that the conversation was over before the landlord closed his door. She stood alone in the hallway outside his room and wondered what she should do now. It was possible that the man was there entirely by chance, that he wasn't following her, that his being in the restaurant, outside the bank, even his being here, was part of a large set of coincidences. Possible, she thought, but highly unlikely.

She heard footsteps on the outside steps. The front door opened and two young men entered the house side by side, their hands entwined.

"Into the trenches!" came the cry from across the hall.

Gail pulled her coat tightly around her and rushed outside.

Despite the cold, the air was still as Gail moved quickly down the street. It felt like rain, she thought idly, her mind back in her cell-like room. She heard the footsteps on the stairs, saw the man across the hall, recognized that she had seen him before, knew that he was following her. Why?

Something I can do for you? he had asked.

Yes, she answered now. You can tell me who you are. Tell my why you're following me. Tell me what you want.

Maybe I'm the man you've been looking for, he said.

No, she answered immediately, shaking her head. It can't be you. The man I'm searching for is taller, slimmer, blonder, younger.

Then why am I following you?

Gail turned the corner.

It can't be you, she repeated, almost out loud. Cindy's killer was fair-haired and slim; he was younger, taller. It can't be you. You're too squat, too stocky, too dark, too old.

Too much. Not enough.

Then why am I following you?

And then she saw him. He was taller, slimmer, blonder, younger. He was walking about a block ahead of her, moving farther away from her with each step. She saw only his back, but it was enough. The boy was of average height and build, with long, light brown hair. He appeared to be youthful. He was wearing blue jeans and a yellow windbreaker. Gail's breathing came to a virtual stop as a light drizzle began to fall around her.

She had found him. She had found Cindy's killer.

Gail waited for several minutes before following him. The boy abruptly turned and disappeared into the last house on the corner. Gail approached the house with caution, wondering even as she rang the landlord's bell what she was going to say.

"Yeah?" the woman asked, her gray hair in old-fashioned pin curls.

"Do you have any rooms?" Gail asked.

"Sorry, full up." She was about to close the door.

"Wait," Gail began, "I'm looking for someone . . ."

"Who's that?" the woman asked curiously.

"Who is it, Irene?" a man yelled from inside.

"I don't know his name," Gail said quickly, aware the woman was eager to be rid of her. "He's about five feet ten, slim, young. He has longish, light brown hair. Wears a yellow windbreaker . . ."

The landlady shook her head.

"I just saw him come in here."

"Irene, who is it, for God's sake?"

"Oh, shut up. It's just some girl looking for a guy with long brown hair and a yellow windbreaker."

"Tell her to try the yellow pages," the man laughed, obviously proud of his feeble attempt at humor. Gail heard him approaching the door, and for an instant feared he might be the boy she had followed; but when he stepped into the doorway, filling it with his vast bulk, she saw that it was not. He waved her away.

"Wait a minute," the woman said as the door slammed shut, "maybe she means Nick Rogers, up on the third floor."

"Never heard of no Nick Rogers," the man said, and Gail heard a sudden burst of laughter from inside.

She stood outside the closed door and stared up toward the third floor. Nick Rogers, she repeated to herself. Nick Rogers.

"Nick Rogers," she whispered into the phone later that same evening.

"I'm sorry, I couldn't hear you. You'll have to speak up." Lieutenant Cole's voice was pleasant, if tired.

Gail raised the level of her own voice while striving to keep it deep, hoping to disguise its basic timbre. "Nick Rogers," she repeated. "He lives at 44 Amelia Street in Newark. He killed the little Walton girl. Last April."

"Who is this, please?" Lieutenant Cole asked, his interest obviously piqued, trying not to sound too eager.

Gail ignored his question, hearing her voice shake as she continued. "It doesn't matter who I am. Nick Rogers," she said again. "Forty-four Amelia Street. The little Walton girl. Check it out."

She hung up the phone and immediately buried her head in her hands, shaking all over. Had Lieutenant Cole recognized her voice? Had he known it was her? Gail slowly drew her hands away from her face, staring back at the phone.

She had been so surprised when Lieutenant Cole had picked up his extension. She had assumed someone else would take the call. It was after eight o'clock. She had thought he would be long gone. Did the man never go home? She wondered what case he was working on now. How had he reacted to her phone call? Would he dismiss it out of hand because she had refused to divulge her identity? Would he bother to investigate? Had he recognized her voice?

"Something wrong?" Jack asked from the doorway.

Gail visibly jumped.

"Sorry, didn't mean to scare you," he said quickly, coming up behind her and rubbing her back gently. "Are you all right?"

"Fine," Gail replied, her voice still husky.

"You sound like you're getting a cold."

"Don't think so."

"That's good." Jack headed for the refrigerator and pulled out the carton of milk. "Want a glass?" Gail shook her head. "Who were you talking to?"

"What?"

"I thought I heard you on the phone."

"No," Gail lied.

"Talking to yourself again?" Jack asked, trying to joke. Gail said nothing, her thoughts on Lieutenant Cole. Had he recognized her voice? Would he investigate Nick Rogers? "Gail, are you all right?"

"Yes, I'm fine," Gail answered, hoping she had heard his question correctly.

"I was thinking," he began, almost nervously, "that maybe we could get away to Florida for a few weeks . . ."

"Not now," Gail said flatly.

"I didn't mean right this minute," he continued, straining to keep things light. "I thought soon, in the next little while . . ."

"Not now," Gail repeated.

When she looked over in his direction a minute later, he was gone.

Gail waited a day, and when she heard nothing from the police, she called Lieutenant Cole.

"I just wondered if there was anything new." Gail hoped she sounded suitably casual.

"I wish I had something to tell you," he said.

"There's nothing?" Gail tried—and failed—to disguise her amazement. "I was so sure that something would have come up," she began, and then stopped, afraid she might give herself away by saying too much.

"Something will," he assured her.

"When?"

"I can't tell you that."

"What can you tell me?"

"That we haven't given up. That we're still working on it."

"On what? Can you be more specific? Are there any new leads?"

"Nothing substantial."

"What do you mean by 'substantial'? Don't you check out everything? No matter how small? Every phone call, every possible clue, no matter how insignificant it sounds . . . don't you check everything out?"

"Of course we do. Gail, what are you getting at?"

"Nothing," Gail said quickly. "I was just hoping that there would be something."

"There will be. Don't give up."

"I don't intend to," Gail told him before hanging up the receiver.

Chapter 23

Halloween night was cold and windy. A night for witches, Gail thought, looking out her kitchen window. A night for goblins and for freaks.

"I told you about this party a week ago," Jennifer was whining from somewhere behind her.

"I'm sorry, honey, I don't remember." Gail searched the sky for stars. There were none. "I never would have agreed. It's a week night and you know you're not allowed to date during the week."

"I *did* tell you. You just didn't listen. You never listen anymore."

"Yes, I do, Jennifer," Gail said patiently, trying not to sound defensive.

"I told you that Marianne was having a Halloween party and you said that sounded great."

Gail turned to face her daughter. "I'm sorry, sweetie, I really don't remember. I'm sure you never told me that it was during the week."

"It's not my fault that Halloween is on a week night this year!"

"Is there some kind of problem in here?" Jack asked, coming into the room wearing an old fright wig.

Jennifer burst out laughing, temporarily abandoning the argument with her mother. "Where did you get that?"

"I wore it to a costume party a few years back. Remember?" he asked, turning to Gail. "At the Thompsons."

"You're not going to answer the door in that, are you?" Jennifer marveled.

"I thought I might," Jack smiled. "What time's your party?"

"Eight o'clock," Jennifer said slowly. "But Mom says I can't go."

"Why not?"

"Ask *her*."

"Gail?"

"I don't remember Jennifer saying anything about a party during the week."

"Sure she did," Jack said. "Last week at breakfast. Mary somebody-or-other . . ."

"Marianne," Jennifer corrected quickly, sensing victory.

"I just don't think that she should be going out," Gail explained, her voice picking up speed. "Halloween is a time for kooks. There are all sorts of crazies out walking the streets tonight, using Halloween as an excuse for their madness. All you have to do is listen to the radio, the warnings to parents to accompany their children, to check out apples for razor blades, to make sure that all packages of candy haven't been tampered with. They're even advising parents with small children to forget about Halloween this year. It's become too dangerous."

"Mom," Jennifer interrupted. "I'm not going trick-or-treating. I'm going to a party with a bunch of friends."

"You are *not* going!"

"Why not?" Jennifer's eyes traveled from Gail to Jack. "Jack . . ."

"Gail . . . ?" he asked in Jennifer's behalf.

"Stay out of this, Jack," Gail snapped and then instantly regretted it. "Sorry, I didn't mean to . . ."

"No, you're right," he agreed quickly. "This is between you and your mother, Jennifer. I have no right to interfere."

"Why don't you?" Jennifer argued. "She's not being fair. You know she's not."

Jack lifted his hands as if to say What can I do? and left the room.

"Why are you doing this?" Jennifer demanded angrily.

"I'm just trying to protect you."

"You're not protecting me. You're smothering me! I can't breathe around you anymore. You're treating me like a little kid. I'm a big girl, Mom. I'm almost seventeen. I'm a good student. I get good grades. Goddamn it, Mom, I'm a good kid."

"I know you are."

"Then why are you giving me such a hard time? Don't you trust me anymore?"

"I do trust you," Gail whispered. "I just don't want you to get hurt."

"I'm not going to get hurt. I promise."

Mommy, when we die, can we die together? Can we die holding hands? Do you promise?

"Okay," Gail nodded, too tired to continue the argument. "Go to the party. But just this once. No more parties during the week."

Jennifer nodded. "Thanks."

There was a long pause. "Something wrong?" Gail asked, watching as Jennifer's eyes darted nervously around the room.

"Mom," Jennifer started, and then stopped, taking a final swallow before spitting the words out. "Are you having an affair?"

"What?" Gail was genuinely astounded. She burst out laughing. "Where on earth would you get a ridiculous idea like that?"

"Is it ridiculous?" Jennifer started to laugh herself, with relief.

"It's the silliest damn thing I've heard in a long time. What would make you think I was having an affair?"

"I don't know," Jennifer shrugged. "Just that you seem so preoccupied all the time. You're never home during the day. I've come home a few times at lunch and you're never here."

"Why would you come home at lunch?" Jennifer shrugged. "Why didn't you tell me?"

"I was afraid you'd tell me to mind my own business, like you did with Laura. I thought maybe Laura found out about it and that's why you weren't speaking to her anymore."

"Jennifer," Gail said, more calmly than she felt, "I am not having an affair. Believe me, it is the furthest thing from my mind."

"Then where do you go all day?"

"Just out. For walks. For drives. Nowhere special."

Jennifer walked to her mother's side and put her arms around her. Gail was amazed to find them the same height. They grow so fast, she thought.

"I love you," Jennifer told her.

"I love you too."

"They say it's supposed to get easier with time." Jennifer took a deep breath. "They don't know what they're talking about, do they?"

Gail hugged her daughter tightly, and then released her. "If you're going to that party, you better get ready."

"What will you do?"

Gail smiled. "Somebody's got to hand out the poisoned apples," she said.

By ten o'clock, only three children had knocked on the door. The first had been dressed as Wonder Woman, the next two had each come as E.T. Gail had dropped several packages of Reese candies into their bags and smiled with the knowledge that Jennifer had been right when she predicted that the majority of trick-or-treaters would come as the rubbery little creature from outer space as they had for the last several years. The only thing they miscalculated had been the numbers. Jack had bought enough candy for at least fifty callers. There had been fifty callers the previous Halloween, over a hundred the year before that. But each year brought fresh warnings, more reports of children swallowing straight pins hidden in chocolates, of children being rushed to the hospital with severe stomach cramps brought on by cyanide discovered in a friendly neighbor's freshly baked brownies. The radio was advising parents to throw out anything that wasn't store-bought and tightly sealed.

Perhaps that was the reason only three children had come knocking. Was it the same everywhere, Gail wondered, or had her house been singled out? Had parents been deliberately keeping their children away?

The fourth knock on the door came just before ten o'clock, as Gail was about to turn off the lights and go to bed. She was tired. She wanted only to go to sleep as Jack had done an hour before. She had hurt him deeply, she knew, despite the fact that she had apologized again and he had told her there was no need, that he had been wrong to interfere. Still, the fright wig he had proudly resurrected had remained in a shapeless heap on the coffee table, and he had excused himself early to go upstairs.

What was happening to her? she wondered, as she had wondered often lately. She had always gone miles out of her way to avoid confrontations.

The knocking at the front door continued, becoming insistent. Gail edged warily toward the door and opened it. What was the matter with some parents? she thought. Wasn't ten o'clock a little late to be dragging youngsters around?

They weren't youngsters, and there were no parents with them. Instead, when Gail opened her door, she came face to face with one wild-eyed teenage boy and two frizzy-haired females. They looked to be Jennifer's age, but there was something truly terrifying about them, their smiles, the look of madness in their eyes. Gail realized as she stood paralyzed before them that she was frightened. She debated calling for Jack, wondering who it was they were supposed to be.

The boy held out his bag. "Trick or treat," he sneered.

Gail wordlessly stuffed several packets of the candy into each of their bags.

"Is that all?" one of the girls demanded.

Gail piled more candies into their sacks, eventually dumping the remainder of the small packages into their open bags.

"That's better," said the boy. "What's the matter with you? Can't you talk or something?"

Gail found her voice. "Aren't you kids a little old for this sort of thing?"

"You're never too old to have a good time," the boy told her with a leer. "You want me to send my friends away? I could show you a good time too, pretty lady."

"I have leukemia," Gail said with a clear voice, watching with satisfaction as the color drained from the young man's face.

The youth backed off several paces. "Yeah? Well, that's too bad." He signaled to his two companions. "We better move on. Old Charlie's got some more houses to invade."

"Charlie?" Gail asked, a queasy feeling building in her stomach.

"We're the Charles Manson gang," he told her proudly. "Didn't you hear? We got paroled!"

Gail slammed the door on his obscene laugh, standing in the hallway shaking, not moving. She thought of Jennifer at Marianne's party. "I'll be back by midnight," Jennifer had promised. She thought of Jack upstairs asleep. "I don't know what's the matter with me tonight," he had said. "I can't keep my eyes open." Gail suddenly reached into the hall closet and grabbed her shabby old coat and purse, opened the front door and rushed out into the cold night.

There were only a handful of other people walking the streets when Gail looked at her watch and saw that it was almost eleven o'clock. Her shoulder bag slapped against her side and Gail looked at it, studying the glow of the white straw bag against the darkness. Nancy would have a fit if she saw this bag, Gail smiled. A white straw purse at the end of October. None of her friends in the shadier reaches of Newark thought there was anything wrong with a summer purse in late autumn. Of course, it could be that they were too polite to comment. At any rate, she'd do everybody a favor and change it when she got home. She had last year's beaten brown leather one somewhere in her closet. She'd have to get it out. Make Nancy happy. Gail laughed out loud.

She was suddenly at Memorial Park with its now empty swimming pool and deserted, netless tennis courts. She stood for a moment at the entrance, surveying the black panorama of trees and pathways, wondering if she had come here deliberately. The park had developed a reputation of late for attracting derelicts and winos at night. Like any other park in cities everywhere, people were advised not to cut through after dark. Gail put her hands in the pockets of her coat and stepped into the park.

She moved with relative speed until she realized how fast she was traveling and slowed down. There was no need to race. Now that she was here, she might as well make the most of it, look for clues, try to pull some facts from the darkness. The killer was a loner, a frequenter of parks. Perhaps he chose this park in which to sleep. Perhaps all the while she'd been renting rooms in Newark and East Orange, the killer was cozily staked out in her own backyard.

Gail slowed her pace further, reaching the tennis courts without having seen a soul.

She stood in the middle of one of the courts, in the spot where the net would normally be, and watched an invisible ball being hit furiously from side to side. The forces of Good and Evil, she chuckled aloud, watching as Evil rushed the net to deliver the winning overhead smash. Gail turned and walked away from the courts.

She moved to a concentration of trees. There were two benches in front of them, both occupied by sleeping drunks, a cheap bottle of wine opened and empty beside them. Her eyes searched their features for traces of their lives, but she saw only years of self-abuse and neglect, and she turned her head away, wishing to see no more.

She heard a scuffling behind some bushes and turned immediately toward them, but then all was quiet, and, feeling suddenly tired again, and cold from the wind, she decided to return home. She would learn nothing here. She was almost out of the park when something was shoved into her from behind.

She gasped and turned, but her assailant was quick and strong, and he pushed her roughly to the ground, kicking at her ribs and grabbing at her shoulders, flipping her over onto her back. It was only when she was in this position, reeling with the pain of the attack, feeling her ribs aching in her chest, that she realized he was not after her but her purse. She rolled over on top of it, but a second kick to her side sent her sprawling away, retching into the dirt. Her assailant tore the purse from her hand, and when Gail looked up to try to see him—the whole episode had taken place so quickly that she hadn't had the chance to determine anything about her attacker except that he was tall and skinny—his fist came smacking fiercely down against her cheekbone, knocking her flat against the cold ground.

She lay there listening to his footsteps recede into the darkness, amazed by the suddenness of her loss of control. As she closed her eyes, she realized she hadn't seen his face at all.

Jack came to the hospital at just after two in the morning to pick her up and bring her home.

A patrolman had found an empty white straw handbag lying on the road by the entrance to the park and become suspicious. He had gone through the park to see if there was any trouble and had found Gail semiconscious on the ground. He had taken her to the hospital. She had no recollection of the drive over, and it took her a few minutes to realize that what had transpired in the park had not happened only in her imagination. For a terrifying time she had thought she might be waking up in the hospital just after the news of Cindy's death and that everything that had happened in the last six months had been a prolonged nightmare she would only have to live through all over again. But then the shooting pain at the side of her face and under her rib cage assured her that the attack in the park had been very real.

She remembered someone sticking something with a very unpleasant smell in front of her nose, being jolted awake, being ushered from one room to another, being poked and prodded and X-rayed, and later questioned extensively. The truth was that she remembered little of the assault, knew nothing of the man who had attacked her. The police, for their part, seemed more curious about *her* motives for being in the park. Didn't she know it was dangerous to go walking alone in the park at night? Had she gone there to meet someone? Was she soliciting? Who *was* she?

Finally, she had told them her name, and they had left her alone. She closed her eyes.

When she opened them only minutes later, both Jack and Lieutenant Cole were standing by her bed. Again she felt disoriented. Was it now or six months ago? Had she imagined everything? Had she really been attacked or was she still trapped in that last awful afternoon in April?

"Mind telling us what you were doing walking through the park at night?" the lieutenant asked her as Jack rubbed his hand across his eyes. She could see that he had been crying.

"I just went for a walk," she answered, wishing there was something she could say that would comfort him, knowing how her words sounded, even to herself. "I got restless at home. I needed some air."

"So you went walking alone through a park on Halloween at midnight?"

"I know it was a stupid thing to do . . ."

"More than stupid, Gail," Lieutenant Cole told her. "Very dangerous. You're damn lucky that guy didn't kill you, that all you got were a few busted ribs and a black eye."

Was she? Gail wondered. "Why are you here?" she asked Lieutenant Cole, knowing how late it must be.

"One of the officers who questioned you recognized your name and called me at home."

"I'm sorry," Gail said.

"You should be, but not because of me."

"Did Jennifer get home okay?" Gail asked Jack suddenly. He nodded, but said nothing.

"Jack," Lieutenant Cole began gently, "would you mind waiting in the hall for a minute?"

Jack obeyed wordlessly.

"Is he all right?" Gail asked, startled by Jack's zombielike state.

"He's understandably upset. The police woke him up when they phoned. He hadn't realized you'd even left the house. How do you think he feels?" Gail said nothing, trying to imagine. "Gail . . . is there something that you want to tell me?"

"Like what?"

"I don't know. Anything. Maybe the real reason you were in that park tonight."

"You know the reason," she said, trying to find one. "There was no reason." Her eyes challenged the lieutenant's. "Can I go home now?"

His voice was sad. "If that's what you want," he told her.

"It's what I want," she said.

Chapter 24

As soon as she was able, Gail was back on the streets of Newark.

Her room at 26 Barton had been rented to someone else when she had failed to show up the next morning with the required rent money. Gail wasn't surprised; she was relieved. She wondered what, if anything, the man with the dark curly hair had made of her absence.

She walked directly to 44 Amelia. Had the police bothered to investigate her phone call at all?

"Do you have a room?" she asked the landlady whose gray hair was still in pin curls. Did she ever take them out? Gail wondered. The landlady obviously didn't recognize her, and though she took note of Gail's black eye, she said nothing.

"Twelve fifty a night," she answered brusquely. "Payable in advance."

"Yes, I know," Gail told her, fishing in her purse for the correct amount and handing it over. "Does Nick Rogers still live here?" she asked as the landlady led her up the first flight of stairs to her room.

"Never heard of no Nick Rogers," the woman said.

She saw him from a distance of about half a block and was about to turn around or cross the street when she realized he had seen her and was coming quickly toward her. Gail braced herself for a barrage of questions, pulling her shabby cloth coat tightly around her.

("For God's sake, Gail, don't you think it's time you got yourself a new coat?" Jack had asked on their way home from the hospital three nights earlier. It was all he had said.)

"Gail," he said, reaching out and touching her arm. "For God's sake, I thought it was you, but what the hell are you doing in this part of Newark?" He looked her up and down. "Going to a costume party?" he joked, his voice growing quickly serious. "And what, in Heaven's name, happened to your eye?"

"Hello, Mike," Gail said, ignoring his questions. "How's Laura?"

"She's fine," he answered. "She misses you, of course. She's just got too much pride to keep calling. You haven't answered my questions. What happened to your face?"

Gail's hand automatically touched the swollen area under her left eye. "I got mugged. Someone stole my purse."

"My God! Did they catch—?"

"No," Gail said quickly, shaking her head before she remembered it was still painful to do so. "But they have several leads." She wondered if Mike was aware of her underlying sarcasm.

"And what are you doing here?" he asked again.

"I have a few things to take care of," she said vaguely.

"In Newark?"

"Why not in Newark? You're here."

"I'm a criminal attorney, and I'm visiting a client. Look, it's damn cold out here. Why don't we go somewhere for a cup of coffee?"

"Follow me," Gail said, knowing there was no point in protesting. She led him across one street and then another. "Here." She stopped suddenly in front of Harry's, her favorite of the local greasy spoons. "They make a good cup of coffee," she said as they walked inside. Mike looked behind him, as if he were afraid that someone he knew might see him entering such a place, then followed her inside.

"Hi there," Harry called from behind the counter as Gail walked past. Gail smiled in acknowledgment and led Mike to her favorite table near the back.

Harry was immediately beside them, wiping the table clean and putting two glasses of water in front of them. "What's the other guy look like?" he asked, turning Gail's chin around with his free hand. "That's a real beaut," he pronounced. "What'll it be?"

"Just coffee," Gail said.

"The same," Mike agreed.

"I got a fresh batch of those pastries with the cherries that you like," Harry winked conspiratorially.

"Not today," Gail told him.

He nodded and went away. That was one of the things that Gail liked about Harry. He asked but he never pestered. And Harry had been very helpful in his own way, gossiping with her about his regular customers, filling her in on neighborhood habits. She smiled and realized that Mike was staring at her from across the table, his confusion almost tangible.

"You come here often?" he laughed, a serious question disguised as an old joke.

"Sometimes," Gail shrugged.

Mike looked around. The restaurant was small and narrow, with a row of arborite tables running down one side and a traditional counter and metal stools on the other. The colors were nondescript greens and grays; the cutlery was only marginally fancier than plastic. There was a smattering of people in the restaurant, the lunch hour having come and gone. Gail studied Mike's face as he made a concerted effort to look relaxed.

"So," Mike tried again, "aside from the mugging, how have you been?"

"Fine," Gail nodded.

"I understand you and Jack spent a few days in Cape Cod." Gail nodded. "How was it?"

"Cold."

"That's what Laura said you told her." Again Gail simply nodded. "How's Jennifer?"

"Fine."

"Doing okay in school?"

"Yes. Fine."

"Good."

Harry brought over two cups of hot coffee, several small containers of cream resting on Mike's saucer.

"You forgot her cream," Mike told him.

"She doesn't take cream," Harry answered before moving away.

"He seems to know you better than I do," Mike observed, not trying to hide his bewilderment.

"We went to school together," Gail said.

It took Mike Cranston several seconds to realize that Gail was putting him on and when he did, he didn't smile. "Gail, what's going on? What are you doing here?"

"I'm having a cup of coffee with a friend," she said, and the look in her eyes told him she would say no more.

"Okay, have it your way." He took a sip of coffee, burned his tongue and quickly added more cream. "Look," he tried again, "why haven't you returned any of Laura's calls? She's been sick about what happened between the two of you. You know she'd never say anything to deliberately hurt you. She loves you. Can't you call her, tell her it doesn't matter . . ."

"I can't."

"Why not, for God's sake?"

"Because it does matter."

"She was only trying to help," Mike continued, eloquently pleading his wife's case. "Ever since this awful thing happened, that's all she's been trying to do—help you. Make things easier for you. She loved Cindy, Gail. And she loves you. She'd cut off her right arm before

she'd do anything that would intentionally hurt you."
His voice caught in his throat.

"I thought lawyers weren't supposed to get emotional," Gail said, reaching across the table and squeezing his hand.

"I wasn't speaking to you as a lawyer, I was speaking to you as a friend."

"Speak to me as a lawyer for a few minutes," she requested. "I need to know some things."

"Will you think about what I said?"

Gail nodded. "Will you answer my questions?"

"Fire away."

"What exactly happens after they arrest someone for murder?"

"Depends on the someone," was Mike's quick retort.

"Are there different procedures?"

"Well, it depends on a lot of factors. If it's some Mafia big shot, for example, chances are he'll be out on bail in a few hours . . ."

"Even for murder?"

"If the judge sets bail at a million dollars and you've got a million dollars, you're out on bail. Even for murder."

"I thought they didn't set bail for murderers."

"Like I said, it depends. If the governor's wife shoots the paperboy, the chances of her getting bail are going to be a lot greater than if the paperboy shoots the governor's wife. There's also a little thing called extenuating circumstances. It becomes difficult to generalize."

"Okay. What about the ordinary guy, the person without the connections or the money or the extenuating circumstances?"

"They'll put him in jail to await trial. Unless, of course, he's mentally incompetent to stand trial, and then he'd be committed to the state hospital until such time that he is judged competent."

"And if he isn't?"

"He stays there."

"Forever?"

"Possibly. More likely, at some point, unless he's a total basket case, he'll be judged competent enough to stand trial."

Gail leaned back in her chair. "Then what?" she asked.

"Well, he'd have a lawyer by that point, either one of his own choosing or someone the court appoints, and together they'd decide how he's going to plead."

"Guilty or not guilty," Gail stated.

Mike laughed. "Well, it's not quite so easy as that. There's murder in the first degree, murder in the second, voluntary manslaughter, involuntary manslaughter, not guilty by reason of insanity, not guilty by reason of temporary insanity. Then there's self-defense. It goes on and on. The days of a simple guilty or not guilty are long gone."

"All right. So the case goes to trial?"

"Sometimes. More usually, unless your client is out-and-out innocent, you'll want to spare the state and your client the time and expense of a trial, so you plea-bargain."

"Which means . . . ?"

"Something in exchange for something else. A compromise. Something that both sides will agree to. Say, you have a guy who shot his poker buddy after he caught him cheating. They'd both been drinking heavily. Chances are you're going to argue diminished capacity and try to reduce the charge to manslaughter. Well, suppose this guy has some information about some other crime and he's willing to help the police out in exchange for a lesser charge and therefore lesser sentence, so you bargain, and chances are the charge will be further reduced to *involuntary* manslaughter and he'll get off with a few years behind bars. Case never has to go to trial. With good behavior and a bit of luck, the guy'll be out on parole in less than a year."

"That's justice?" Gail scoffed in amazement.

"It's the best we've got."

"Doesn't sound like much."

"Listen, if we took the other route, if the guy goes to trial charged with voluntary manslaughter or second-degree murder, then first you start with a whole lot of costly delays and various motions and postponements, and when the damn thing finally does get to trial, chances are you'll end up with the same verdict anyway. Guy winds up serving the same amount of time."

"And he's out on the streets in less than a year."

"Can't keep people locked up forever."

"What about someone found guilty of first-degree murder?"

"Well, they've reinstituted the death penalty, but we haven't executed a man in this state for a very long time. A more likely sentence is life imprisonment."

"Which means what?"

"Twenty years. Maximum. With parole, probably less than half that."

"And the man who killed my little girl?" Gail asked quietly.

"Well," Mike said gently, "any man who rapes and murders a six-year-old girl is obviously crazy, but insanity is a very tricky line of defense, and the legal definition of what constitutes sanity rests on whether or not the defendant could distinguish between right and wrong at the time of the crime. Very difficult to prove." He shook his head. "My guess is that the police won't make an arrest without either a confession or a solid case of circumstantial evidence. A jury would find him guilty and he'd probably end up in some form of solitary confinement to protect him from the other prisoners."

"Protect him?"

"The man has certain rights under the law." He lowered his head. "Look, I know it sounds like shit, and I guess in many respects, it *is* shit, but you have to remember that these laws went on the books originally to protect innocent people."

"And the guilty?"

Mike shrugged helplessly. "What can I say?" Gail

nodded. "I wish there was something I could do. I'd shoot the guy for you myself if I could."

"We have to find him first," Gail said.

"They will," Mike told her, unconsciously altering the pronoun. He stood up. "I'd better go. My client will be wondering what the hell happened to me." He put a dollar bill on the table under his empty coffee cup. "Is there anything you want me to tell Laura?"

Gail felt the invisible presence of her former friend, the words of an old song from her high school days running through her mind. Tell Laura I love her, the plaintive voice rang out in the recesses of her memory. Tell Laura I miss her.

The words stumbled to her lips. "Tell Laura . . ." she began, one word swallowing the other. She shook her head, then looked back down at her coffee.

Mike waited for her to look up again, and when she didn't, he proceeded with hurried determination out of the small diner. Gail heard the front door open and close but she didn't look up, and she didn't see which direction he took.

After a few minutes she became aware of the uncomfortable sensation that someone was watching her. She raised her eyes from the table.

He was standing at the front counter, and as soon as Gail looked up, he turned away, apparently concentrating on his cup of coffee. Gail recognized him immediately, his casual clothes carelessly arranged over his squat frame, his dark curls falling low over his forehead.

There could no longer be any question—whoever the man was, he was definitely following her. The only question that remained now was why.

Chapter 25

Gail spent her fortieth birthday cleaning every room in the house.

It was Saturday morning and Jack had planned to spend the day with her, but his receptionist had called first thing in the morning with an emergency, and so he had kissed her goodbye while she was still in bed, and gone to work. Gail debated whether to drive into Newark, but the roads were bad with the recent first snowfall of the season, and she wasn't sure how long Jack would be gone, so she decided to stay home.

She showered and dressed and stood for a long time staring past her blue bedroom curtain at the snow which had been falling continuously since the previous afternoon. It had made driving home from the rooming house very difficult. She'd narrowly missed several accidents. People seemed to forget how to drive the minute there was the slightest precipitation. Drive defensively, she'd heard the radio announcer warn. Watch out for the other guy.

Cindy would have loved this snow, Gail thought, pulling away from the pale blue curtain. In seven weeks, as unbelievable as it seemed, it would be Christmas—Gail's first Christmas in over six years without her.

A sudden childhood memory caught her by surprise,

and she found herself smiling at the image of her father, his body clad in striped pajamas, his face pinched tightly with exasperation, trying to force their errant Christmas tree into an upright position. The tree was overladen with ornaments, and the stand her father had purchased earlier was proving inadequate. Try as he might, sing to it as sweetly as he could, swear as loudly as he did, he still couldn't make the stubborn tree stand straight. After almost an hour, her father, his body scratched and sore from the tree's branches, his face bathed in sweat, his bare feet cut by the tiny, bright chips of the many broken bulbs and gaily decorated balls that now lined the floor, had ordered his near hysterical wife to "hold the goddamn tree" while he went to find a hammer and nails, and returned to nail the tree right into the floor! "Let's see if it falls over now," he proclaimed triumphantly as his wife and two daughters looked on in amazement.

How old could she have been then? Ten? Twelve? The memory was still so clear. Now she was forty. Somewhere in between, thirty years had passed.

Somewhere in that time she had grown up and borne two daughters of her own, just like her mother before her.

And then there was one, she thought, a sudden chill shooting through her body, the image of two men before her eyes. One was not very tall, with a headful of black unruly curls; the other had light brown hair and wore a yellow windbraker.

She had not seen the dark-haired man since the afternoon in the restaurant earlier in the week, although several times she had felt his presence. She had not seen Nick Rogers at all.

("Are you sure you don't know a man named Nick Rogers?" she had asked the landlady again, describing him for the wary woman. "On the third floor maybe," she had continued. "That might not be his name." Gail had described him again to no avail. "Who is it, Irene?" the fat man had bellowed from inside their room, and Irene had unceremoniously closed the door in her face.)

The previous afternoon Gail had actually gone up to the third floor and waited on the landing, but no one had gone in or come out of any of the rooms. When she had left the rooming house that afternoon to return to Tarlton Drive, the landlady had been standing at the foot of the stairs regarding her suspiciously.

Gail remained standing very still in the middle of her bedroom for what felt like a long time. The house was quiet; Jennifer was spending the weekend with Mark and Julie, having given Gail her birthday present—a pair of black leather gloves—the night before.

Gail decided that her fortieth birthday was as good a time as any to get her house in order. Jack had been complaining lately that he couldn't find any of his winter clothes. The very least she could do for him would be to reorganize the closets.

She started with her bedroom, removing every article of clothing from each drawer and wiping and scrubbing the wood, before reorganizing and returning each item. She then moved on to the closets, pushing the light cottons to the rear, pulling the more somber winter fabrics to the forefront. Next, she got down on her knees and shuffled through the many shoes that lined the bottom of the closet, exchanging white sandals for black pumps, espadrilles for boots. Suddenly, she saw a bag scrunched into the far corner just beyond the last pair of shoes. She felt her pulse begin to quicken as her hand reached inexorably toward it.

The bag was large, its pattern familiar. Gail hadn't seen it since the afternoon of April 30 when she had turned the corner to find police cars waiting in front of her home. Then she had dropped the bag to the sidewalk, along with several others which she now saw buried behind this one. Her purchases, she remembered, carrying the parcels to the bed and ripping them open, bought while her youngest daughter was being raped and strangled behind a clump of bushes in a friendly neighborhood park.

Someone must have found them and brought them to the house. Her name and address were on the bill. She pulled out each item, one at a time—some shorts and tops for Jennifer, a pretty cotton dress; two wonderful little outfits for Cindy.

And what of her own purchases? What clothes had she needed so badly? What couldn't have waited until another day, a more suitable hour? She pulled out a blue and white cotton print dress. It was summery and bright and it filled her with loathing. She stuffed it back into the torn bag along with the gaily printed purple and white striped bathing suit.

Gail pushed the torn parcels into a large green garbage bag, along with a once favorite blouse she angrily yanked from a hanger.

She attacked Jennifer's room in a similar fashion, freshening and deodorizing, replacing the light cottons of summer and early fall with the heavy wools of winter.

What had her family been wearing these past few months? she wondered, realizing she hadn't noticed.

Gail stopped when she came to Cindy's room.

No one had gone into that room since the previous April. Not even the robbers had dared to step inside. Gail stood outside the closed door, her breath held tightly. Slowly, she reached out and touched the door handle. She held it without moving, swallowing hard, looking to either side to make sure that no one was watching. After a few minutes, her hand seemingly stuck to the door, she twisted the handle, standing back as the door fell open.

For a minute Gail half expected to see Cindy kneeling by her bed, Barbie dolls in hand. But the space in front of the bed where the child used to play was empty, and the bag full of Barbies—at least ten by the last count—that was usually sprawled open, its contents spread across the floor, was neatly put away in its proper box, the lilac carpet on the floor lying smoothed and undisturbed.

Gail dropped the green garbage bags she was holding and walked over to the white canopied bed. Cindy's room had always been done in shades of lilac and white. Originally, the walls had been white with big purple flowers and magic butterflies and birds. It had been replaced only two years ago by a slightly more sophisticated paper of white background with tiny delicate violets that Cindy had chosen herself. The lilac broadloom had remained the same. The white crib had been replaced by the canopied bed for a princess. Except that there was no longer a princess.

Gail stepped inside the room and closed the door.

"Mommy, will you play Barbie with me?"

"Oh, sweetie, not now."

"Please. Just for a few minutes."

"Oh, all right. Just for a few minutes."

"Okay. Sit down."

Gail sat down on the floor beside the bed and ran her hand across the soft carpet. It still felt warm, she thought.

"You can be Western Barbie."

"Who are you going to be?"

"I think I'll be Angel Face Barbie."

Gail pulled the box full of Barbie dolls toward her. Inside the square cardboard box was what they called the Barbie bag. It was where all the Barbies slept when they were not being played with. Gail reached inside the bag and took them out one at a time.

They were all neatly dressed, their hair perfectly groomed. The first one she pulled out was known, appropriately enough, as My First Barbie, so-called because it was supposedly suited for little hands, the easiest of all the Barbies to dress and undress. Sure, Gail thought, fingering the yellow pantsuit, silently calculating the hours she had spent sliding the miniature clothes over and off those well-developed hips. Next she took out one of the two Western Barbies.

(Jack's mother had bought one although she knew Cindy already had one just like it. It was the only one the store had, she had explained, and Gail could always exchange it.) But Cindy had loved the second Western Barbie just as she loved the first and all the others, which Gail now spread across the floor. The second Western Barbie was missing one of her boots, and Gail hunted in the bag until she found it and then thrust the tiny plastic foot inside. She slowly let her eyes travel across the open blue eyes of the dolls, smiling with recognition at the sight of Angel Face Barbie, her perfect cheeks shining red with the makeup that Cindy had applied. Gail couldn't remember the names of the others; Cindy had known them all. To her they were as individual as children to a mother. Even the two Western Barbies were like identical twins, and she could always tell which one was which.

"Come on, play."

"Okay. 'Hi, I'm Western Barbie.' "

"No."

"No?"

"Not that. You're supposed to say, 'I have a prettier dress than you do.' "

"Oh. All right. 'I have a prettier dress than you do.' "

" 'No, yoo-hoo don't.' "

" 'Yes, I do-oo.' "

" 'No, yoo-hoo don't.' "

" 'Yes' . . . Cindy, how long does this go on?"

"Mommy!"

"Oh, all right. 'Yes, I do-oo.' "

" 'You're ugly.' "

" 'That's not a nice thing to say.' "

"Mommy, that's wrong!" Cindy's formidable pout occupied the lower half of her face. "You're supposed to say. '*You're* ugly.' "

"I don't want to say that."

"That's what you're supposed to say."

"Says who?"

"Me."

"Why do I have to say what you want me to say? Why can't I say what I want?"

"Because you can't."

"Cindy, if I'm going to play with these silly Barbies, then at least I get to say what I want to say."

Gail would realize how ridiculous she sounded at the same moment that Cindy's pout would spread up to her eyes, spilling tears down her cheeks.

"They're not silly."

"No, you're right. Of course you're right. They're not silly." Cindy would now be cradled in her mother's lap, Gail's kisses dotting the child's forehead. "I'm the silly one. Come on, let's play." It would require several minutes of coaxing before Cindy was ready to resume her former position. "Now, what is it I'm supposed to say?"

Gail studied the faces of the various dolls as she lifted each one up and returned them to the plastic Bloomingdale's bag. Then she pushed herself off the floor and walked to the closet. Cindy's dresses hung in a neat row. There were some that had to be lengthened, and a few recent purchases that required shortening, others that were, pure and simple, too small. Cindy was growing up so fast. Too fast, Gail had often thought, a recollection that now sent shivers down the length of her spine.

Gail's hand shot through the small dresses, searching for the feel of purple velvet, realizing as she came to the end of the rack that it was not there, that the police were still holding it as evidence. She grabbed the dresses off the rack in one sweeping movement and piled them into one of the large green garbage bags she had dropped by the door. Within minutes she had emptied the closet and all the dresser drawers. She had tossed stuffed animals and other toys on top of clothes, thrown in the various games and puzzles and, ultimately, pushed even the Barbie bag down on top of everything else. Then she had knotted the bags at the top and left them sitting in the middle of the room.

She rushed to her own bedroom, picked up the phone and dialed the Salvation Army. She had several bags of articles, yes, clothing and toys, she stammered, aware suddenly that they were having difficulty understanding her because she was crying and swallowing her words. When could they come and pick them up? No, next week would be too late . . . yes, the day after tomorrow would be fine. No, nothing was wrong. She'd see them in two days.

Gail sat on her bed and shook with grief and rage, her hands trembling. She needed to talk to someone, she realized, feeling the weight of the phone in her hand. She called Jack's office, but his receptionist told her he was still in surgery. Did she want to leave a message? Gail declined, about to return the receiver to its carriage, when without stopping to think about what she was doing, she pushed down on the buttons again, listening to their careless tune and waiting.

"Hello?" came the familiar voice.

"Nancy?" Gail whispered.

"Who is this?"

"It's . . . Gail," Gail said, almost under her breath.

"Who? Sorry, you'll have to speak up."

"It's Gail," she said louder, clearing her throat.

There was a moment's silence. "My God, Gail! I didn't recognize your voice."

"I've been crying," Gail admitted helplessly, feeling Nancy's discomfort through the telephone wires.

"Oh, you poor dear," Nancy said. "I wish I could help you. It's this damn weather. The snow. It's depressing the hell out of everyone. And just think, Sally Field and Tom Selleck are in town shooting a movie, and look at the weather they get. I mean, can you imagine the picture of New Jersey they'll take back with them to California? It gets me so upset whenever we have a visiting celebrity and there's bad weather."

"It's my birthday," Gail broke in. "I'm forty."

"Oh my God, no wonder you're depressed, you poor thing. I remember how depressed I was! I spent the whole day in bed. You know what you should do?" Nancy asked, and Gail realized that there was no way that Nancy would ever let her get to the heart of what was really bothering her. Nancy was shallow and self-centered, but she was not stupid. She had made a conscious decision regarding those things she could deal with and those things she could not. Gail, and the real reasons she was depressed, were among the things she could not. "You should go out and get your hair done. That always picks me up. I found a wonderful new guy at Tyler's. His name's Malcolm. He works miracles. Why don't you give him a call. Tell him it's your birthday. Maybe he'll be able to squeeze you in this afternoon . . ."

"I'm cleaning the house," Gail offered, anxious now to get off the phone.

"Cleaning? Are you serious? Gail, when are you going to get smart and get yourself a cleaning lady, for God's sake? Do you want the name of a good one? One time when Rosalina got sick and I was absolutely desperate, someone gave me the name of a wonderful girl. Wait, here it is. Daphne. I don't know her last name. It doesn't matter anyway. She was wonderful. Here's her number. Have you got a pencil?"

Gail pulled open the drawer of the night table, retrieved a pen and a piece of paper and dutifully wrote the number down as Nancy dictated.

"Now, you call her right away. Do you hear me? You shouldn't be cleaning. Especially on your birthday. Now take my advice. Go out and get your hair done. Last time I saw you, it looked like it could use a good trim. And treat yourself to a massage. You know how relaxing they can be. God, I don't know what kind of state I'd be in without my weekly massage. Especially with the way my back's been bothering me lately. Look, honey, I really have to run now. Is there anything else you need?" she asked timidly.

"No. No, thank you." Gail returned the pen and paper to the drawer and closed it.

The line went dead in her hands.

Gail sat holding the receiver against her chest until it began to make the funny sound indicating it had been held too long off the hook. She jumped up in fright, the phone falling to the floor at her feet. Carefully, she bent over and replaced the receiver. The noise stopped.

She thought of calling Laura but decided against it. Laura would forgive her immediately for the things she had said, apologize profusely for her own mistakes, try to cheer her up, then urge her to get professional help. She didn't want professional help. She didn't want to cheer up.

Gail dragged herself out of her bedroom and down the stairs into the kitchen, and spent the next hour cleaning out the kitchen cupboards.

The dishes that she and Jack had purchased for their wedding still occupied the majority of shelf space. Over the years, they had broken only one plate, and chipped two saucers in the dishwasher. Now she watched as first one large plate fell to the floor and then another, shattering on contact with the hard tile floor. By the time Gail had finished emptying the cupboards and re-filling them, she had lost half the set to the pail under the sink. She wasn't sure whether to laugh or cry. She had always liked those dishes—red and yellow flowers in the middle of white green-rimmed plates—and she'd read that the pattern had since been discontinued. The broken dishes would be hard, if not impossible, to re-place. Cindy had loved these dishes with their happy flowers, as she had called them.

Gail got down on her knees and began picking up the broken bits of china, its flowers uprooted and scattered. She'd have a hell of a time explaining this one, she knew, tossing each piece into the container under the sink. As she leaned over to pick up one almost perfect crescent of china, its yellow flower severed at the stem, her wrist pressed down against another smaller piece. It stuck into her skin, drawing blood, and Gail watched with fascination as the drops of blood continued to fall, like small red tears, to her lap, staining her jeans. But it was a small cut and the bleeding soon stopped.

Gail held up the perfect crescent shape of what was once her dish. She held it to her wrist and mimed a slice across. No, that wouldn't do it, she thought, turning the piece of china in the other direction, drawing it lengthwise down her arm. If you wanted to go to the hospital, you slit across; if you wanted to die, you sliced lengthwise along the vein itself. Then no one could stop the bleeding.

She pressed the edge of the dish against her arm, but discovered it wasn't sharp enough to do serious damage. She'd need a knife. She had several in the top drawer. She stood up and dropped the final pieces of broken china into the garbage container. Then she opened the top drawer.

The knives were laid out side by side. Gail reached for one, letting her fingers clasp its wooden handle. She lifted it out and held the knife against her arm, measuring it against the length of her vein.

It would be over quickly, she calculated. In a matter of minutes, she would be dead on the floor, sprawled in a pool of her own blood. She pressed the knife against her skin.

The phone rang.

It was almost funny, she thought, and she almost laughed.

Gail listened to it ring three or four times before deciding that she had better answer it. If it was Jack and she didn't answer, he might become suspicious and come home quickly, finding her in time to rush her to the hospital. Or maybe it was Lieutenant Cole, calling her with news that they had found the killer. She could not allow her daughter's murderer that final, bitter irony.

"Hello, darling, happy birthday," came her mother's voice when she picked up the receiver.

Gail smiled. Her mother was watching out for her,

protecting her without even being aware that she was doing so, something Gail had been unable to do for her own little girl.

Gail listened while her mother told her that she had her whole life ahead of her, not interrupting to say that the rest of her life would be spent just waiting to die.

After Gail finished speaking to her parents, she put the knife back into the drawer. Now wasn't the time. Not before she had accomplished what she had set out to do, not until Cindy's killer had been brought to justice.

First things first, she decided.

Chapter 26

Gail was sitting on the bed in her room at number 44 Amelia staring at the wall in front of her when someone knocked on the door.

"Who is it?" she asked, startled. She had been living in this room for almost two weeks. It was the first time anyone had knocked on her door. "Who is it?" she repeated when no one answered. Probably the landlady, she thought, trying to remember, as she walked to the door, if she had paid today's rent. Gail pulled the door open slowly.

"I understand you've been looking for me," he said, casually pushing his way into her room and shutting the door behind him.

Gail said nothing, her voice having disappeared at the sight of him.

"Nick Rogers," he told her, enjoying her discomfort. "Just in case the name slipped your mind."

He wore a black T-shirt and the standard regulation pair of blue jeans. His light brown hair had been cut shorter than the last time she had seen him, so that it now fell in uneasy layers above his square chin. Otherwise, he was the same boy she had followed to this house two weeks before and had almost given up hope of seeing again. Now here he was in her room, his eyes openly challenging her, his voice daring her to speak.

Gail studied his smooth, unlined face. He was barely out of his teens, with eyes the clear light blue of a tropical ocean. His nose was narrow and straight, his mouth small and full. In other circumstances, in different surroundings, he would undoubtedly be considered handsome, she thought, surprised by her own objectivity.

Her eyes moved down his body. He was Jack's height, she estimated, perhaps five feet ten inches, about 145 pounds, maybe less. Below the tight, faded jeans she saw the toes of his black leather boots. How was it, she asked herself, that no matter how poor, they all had enough money for leather boots?

"You want to smoke?" he asked, pulling a self-rolled cigarette out of his jacket pocket and lighting it. The heavy, sweet odor of marijuana filled the room. Gail shook her head. "You should," he told her. "Takes your mind off your troubles." He smiled, but the smile was without mirth. "And you got troubles," he added somewhat unnecessarily. He held the cigarette out to her.

Gail cleared her throat, trying to shake her voice loose. "No," she finally managed, though it was barely audible.

So often, she thought, watching as the boy inhaled deeply and held the smoke inside his lungs, she had wished she could be the sort of person who could bury her grief in either alcohol or drugs. But more than one glass of wine at dinner simply made her sleepy and unsteady, and she didn't like the taste of hard liquor enough to get herself good and drunk. More likely, she'd only end up making herself sick. As for dope, she'd never developed the necessary interest, had smoked pot once in college and then once more with Mark before deciding that it was definitely not for her. She liked to be in control. Control, she thought, staring at the boy, that was a laugh.

"What did you want to see me about?" he asked almost pleasantly.

"I . . ." Gail's eyes traveled awkwardly from the

boy to the floor. What was she supposed to say now? she wondered.

"Irene told me you've been asking about me. I've been away for a bit 'cause I ran into some trouble around here. Irene told me there's this broad on the second floor who's been looking for me. Said you asked for me by name."

"I thought you might be someone I know," Gail told him, surprised by the strength of her voice.

"How's that?" he asked, curious. "Mind if I sit down?" He didn't wait for her answer before stretching out across her bed, his back against the wall, feet fully extended, in much the same position Gail had been in before his knock at the door.

"I saw you one afternoon walking down the street. I thought you looked familiar, like someone I knew, a friend's son who disappeared," she continued, her voice losing its sureness with the lie. "I followed you, asked the landlady about you. She said she didn't know you."

"Your friend's son's name is Nick Rogers?" he asked with just the right touch of irony.

"No," Gail said quickly. "Of course not. I overheard Irene call you Nick Rogers. I thought you might have given her a false name."

"And so you moved into the same place as me and hung around waiting for me to show up?" Gail nodded weakly. "Kind of a lot to do for a friend, isn't it?" He leaned forward, pulling his knees up and resting his hands across them. Gail remained silent, knowing that anything she said at this point would sound as false to the boy as it obviously was. "Unless of course you were being paid to stick around."

"Paid?"

"Like a detective or something. Like one of them Charlie's Angels." He paused. "Like a cop or something." He took a final drag on his joint and dropped it to the floor, one of his legs automatically reaching off the bed to stamp out what was left.

"I'm not a detective," Gail said. "Or a cop."

"But you did send the cops after me, didn't you?" he stated rather than asked, catching the look of astonishment that crossed Gail's face. "It *was* you," he marveled, getting up off the bed. "You sent those cops down here." Gail found herself backing up against the door as the boy walked steadily toward her. "Who the hell are you, lady? What do you want from me?"

Gail stared at the boy with wonder. So, the police had followed through on her phone call; they had sent officers to question him. And they had let him go. Why? "I'm her mother," Gail said softly.

"Her mother?" he asked. "Is that supposed to mean something? Whose mother? What are you talking about? And let me tell you, you better start making sense pretty fast."

"Cindy Walton's mother," Gail said slowly. "The little girl you raped and murdered."

Nick Rogers' face broke into a wide, expansive smile. He said nothing for several seconds. "The little girl I raped and murdered," he finally repeated. "You're going to have to be more specific," he continued. "There've been so many."

"Last April," Gail told him calmly. Numbly. "In Livingston. In a small park down from Riker Hill Elementary School. She was six years old. I was her mother."

"This is real interesting," Nick Rogers said, nodding his head. "Now I'm starting to understand what all those questions the police kept asking me were about." He paused. "Tell me more."

"I'm not sure what you want me to say."

"Details. I want details."

"You know the details."

"Refresh my memory."

Gail looked directly into his eyes. "My little girl was walking home alone from school. You were waiting for her behind some bushes in a small park about a block away. You . . ." she stumbled briefly, then regained control. "You pulled her into the bushes and you raped her. Then you killed her." Gail felt the tears traveling down her cheeks.

The boy's grin grew wider. "Not a very nice guy, am I?" he asked.

Gail caught the look of contempt in his eyes, saw those eyes watching her young daughter as the child ambled down the street, observed him crouched behind the bushes, waiting for his chance to attack. Suddenly, Gail lunged at the boy, her nails catching at the skin just beneath those eyes, tearing across his flesh. She watched as the blood ran down his cheeks, mimicking her tears.

"You crazy bitch!" he screamed, knocking her hands away and pinning them behind her back, locking his own arms around her waist as he picked her up and threw her across the bed. He caught hold of her kicking feet with his legs, straitjacketing her hands with his arms.

Gail marveled at his strength. He was not that much bigger than she was, only a few inches taller, perhaps twenty pounds heavier, and yet he could easily overwhelm her, render her helpless. How little effort it must have required with her child.

"What the hell makes you think it was *me*?" he was yelling. "Why would you sic the goddamn cops on *me*? You think I need that kind of hassle? You don't think I got enough trouble? I've *been* in jail, lady. You think I need that kind of shit again?"

"You killed my little girl!"

"I didn't kill anybody! And you can send all the police you can find after me, or follow me until we're both too old to walk anymore, and you are *never* going to pin that rap on me!"

"You said you did it," Gail sobbed. "You said you did it. You admitted it."

"What the hell are you talking about?" He was getting angrier. His hands on her wrists were pressing down harder into the mattress.

"Just now, in this room, you as much as admitted it . . ."

Gail watched his eyes. "I was just being a smart ass," he spat contemptuously. "Trying to put you through it a bit because of what you put me through. I didn't admit anything . . ."

Suddenly he jumped off her and got down on the floor, fumbling wildly under the bed, his hands running along underneath it, tearing at the bed sheets. "You aren't going to pin this crap on me!" He jumped back up on his feet, his hands now racing along the sides of the walls, reaching the end table, knocking it over on its side and feeling underneath it.

"What are you doing?" Gail cried.

He was suddenly more agitated than ever, moving back and forth from one foot to the other, unable to stand still. "For this," he screamed, throwing something that looked like a thimble at her face. It hit the side of her cheek, then bounced to the floor.

"What is it?" Gail felt her own hysteria building.

"Don't give me the Miss Innocent routine, copper! I know a goddamn bug when I see one."

"Bug? What are you talking about?"

"You are not going to pin any goddamn child murder on me, bitch! Do you understand me?"

Gail jumped off the bed and raced toward the door. Instantly, she felt his hands on her shoulders. "No!" she screamed, hoping someone would hear her, frantically feeling for the doorknob and twisting it, pulling it open.

The squat man with the dark, unwashed curls suddenly stood before her, and Gail's first thought when she saw him was that her life was over. She had been right; he had been following her. The two men were somehow connected.

"Police!" she screamed instinctively as the man with the dark curls caught hold of her arm. Nick Rogers pushed both of them roughly against the side of the door and ran from the room. She heard his footsteps as he tumbled down the stairs. The dark-haired man led her back inside. "Police," she whispered, looking up into his eyes as he sat her down on her rumpled bed, and she suddenly knew, even before he spoke the words, that that was precisely who he was.

"How long have you been following me?" she asked Lieutenant Cole less than an hour later. They were both sitting on the bed in her room at 44 Amelia.

"Since you started this business," he told her. "Oh, not right away. It took me a while to twig to what you were doing. I got suspicious when I kept calling your house and you were never there. You were so evasive when I finally spoke to you that I decided to follow you, see where it was that you disappeared to."

"Why didn't you stop me?"

"It's a free country," he said. "I can't stop you from driving into Newark. But I thought that I better keep an eye out for you, so I had Peter following you."

"You put the bug in my room?"

"In all your rooms," he told her.

"What about Nick Rogers?"

"We checked him out right after you phoned."

"You knew it was me?"

"I had a pretty good idea."

"And?"

"He claims he knows nothing about your daughter's death. Says he was in California all last April and May. We haven't been able to verify his story yet, but we have no evidence, no evidence at all, to link him to your daughter's killing. We got a search warrant and searched his room. There was nothing. His boot size is a good size smaller than the footprint impression we took from the mud at the scene."

"But he has a record. He told me he's been in jail."

"For robbing a local grocery store when he was fifteen years old, and it was a reformatory, not a jail. He's one of life's losers, Gail. But I don't think he killed your daughter." Gail's shoulders sagged as Lieutenant Cole's arms reached around her. She buried her face in the side of his jacket, felt the bulk of his gun under his arm. "Go home, Gail. Leave the police work to us. Don't give us any extra."

"Please don't tell Jack," she whispered.

"He already knows." Gail pulled back, her eyes searching the lieutenant's. "I called him as soon as I got word about what was going on here. I felt I had an obligation to tell him. He's waiting for you at home. I'll drive you there now."

"I have my car," Gail said, though her voice felt like it was coming from someone else. It was weak, disembodied.

"Let me have your keys," Lieutenant Cole said. "One of my men will bring your car home."

Gail did as she was told, handing over her car keys, standing when she was directed to do so, following Lieutenant Cole to the door.

She took a final look around the desolate room.

Lieutenant Cole was at her elbow, reading her thoughts. "Say goodbye, Gail," he told her.

Chapter 27

Jack was waiting for her when she stepped inside the front door. He said nothing as Lieutenant Cole's car pulled away from the curb and Gail closed the door behind her. He watched as she walked slowly into the living room, not bothering to remove her coat, and sank down on the sofa, staring blankly ahead of her.

Gail heard Jack follow her into the room, was aware of him standing a few feet from her, knew he was staring down at her, waiting for her to speak, to explain. She owed him that much, she thought, but was unable to find the right words.

It was over, she thought. Her search had ended. She had failed her daughter a second time. She had broken yet another promise.

"Gail . . ." Jack began, his voice breaking.

"A policeman is bringing my car back," she told him lifelessly.

"I don't care about the goddamn car!" he snapped impatiently. "I'm sorry," he said immediately. "I promised myself I wouldn't lose my temper."

"You have every right to lose your temper," she said, relieved to find that there were promises that he was also unable to keep.

"What will getting angry accomplish?" he asked

wearily, lowering himself into the seat beside her. "Are you going to tell me what's been going on?"

"I thought Lieutenant Cole already filled you in on everything."

"He told me that my wife was in a rooming house in Newark, that she had come very close to adding a few more broken ribs to her repertoire, that he was bringing her home and that he thought it would be a good idea if I were there when she arrived."

"Where's Jennifer?" Gail asked suddenly.

"I sent her to Mark and Julie's."

"That's good."

"Tell me what the hell's going on, Gail," Jack pressed.

Gail looked directly at her husband, saw the pain etched deeply into his face and turned away again. "I've wanted to tell you," she began.

"Why haven't you?"

"Because . . . because I was afraid you'd try to stop me."

"Stop you from doing what? Tell me, Gail. I'm trying very hard to understand."

The whole story began spilling from Gail's mouth. She watched as Jack's expression changed from curiosity to alarm to outright horror as she poured detail on top of detail. "I knew I was going to have to do it, Jack," she began. "I knew it right from that first day in the hospital, when they kept asking all those questions about Mark and Eddie. I knew that Mark and Eddie couldn't have killed Cindy, and I knew right then that the police were never going to find Cindy's killer; but I decided that I had to give them a chance, and I did, sixty days, Jack, I gave them sixty days to find her murderer. But of course, they didn't, and then she sort of became old news to them. Not that I blame them. She's just another case to them. She's not their child. And they had so many other murders to solve. Meanwhile, the man who murdered Cindy was getting farther and farther away from them, and somebody had to try to find him. So, I started reading about sex killers and combing the newspapers for details of crimes in the area. I kept track of where most crimes were occurring around Livingston, and then I started to go there. Mostly to East Orange and to Newark. I drove out on the highway after those murders, because the suspect sort of fit the description of the man who killed Cindy. I thought maybe I could flush him out. But the police stopped me, they made me turn back."

Gail ignored the sudden flash of fear in her husband's eyes. She continued, hoping that Jack would not try to interrupt. "After that MacInnes woman was found murdered, I knew I had to start doing more, I had to get right into the thick of things. I started renting rooms, following men who looked suspicious. I found a good suspect right away, a boy with a crew cut and a stack of dirty magazines hidden under his bed." She caught the question in Jack's eyes. "I know about the magazines because I searched his room. I used a credit card to break in. But he must have figured out that somebody had been in his room, because by the time I got back to the rooming house the next day, he was gone. And I never saw him again, so maybe it *was* him. Maybe he was the one . . ." She drifted off.

"Gail . . ."

"Anyway, I kept looking. My car wouldn't start one day," she said, remembering, "and so I hitchhiked. I thought maybe Cindy's killer might be the one to stop and pick me up, but he didn't. Just some kid, a nice kid really who was kind of worried about me, and then this awful man who wanted me to . . . Anyway, nothing happened."

"Gail . . ."

"I went for a walk in the park on Halloween. I thought maybe there was a chance he might be hiding there. Well, you know what happened. Maybe it was him; we'll never know. I never saw his face." She sensed Jack's growing impatience, knew he was about to interrupt her again, and continued, one word tumbling on top of the next. "I kept moving around. I became aware that there was a man following me. I didn't think he was Cindy's killer. He didn't match the description, but then I thought the description could be wrong. I mean, why was he following me? And then I saw him, this boy who fit the description perfectly. He was even wearing a yellow windbreaker. I took out a room in the same house he was living in. I even called the police and reported him, but nothing happened. And then suddenly he was at my door, and I asked him if he had killed Cindy and he said something like he couldn't remember, there'd been so many, and next thing I knew, I jumped at him, and we were fighting, and suddenly, he threw something at me and said it was a bug and that I was from the police and that I wasn't going to pin Cindy's murder on him. I tried to get out, and when I opened the door, there was the man who'd been following me, and he was with the police—they'd been bugging my rooms, listening. They said they didn't think this man was the killer, his shoe size didn't match the impression they took—"

"Gail, stop—"

"We don't know too much about Cindy's killer, but we do know a few things. We know that he's young, that he's got dirty blond hair, that he's slim, of average height, and that he wears a size ten and a half boot—"

"Gail . . . for God's sake," Jack exploded when he could keep silent no longer, "what the hell are you telling me?" He was up and pacing the room.

"That I've been trying to find Cindy's killer!" she exclaimed. Couldn't he see that?

"Gail, listen to me. I want you to see a psychiatrist."

"Why?" Gail scoffed. "Can he tell me who killed Cindy?"

"I'm not *asking* you to see a psychiatrist, Gail, I'm insisting."

"I don't need a psychiatrist. This is exactly why I didn't tell you what I was doing. I don't need a psychiatrist. I am not crazy!"

"You don't think that going for drives at night alone along a highway where there's some lunatic loose, following strange men, breaking into their rooms— what else?—oh yes, hitchhiking, and taking walks in parks after midnight and getting yourself mugged—"

"I didn't plan to get mugged!"

"No, you're right," Jack yelled. "I don't think you planned to get mugged! I think you planned to get killed!"

"What are you talking about?"

"Listen to yourself, Gail. Did you hear the things you just said? What am I *talking* about? I'm talking about a woman who repeatedly puts her life in jeopardy, who moves from one seedy room to another, from one dangerous situation to the next, waiting to be found out, *begging* to be found out. I'm talking about the fact that you are not looking for a killer. Goddamn it, Gail! You're looking to get *yourself* killed!"

Gail sank against the back of the sofa, the wind gone from her sails. There was no point in further discussion. There was nothing else to say.

He was right.

Chapter 28

"How do you feel about being here?"

"How do you think I feel?"

The man behind the wide desk smiled and scribbled something on the notepad in front of him. "You're stealing my technique," he told her and waited for her to smile. Gail stared at him in resolute seriousness.

Dr. Manoff was young. (Everyone was young, Gail decided. Certainly everyone was younger than she was.) He had black hair on either side of his head but he was completely bald in the middle and made no attempt to hide any of his bald spot. Gail liked him for that. She also liked it that he didn't wear a white jacket, or a jacket at all, for that matter. In fact, he was remarkably casual for a doctor. He wore a pink checked shirt with a navy tie, slightly open and loose at the neck. The pink shirt was probably designed to show his lack of concern for his masculine image, his security with his own maleness. She wasn't sure what the navy tie signified, why it wasn't done up properly. Was he trying to tell her that he was just one of the boys? Gail found herself wishing that he had worn the white jacket after all. It would have been less complicated.

"What are you thinking about?" he asked.

"My childhood," she lied.

"Your childhood?" He leaned forward, interested.

"I had a crazy mother."

"Do you want to tell me about her?"

"Not especially."

"How was she crazy?"

Gail shrugged. This was fun. And very easy. No wonder the mentally ill were out wandering the streets long before they were ready.

"Tell me about your mother," Dr. Manoff repeated. "How was she crazy?"

"She liked being a mother."

"That made her crazy?"

"In today's world it made her crazy. She didn't realize that children were supposed to drive her nuts, that she would have been much happier working at a job outside the home, that her children were a nuisance and an outright pain in the neck."

"Didn't most women of your mother's generation stay at home and look after their children?" Gail found herself drawn to his eyes. "Who are we really talking about here, Gail?" Dr. Manoff asked.

So, it wasn't quite that easy, she thought, giving the good doctor some extra points. She would have to be more clever. Gail withdrew her eyes from his and looked into her lap.

"How old are you, Dr. Manoff?" she asked.

"Thirty-five," he told her.

"I'm forty." She paused. Each waited for the other to speak. "You're supposed to say 'Really? You don't look it.'"

"How do you feel about being forty?" he asked instead.

Gail shrugged. "Age never mattered to me."

"You're the one who brought it up."

"It was something to say. I'm supposed to say things, aren't I?"

"If you want."

"I don't want. I don't want to be here at all."

"Why are you?"

"Because Jack insisted."

"You did it for Jack?"

"I didn't feel I had any choice after what happened in Newark. I thought that if I agreed to see you, he might leave me alone for a while."

"You want to be left alone?"

"That's exactly what I want."

There was silence.

"I can't help you if you won't let me," Dr. Manoff said when it became obvious she wasn't about to continue.

"I won't let you," Gail told him.

"Why not?"

"Because I don't want to be helped. I want to die."

She saw the frown that passed over Dr. Manoff's face. "I have two sons," he said softly. "One is five, the other is almost three. I have nightmares sometimes about something happening to one of them. I can't imagine anything worse. I don't imagine there are many parents who can." He swallowed, and Gail sensed genuine emotion lurking behind his words. "We're trained to accept all sorts of losses. Friends go away; parents die; entire nations disappear. But nothing on earth, I'm convinced, can prepare you for the death of a child. And when a child dies the way your daughter did . . . I can't begin to fully comprehend the depth of your sorrow. I won't try to fool you. I can put myself in your shoes, but only to a point. I believe you when you say you want to die. I think I would probably feel the same way."

"Then how do you think you can help me?" Gail asked, thankful for his honesty.

"By listening," he said simply.

Gail searched his eyes with her own. "What am I supposed to say?" she pleaded. "I've gone through all the prescribed stages. I've been angry; I've been disbelieving; I've bargained with God; I've denied any of it happened; goddamn it, I've even accepted it. And I still want to die." She let out a breath that trembled into the space between them. "I appreciate your being here, Dr. Manoff. I am thankful that you are here to listen to people who want to talk. Who need to talk. But I'm not one of those people. I have nothing to say to you." Gail looked around the room, searching for words which would carry her to the exit door. "The only time in the last eight months that I have felt any spark of life in me at all was when I was out trying to get myself killed! And you can sit here and tell me about my husband who loves me and my daughter who needs me, and I'll tell you that I know all that, that I love them too, but it doesn't help me. It doesn't change the way I feel. I used to be a happy person, Dr. Manoff. If you showed me a half-empty glass of water, I'd tell you it was half full. I really used to believe that each day was the first day of the rest of my life."

"I used to have hair," Dr. Manoff said gently, and Gail found herself laughing, then suddenly crying. She wiped quickly at her tears.

"I have a friend," she began again, erasing the final tear from under her eye. "Her husband left her a few years back. He left her for the woman who used to manicure his nails. Anyway, when he left, he told my friend, my ex-friend, well, she was never a friend, really, just someone I used to know. Anyway, when he left, he told her he was leaving because he was tired of all the hassles. He didn't want any more hassles." Gail smiled at Dr. Manoff. "Do you know what my friend, this woman I knew, what she told him?" Dr. Manoff watched her expectantly. "She said, 'You don't want any hassles? Then die.' That's what she said to him. That was probably the most profound thought she ever uttered," Gail said with growing amazement. "I just never realized it until now." She shook her head. "I don't know why I told you that story."

"You don't want any more hassles," he said simply.

Gail brushed an invisible hair away from her forehead. "I guess that's what I'm saying, yes." She let out a deep breath. "I'm tired, Dr. Manoff. And I don't want anything that's going to make me feel better. Life is too many hassles. I want to die."

"Why haven't you?" he asked.

Gail was momentarily stunned by his question. She felt her heart beginning to race. "I don't know," she answered finally. "I guess wishing doesn't always make it so." She shook her head. "No guts, I guess," she said, recalling a similar remark she had made to her mother so many months ago. "No gun," she added softly, remembering what else she had said.

"There are other ways," Dr. Manoff continued, and Gail recognized that, quite the opposite of trying to educate her in alternate methods of suicide, he was trying to force her to admit that despite these alternatives, she had selected life.

"Like I said," Gail repeated, "no guts." She paused. "Besides, Jack has already told you, I was trying to get someone else to do the dirty deed."

"Yet when you were mugged in the park, you fought back; when you were cornered in the rooming house, you screamed for the police."

"I was afraid. I didn't have time to think. I just reacted."

"You instinctively fought back."

"Yes. Instinct, a wonderful thing," she said sarcastically.

"The instinct to survive is strong in all of us."

Gail said nothing.

"I'm just saying—"

"I know what you're saying," Gail cut him off. "You're trying to tell me that there's a small part of me that doesn't really want to die, because if I did, I would have taken a bottle of pills or slashed my wrists or swallowed the Drano, or whatever it is that people who really want to die do. And maybe you're right. I don't know." She looked back down into her lap. "And I really don't care."

She stood up. The interview was over as far as she was concerned.

"And if they catch the man who killed your child?"

"They won't."

"If they do?"

"If they do, they'll slap him on the wrist and ask him not to do it again. Then they'll let him go."

"You have very little faith in our justice system," he noted, not disagreeing with her assessment.

"The man has rights, after all," Gail reminded the doctor.

"And the rest of us? What about our rights?"

"Haven't you heard?" Gail asked. "You don't have any rights until you kill somebody."

After that, there didn't seem to be anything left to say, and Gail left his office in silence.

Chapter 29

Gail hoped that Christmas would pass with a minimum of fanfare—Christmas is for children, she had protested weakly—but Jack insisted that they have a tree and Gail didn't have the heart or the strength to argue.

"Why don't you open this now?" Jack asked, bringing an enormous box into their bedroom where Gail was already in her nightgown, brushing her hair as she sat on the edge of the bed.

"Christmas isn't until tomorrow," she reminded him.

"Lots of families open their presents on Christmas Eve," he told her, putting the box on her lap and waiting.

"Okay," she said, pulling at the bright red ribbon. It came apart easily and seconds later, the box fell open. "Oh, Jack, it's beautiful," Gail said, pulling the luxuriant black mink coat out of its wrapping and holding it up.

"I thought you could use a new coat," he smiled shyly.

"I didn't get you anything like—"

"I didn't expect you to."

"I can't accept this. It's too much. I don't deserve—"

"I love you, Gail," he told her, sitting beside her on the bed. "Try it on."

"Now? I have my nightgown on."

"I've always liked mink and flannel," he laughed, and Gail found herself laughing with him. She jumped up and wrapped the rich, dark fur around her shoulders.

"How does it look?" she asked, twirling around, still laughing.

"Beautiful," Jennifer said from the doorway. "Can I come in, or is this a private party?"

Gail held out her arms for her daughter.

"I have something for you too," Jennifer said, holding out a small, carefully wrapped package.

"You want me to open it now?" Jennifer nodded. "Okay." Gail sat back down on the bed, the black mink coat spilling across the soft white of the bedspread, and tore open the silver paper, gingerly extricating a delicate gold chain, in the center of which sat a single pearl, framed on either side by tiny diamonds. Gail turned to her daughter unable to speak. "I can't take this, Jennifer," she said at last.

"Don't you like it?"

"Like it? How could I not like it? It's beautiful. *You're* beautiful. But I can't let you spend all your money on me. It's much too expensive—"

"It's all right," Jennifer said quickly. "Dad helped me."

"He did?" Gail asked in surprise, remembering that the only time Mark had been generous with gifts was when he was feeling his most guilty. "I wanted you to have something special, and Dad agreed. He thought you should have it." Jennifer looked toward Jack. "Do you like it?"

"I think it's lovely. And I think it'll look even lovelier around your mother's neck. Here, let me help you."

He slipped the necklace around Gail's throat and fastened the clasp.

Gail walked toward her reflection in the mirror and

stared at the woman wearing white flannel, black mink and a jeweled necklace, feeling as unreal as she looked. "All dressed up and no place to go," she smiled as Jack and Jennifer surrounded her with their arms.

"Merry Christmas," someone said.

"Are you guys doing anything for New Year's?" Jennifer asked after a pause, unwittingly breaking the spell.

"I don't think so," Gail answered.

"We're having dinner with Carol in New York," Jack said at the same time.

"We are?"

"I spoke to her yesterday. She has a new fellow she wants us to meet. I thought we'd have dinner with them, then stay overnight at the Plaza."

"What about Jennifer?"

"I'll be all right. Eddie and I are going to a party. And I can sleep at Dad's."

"I don't know," Gail hesitated. "Maybe Mark and Julie have plans of their own. They might be going out of town—"

"They're not," Jennifer said quickly. "Julie hasn't been feeling very well lately."

"She hasn't? Well, if she's sick, then the last thing she'll want is—"

"She's not sick. She's pregnant," Jennifer said.

"She's what?" Gail asked, though she had heard Jennifer the first time.

"Julie's pregnant," Jennifer repeated.

"When?" Gail asked, feeling for the necklace at her throat.

"Not till next August. She just found out."

Gail let the mink coat drop from her shoulders. "I hadn't realized they were planning on children."

"I don't think they were," Jennifer agreed. "At least not until recently."

Gail fumbled with the clasp at the base of her neck. "Well, be sure to give them my congratulations," she said. "And thank your father for me . . . for helping you with the necklace. It was very generous of him."

"He wanted you to have it," Jennifer said, as she had said earlier.

"Merry Christmas," someone said.

"Well, what do you think of him?" Carol asked.

"I think he looks like Dad," Gail told her. They were standing in the kitchen of Carol's tiny apartment, having just completed the main course of the evening meal, waiting for the coffee to perk.

"You're kidding?! Dad?! Are you serious?"

"Don't you think so?"

"I think he looks kind of like Jack Nicholson."

"Jack Nicholson looks kind of like Dad."

"I never noticed."

"There's nothing wrong with Dad," Gail reminded her younger sister, chuckling. She had been giggling most of the night, genuinely enjoying herself, periodically amazed that she had been somehow able to push her unhappy memories aside.

"Except, can't you see?" Carol was asking. "Now the transformation is complete. I've been sounding more like Mom every day. Do you know that I've even started moving the furniture around all the time, you know, like she used to do? And now you tell me that the man I'm involved with looks like our father! It's too much."

"What the hell," Gail joked. "It's only for two years."

There was a moment's silence while the two sisters exchanged warm glances.

"You seem much better," Carol told her.

"Do I?" Gail asked, disconcerted by the thought, not sure why. At midnight they raised their glasses, toasting in the new year. Gail abruptly put down her glass and stood up before Jack had the chance to kiss her.

"What's the matter?" Jack asked.

"I think we should go."

"Go?" Carol exclaimed. "It's early. Are you all right?"

"I want to go," Gail repeated, offering no further explanation.

"She's tired," Jack said for her. "We'll go back to the hotel, get some sleep."

"I don't want to go back to the hotel," Gail said adamantly. "I want to go home. To Livingston."

"Tonight? Gail, we can leave first thing in the morning."

"This *is* first thing in the morning," she reminded him.

"But what happened?" Carol asked, confused. Her new friend, Steve, sat silently on the couch, watching the proceedings with a combination of interest and embarrassment. "A minute ago we were laughing and having a good time."

"That's precisely the point," Gail cried, turning in an anguished circle around the room. "I have no right to enjoy myself, to have a good time. Can't you understand? To forget, to have a good time, to suddenly start enjoying life again, even in a small way, is a betrayal of Cindy! How can I allow myself to find pleasure in anything when my six-year-old daughter has been murdered? How?"

The question hung unanswered and unanswerable in the room as Jack helped Gail on with her new fur coat. It lingered in the air between them on the long, silent ride back home.

Less than an hour later, they pulled into their driveway at 1042 Tarlton Drive.

"Isn't that Eddie's car?" Gail asked, referring to the blue Trans Am that was parked out front.

"Maybe Jennifer had to come back for her things," Jack offered weakly.

"Why is the house so dark?" Gail was becoming increasingly agitated.

"Take it easy, Gail," Jack cautioned. "It might not be Eddie's car."

"It's Eddie's car," Gail said with certainty. "And I want to know what it's doing here."

Gail was out of the car before Jack had a chance to stop her.

"Gail, wait a minute, will you? Don't do anything you'll regret. Stay calm. Jesus, will you wait for me."

But Gail was up the front walk and at the door before Jack had time to get out of the car, and before he could catch up to her, she was already inside.

They were sitting together on the couch, and at first Gail didn't see them. Certainly, they neither saw nor heard her, so wound up were they in each other. Gail walked through the front hallway without bothering to flip on the light or close the door. She headed straight for the living room, aware of the low moans that filtered through the room like Muzak. Then she saw them.

His arms were around her and even in the darkness Gail could see her daughter's white expanse of thigh. Jennifer's arms were wrapped around the boy's neck, their lips crushed against each other, their entire posture a parody of teenage passion.

Gail walked to the corner table and flipped on the light.

Immediately, they pulled apart. Jennifer's hands shot to her skirt, which she quickly pulled down around her knees. Eddie's hands went to his sides. Their faces looked bruised and sore.

"Mom," Jennifer cried, jumping up, smoothing her clothes. "What are you doing home?"

"Funny, I was just about to ask you the same thing." Gail's eyes moved to Eddie, who was trying to hide his erection with his hands. "Happy New Year," she said, her voice ringing with sarcasm.

"Mom, please . . . We weren't doing anything." Jennifer started to cry.

"I saw exactly what you were doing!"

"It was my fault, Mrs. Walton," Eddie offered. "I convinced Jennifer to leave the party early."

"Did you convince her to lie to me?" Gail snapped.

"I didn't lie! We *did* go to a party. I *was* going to sleep at Mark's," Jennifer pleaded.

"After you finished sleeping here, that is."

"Gail, take it easy," Jack warned from the doorway.

"We weren't doing anything!" Jennifer cried, running to her stepfather. "We weren't going to go too far. I swear!"

"I think you better leave, Eddie," Gail told the hapless boy.

"No!" Jennifer protested.

"It's okay," Eddie said. "Your mother's right. I'll speak to you in the morning." He moved toward the hallway.

"I don't think that's a very good idea," Gail said pointedly. "I don't want you speaking to my daughter tomorrow. Or the next day. Or any day, for that matter."

"Gail . . ."

"Mom! What are you doing?"

Gail turned on her daughter with a vehemence that shook the room. "How could you? Have you no memory? Is April too far back for you to remember? Do I have to remind you?"

"Mom, please stop."

"You had a little sister. You remember her?"

"Gail . . . stop!"

"Mrs. Walton," Eddie interrupted, "please don't—"

"You, shut up!" Gail snapped, turning her attention back to her daughter. "Her name was Cindy and she was six years old. She was raped and strangled by some man who put his hands on her the way you let this man put his hands all over you."

"Mrs. Walton . . ."

"Who knows?" Gail continued, recalling that Eddie had never been able to provide the police with an alibi.

"Maybe even the same man." Instantly, she regretted her words. She saw the anguish in Eddie's face, the horror in her daughter's eyes, the defeat in Jack's stance, and knew she had gone too far. What had she done? Of course she knew that Eddie had nothing to do with her daughter's death. She'd known that all along. She let her eyes drop from the boy's ghostly features to his trembling hands.

"Go home, Eddie," she heard Jack say softly. Several seconds later she heard the front door close.

No one else in the room moved, their energy drained. They were like three lifeless statues, Gail thought, lifting her eyes to her daughter.

"You hate me," Gail said, sickened by her outburst.

"No," Jennifer told her. "I could never hate you."

"I didn't mean to say those things. They just came out. Seeing you with Eddie that way . . . I lost control."

"I know, I understand."

Gail searched her daughter's eyes eagerly. "Do you? Do you really?"

Jennifer nodded silently. "I'd like to go to bed now, if that's all right with you."

"Of course."

"I'll call Dad from upstairs and tell him I won't be over."

Gail nodded. "I love you," she whispered, but Jennifer had already left the room.

Chapter 30

Jennifer didn't come downstairs the next morning until almost noon. Gail wasn't surprised; she knew that Jennifer hadn't slept much, if at all. Neither had she or Jack.

Several times during the night, Gail had heard Jennifer going to the bathroom, getting a drink of water, pacing back and forth. Gail had debated going to her to try to explain herself again, but she knew there was no point in that. She had overreacted, to be sure. Some simple teenage groping, she tried to tell herself, repeating the words over and over in her mind until at last, she had drifted off to sleep.

Jack had gotten out of bed early that morning, telling her that he needed to get out into the cold fresh air and clear his head. He had been greatly upset by the scene she had created, although he had said nothing, recognizing, as she did, that everything had already been said. He was still out when Gail had finished her shower and come downstairs.

She had settled herself at the kitchen table with the latest edition of the Sunday *Times* and read a story about a woman put in jail for contempt of court after refusing—because she feared for her life—to testify against the two men accused of raping her. The two men were free. Another story concerned a convicted killer, due for parole after serving seven years of a life sentence, who had had his parole rescinded because of the vehement protest of the outraged citizens of the area. However, the state appeals court had ruled that public outcry was no reason for denying someone parole, and there was still a good chance that the killer might be set free. According to one prison official, this killer of one teenage boy, rapist of three young women, and a person who had committed close to a dozen lesser felonies, had a "less than average" potential for violence.

Gail was still reading the paper when Jennifer came into the kitchen just before noon. She immediately folded up the newspaper and rose to greet her.

"Do you want some breakfast?" she asked, noting that Jennifer had been crying. Her eyes were red and puffy, her face covered with blotches. Jennifer avoided looking directly at her mother, picking at her fingers and scratching at something on the kitchen table. "I'm not hungry," she said.

"Thirsty? Some orange juice?"

Jennifer closed her eyes and looked at the floor. "Okay," she answered at last.

Gail went to the refrigerator and poured her daughter a tall glass of juice. "Did you manage to get any sleep?" Jennifer shook her head, taking the glass from her mother's outstretched hand and lifting it to her lips, though she made no attempt to drink. "I thought maybe you were able to fall asleep this morning," Gail continued, afraid, though she wasn't sure why.

Jennifer shook her head. "I've been on the phone most of the morning."

Gail was clearly surprised. "Oh? I didn't hear you."

"I was talking to Eddie." Jennifer lowered her glass of juice to the table without having taken a sip.

"How is he?" Gail asked, genuinely concerned. "I'll have to call him later and apologize."

"I don't think he'd want you to do that."

"I think I should."

"Please, Mom," Jennifer begged, "don't make things any worse than they are."

"Okay," Gail acquiesced. "I won't call him if you don't want me to. You can tell him for me how sorry I am about the things I said."

Jennifer raised her gaze from the floor to her mother. "I won't be speaking to him," she said slowly, fresh tears springing to her eyes. "He says he doesn't think we should see each other for a while." Her voice was plaintive, disbelieving.

"Oh, sweetie, I'm so sorry—"

"Sorry?! How can you say you're sorry?" Jennifer demanded. "It's what you wanted, isn't it? You wanted us to break up. You've been after me for months. Well, you did it, you finally did it. You got what you wanted, so don't you dare try to tell me that you're sorry. Because you're not. You're glad!"

"No, honey, I'm not. I'm really not. Please let me go over there. I'm sure if I talked to him, explained—"

"No," Jennifer said strongly. "I don't want you to go over there. He said he was up all night with pains in his stomach, and that he talked it over with his parents, and they think it's for the best this way." There was a long pause. "There's something else."

"What's that?" Gail asked.

"I spoke to Dad. Right after I finished talking to Eddie."

"And?" Gail waited for the second shoe to drop.

Jennifer took a long, deep breath, then plunged in. "I want to go and live with them." Gail felt instantly light-headed and grabbed onto the back of the chair in front of her. "They said that if that's what I really wanted, then that was fine with them. They have the room; they said it was okay. Julie could use some help around the house, and I'll be able to help out more when the baby comes."

"What are you talking about?" Gail demanded.

"I'm going to move in with Dad and Julie," Jennifer repeated.

"But why? Just because a boy says he doesn't want to see you anymore . . . ?"

"Not just because of that. Because of a lot of things, not just because of Eddie or even because of what happened last night."

"It won't happen again, honey, I promise."

"Mom, you're not listening to me. It's not just what happened last night. Oh, that's part of it. It's what brought things to a head. But it was bound to happen sooner or later. If not last night then some other time. Mom, I feel like I'm in jail. I can't breathe. I need some room to breathe."

"I'll give you room."

"You can't, Mom. You can't."

Gail sank down into the chair. "When are you planning on leaving?" she asked, hearing her voice break.

"Dad should be here in a few minutes." Gail was stunned by the speed with which everything was happening. "I'm already packed," Jennifer explained.

"You've been very busy," Gail said. "Sorry," she apologized quickly. "I didn't mean to be sarcastic."

"It's okay." Jennifer retrieved her glass of juice from the table and downed its contents in one long gulp.

When Mark came to pick Jennifer up some twenty minutes later, Jack was waiting for him at the front door.

"Hello, Jack," Gail heard Mark say. If he was at all uncomfortable, it didn't register in his voice.

How ironic, Gail thought. Now Mark would be the one to have two children while she had none.

"Jennifer's doing a last-minute check of her things," Jack explained as Gail walked into the room. "I'm not sure I understand what's happening here," he continued. "I just got home ten minutes ago. Gail said Jennifer has decided to live with you and Julie for a while."

"It wasn't my idea," Mark said, more to Gail than to her husband.

"It never is," Gail told him simply.

"I'm sure that after she's had time to cool off, she'll

want to come back," Mark continued, ignoring the inference.

Gail said nothing as Jennifer joined them in the living room.

"All set?" Mark asked, obviously relieved by her presence.

Jennifer nodded. Mark picked up her suitcases and quickly headed for the door.

"You can always change your mind," Gail told her daughter quietly.

"I know."

Gail leaned forward and hugged Jennifer tightly to her chest. "Bye, baby."

"Goodbye, Mom."

Minutes later, Gail and Jack stood alone, facing each other from opposite sides of the room. Jack made no attempt at conversation; he didn't have to. Soon there will be nothing left, his eyes were saying clearly. There has to be some solution.

Chapter 31

His solution was for them to go to Florida.
She heard him on the phone making last-minute arrangements, booking the airline tickets for three days hence. He lined up several other veterinarians who were prepared to take on any sudden emergencies. He called Lieutenant Cole and explained that they'd be away for two weeks, giving him the number at which they could be reached. He phoned Dr. Manoff and arranged an appointment for as soon as Gail returned. He let Gail's parents know the exact time of their arrival. They had been after them recently to come down. They were planning a trip to New York to see Carol and her boyfriend, and they would stay in Florida with Gail and Jack for a few days before heading for New York and leaving them on their own in the condominium. It might be their last chance to see the Eden Rock, Gail's mother had warned her son-in-law. They were thinking of moving to another building just down the beach.

"We land in Miami," he told Gail.

"Miami? How come?"

"Only flight I could get. We'll have to rent a car and drive up to Palm Beach. We did it once before," he reminded her. "It's only about an hour's drive, maybe a little more."

"It's a pleasant drive," Gail agreed.

"You haven't seen your parents in a while," he continued. "It'll be good for you to see them again."

Gail nodded. "And I'm sure you can use a holiday."

"That's certainly true. I think it'll do us both good to get away."

There was a pause that Gail immediately sought to fill, anxious to continue the steady stream of harmless chatter.

"Apparently, they're having a terrific winter in Florida. The papers say it hasn't rained there since November. The natives are complaining like crazy about the crops—you know how they go on about the drought—but the tourists are in seventh heaven."

"Sounds wonderful," Jack said, but his voice carried worry, not wonder.

Gail realized that this would be their first trip to Palm Beach without Cindy. She saw herself walking with the child along the beach, advising her not to step on anything that looked like a blue bubble ("They're called man-of-wars, and they sting," she had cautioned) and to hold on to her hand tightly when they went near the ocean. She thought back to when Cindy was not quite a year old and she had taken her for a walk to find seashells. It had been very windy that morning, and she had picked Cindy up and carried her close against her chest through the difficult sand, her feet sinking repeatedly up to her ankles. Ultimately, the wind and Cindy's weight combined to defeat her. She had turned back, facing directly into the wind, only to find Jack waiting by the dunes with his camera. He had snapped a picture of the two of them, their faces pressed tightly together, their hair blowing around them as if from one head. Gail had thought at the time that it was a waste of good film, but when the picture was developed, it had been so good that they had had it enlarged and framed. It hung on the wall of her mother's living room. It would be there for her to see when they reached the Eden Rock.

"We need some sun," Jack said, and Gail realized he was trying to convince himself as much as her.

Gail looked out their bedroom window at the gray sky. It seemed that no matter how moderate the winter, what ultimately wore people down between November and April was the perpetual cover of gray.

The day before they were scheduled to leave, Jack's new receptionist quit. He had just spent a month training her, breaking her in, when she announced her intention to leave without notice. When he pressed her for a reason, she confessed to a deep fear of snakes. He explained that the ailing boa constrictor which had been brought in that morning was the first snake he'd treated in ten years, that his practice consisted almost entirely of dogs and cats, with the occasional parakeet thrown in to keep him on his toes. She mentioned the possibility of contracting cat scratch fever or psittacosis. She was afraid she might get AIDS, she continued, and Jack had stared at her in helpless fury and said nothing. She wouldn't even agree to remain for the two weeks of Jack's holiday. At literally the last minute, Jack was forced to hire a temporary worker and pay her extra to come in that night to learn the way the office was run so that he would be able to leave the next morning.

"We could cancel the trip," Gail offered when he got home at midnight and started to pack. Their plane was due to leave at 8 A.M.

"We'd never get another flight," he told her. "I checked. Besides, I've just spent the last four hours going over everything with this new girl. I think she'll be all right." He flopped across the bed. "Why do these things always happen when you're trying to get away?"

"I thought AIDS was a homosexual disease," Gail said with genuine curiosity.

"What are you talking about?" Jack asked, sitting up and staring at her as if she had gone completely mad.

"You said that Mandy was leaving because she didn't

want to contract AIDS. I thought AIDS was a homosexual disease."

"Nobody knows exactly what it is. Apparently, it can be passed on through the blood. Like hepatitis. I guess she's afraid that someone who has AIDS and also has a cut finger is going to hand her his sick pet and that his finger is going to come in contact with a cut that she also happens to have on her finger, and that their blood will mix and her entire immune system will break down and she'll die." He smiled at the thought. "I think I have just summed up the essence of my receptionist."

"It sounds like you're well rid of her."

"I would have been better rid of her two weeks from now."

"It would have been Cindy's seventh birthday in two weeks," Gail reminded him. She saw him wince.

"I know."

"She would have been seven," Gail repeated to herself, and sat down at the foot of the bed.

Chapter 32

Jack took the ocean route from Miami up to Palm Beach. It added over half an hour to the drive, but it was lush and scenic, and the sun shone down as promised. The radio blasted out the latest in country and western tunes, a song about illicit love in a dirty old motel followed by something about the evils of liquor. Next came the weather report: there would be nothing but sunshine for the next five days, with a zero percent chance of rain. This was followed by the news of the hour. Trouble in Miami, the voice decreed sadly. A family of four had been found dead in a burning automobile: a man, his wife and their two children, boys aged two and four, were discovered in the wreckage with their hands tied behind their backs. The police were trying to determine whether they had been placed in the burning car dead or alive.

Jack's hand moved to the radio.

"What are you doing?" Gail asked him, her hand blocking his.

"I'll find some music," he said.

"I want to hear this," Gail told him.

"Why, for God's sake? It's so grisly."

"It's important to be aware of these things," Gail said.

"Aware of what? That there are a lot of sick people in

this world? I thought that was one of the things we came down here to forget." He pressed the button and changed the station.

They caught the tail end of a song about unrequited love, and then the news reasserted itself. A family of four, the announcer began, before Jack unceremoniously cut him off with the press of another button.

"It's everywhere," Gail said quietly, closing her eyes to the deep greens of the immaculately kept lawns and neatly trimmed trees, blocking out the sight of the sprawling yellow and pink homes. The storybook world of Palm Beach, she thought, remembering that even fairy tales were full of evil witches and ugly monsters.

"We're here," Jack said as she opened her eyes, looking around in astonishment. "You fell asleep," he told her. She looked out the car window at the six-story white building, palm trees framing and enhancing it. "Welcome to the Eden Rock," he said, and hopped out of the car. "The air smells terrific." He always said that. Every time they came to Florida, every time they arrived at her parents' condominium, every time he first set foot out of the rented car and looked over at the luxury building, he said the same thing: "The air smells terrific." Gail smiled to herself and got out of the car.

The guard greeted them at the door and promptly buzzed up to her parents' apartment, which was on the fourth floor overlooking the ocean. Jack spoke to her father on the intercom while Gail looked around the lobby for any changes. There were none.

That was the nice thing about Florida, Gail decided. It never changed. It was like a soap opera that you could leave for a year, even two, and when you came back, it was as if you had never left.

The floor of the lobby of the Eden Rock was of beige marble tile, covered in part by a beige rug on which sat two streamlined sofas of beige with burgundy highlights. Very tasteful. Nothing to which anyone could possibly object. But as with most of the condominiums in the area, the people who inhabited this building found plenty with which they could, and consistently did, take umbrage.

Children were what they seemed to object to most. Because the majority of the residents were of retirement age and had only themselves to worry about, they tended to become crotchety about small annoyances. They didn't like noise or loud music, which meant they had a particular aversion to teenagers. They didn't like sudden cries, or anything sudden for that matter, and since small children could rarely be relied on to do things in an orderly fashion, children made them nervous. They were terrified that one of them might leave something untoward in the pool, and they were always testing the water for sudden warm spots. Gail had pointed out to some elderly gentlemen that they probably had more to fear from the older bladders than the young ones, a remark that spread through the condominium and caused her mother embarrassment at her next bridge game.

It seemed that every time Gail and her family came down for a visit, there were new rules posted. When Gail's parents had moved into the building, it was brand-new and there were no rules. By the next year there were signs everywhere. No eating or drinking by the pool; no running; no jumping; no toys around the pool; children must be toilet-trained; no inflatable rafts; showers were obligatory before entering the pool; tar had to be removed from feet after a walk on the beach; no reserving of beach chairs around the pool. When Gail finished reading through the growing list she remarked, "Why don't they just put up a sign that says No Fun Around the Pool?" Again this comment spread like wildfire through the condominium.

The year the residents installed an outdoor whirlpool bath, Gail had taken Cindy in with her for a few moments. On their next visit there was a sign by the whirlpool stating that children under the age of thirteen were not allowed to use it.

Gail wondered now what new rules they would encounter, then realized that without her children she probably had nothing to worry about. It wasn't that these people didn't like children—most of them had grandchildren of their own—it was that they preferred them from a distance. They didn't want the inconvenience of children. In that respect, Gail thought, they really weren't that much different from the rest of the world.

Gail's father was suddenly at her side. "Hello, darling," he said warmly and took her in his arms. Gail returned his hug, glad to see him, happier than she had expected to be.

"Come on up," her father said, grabbing one of the suitcases from Jack. "Your mother's waiting for you upstairs. She's fixed up the apartment a bit, changed a few things around. You'll see."

They got inside the elevator and pressed the appropriate button. "What's this?" Gail asked, pointing to a cannister hanging on the wall.

"Oxygen," her father said.

"Oxygen? What for?"

"Well, you know," her father began, "there are a lot of old people in this building, and they get worried that one of them might have a heart attack in the elevator or that they might need oxygen, so they put some in. That's one of the reasons your mother wants to move. She says the place is starting to fill up with old fogies."

The elevator doors opened, and they followed the beige and burgundy squares of the carpet to the apartment at the end of the hall. The door was already open and the inside balcony windows pulled wide apart so that the ocean seemed to spill over into the living room, an effect that was enhanced by the bright blue of the ceramic tile covering the floor.

"Gail," her mother called, coming toward her and stretching out her arms. Gail pressed her mother's body tightly to her own. "Let me look at you," her mother said, pulling back. "Are you all right? You look like you lost more weight."

"I don't think so," Gail answered. "I've been eating. Sometimes it feels like that's all I do."

"Yes?" her mother asked skeptically. "Well, eat some more. I made reservations tonight at Capriccio's."

"Sounds nice," Gail said, hoping she sounded enthusiastic. "What have you done here? You changed everything."

"I just moved the furniture around a bit, put the sofa against the wall, and moved the television into the bedroom."

"Where I hate it," her father interjected. "She did it just to annoy me."

"Don't be silly," her mother said. "I did it because it doesn't look nice to have a television in the living room."

"It looked nice that way for four years."

Her mother dismissed him with an impatient wave of her hand.

"And you had the chairs recovered," Gail noticed.

"Do you like them?"

Before she could answer, Gail's father interrupted. "She had a beautiful swatch, a lovely thing with green and white flowers . . ."

"It didn't go with the tile, and besides I was tired of flowers. I thought the blue and white stripes were more sophisticated."

"Who needs sophisticated?" her father demanded sharply. "I don't need to impress any bridge ladies."

"I wasn't trying to impress the bridge ladies. I thought that it would look nice. What do you think, Gail?"

"I like it," she said honestly.

Her mother turned to Jack for the first time, as if she had just noticed he was there. "Hello, Jack," she said, taking him into her arms.

"Hello, Lila," he said warmly. "I like it too."

"None of you has any taste," Dave grumbled.

"It looks like a beautiful day," Lila enthused, changing the subject.

"Looks like rain," Gail's father replied automatically.

"It hasn't rained in months," Lila told them. "Do you want to see how I changed your room around?" she asked her daughter and son-in-law.

"It's a mess," her father said. "She made a mess."

"Where's the picture?" Gail asked when they were almost out of the living room.

They looked toward the wall for the enlarged photograph of Gail and Cindy being buffeted by the wind. "I took it down," her mother said softly. "It was too painful for me to look at."

"That's when she got the itch back," her father pronounced. "Once she moved that picture, she couldn't stop till she'd moved everything. When she finally finished shuffling the furniture around, she decided it was time to find a new building."

"It's just time for a change," Lila said, leading them into the guest bedroom.

"Time for a change," her father grumbled from behind them. "Time to get your head examined, you mean."

"Oh, be quiet, Dave," Lila exclaimed.

What was the matter with her parents? Gail wondered, pretending to study the furniture in the guest bedroom. They rarely argued; she couldn't even remember her father raising his voice before unless it was in song. Now it seemed all they had to do was look at each other for the bickering to start. Why?

"Is he all right?" Gail asked her mother after her father had left the room.

"He's changed," Lila said, as if she couldn't quite accept the truth of her words.

"In what way?"

Gail's mother shrugged, fighting unsuccessfully to hold back her tears. "He stopped painting. He never sings, not even in the shower. Says there's nothing to sing about. He's angry all the time. I can't say or do anything right. He's just—changed." She looked from Gail to Jack and back to Gail. "So, you unpack and have a rest," her mother directed pleasantly, regaining her composure, "and we can go to the pool if you'd like, or maybe a walk along the beach." She stopped on her way to the door, hesitating. "You're not mad, are you? About the picture?" She looked at the floor. "I just fell apart every time I looked at it."

"It's all right," Gail said, sitting down on the edge of the bed. "I know." Her mother smiled sadly, her lip trembling. The she nodded a few times to herself and left the room.

"The room doesn't look any different to me," Jack said after she had gone.

"The bed was against the other wall before," Gail told him. "And the drapes are new."

"You want to go for a swim?" he asked, not really listening.

Gail shook her head. "No," she said, lying back. "I think I'll try to sleep for a while."

"You're wasting a nice afternoon," he told her.

She heard him opening his suitcase and changing his clothes. When he was finished, she was almost asleep. His voice caught her at the tip of consciousness. "You sure you don't want to join me?"

She fell asleep before he could ask her again.

It took them thirty-five minutes to reach Capriccio's. Not that it was such a long way, but the drivers in Palm Beach seemed uncomfortable at speeds over twenty miles an hour. ("What can you expect?" her sister Carol had once joked. "They're half blind and they can't hear if a horn honks. Besides, they're not in a hurry.")

"How's Carol?" Gail asked, her thoughts on her sister.

"She sounded a little depressed when I spoke to her," her mother answered.

"Why is she depressed?" Gail asked, hoping that nothing had happened between her sister and her new boyfriend.

"She missed out on another part," her mother said, "and I think she's a little nervous about our visit."

"Why would she be nervous about your visit?"

"I don't know. She seems nervous about our meeting this Stephen she's living with. You met him, didn't you, Gail?" Gail said she had. "What's he like?"

"Very nice," Gail told her. "He looks a bit like Jack Nicholson."

"I always thought your father looked a bit like Jack Nicholson," her mother said.

"You're crazy, Lila," Dave Harrington grumbled, and after that nobody said anything until they arrived at the restaurant.

Capriccio's was filled when they arrived, and they had to wait another half hour for their table, despite having made reservations. When they sat down, Gail surreptitiously glanced around the opulent room at the other diners. For the most part, they were extravagantly dressed and coiffed. Gail estimated their median age to be sixty-five.

The service was slow and Gail found herself filling up on wine. When the food arrived, she discovered that she wasn't very hungry anymore, and so ate little but continued drinking a lot. Her mother wondered aloud if she shouldn't go a bit easy. Her father said she was entitled to tie one on occasionally, and refilled her glass. Gail shrugged and drank some more, beginning to feel vaguely dopey and very giddy.

"Slow down," Jack advised quietly.

"Is there anyone in this room under eighty?" Gail chuckled out loud.

"Just the four of us," her father replied every bit as loudly. Gail thought of the oxygen in the elevators of the condominium. "They certainly cling to it," she stated on the way to the car, feeling herself more than slightly off balance.

"Cling to what?" Jack asked, helping her into the back seat.

"Life," she muttered, resting her head against his shoulder.

Before she closed her eyes, she noticed that the car pulling away beside them had an interesting bumper sticker on its rear fender. God, Guns, and Guts, it proclaimed boldly, Made America Great.

Chapter 33

The weather predictions proved accurate. The skies were the blue of travel folders. The temperature rarely dropped below eighty, even at night, and the ocean, while often rough, was inviting and warm. There were surfers everywhere.

Gail lay on her lounge chair by the side of the multi-shaped pool (a square at one end which swerved to the right and opened into a larger rectangle at the other) and watched the other sun worshipers. Her father lay beside her, his eyes closed, his ears plugged by the omnipresent Sony Walkman. He rarely stirred, arranging his body in place at just after eight in the morning and remaining that way until exactly twelve o'clock, when he would suddenly, as if on an automatic timer, sit up and go in for lunch. By one o'clock he was back in poolside position, not stirring until the sun disappeared from his corner, when he would pack up his towel and retreat indoors. He rarely spoke. If he did, it was usually to disagree with something someone had said or to tell someone's grandchild to be quiet. Gail wondered what he did when it rained. Her mother, who rarely came out to the pool (she was afraid of the sun's rays, she explained, in the face of much derision from Gail's father), told Gail that on rainy days Dave Harrington rarely got out of bed at all anymore. They used to take little trips to the shopping malls, go to an early movie, perhaps visit with friends, but they didn't lately, she said without further explanation, and Gail didn't ask for one.

Gail looked toward the pool and watched Jack as he completed the last of the fifty lengths he had taken to swimming every day since they arrrived. He raised his head triumphantly out of the water and shook his hair free, like a dog after a bath. He caught her staring at him and waved. She waved back, watching him climb from the pool and jog over in her direction.

"Tired?" she asked, handing him a towel.

He took it and ran it roughly through his hair. "No," he told her. "It gets easier every day. I may increase it tomorrow. Try for fifty-five lengths."

"Don't strain," Gail cautioned.

"Don't worry," he smiled, obviously pleased that she had. "Feel like a walk on the beach?"

Gail shook her head. "Not now."

He looked disappointed. "Mind if I go?" he asked.

"No. Why should I mind?"

"No reason," he said, dropping the towel to the chair beside her. "I'll be back in about an hour."

"Take your time." Gail watched as he disappeared over the grassy dunes, down the steps to the ocean. She looked back over at her father. His eyes remained closed. His skin was as brown and wrinkled as his swimming trunks. It was almost as if he were daring the sun to harm him. Gail lay back against her own chair and let her eyes drift back to the pool.

She heard voices approaching and turned to see three impossibly slim young men laying their towels across three vacant chairs on the other side of her father. They were effeminate and theatrical, their movements highly exaggerated, as if everything they said was of the utmost importance. They must be the young men she had heard about the other day. They were the scandal of the building, as it turned out, having rented an apartment for the season from old Mrs. Shumacker.

One was rumored to be her nephew, it was reported with raised eyebrows. Poor thing—to have such an obvious stereotype in the family.

Gail stared openly at the three men, who seemed mindful only of each other. They wore the briefest of bikinis, something that would further enrage the residents, no doubt, and they rubbed suntan oil on each other as if it were their mission on earth. Gail wondered if they ever worried about AIDS. She looked away when one of them caught her staring, closed her eyes against the sun and tried to ignore their conversation. But their voices were too deliberate, too studied to be ignored. Gail allowed herself to be drawn into their dialogue, like a university student auditing a class.

"The worst blow," one was saying, "was when they hired that awful woman, Helene Van Elder, to do the sets. Here I've slaved my ass off for two and a half years writing this damn play and she tells me that she wants to do the whole backdrop in silver foil, and I thought, I wish I was dead."

"How was it resolved?" another of the men asked.

"It wasn't. They never did the play. The director had some sort of a nervous breakdown."

"Who was the director?"

"Tony French," came the reply. Gail recognized the name. He was a noted Broadway light. Gail wondered if she would recognize the names of these three men as well. She tried to steal a glance back in their direction, but the sun was now obstinately in her eyes.

"Poor Tony," the highest of the voices proclaimed. "He's just never gotten over Auschwitz."

"Jesus, Ronnie," laughed one of the others, "you've never gotten over high school."

The writer chuckled. "High school was no laughing matter." He paused dramatically. "Anyway, I suppose it was for the best that they killed the play. You'll never guess who they were thinking of for the lead?"

"Who?" the others asked in unison.

"Raquel Welch! Can you imagine? For the part of a

sixty-year-old woman with scars all over her body. They thought she might give it sex appeal. Naturally, I screamed bloody murder. I told them whoever heard of a sexy sixty-year-old woman, and of course, they hit me with Marlene Dietrich and Mae West. I told them that the last I heard, Mae West was dead. They told me I didn't know a tinker's damn about sexy women to begin with. I suggested Monica Campbell."

"Monica Campbell? That dinosaur!"

"She couldn't act her way out of her last face-lift."

"Come on, you guys, be generous."

There was laughter. "None of us, Ronnie," he was told, "is particularly known for his generosity." There was more laughter.

Gail let herself be drawn into another conversation that was taking place on her other side. It was a debate much more common to the area—where to eat dinner. "I don't like Bernard's," a woman was saying to the great protestations of her colleagues. "Oh, I know it's your favorite restaurant, but it's just too rich and too noisy for me. I like somewhere quiet and intimate."

"You like somewhere cheap," she was told.

"Did you see the couple who moved into 502?" another woman interrupted. "I went up in the elevator with them yesterday. He's absolutely gorgeous—looks just like Don Ameche."

"Isn't Don Ameche dead?"

"Is he?"

"I didn't say it was Don Ameche; I just said he looked like Don Ameche. My second husband looked just like Don Ameche," she continued. "Who told you he was dead?"

Gail turned her head back toward the three homosexuals.

"Did you see the movie with that gorgeous Mel Gibson, *The Year of Living Dangerously*, I think it was called," the voice she recognized as Ronnie's was saying. The others muttered something Gail couldn't quite make out. "I thought I'd write a play for that woman who played the man, you know, the dwarf."

"She died," one of the others said.

"She died? My God, when?"

"I think you're wrong. I never read that she died."

"Oh well, there's always that little guy who used to be on 'Fantasy Island.' You could write something for him."

"He died."

"What? What are you talking about? He isn't dead. What did he die of?"

"I don't know." He paused dramatically. "Dwarfs die," he pronounced finally, shrugging his bony shoulders.

Gail got up from her chair and headed for the ocean. It seemed that there were only two things that people talked about anymore—death and food. These were certainly the two preoccupations of life in Palm Beach—who died and where they had eaten dinner the night before.

She climbed the steps to the top of the dune, watching out of the corner of her eye for snakes in the wild grass. She had heard the caretakers talking on her way out to the pool. A family of black snakes was supposedly living out here, well hidden by the strip of dense foliage that the government refused to allow the residents to cut back. Something about the natural protection from the ocean, Jack had tried to explain. Gail cast a wary glance around for the snakes, even though they were said to be harmless. She reached the top of the steps and looked out at the immense expanse of salt water.

As it did every time she climbed these steps, the sight took her breath away. Thousands of miles of rolling ocean suddenly stopped right under her feet. It just stopped, she thought, amazed as always. And yet, there was fear it might one day choose to continue, sweeping away the high-priced residences and elaborate highways. Indeed, it was rumored that the old highway was lying out there somewhere, covered by sand and seaweed. Jack dismissed this as romantic babbling, and Gail had wondered how something that had meant death and destruction could be described as romantic.

She was about to proceed down the steps when she saw the sign. It stood right in the middle of the stairway, and Gail marveled that she had almost missed it. Sharks, the sign proclaimed boldly in black letters, had been spotted migrating south. It was strongly advised that swimmers avoid the ocean and stick to the pool. Gail looked past the sign to the ocean. There were at least half a dozen people cavorting in the high waves despite the dire admonition. Gail studied the white peaks for shark fins but saw none. Overhead, she heard a plane cruising at a low altitude and she looked up, thinking it might be the helicopter shark patrol, but instead she saw a biplane trailing a long advertisement streamer for some product to be used against jock itch. Somehow, it seemed an appropriate enough send-off, and she took the steps down to the ocean two at a time.

If the ocean contained only a handful of people, the beach was unusually crowded. People were everywhere—they lay on towels, on beach chairs and on the sand itself. Children dug great tunnels; adults kept a grudging eye on their whereabouts while trying to maintain maximum exposure to the sun. Gail walked through the maze of bodies, careful not to step on any of the blue man-of-wars that had been swept up on the shore. It had always amused her that the numbers of these hurtful little creatures seemed to increase directly in proportion to the number of tourists. Gail inched her feet carefully between two deceptively pretty blue bubbles and marched purposefully into the ocean.

It was colder than she had anticipated and very dark. The waves overlapped in furious abandon, crashing against her body and knocking her over. Her foot slipped against a rock she hadn't seen, and she felt the strong pull of the undertow, immediately surrendering herself and letting her body be carried away from the shore without a struggle. She suddenly found herself reluctantly on her feet again, only to be knocked forward seconds later by another wave and then sucked back farther still. She peered through wet eyelashes at the horizon, wondering how she would feel if she saw the telltale fin.

She didn't see him until he was almost on top of her.

"What the hell are you doing out here?" Jack was bellowing, his voice incredulous. "Didn't you read the sign?" He pulled her roughly toward the shore.

"There are a lot of people swimming," she argued weakly.

"And a lot more sharks," he answered, dragging her by the elbow out of the water. Gail tripped on the sand and almost fell. "Why would you go for a swim in the ocean today of all days? You haven't been in the ocean since we got here."

"I thought it was time," she told him stubbornly. "I didn't think there was really anything to worry about."

"Gail," he told her patiently, "we've been coming down here for years. Have you ever seen a sign like that before? Doesn't that tell you that there may be something to worry about?" Gail didn't answer. "Do you want to walk with me?" he asked. "I think you better," he said when she didn't answer.

They skirted the water's edge for many minutes without speaking. Periodically, she perused the water for sharks but saw none. There were no surfers either, she noticed, feeling cold from the breeze.

"Is your mother all finished packing?" Jack asked, straining for something to say.

"I think so. My father, of course, is determined to get his last few hours in the sun before they have to leave."

"They stayed with us longer than they originally planned."

"It was nice to see them," Gail said. In truth, she was glad they were leaving. While it had been nice in the beginning, their concern had soon become stifling, their bickering oppressive. She felt reduced to her girl-hood and for the first time understood how Jennifer must have been feeling. She was glad they would be leaving in a few hours.

"Careful," Jack cautioned, as she narrowly missed stepping on a large purple-tinged man-of-war. "Now that one," he said, bending down to examine it more closely, "looks like it could inflict some serious damage."

Gail viewed the large, ripe bubble with its long, stringy tentacles, trying to imagine what it would feel like to be stung, to feel the poison propelling through her veins. Every apartment building kept a bottle of something-or-other down at the pool for just such an emergency. Supposedly, it relieved the sting. But often, those bitten were rushed to the hospital. It depended on the extent of the injury.

Gail turned her head back to the ocean, following the rhythm of the turbulent waves, noticing that Jack was similarly preoccupied. She glanced back at the sand, at the blue monster to the right of her feet. Then she slowly lifted her left foot and brought it squarely down onto the middle of the juicy round ball.

It took Jack a minute to realize what happened. Gail said nothing. She didn't cry out, didn't grab frantically for his arm. Indeed, at first, she did nothing because she felt nothing. For an instant she thought that all the forbidding tales about these creatures were no more valid than the stories about the old highway.

Then she felt it. It started as a small, prickly sensa-tion on the bottom of her foot, but within seconds, it had engulfed her entire leg, then spread to her torso, until the pain seemed to stretch clear into her brain, ripping at her insides, as if she had swallowed a thou-sand tiny pins. She felt sick to her stomach and weak at the knees, which, she realized, were about to buckle out from under her. Jack caught her as she was starting to fall.

"Jesus Christ," he screamed. "What the hell did you do?"

His cries brought forth a few concerned onlookers, and together they sat Gail on the sand and began furiously trying to extricate her leg from the now squashed ball of jelly which clung like a leech to the bottom of her foot.

"Sand," someone yelled. "Get lots of sand on it."

Gail waited until she saw her foot was free of the creature before succumbing to the urge to faint.

"A fine send-off this is," her mother was saying when Gail opened her eyes.

"What time is it?" Gail asked, sitting up in bed. She was in her parents' apartment.

"Almost four o'clock," her mother said.

"Your plane?"

"It leaves at six-thirty," her father said from her other side.

"We don't have to go today," her mother told her. "We can wait a few days."

"No," Gail protested. "I'll be fine." She winced at the thought of what had happened, envisioning the squishy blue mass plastered underneath her toes.

"Are you in pain?" her mother asked quickly. "The doctor said he gave you painkillers."

"I don't feel any pain," Gail told her and realized it was true. "What doctor?"

"We took you to the hospital," Jack said from the doorway. "You were lucky," he continued, his voice a monotone. "The doctor said it could have been a lot worse, but you'll probably have to stay in bed for a few days and you might be pretty uncomfortable."

"You have to be more careful, darling," her mother cautioned sadly.

Gail felt tears running down her cheeks. "I'm sorry," she said. Her mother reached over and grabbed her hand. Her father bent down and patted her shoulder.

Only Jack, standing resolutely still in the doorway, made no move to comfort her. He stared at her from across the room, and she knew he didn't believe her apology.

Chapter 34

During the two days she spent in bed, Jack met another couple at the beach who had recently moved to Florida on a permanent basis. He quickly arranged a host of activities—tennis, jogging, even golf, which he had never played. Gail listened as he rattled on about Sandra and Larry Snider with bemused detachment until she realized that he meant to include her in these activities.

"My foot's still sore," she protested.

"It'll be fine by tomorrow," he told her. "Besides, it's just doubles. You don't have to do a lot of running."

"I'm a rotten tennis player," she reminded him. "They'll never play with us again."

"One game is better than none," he said, considering the matter closed.

"Who are these people anyway?" Gail asked.

"They're originally from Toronto. They got tired of the long winters, and his business wasn't doing too great, so they decided to chuck the whole thing and start over again down here."

"Children?"

"No."

"What do they do?"

"He has some sort of roofing company. She works for him, combination bookkeeper-secretary. Very nice people. They belong to the golf club. I think she comes from a lot of money. At least that's the impression I get."

"Does that account for your sudden interest in golf?" she smiled.

"They've invited us to their club for a game tomorrow afternoon. Then we'll be their guests for dinner."

"Sounds very nice," Gail told him.

"I think it will be," he said. "I think it's a good idea for us to keep busy, get out and do things, get lots of exercise instead of just lying around all day."

"Just like summer camp," Gail said. Tennis in the morning, she thought, golf in the afternoon. Everybody out of the pool!

Sandra and Larry Snider were an attractive couple in their early forties. She had short dark hair and the kind of slim but full figure that Gail had always wished for for herself. Her face was unlined and pleasant, and she was obviously careful not to get too much sun.

"I made a decision when we first moved down here," she told Gail on the way to the tennis courts, "that I was not going to allow myself to look like a shriveled-up old prune after only a few years. So, I only sit out for maybe a half hour a day total, if that. Half the time I don't go out at all."

Gail wondered why, that being the case, they had chosen to move to Florida, but she didn't ask and only smiled in agreement.

Larry Snider was very tall, well over six feet, Gail estimated. He was neither slim nor fat, and he looked distinctly nonathletic, but he moved with surprising grace on the tennis court. He had a friendly voice and an engaging manner, and Gail found herself liking him immediately.

She and Jack were paired against the Sniders and they lost, six games to four. Gail was pleased in spite of herself at their good showing. She was surprised too when she found no small degree of satisfaction in smashing the hapless tennis ball.

They left for the golf club at just after one o'clock, taking South Ocean Boulevard to Southern Boulevard and then to Dixie Highway. Dixie Highway was an unimaginative and flat street, lined on both sides with a series of drab fast-food chains and gas stations, windowless bars and one-story shops and clinics. There was nothing about it to suggest the ocean to its east.

Normally, Gail would have closed her eyes to such a drive, but Larry and Sandra kept them regaled with a continuous series of amusing anecdotes about their respective in-laws—they never asked Gail about her family, and she concluded that Jack had already informed them of their "tragedy"—so Gail kept both her eyes and ears open.

They were stopped for a red light when Gail became aware that the store she was staring at across the intersection, a store without windows whose surface was covered with brightly colored lettering, was a gun store. MOTHER'S, the blood-red letters spelled gaily, and just underneath, in equally large lettering of black and blue, WE SELL, BUY, TRADE. GUNS, GUNS, GUNS. OLD, NEW, USED. THE BIGGEST, BEST SELECTION IN FLORIDA. And still more: GUNS, GUNS, GUNS.

The store sold other items. These too were listed on the outside walls of the squat white building. Camping equipment, fishing gear. Hard-core hardware, Gail thought as the car advanced with the green light. She noticed as they drove past that the front door, hidden in a small alcove, was covered in wire mesh. A fortress, she thought, straining her neck to catch a last look. Mother's, she repeated silently to herself, a name she was unlikely to forget.

"That's quite a store," she said aloud.

"Great store," Larry agreed. "They have everything in there. Every type of gun imaginable."

"Do you have a gun?" Gail asked him, genuinely curious.

"Bought one as soon as I got down here," he answered.

"Why?" Gail sat forward in her seat.

"You've got to have a gun these days. It's common sense. The good guys have got to start fighting back."

Jack chuckled. "Then how will you be able to tell the good guys from the bad?" he asked.

"Whoever's left standing," Larry told him, and Gail found herself smiling at his response.

"The gun regulations down here are such a joke anyway," Sandra said. "It's like going into a supermarket and picking whatever you like off the shelf. You fill out a form that says you've never been convicted of a felony, you hand over your money, and you walk out with a gun."

"There's no waiting period?" Gail asked.

"They keep trying to introduce a law to bring in a three-day waiting period, but it keeps getting defeated," Sandra laughed. "I mean, just think of all the spur-of-the-moment hunting trips you'd have to pass up if you had to wait three days for a gun."

"So anyone can just walk in off the street and buy a weapon," Gail reiterated.

"Anyone can just walk in off the street," came the reply.

The golf club was typical of the genre—rolling green hills, jaunty little golf carts being wheeled around by even jauntier people in bright Lilly Pulitzer prints and Lacoste T-shirts. Gail and Jack were properly outfitted with the correct shoes and bag of clubs from the pro shop, and out they went to the putting green.

Jack, a natural athlete, picked up the rhythm in short order; Gail never did seem to catch hold of it, and after endless delays—there were others lined up to get on the tee—she offered to drive the cart and ferret out the wayward balls. Though this decision was gallantly protested by all, it was quickly accepted, and she became the official driver and ball collector for the balance of the afternoon.

On one of Sandra's subsequent shots, the ball went wide of its mark and splashed into one of the many water traps. Gail ran forward to retrieve it.

"No," Larry called after her. "Just leave it. Never try to get a ball out of the water down here. Believe it or not, there are crocodiles in some of these traps."

Jack laughed, refusing to take him seriously. "Now that's what I call a trap," he joked.

"I'm not kidding," Larry said. "This is swampland out here. You don't know what's in those bushes. And people have seen water moccasins and small crocodiles in some of these water traps. You're advised strenuously not to go after your ball if it goes in the water."

Gail looked down at her feet. She saw nothing crawling. Her eyes traveled to the water's edge, quickly scanning the surface for the potentially deadly water moccasin. She saw nothing disturbing the calm surface of the water, no crocodile heads she might mistake for rocks. When the others were busy with their shots, she inched closer to the edge of the trap until she was right beside it, her eyes darting in every direction.

She could see the golfball clearly. All she had to do was reach out her hand. She knelt down and slowly reached her hand forward until her fingers were directly over the ball. She heard the squish of the mud under her shoes as her weight shifted, and she quickly turned her head to see if she was being observed.

Gail could hear the others laughing and they seemed unaware of her absence. She lowered her hand deliberately into the water and waited. When nothing happened, she lowered it further still until her right arm was submerged to just under her elbow. Then she began to snake it back and forth.

She felt something behind her and turned sharply, quickly drawing her hand up out of the water. Jack stood only a few feet away. He stared at her wordlessly until she pushed herself up to her feet, and then he turned around and walked back to the others.

The next day she declined their invitation of another day on the links, and stayed out by the pool while Jack accompanied Sandra and Larry to the club. She would see them later at the dinner she had volunteered to make.

She sat by the pool in her father's chair and watched Ronnie and his friends go through their morning ritual of applying suntan lotion to their already well-oiled bodies. She wondered how it was possible that some men seemed to be born with no hips at all and if that was one of the prerequisites for becoming homosexual. They were discussing the decline of Tennessee Williams in the years before his death, and dismissing Edward Albee. One man pondered aloud on where the American theater would be without homosexuals, and Gail thought that was potentially a most interesting topic of discussion, but the question was not seriously examined and the talk quickly turned to where they would go for dinner.

Gail felt a tightness in her cheeks and decided she should apply some suntan lotion herself. She reached inside her beach bag and pulled out the sunscreen. Then she stopped and returned the bottle to its place. One day without it couldn't do too much harm. She closed her eyes and fell asleep.

When she woke up two hours later, the tightness in her cheeks had spread to the rest of her body, and when she opened her eyes and looked down at her legs, she could see they were orange and swollen. She closed her sore eyelids again and lay still.

"You're getting awfully red," a voice said.

She covered her eyes with her hand and looked up at the voice. It was one of the three men whose conversations she had been following. "You think so?" she asked, not sure of what else to say.

"Well, of course, I don't know your skin type, but

you look awful sore to me. What kind of cream are you using?"

"I didn't use any," she told him.

"Oh God," he gasped. "You always have to use cream. You could get sunstroke. That's very dangerous. I wouldn't stay out much longer," he said as a parting gesture. She watched as he and his friends gathered up their towels and headed for the ocean.

The clock by the side of the pool said it was almost lunchtime, and she felt suddenly hungry, knowing she had a dinner to prepare. She decided that she would skip lunch, and that four o'clock would be more than enough time to start getting dinner ready. She flipped over onto her stomach.

At four o'clock she tried to stand up. Her front and back hurt in equal measures and her head was spinning. She tried to slip her foot inside her sandal but it wouldn't fit. Now she'd never get to marry the prince, she decided, and scooped up the sandals by their thin straps, pulling her towel free from the chair and heading for the apartment.

When Jack saw her, he called the Sniders and canceled dinner. His wife had fallen asleep in the sun, she heard him explain. She looked like a lobster. Obviously, she was in no condition to eat, and in even less a condition to cook. He was sorry, he told them. He'd speak to them soon.

"I'm sorry," Gail apologized from her bed. "I didn't realize I was getting so much sun."

Jack said nothing. He roughly opened the closet door and pulled out his suitcase.

"What are you doing?" she asked, startled.

"Packing," he said simply.

"I can see that," she said, watching as he emptied the drawers and began piling his belongings inside the worn leather bag. "Why?"

"Because I'm leaving," he told her.

"You're going back to Livingston?" she asked, disbelieving. "Because I let myself get too much sun? Because I couldn't make dinner for the Sniders?"

Jack stopped what he was doing. "I'm leaving," he began, "going back to Livingston, because I can't sit around anymore and watch what you're doing to yourself. I can't watch you step on another man-of-war, or swim out into an ocean full of sharks. I can't watch you stick your hand in a potential nest full of deadly snakes—"

"There weren't any snakes in that water trap," she protested.

"You didn't know that," he said, resuming his packing. "You hoped there were. You were hoping one would bite you, just as you deliberately made yourself sick with the sun. You're trying to destroy yourself, Gail. The same as you were doing back home. I was wrong to think I could do anything to stop you."

"You think I'm crazy?" she asked.

Again he stopped his packing. "No," he said, shaking his head. "I think you know exactly what you're doing. I think you've made a conscious choice to die, and I don't think there's a damn thing that I, or anyone else for that matter, can do to change your mind. I think that *I*, not you, am the crazy one. Or at least that I will be crazy if I stay around any longer to watch it happen. I can't do it. I'd be aiding and abetting a suicide if I did." He finished throwing the balance of his things into the suitcase and zipped it up. "I'll see if there's a plane out of here tonight. If not, I'll sleep at a hotel and leave in the morning."

"What about the Sniders?" she asked.

He stared at her in disbelief. "The Sniders?" he repeated incredulously. "I guess I'll call them from the airport and say goodbye." He stood still, looking at her. "That's all you have to say to me?" he asked.

"Tell Jennifer I love her," Gail whispered and then lay back against her pillow and watched him leave.

Chapter 35

The next day Gail arranged for another rental car and drove to Mother's. She parked the car around the back in the designated parking lot and walked in through the rear entrance.

At first glance, it didn't look any different than some of the larger hardware stores at home. It was just bigger. Everything was on a grander scale. The choices seemed limitless. Gail made her way down through the rows of various types of equipment, past the folding pup tents and flashlights, past the fishing tackles and toolboxes, to the front of the store. Here everything changed. The friendly camping gear gave way to the not so friendly world of the hunter. Rifles and guns of every shape and size lined the walls and the front counters and cabinets. Gail stared wide-eyed at the display.

"Can I help you?" a deep and knowing voice drawled from across the counter. "My God, would you just look at you," the man continued when she lifted her head to meet his eyes. "Somebody got themselves good and charcoal-broiled," he whistled.

"I fell asleep," she told him.

"That does look sore," he said, every word in invisible italics.

"It doesn't feel too bad," Gail lied. She had been up half the night throwing up, and every inch of her skin felt as if it had been stretched between two distant poles and scraped with a cheese grater.

The man, whose tag on his floral print Hawaiian shirt announced his name as Irv, winced at the imagined pain. "What can I do for you?" he asked.

"I want to buy a gun," Gail told him, straining to keep her voice steady.

"Any particular kind?" he asked easily, unaware of her discomfort.

"Well, I don't know anything about guns," Gail began, "but I do know what I read in the papers, and I think I need something for protection. My husband is away a lot and I worry . . ."

"With good reason," he agreed. "There's lots to worry about these days. So you want something for yourself then?"

Gail nodded. "I don't know anything about guns," she repeated, as he reached into the locked cabinet and pulled out a small black weapon that looked like a toy. "It looks like a toy," she said out loud.

"It isn't," he told her. "Here, feel the weight of this one."

He put the gun into her outstretched palm. Gail was startled by its weight. "It's heavy," she announced, looking from the gun in her hand to his eyes.

"It's no toy," he repeated.

"What kind is it?"

"It's an H & R nine-shot .22," he told her. "I think that's the best for someone like yourself, for what you want."

"Will it kill?" Gail asked quietly.

"Oh shit yes," the man said. "Pardon the language. Oh hell yes," he substituted. "This thing'll kill. You aim it at someone's head or heart and you fire, and you got yourself one dead prowler. I got something bigger, if you want. I can give you a .357 magnum that's more powerful and everything, but it's not as easy to handle as this is. Why don't you try this one," he offered.

Gail positioned the gun properly in her hand, still astounded by its weight. Irv came around from his side of the counter.

"That's right," he told her. "You been watching television, I see." He laughed. "The bullets go in here," he indicated, pointing. "Nine of them."

"Nine? I always thought six."

"Depends on the weapon. This is a nine-shot. You get nine chances," he smiled. "Put your finger on the trigger. That's right. You don't have to cock it. You just have to pull it."

Gail tried, but the trigger didn't move. "It won't move," she said, trying again.

"You gotta pull harder than that, honey," Irv instructed. "They're not built to go off with just a slight flick of the finger. You gotta give a good pull."

Gail pulled on the trigger as hard as she could. It clicked. "Oh," she gasped.

"Bull's-eye," Irv said proudly.

"How much?" Gail asked, as he returned to his side of the counter.

"Well, they're usually a hundred and twenty-nine dollars, but they're on sale for the next few weeks for just ninety-nine. The bullets are extra."

"I'll take it," Gail said quickly.

He pushed a yellow piece of paper in her direction. "You gotta fill this out," he told her.

"What is it?" Gail asked, perusing the yellow sheet.

"Firearms Transaction Record," he said, the words sounding strange and formal in his mouth. "You have any children?" he asked, catching Gail by surprise.

"Yes," she answered, "two."

"How old?"

"Seventeen," Gail said, then hesitated. "My little one," she continued softly, "will be seven in three days."

Irv smiled. "Still a little young," he said. "I'd wait another year till he's eight, and then I'd teach him how to use it."

"Teach a child to use a gun?" Gail asked, astonished.

"This is a great gun for kids," the man said earnestly. "Sure, listen, you don't know what's liable to happen. Someone could break in when you're out and the baby-sitter won't know what to do, and if your kid knows how to operate this thing properly, it just might prevent a tragedy."

"It could also create one," Gail argued, though her heart wasn't in it.

"Not if you've taught the little bugger well. But seven's still too young. They're not strong enough yet. Give him another year."

"It's a her," Gail said, and immediately wondered why.

"Give her another year," Irv said without missing a beat. "In the meantime, you get a piece of string and secure the trigger like this." He demonstrated. "That way there won't be any accidents."

Gail fished in her purse for a pen but couldn't find one. Irv pushed one in her direction and began wrapping up the gun. Gail read through the yellow piece of paper. "Firearms Transaction Record," it said at the top, and just underneath, "Part 1—Intra-State Over-the-Counter." She was asked for her name and address. Gail Walton, she filled in, and gave her parents' address. They wanted to know her height, her weight, her race, and date and place of birth. She obliged them with the details. The rest of the questions, to which she was to respond with a simple yes or no, were much more interesting: Was she under indictment for an imprisonable offense? Had she ever been convicted of a crime punishable by a prison term of more than one year? Was she a fugitive from justice? Was she an unlawful user of drugs or a drug addict? Had she ever been judged mentally defective or spent time in a mental institution? Had she ever been discharged from the Armed Forces under dishonorable conditions? Was she an illegal alien? Was she a U.S. citizen who had renounced that citizenship?

She was warned in print that an untruthful answer

might subject her to criminal prosecution. Gail felt
duly chastised and wrote no beside all the questions.
Did anyone, she wondered with some amusement, ever
write yes? All that was required of her now was her sig-
nature and the date. The rest of the form was to be
filled out by the seller. Gail pushed the paper back in
Irv's direction. She was about to put the pen in her
purse, when she realized that it wasn't hers, and guiltily rolled it over to his waiting fingers.

He read through her list of answers. "You're forty?"
he asked taking a longer look at her. Gail nodded.
"Never would have guessed," he said. "Of course, it's
kind of hard to tell with that bright orange skin." He
glanced back at the piece of paper. "I'll need your driver's license," he said.

Gail fished in her purse for her wallet, retrieved it
and pulled out her license.

"What's this?" he asked after she'd handed it over.

"My license," Gail said, confused.

"This is from New Jersey," he told her, as if she
might not have known.

"That's right," Gail agreed. "I'm from New Jersey.
We just moved down a few months ago."

"You need a Florida license."

Gail was silent. She didn't know what to say. He
sensed her confusion.

"Nothin' to get yourself upset about," he said gently,
looking at his watch. "It's kind of late now. I don't
think you'd have time to get there before the office
closes, it being a Friday and all, but, look, there's no
problem. I'll just put the gun away for you, and I'll
keep this here sheet until Monday, and first thing on
Monday morning, you go on over to the city hall in
Lake Worth," he continued, rechecking the information on her sheet. "That's the closest one to where you
live, and you take your little driving test and you get
your Florida license."

"I have to take a test?"

"It's just a formality. We already know you can

drive. All you gotta do is take a written test, and ten minutes later you'll have your license. You bring it on down here and you'll have your gun."

"I have to wait till Monday," she repeated.

"Husband gone for the weekend?" he asked. Gail nodded. "Wish I could help you," he said sincerely. He raised his hands in a gesture that asked, What can I do?

Gail folded her license back into her wallet. "I'll be back on Monday," she told him, realizing as she spoke that Monday was Cindy's birthday. Somehow, it seemed appropriate.

She spent the weekend in the apartment. Her mother called. New York was glorious, if cold. Carol looked wonderful. Stephen was an absolute dream. They had gotten them tickets to two Broadway shows, and each one had been exhilarating. They had eaten dinner at the Four Seasons, where the menus didn't have prices, and where they spotted David Susskind with a pretty blonde. The bill for the four of them—Steve had insisted on picking up the tab—was over three hundred dollars. Lila asked how Jack was doing, what the weather was like, and if she was having a good time. Gail answered that Jack was fine, the weather was great, and that she couldn't be enjoying herself more.

Gail's father came on the line to repeat the same information from a different perspective. The weather in New York was miserable; Carol looked tired; Stephen was a pompous bore; the plays they had been subjected to were tuneless and drab—he had barely managed to stay awake. Dinner, he concluded, had been overpriced.

The last speaker was Carol. Their parents, she confided, were driving her crazy and she didn't know how much more of them she'd be able to take. What was the matter with them? Steve didn't know what to make of their behavior. They'd tried to make their visit pleasant, she admitted in defeat at the end of the conversation, but nothing seemed to make them happy. Regrettably, she would be glad to see them leave.

The only other people who called were the Sniders. Jack had phoned them from the airport to explain that an emergency had come up at the office with which his temporary girl was not equipped to deal, and he had to return that night. Gail, he had explained, was staying on for a few more days. How was she feeling? they inquired. Did she want to go out for dinner one night before she left? She declined with thanks and told them she would be leaving Monday. Wasn't it a shame how you couldn't depend on anybody these days? Sandra asked, and Gail agreed, forgetting to say goodbye before she hung up the phone. She spent the rest of the weekend in bed.

Irv was right—it was a joke.

Gail stared down at the list of questions on the test in front of her. She had as long as necessary to answer twenty elementary questions on driving. What's more, the questions were multiple choice, and she had been allowed to bring the information booklet in with her. If she didn't know an answer, all she had to do was look it up. Furthermore, she had been informed when she arrived to take the driving test, she was free to bring someone in with her who could assist her. Gail looked around the room. There were half a dozen other people taking the test, leaning forward in the old wooden chairs, giving all their attention to the project at hand. One young Cuban was having noticeable problems, probably with the language, Gail thought, looking past him to a teenage girl who had brought her father along as adviser.

Gail picked up the pen beside her and quickly ticked off the correct answers to the questions: An octagonal-shaped red sign meant (a) yield, (b) stop, (c) danger, (d) curves ahead. An arrow which pointed right indicated (a) the road continued straight ahead, (b) the road turned to the left, (c) the road turned to the right,

(d) a dead end. Eighteen more of the same. Gail finished and handed her test paper to the woman in charge, who took more time to mark it than Gail had needed to complete it. They must take lessons in slowness, Gail thought, waiting for the woman to finish marking. "You got them all right," she smiled. "Take this to Mrs. Hartly in the other room. She'll give you your license."

Gail thanked her, took her results firmly in her hand and left the room. Just as Irv had predicted, ten minutes later she had her license.

"Here it is, brand spanking new," Gail said, producing her newly acquired driver's license and handing it across the counter to Irv. He was wearing another one of those bright Hawaiian numbers, this one filled with pictures of women in grass skirts and bikinis. "I got perfect marks," she said with some pride, and laughed.

"Good for you," he said, retrieving her yellow form from the drawer where he had placed it and copying her license number into the appropriate box. "You're looking better too. Not so sore."

"I'm peeling like crazy," Gail informed him. "My legs look like snake scales."

"Always liked snakes," the man confided, with a wink at her legs. She was wearing slacks to hide them.

"I've never liked them," Gail shuddered. "I'm afraid of them. I always have been."

"It's my experience," Irv said, "that the only snakes you have to be afraid of are the ones that walk on two legs." He pulled the H & R nine-shot .22 out of its box and marked down its serial number and the other required information in the appropriate squares. Then he signed and dated the form.

"You survived the weekend, I see," he said, returning the gun to its box.

"Barely," Gail told him. "I was kind of nervous about that stupid test." It was true. She had always gotten very nervous over tests. In her several years a college, she had often lost as much as eight pounds over a set of exams, and even term tests in high school had thrown her into a panic. She was always prepared, and she always did well, but every year her anxiety increased. Leaving school to marry Mark had been something of a relief.

"Better not forget the bullets," Gail reminded him.

Irv secured the box, located the proper bullets, and put the whole package in a plastic bag before handing it over. "Don't shoot till you see the whites of their eyes," he smiled.

Chapter 36

On impulse, Gail stopped at a bakery on the way home and purchased a small birthday cake. " 'Happy Birthday' will be fine," Gail told the saleslady when she asked if there was a name Gail wanted added. The cake was round and covered with white icing and pink flowers. Gail also bought a small box of birthday candles. She drove back to her parents' condominium with the cake and the gun sitting in the seat beside her.

When she got inside the apartment, she set the cake on the kitchen table and unwrapped the box containing the gun. She laid it on the table beside the cake and then changed into her bathing suit and went for a walk on the beach.

It seemed there were fewer people out today, although the sky was as relentlessly blue as ever. There was only a handful of people by the pool. The three homosexuals had departed over the weekend. The season had another month or so to run, then most of the tourists would disappear, leaving behind the locals. Half the stores and a good number of the restaurants would close their doors until next October. The houses would be boarded up. Hurricane shutters would be firmly in place. Like a cottage closed for the winter, Palm Beach would effectively shut itself up for the summer.

Gail walked along the wide expanse of beach. The sand was hard and good for walking. She had always loved this stretch of beach. Even at its most crowded, its numbers never approximated the hordes of people who flocked to Fort Lauderdale or Miami. Gail moved her eyes from the ocean to the line of low white buildings. The newer condominiums displayed interesting curves and angles, with a maximum exposure to the ocean view, and as much window frontage as the rules allowed. Balcony railings curved around corners; people sat sunning themselves on their private deck chairs, a bottle of expensive wine at their feet. Could life be more perfect than this? they seemed to ask.

Gail continued walking until she reached the bridge at Boynton Beach, marching past the men fishing off its sides, to its tip. The ocean was calm, its waves scarcely more than ripples. Gail watched it, thinking of how calm it had always made her feel, and realized that even now, it was having that effect. Nothing was that important, it said to her. Life was never meant to be taken this seriously.

Gail turned around abruptly and headed back for the apartment. When she reached the pool, she glanced up at the clock and calculated she had been gone over two hours. Her legs were sore and she'd gotten more sun. Oh well, she thought, jumping into the pool to cool off, she would look glorious in death. She looked so well, she could hear them mutter as they filed past her open coffin. No, she thought, coming up for air, her coffin would undoubtedly be closed. Most people would not like to witness a head half blown away by a bullet, no matter how deep the tan on the remaining flesh.

She laughed out loud, feeling silly. A woman, she noticed, was making motions at her from the side of the pool. Gail swam toward her. "Yes?" she asked, shaking her head to get the water out of her ears.

"I said you're supposed to take a shower before entering the pool," the woman repeated testily, pointing at the nearby sign. "It says so right in the rules."

Gail made herself a nice salad for dinner. There were some shrimps that Jack had bought before he left, and Gail wondered if they were still good. She smelled them, couldn't be sure, and added them to the salad. Then she removed a bottle of her favorite white wine, Verdicchio, from the fridge. She uncorked it and poured herself a tall glass. Then she sat down with the salad, the wine, the birthday cake and the gun in front of her.

"Cheers," she said.

She ate her salad. When she was finished, she took the plate to the sink and washed it. She didn't want to leave any dirty dishes. The apartment would be spotless for whoever found her. Who would find her? she wondered, finishing off her glass of wine and pouring herself another. Most likely the superintendent. Someone would report they hadn't seen her. Perhaps someone would phone and become concerned when no one answered. She hoped it wouldn't be her parents. No, that was unlikely. Someone would find her before her parents were scheduled to return. They would search through the rooms and ultimately find her in the bathroom, in the shower. That way there would be the least amount of mess. She didn't want to leave a mess. Her suicide was probably against the rules as it was.

She sat down with her second glass of wine and contemplated leaving a note. What would she say? Goodbye, cruel world? I took you too seriously. I leave you to your monsters. I don't want to live in a world where children die before their seventh birthday. She looked toward the cake.

There was no need for a note. Everyone would know her reasons. They would remark, correctly, that she just hadn't been the same since Cindy's death. Laura would blame herself for her ill-conceived remarks; Nancy would say that she had tried to make herself available, but that Gail never phoned. She would not attend the funeral, although she would doubtless send a huge arrangement of flowers. Laura would send food. Her parents would be numbed, but perhaps her death would propel them back toward each other.

And what of Jennifer? She would be devastated by her mother's suicide, would bear the scars of it all her life. She would blame herself, just as Gail had blamed herself after Cindy's death. If only she *hadn't* done this, if only she *had* done that. Guilt—the most useless of all human emotions, and the most pervasive. Gail prayed that Mark and Julie would be able to help Jennifer, convince her that what her mother had done was beyond anyone's control. They had all tried so hard to help her.

And Jack. How would he feel? What would this do to him? Like Jennifer, he would blame himself. If he hadn't left her, this never would have happened. If he'd stayed and been the friend he always claimed to be.

It wasn't true, and Gail hoped he would recognize that fact in time. He'd never meant to leave her, she knew that. He hoped only that this last desperate measure would pull her to her senses, force her to confront what she was doing to everyone, but mostly to herself.

She pictured Jack sitting on their bed in Mrs. Mayhew's house in Cape Cod. What had he said? Something about Cindy's killer. Don't let him take everything. Words to that effect.

She was going around in circles, she thought, rubbing her forehead and pouring herself another drink. She was also getting drunk, she realized, admonishing herself to be careful. When she fired the damn gun into her brain, she didn't want to miss and shoot the shower curtain instead.

Gail stumbled to the counter and located the small box of birthday candles. She pulled out eight—one for each year and one for good luck. She arranged them around the circumference of the cake, placing the one for good luck right in the center, and then rummaged through the drawers looking for a match. She found a matchbox from a place called the Banana Boat and managed to light one of the candles before the match burned down to her fingers. It took one match per candle to finally get them all lit. "Make a wish," she said to herself and then complied. "I wish I was dead," she said.

Mommy, when we die, can we die together? Can we die holding hands? Do you promise?

She blew out all the candles, struggling with the one for good luck.

She cut herself a small piece of cake, ate it quickly and washed it down with the last of the wine. Then she sat staring at the small black gun, so much heavier than it looked, so much deadlier than it seemed.

She pulled it toward her and lifted it to her head. Through the temple or through the mouth? It was a tricky question and an important one. If she put the gun in her mouth, there was the chance that the bullet would be misdirected and would lodge somewhere inside her skull, causing blindness but not death, putting her in a coma but not into her grave. That wasn't good enough. She lifted the gun to her temple.

Then she started to laugh, throwing her head back and dropping the gun to the table. "Bullets," she said aloud. "It helps to have bullets." She stumbled to the kitchen counter and retrieved the bag with the bullets. Her head was very woozy; the room was barely standing still. Her hand shaking, she gripped the gun and raised it in front of her eyes, dropping a small, deadly bullet into each of the nine cylinders, the way Irv had showed her. "Ready, aim, fire," she said, lifting the gun back to her head.

She had to go to the bathroom.

Can't you wait? she asked her stomach silently, and then decided that she couldn't, remembering as she tried to stand up that she had intended to do it in the bathroom anyway.

She sank down onto the toilet, the gun resting against

its white porcelain base. Her head was throbbing. She would be glad to miss this hangover.

The phone was ringing. At first, she thought maybe the noise was coming from inside her head, but after four rings, she knew someone else was responsible. She debated for an instant, which felt like much longer, whether or not to bother with it, then decided she might as well. Her final words. She pushed herself off the toilet seat and stumbled toward the phone in the bedroom.

"Hello," she murmured into the phone, balancing on the side of the bed.

"Gail?"

It was Jack. She tried to clear her throat, almost gagged on the effort, and concentrated very hard on keeping her eyes open.

"Hello, Jack," she managed, wishing she weren't so drunk.

"Is everything all right? You sound funny. Did I wake you up?"

"I'm drunk," she told him.

There was silence. "Jesus Christ," he swore softly, upset, not angry. "Are you by yourself?"

"As far as I know," Gail answered, straining to make her words coherent. "Is everything all right?"

"Everything's fine here. I spoke to Jennifer. She's okay."

"Good."

"Gail, I want you to come home."

"No." She shook her head and watched the room spin.

"Then I'll come back and get you."

"No, Jack, please."

"I don't think you should be alone. It was such a stupid thing for me to do. I guess I thought it would slap some sense into you, but . . ."

"I know. Please don't feel guilty."

"I can't hear you, Gail," he said. "You're slurring your words."

Gail was surprised. She had thought she was managing rather well. "Please don't feel guilty," she repeated clearly.

"I'll fly down tomorrow," he told her.

"No, please don't, Jack. There's no need. It's almost over."

"What? I can't hear you."

"I don't want you to come," Gail said loudly. "Jack . . ."

"What?" he asked quickly.

"I want," she began, then swallowed hard. Her throat was very dry. She needed a glass of water. "I want you to get a divorce," she said, knowing that as a widower a divorce would be somewhat redundant, but wanting to spare him as much guilt as possible.

"Gail, you're drunk. This isn't the time . . ."

"I want you to divorce me."

"I love you, Gail."

Gail lost her already shaky grip on the phone. "I love you too," she muttered, her words just missing the receiver.

"What? What did you say? I couldn't make it out."

"I have to hang up now, Jack."

"Gail . . ."

She hung up. "I need a glass of water," she said aloud, and tripped into the bathroom to get one. She drank two glasses in rapid succession, realizing as she put the cup back on the side of the sink that she had left the gun on her bed. "Dumb," she cursed, and guided herself along the walls of the narrow hallway to her room. So it would be Jack who found her, she thought as she reached across the bed for the weapon. Her knees gave out as they slammed against the low baseboard, and she fell forward. As her head hit the soft, quilted bedspread, she felt the tip of the gun smack against her temple, and she wondered, as her eyes closed, if she had managed to pull the trigger.

She heard the ringing as if it were coming from somewhere far away, and so she didn't bother to open her eyes. Then she remembered the events of the night before—she quickly realized it was morning—and she forced them open. She was not dead, she knew. The gun, despite its proximity to her temple, had not been fired. She had gotten herself too drunk to pull the trigger. There was no blood. Oddly enough, there was no hangover either. Perhaps, she thought, reaching over to silence the ringing phone, she was dead after all.

"Hello," she said, sitting up very straight.

"Gail," she heard Jack say, his voice strong and full of urgency, not hesitant like the night before. "Listen to me. Can you hear me all right?"

"Yes," she told him, angry with herself and her failure. She had the gun, she thought, moving it into her lap, but she still lacked the guts. The governor had granted her yet another, unwanted reprieve, condemning her to the rest of her life. She was doomed to survive.

"I have something to tell you, and I want to make sure you're not too drunk to understand."

"What is it?" Gail asked, feeling frightened and unsettled. "Is Jennifer okay? You told me Jennifer was okay . . ."

"Jennifer's fine. This isn't about Jennifer."

"What then?"

"I just got the call a few minutes ago. I literally just hung up the phone. The police called . . ."

"Jack, for God's sake, what is it?"

"They found him," Jack said simply, and at first Gail didn't understand. "The man who killed Cindy. Some drifter. He's confessed." Gail felt her entire body beginning to tingle, every nerve beginning to twitch. She couldn't sit still. She began rocking back and forth, standing up and then immediately sitting back down. She didn't know what to do with her hands. She knocked the gun up and down against the bed, tightening her grip on its handle, loosening it until it almost fell. "Gail, did you hear what I said? They found the man who killed Cindy. He's confessed."

"I'm coming home," Gail informed him, her fingers firmly closing over the top of the gun. The airlines might give her trouble if she tried to carry it on board. "I'm going to drive," she said, calculating that she could drop the rental car in Livingston. "I should be home in a few days."

"Drive?! Gail, you can't drive all that way alone. It's much too far for one person to drive all by themselves."

"You forget that I'm used to highway driving," Gail told him. "I'll be fine, Jack. Really, it'll relax me. Are they sure he's the right man?"

Gail could sense Jack's confusion through the telephone wires. "The police seem satisfied," he said. "He's confessed." He paused. "Look, let me fly down—we'll drive back together if that's what you want . . ."

"I'll be home in a few days," Gail told him, not letting him continue.

She hung up the phone, packed her suitcase, tucked her gun inside her purse and carried her belongings out to the car.

Then she drove straight through to Livingston in twenty-four hours without stopping.

Chapter 37

By the time Gail got back to Livingston, the drifter had retracted his confession. He claimed he had been denied his legal rights, that he had been pressured by the police into signing his confession. The police said otherwise. The accused had been read his rights in the presence of many witnesses; they had needed to create no pressure whatsoever to extract his confession. Indeed, they continued, the man seemed eager to talk about what had happened, almost boastful. At any rate, they continued in the radio reports, they remained confident of a conviction with or without the confession.

Gail was initially stunned by the retraction. She had arrived home hoping to have all the loose ends bound, the killer on his way to a speedy conviction. She found, instead, added tangles to the strings already left dangling too long.

Her family was waiting for her, huddled together in the living room as they had been nine months before. The sense of déjà vu was startling but not overwhelming, as it would have perhaps been earlier. Now there was no question about what time it was or if she had been living a dream these past months. She knew with certainty that her nightmare was horrifyingly real and that she had been awake for the duration.

Nine months ago, she thought, aware of the irony, she had returned from the hospital to find a similar scene. Now she saw her parents, looking no less tanned but somehow less substantial; Carol, drawing nervously on her ever-present cigarette; Jennifer, fragile and pale, surrounded on either side by Mark and Julie. Lieutenant Cole was talking animatedly in the far corner between Laura and Mike. Jack stood alone by the window.

Gail rushed into her husband's arms. In the next minute the room converged, everyone surrounding her with their arms, with their tears. Tears of anger, of joy, of relief.

"Tell me everything," Gail said, clinging tightly to Jack's hand. "The radio said he's retracted his confession. Are they still sure he's the one?"

Jack led her toward the sofa. Everyone automatically arranged themselves around her.

"We're sure," Lieutenant Cole said, his voice leaving no room for doubt.

Gail noticed the newspapers on the coffee table in front of her. She leaned forward to get a better view of the grainy black and white photographs spread across the front pages.

"His name is Dean Majors," the lieutenant began. "We were on the right track—he's a drifter, no permanent address. A history of arrests for drunk and disorderly conduct, served six months for assault a few years back."

Gail pulled one of the papers closer toward her. The face that stared blankly back at hers was that of a middle-aged man.

"He's forty-two," Lieutenant Cole said, reading her thoughts. "He'd been living in a rooming house in East Orange . . ."

"What street?" Gail asked quickly.

The lieutenant smiled. "Shuter."

Gail shook her head. It was not one of the streets with which she was familiar.

"Apparently," the lieutenant continued, "a new boarder had moved in, a man named Bill Pickering. Young guy, but with the same kind of background as Majors. They got together one night over a few drinks, started trying to one-up each other about crimes they'd pulled off, and Majors started boasting that he'd been the one who killed that little girl in a park the previous spring. Well, this Bill Pickering had spent some time in jail himself for breaking and entering, and if you know anything about convicts, you know that they consider sex offenders the lowest of the low, especially where children are concerned. Pickering and Majors ended up in a real brawl, and Pickering beat him up pretty badly, in fact, might have killed him if the landlord hadn't broken it up and ordered Pickering out of the place. Pickering went. He spent the night breaking into half a dozen homes in Short Hills. We arrested him after someone reported seeing a prowler. That's when he told us about Majors." He paused. "We got a warrant and searched Majors' room. We found the yellow windbreaker, boots that match the footprints, everything we need. Majors confessed immediately. He was very arrogant about it, kept asking us what took us so long."

"When did he retract his confession?" Gail asked.

"He was assigned a public defender . . ."

"I understand," Gail said. "He received legal counsel."

"Please don't blame the lawyers," Mike Cranston urged. "Apparently, from what I read in the papers, his lawyer claimed that Majors was roughed up pretty badly by the cops, and there's no question about his being covered with bruises. The police say they're the result of the beating he got from Pickering, but it'll be up to the courts, of course, to decide."

"So where exactly do things stand?" Gail pressed.

"They'll probably push for a change of venue. There's some speculation that Majors couldn't get a fair trial in this county. The district attorney will fight it, of course. Right now Majors is in jail. Bail was denied. So he'll sit there until the case comes to trial."

"Which is when?"

Lieutenant Cole shrugged. "Could be a month, could be a year. But I suspect that his lawyer will press for a speedy trial."

"And Majors will plead not guilty," Gail said, acknowledging their nods.

"Don't worry, Gail," the lieutenant assured her. "There's no question of his guilt. His confession was only icing on the cake."

"Somebody should just shoot the bastard," Dave Harrington muttered.

"I think I need to be alone for a while," Gail pleaded softly.

"Gail . . ." her mother began solicitously.

"Please," Gail urged, effectively stopping her.

Jack came to her support. "I think Gail needs to rest. Let's give her time to digest everything that's happened, okay?"

Laura nodded. "Let's grab some lunch," she said, ushering everyone out the front door. Gail twisted her head to watch them leave.

"I love you," Laura mouthed from the doorway, and Gail smiled and repeated Laura's words with her eyes.

Gail watched Mark and Julie, neither of whom had said a word, walk out with Jennifer between them. At the doorway Jennifer suddenly broke away from her father's protective arm and ran back to Gail, falling to her knees and laying her head in her mother's lap. "Oh, Mom," she cried.

"It's okay, sweetheart. It's okay now," Gail comforted her, running her hands along the top of her daughter's soft hair. "Don't cry, darling. Don't cry."

Jennifer raised her eyes to her mother. Gail wiped the tears off her daughter's cheeks. "Can I come home?" Jennifer asked.

Gail hugged her daughter tightly. "Of course you can. Of course you can."

Jennifer pulled herself up and threw her arms around Jack before rejoining her father at the door.

"Lila," Gail's father called, "you're holding up the works."

"We'll be back soon," her mother advised.

"Do you want me to go too?" Jack asked after the others had left.

Gail reached over and grabbed his hand. "No," she said softly. "I don't want you to go."

Gail spent over an hour studying the photographs of the man on the front pages of the newspapers. The face of average America, she thought, realizing that it was a phrase she would have once used to describe herself. She might have passed him dozens of times on the street.

There was nothing very distinctive about him. He was neither good-looking nor bad. His eyes were neither overly large nor noticeably small. They were an ordinary distance apart, and in one picture they almost sparkled, if not with intelligence, than at least with a certain vitality. His nose was crooked but not unpleasant. It had apparently been broken several times in various fights through the years, and he had never bothered having it fixed. His mouth was thin and curled into a knowing half smile that stopped just short of a smirk. His hair was straight and light brown, a little longer than the current trend. Gail found him not nearly as threatening in appearance as the youth with the crew cut whose room she had searched. His shoulders were rounded, his back slumped forward as he walked between the two policemen in the pictures. His hips were narrow. Gail ran her fingers through her hair. He was so *ordinary*.

Gail's eyes moved from photograph to photograph, her eyes skimming the text beneath. This was the man who had raped and strangled her six-year-old child, this man who had himself been raped by his own father when he was barely five, this man with an IQ of just under one hundred—low normal. Normal, Gail repeated to herself. *Normal.*

For a minute she tried to imagine what life had been like for this man, born into a hostile home through an accident of birth. He had not asked to be born. He had been created and then left to the deranged whims of his so-called family. He had never stood much of a chance, she realized, trying to feel some sympathy for him, and stopping when she realized that she couldn't.

Somewhere, she knew, there were better people than herself, people who could survive this kind of brutality and still manage some compassion for those responsible. She was simply not one of those people. It was easier to be understanding when the horror was happening to somebody else. Magnanimity was simple as long as it was abstract. It was not so easy when events struck closer to home, when the home itself was almost destroyed. No, Gail thought, folding up the newspapers and pushing them aside, she did not feel compassion for this man. She did not want to feel it. It was too late to help him, just as it was too late to help her dead child.

She wondered if it was too late for the rest of them.

Chapter 38

In the end, it took six months for the case to come to trial.

July was very hot, the summer having arrived late, then settling in with a vengeance. April had been cold and wet, its last afternoon passing in a downpour of vicious rain. If only it had rained like this a year ago, Gail had thought, and then tried to find some comfort in the fact that at least Cindy's killer had been apprehended.

May had continued cool and unpleasant, the unseasonably cold temperatures carrying over into June. And then suddenly the weather had turned around; the sun had come out and stayed out; the temperature had begun its steady climb. The July 4 weekend had been the hottest in recent memory.

Gail and her family went to the courthouse on Livingston Avenue every day as the trial unfolded. After a lengthy, heated debate, a change of venue had been denied. The case was being heard in Livingston. The pretrial publicity had been determined not to be too prejudicial; the defendant's chances of a fair trial were ruled to be as good in Essex County as anywhere.

The defendant's confession had been ruled inadmissible. There was some evidence to suggest coercion, the judge decided, disallowing the signed confession.

The state remained confident. They had a witness who would testify that the accused had confided in him all the details of the killing, and while they would concede that Bill Pickering was not one of New Jersey's more outstanding citizens, and that he had, in fact, been granted "consideration" for his testimony, his alibi had proved sound for the afternoon of the murder, and he was, himself, above suspicion for the grisly crime.

The accused had no alibi for his whereabouts at the time of the murder; he was known as a loner; no one at the house where he roomed could ever remember having seen him with a woman. Worse still, the police had uncovered a stack of kiddie-porn magazines hidden deep inside his closet.

The circumstantial evidence was indisputable. Majors' footprints matched those found at the scene; his clothing matched the description provided by the boys who saw him fleeing the area; most damning of all, the forensic evidence provided an undeniable link between man and child.

The first day of the trial, the Walton family arrived early and watched outside as the curious trickled in; gradually, people overflowed onto the street. Scores were turned away at the courthouse door as Gail and those closest to her were escorted inside. Reporters snapped their cameras within inches of her face, blinding her temporarily, mounting and framing her confusion for their front pages. Their microphones appeared like lollipops in front of her mouth. Did she think Dean Majors was guilty? Was she hoping for the death penalty? Gail had stopped at the courtroom door and faced them squarely as, all around her, cameras clicked and lights popped. Yes, she answered simply to the first question, she was convinced Majors was guilty. Was she hoping for the death penalty? She shook her head— she no longer hoped for anything, she told them.

After that the reporters were silent. The lights stopped flashing. Everyone left her alone. Gail went inside and took her seat in the front row of the crowded courtroom.

The extended family sat huddled in close proximity throughout the proceedings: Gail and Jack, with Carol and her parents beside them; Mark Gallagher sitting beside Jack's mother in the row directly behind, his wife Julie, now hugely pregnant, remaining at home; Laura and Mike—all within arm's reach. After the first day, Gail had been able to persuade Jennifer to keep Julie company. She didn't want Jennifer to be part of the agony of the trial.

So much had happened, Gail thought, looking them all over, reviewing the last fifteen months, silently calculating everything that had changed. They were no longer the same people they once were—they would spend the rest of their lives paying for what this man had done.

Gail looked over at her husband, his face directed at the floor, his hands entwined with hers. He had finally persuaded her to attend the meetings of the victims-of-violence organization, and after her initial claustrophobia had subsided, she found that these people *did* help her.

"We all want vengeance," Lloyd Michener had assured her, the group nodding in silent understanding when she had finally allowed the pent-up rage of the past year to burst forth.

The release of her hatred had carried her through the next six months, though Gail was aware that something was missing. She had come to terms with her fury, given voice to her bitterness and frustrations, recognized that her mother had been right—life did go on no matter how one tried to stop it, no matter what one tried to do. And while it wasn't true that time was the great healer everyone claimed it to be, eventually life did return to a semblance of normalcy, however different it was now from what it had been before.

And yet there was still something missing, something intangible, that she couldn't quite put her finger on.

Sometime in the last six months Gail and Jack had miraculously started making love again, drifting into it naturally one night as they lay in each other's arms. The feelings of disgust and shame she had thought would never leave her had somehow dissipated. And although both recognized that their lovemaking would never be performed with the same carefree abandon it had once been, Gail was astonished to find how much comfort could be drawn from the sexual act.

She remembered her early gropings of her teenage years, the first discoveries of what her body was capable of feeling, the initial thrills of being touched by another, the deep satisfactions inherent in giving herself to someone else. Cindy had been denied that knowledge. She would never know the tenderness that was possible in such an act.

The coroner testified that Cindy had been unconscious at the time of the sexual attack. She had been spared the more obvious physical pain. Gail sighed audibly when she heard this, was aware of tears dropping into her lap.

She found herself staring at the jury. After three days of intense haggling on the part of the two attorneys, eight men and four women had finally been selected. Though collectively they appeared as indistinguishable as the accused, individually they had been selected with great care. The defense had fought hard—and successfully—to keep mothers off the jury. Their one concession had been a woman whose children, both boys, were well in their teens.

The other three women consisted of a young divorcee and two who had never married, one a dental technician the same age as the defendant.

The men had been similarly inspected, and wherever possible, fathers of young daughters had been immediately weeded out. The only exception was the young father of an infant girl. The defense had looked for work-oriented individuals whose time at home was limited.

Gail's eyes drifted across the twelve serious faces. They looked more nervous than the accused, Gail thought at one point early in the trial. When the judge was forced to explain a point of law, they fidgeted noticeably and appeared anxious, afraid that something might slip past them, that they would fail to understand a key point. They looked alternately bored or horrified with certain of the technical details. One woman cried as pictures of the dead child were passed among them. Gail studied each face as each face studied the accused. She tried to crawl inside their minds, to feel what they were thinking, but she was unable to project herself beyond their somewhat bland exteriors. She had no way of knowing, she thought, just as she understood that *they* had no way of knowing the depth of the tragedy with which they were dealing.

Gail listened intently as each prosecution witness took the stand. She forced herself to hear each gruesome detail, refusing to block out what she did not wish to relive, forcing herself to dissect each sentence as if she were in grammar school. She listened to the police descriptions of the murder scene, to the boys' vague recollections of the man they saw fleeing the scene, to the indisputable weight of the forensic evidence. She heard Lieutenant Cole's steady, strong description of the discoveries they had made in Dean Majors' bedroom. She recognized that the prosecution was putting forward an airtight case.

She paid particular attention to Bill Pickering, the informer, looking from his unkind face to the faces of the jury. They didn't like him, she could see at a glance. Nor did she. He was arrogant and disreputable-looking, though he had made an awkward attempt at propriety by wearing a suit. He sweated and twisted uncomfortably in his imposed civility.

The defense made much of the fact that he was an ex-con and a snitch, protecting his own skin. He had told the police about Majors only after it could do him some good. Was it not possible, the defense postulated, that Pickering had planted the incriminating evidence in Majors' room? A reasonable doubt, the lawyer continually repeated during the course of Pickering's testimony, harping on the point that Pickering was not a man to be trusted, that there was more than a reasonable doubt to discount everything he said, conveniently neglecting to mention the certitude of the forensic disclosures.

Dean Majors sat beside his lawyer without moving or speaking, as he had done every day since the start of the trial. Gail had wondered how she would feel the first time she saw him. He was a strange figure, pale, obviously uncomfortable, his nails chewed to the quick, his head moving restlessly from side to side, but nevertheless defiant.

Gail hated him on sight. Could he feel her loathing? she wondered. Turn around, she commanded silently. Look at me. But he stopped just short, turning back to face the front just when it looked as if he might confront her.

The defense called no witnesses. Dean Majors did not take the stand. His attorney made a final, eloquent plea on behalf of the reasonable doubt, but the simple fact was that there were no doubts. The jury deliberated for less than an hour before returning with its verdict of guilty.

Gail fell into Jack's arms and cried as all around her she heard words of congratulations. She looked up just as Majors was leaving his seat, his eyes inadvertently stumbling across hers, returning her gaze as if caught in a trap and unable to do otherwise. The intensity of her feelings held him immobile.

The rest of the crowd in the courtroom seemed to disappear. There were only the two of them, confronting each other directly, leaving no room between them for anything but the truth.

It was only a matter of seconds but it felt like a life-time before his eyes admitted to hers what his tongue would not, that he had raped and murdered her child, that he had dragged the little girl behind the clump of bushes and rendered her unconscious with his hands, that he had ripped her clothing from her child's body and brutally forced his way inside her before returning his fingers to her small delicate throat.

I'm the man you've been looking for, he told her wordlessly—the man in the bookstore, in the pawn-shop, down the hall. The man on the highway; the man on the street. It's my face in your nightmare, the nightmare that began at precisely seventeen minutes past the hour of four on the last afternoon of an espe-cially warm, sunny day in April. A nightmare that had a beginning but no end.

Somebody should just shoot the bastard, she heard her father say.

Mommy, when we die, Cindy's voice intruded, *can we die together? Can we die holding hands? Do you promise?*

Gail thought of her old life—of the ease with which she used to walk through her days, the comfortable values she woke up with each morning, the casual ide-als that had carried her through till night. All gone. The afternoon of her innocence had been destroyed. It was lost to her forever.

She thought briefly of how far she had strayed from her core, how her mirror image no longer reflected the face of middle America, how very different she was from everything she had been.

And suddenly, Gail understood what it was that had been missing from her life these past months—what, precisely, this man had robbed her of on that last April afternoon, and all that she had permitted him to take.

Thoughts of him had occupied her days and directed her dreams. She had gone nowhere without him. Even now, from behind bars, he continued to control her every move, filling her head like the scent of a strong and unwanted perfume, leaving her little room to breathe. It was *she* who was the prisoner. She had allowed a stranger lurking behind a clump of bushes to seize control of her life.

Gail watched as Dean Majors' lips curled into that curious little half smile she recognized from the photographs in the newspapers, the smile that stopped just short of a smirk. Now, she told him, the smile transferring itself subtly from his lips to her own, she wanted that control back.

The smile stretched across her face as the feeling of control spread through her body, as tangible to her as the gun which suddenly slipped from her purse into the palm of her hand.

Somebody should just shoot the bastard, a voice repeated, and this time the voice was not her father's but her own.

From the time of the first shot to the time Dean Majors fell to the floor dead, five holes in his chest, till the moment someone wrenched the gun from her hand before she could fire more, Gail was aware only of this feeling.

Gradually, she became aware of other things—of sounds, of screams, of cries, of shuffling and running. She felt hands all around her, restraining her though she was not trying to move. She saw people pushing against each other to see what she had done, watched the omnipresent cameras trying to make sense of what had happened, heard cries of "My God" and "He's dead" on top of pleas to give the dead man room to breathe.

Gail marveled silently at what she had done. Her eyes locked on Jack's. She wondered briefly what would happen to her. Perhaps a jury of peers, as a lesson to others about straying too far from the fold, would sentence her to die. If so, she was prepared to accept their decision.

And then she heard it, another sound which told her that perhaps she hadn't strayed so far from the fold after all. Gail threw her head back, soaking up the sound and letting it envelop her. It grew, spreading like a fire across dry wood, until it filled the courtroom.

The sound of applause.

About the Author

JOY FIELDING is the author of two recent best sellers: *K Mommy Goodbye* and *The Other Woman*, both availab in Signet paperback editions. With her lawyer husba and two young daughters, she divides her time betwe homes in Toronto and Palm Beach, Florida.

ecommended Reading from SIGNET

*Prices higher in Canada

**Buy them at your local
bookstore or use coupon
on next page for ordering.**

Great Horror Fiction from SIGNET

World Renowned Authors from SIGNET

(C

- [ ] **THE MIRACLE** by Irving Wallace. (135962—$4
- [ ] **THE CHAPMAN REPORT** by Irving Wallace. (138287—$4.
- [ ] **THE PRIZE** by Irving Wallace. (137590—$4.
- [ ] **THE FABULOUS SHOWMAN** by Irving Wallace. (113853—$.
- [ ] **THE THREE SIRENS** by Irving Wallace. (125843—$3.
- [ ] **THE SECOND LADY** by Irving Wallace. (138279—$4.
- [ ] **THE SINS OF PHILIP FLEMING** by Irving Wallace. (137604—$3.
- [ ] **THE TWENTY-SEVENTH WIFE** by Irving Wallace. (137612—$4.
- [ ] **DANIEL MARTIN** by John Fowles. (122100—$4.
- [ ] **THE EBONY TOWER** by John Fowles. (134648—$3.
- [ ] **THE FRENCH LIEUTENANT'S WOMAN** by John Fowles. (135989—$3.
- [ ] **BREAKFAST AT TIFFANY'S** by Truman Capote. (120426—$2.
- [ ] **THE GRASS HARP** and **TREE OF NIGHT** by Truman Capote.
  (120434—$2.
- [ ] **MUSIC FOR CHAMELEONS** by Truman Capote. (138805—$3.
- [ ] **IN COLD BLOOD** by Truman Capote. (121988—$3.
- [ ] **OTHER VOICES, OTHER ROOMS** by Truman Capote. (134516—$2.
- [ ] **THE ARMIES OF THE NIGHT** by Norman Mailer. (123174—$3

*Prices slightly higher in Canada
†Not available in Canada